THE SISTERS

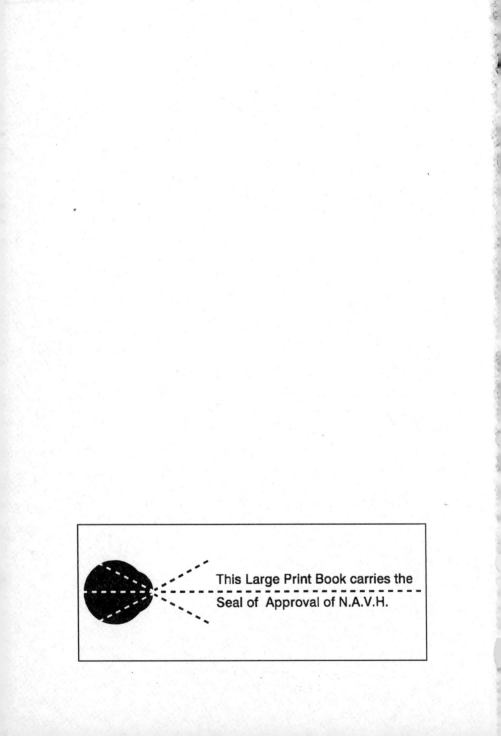

This Large Print Book carries the
Seal of Approval of N.A.V.H.

THE SISTERS

NANCY JENSEN

THORNDIKE PRESS
A part of Gale, Cengage Learning

GALE
CENGAGE Learning®

Detroit • New York • San Francisco • New Haven, Conn • Waterville, Maine • London

GALE
CENGAGE Learning·

Thorndike Press® Large Print Basic.
The text of this Large Print edition is unabridged.
Other aspects of the book may vary from the original edition.
Set in 16 pt. Plantin.

LIBRARY OF CONGRESS CATALOGING-IN-PUBLICATION DATA

Jensen, Nancy, 1961–
   The sisters / by Nancy Jensen.
     p. cm. — (Thorndike Press large print basic)
   ISBN-13: 978-1-4104-4500-1 (hardcover)
   ISBN-10: 1-4104-4500-3 (hardcover)
   1. Sisters—Fiction. 2. Separation (Psychology)—Fiction. 3. Family secrets—Fiction. 4. Kentucky—Fiction. 5. Indiana—Fiction. 6. Domestic fiction. 7. Psychological fiction. 8. Large type books. I. Title.
PS3610.E573S57 2012
813'.6—dc23
                                2011041265

Published in 2012 by arrangement with St. Martin's Press.

Printed in the United States of America
1 2 3 4 5 6 7 16 15 14 13 12

For my mother, my mooring

CONTENTS

. . . I, being poor, have only my dreams;
I have spread my dreams under your
feet;
Tread softly because you tread on my
dreams.
— **W. B. Yeats**

We always keep the dearest things to ourselves.

— **James Joyce**

THE FISCHER FAMILY TREE

Albert Fischer ⁓ Imogene East ⁓ Jim Butcher
(1889~1918)   *(1890~1922)*

Charles
(stillborn, 1922)

Mabel
(b. 1908)

Bertie ⁓ Hans
(b. 1913)

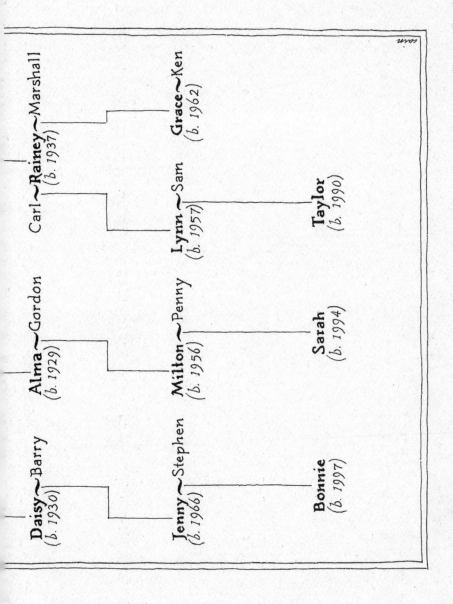

ONE:
COMMENCEMENT

June 1927
Juniper, Kentucky

BERTIE

It was a lovely dress, soft and pink as a cloud at dawn. Bertie admired the way the chiffon draped from her neck in long, light, curving folds, seeming to narrow her square shoulders, and it pleased her to imagine how the skirt would swish around her calves when she walked to the stage to get her eighth-grade diploma, but she was most fond of the two buttons, small silver roses, that fastened the sleeve bands just below each elbow. Two months Mabel had worked for the dress, going into Kendall's an hour early every day, fixing it with Mrs. Kendall so, come commencement week, Bertie could choose any one she wanted. Bertie twirled before the mirror, then lifted her hair to see how it would look pinned up,

15

and, yes, suddenly she was taller, almost elegant. She couldn't remember feeling pretty before. In this dress, she did, and it was wonderful. She even felt a little sorry for Mabel. Her sister had always been beautiful — slim and doll-like, with big eyes and glistening bobbed hair, Juniper's Clara Bow — so Mabel couldn't appreciate the wonder of suddenly feeling transformed, caterpillar to butterfly.

Bertie swooshed out her arms, letting her hair fall again down her back. Stooping to pull open the bottom drawer of the dresser, she reached into the far back corner for Mabel's photograph — the one made specially for the stereopticon, with two of the same view, printed side by side. There was Mabel, sitting on a swing, a painted garden behind her — a pair of Mabels, as if she were her own twin — looking like an exquisite, unhappy bride in a lacy white dress, her dark hair, still long then, longer and fuller than Bertie's had ever been, spilling round her shoulders.

Bertie slid her fingertips across her own hair — not heavy, but fine and smooth. Very soft. Sometimes, just before he kissed her cheek, Wallace stroked her hair like this. He'd never told her if he thought it was pretty — but he must think so. Why else would he have made her a Christmas present of the pale green ribbon she'd pointed out to him in the window at Kendall's?

She'd never worn it, not once. It stung her suddenly to realize this must have hurt Wallace, made him think she didn't appreciate him. No one but the two of them knew about the gift — not even Mabel. Bertie had brought it home and hidden it, taking it out to hold against her cheek only when she was alone in the house — too afraid of her stepfather's angry questions, demanding to know how she had come by it.

Well, she *would* wear it. This Saturday, her graduation day. She would wear Wallace's ribbon and not care what anyone said. Such a pretty green to go with her dress, pretty as the spring-fresh stem of a rosebud. She would wear it and Wallace would know that she loved him, and then maybe, just maybe, in another year, after Wallace had finished high school, they could talk to his folks about getting married. Even if the Hansfords said they had to wait awhile longer, until Bertie was sixteen or seventeen, she could leave school and get a job, and with her and Wallace both working and saving up, they could get a place of their own straight off.

Mabel would be upset to know Bertie was thinking this way. Lately, Mabel had talked as hopefully about her finishing high school as Mama once had — all through that sad winter after the doctor, fearing for the baby, had put Mama to bed. Every afternoon when nine-year-old Bertie got in from school, she hurried into Mama's room, not pausing long enough even to take off her damp coat. She would lean in, kiss Mama with her wind-frozen lips, then turn to hug Mabel, who would take the coat to the kitchen to dry. While her sister started supper, Bertie sat in the bed beside her mother.

"When the baby comes," Bertie said, "I'll stay home to help."

"You'll still be in school." Mama pulled her close. "Don't you mind what your stepdaddy says. We'll work it out. Mabel's here now, and I'll have both my girls to help me through the summer." Mama's voice was tired, tinged around the edges with uncertainty, but firm at the center. "Come the autumn, I want the two of you back in school where you belong."

When Mama talked, Bertie believed her, but then at supper, in between mouthfuls of stew, their stepfather, Jim Butcher, not looking straight at either of them, would tell the girls what was on his mind. "You've had enough school," he said to Mabel. "Reckon even too much." He stabbed his fork toward Bertie before filling it again. "Even she's had more than I had, and I had more than my daddy. You know how to read, write, do all the sums you're liable to need. That's plenty enough."

"But when Mama's stronger —" Mabel began.

"Then there'll be another one along."

At one time or another, it seemed like everybody in Juniper had heard Jim Butcher tell his story — always when he was drinking — about how, when he'd made it across the field of wheat and lay alone in a thicket in Belleau Wood — lay gasping, covered in the mixed muck of rotting leaves, pine needles, blood and flesh — God had spoken to him and promised him three sons.

But Jim Butcher's only son had died before he could take even one breath. Two days the baby had battled to be born, and when he gave up, he took Mama with him. That — losing Mama — had been the worst thing possible, and yet Bertie couldn't help feeling that for Mama it might have been best, dying before three, four, five years of new babies could make her older and ever more tired, make her worry more about the burden she was leaving on her girls.

Only because of Mabel, who did every-thing Butcher wanted — tending the house and working a job, too — had Bertie been able to go back to school. Her sister had just stepped into Mama's shoes, seeing to all the cooking, the washing, and the dream-ing for Bertie's future. How could she tell Mabel that going on to high school didn't matter to her? She wasn't quick like her sister was — Mabel loved everything about books and learning — but Bertie struggled mightily whenever she had to read some-thing. All she really wanted was to make a life with Wallace, to stand by him, and raise his children, and smile on him until death.

Bertie reached again into the open drawer until her hand found the fold of tissue paper protecting Wallace's ribbon. Mabel would be in the kitchen now getting breakfast, and Jim Butcher would be sitting on the chair beside the bed that used to be Mama's bed, pulling on his work boots, probably figuring up some new way he could make Bertie feel small, some reason to call her stupid and clumsy, like the way he did when he saw her slosh a little milk out of the pail after stumbling in a rut outside the barn.

But Bertie didn't care. She stood before the mirror, drawing the ribbon out to its full length. It *was* beautiful against the dress. She might wear the ribbon as a band, leaving her hair loose as a waterfall down her back. Or she might gather the hair at her neck to show off the ribbon in a shimmery bow. What mattered was that, however she wore the ribbon, Wallace would see, and then — at the party after the commencement service, since no dancing would be allowed in the church hall — then Wallace would keep his promise to her by dancing her outside, and he would glide her in circles across the grass, and, flushed and dizzy, they would stop and he would look right at her, touch the ribbon, and tell her she was beautiful.

She picked up Mabel's portrait again, turning it to face the mirror, just to see how she measured against her sister. But no — *she would not look.* She was done comparing herself with Mabel. And she was done trying to work out why Mabel hated this picture of herself, why she'd cut off her hair the night after it had been taken, why she had wanted to burn the card the very day Jim Butcher had brought it back from that Louisville photographer.

Right now, this moment, Bertie was determined to be happy. She had made it through Saturday and Sunday, and now it was Monday again and she had only to make it through the school day until she would see Wallace, waiting for her on the stoop like he always did, ready to hold her hand on their slow walk away from school, through town, and to the corner, where he would kiss her cheek before leaving her to turn for home.

"Alberta!" Butcher's growl flung out ahead of his familiar heavy step.

She dropped the ribbon into the open drawer and pushed it closed, waiting to answer her stepfather until he appeared in the doorway. "Sir?'

He pulled back a little when he saw her, and stared. Raking his eyes up and down her body, up and down, like he didn't know her. For a moment, Bertie stopped breathing and reached out a hand to steady herself on the dresser. She'd been caught trying on the dress when she ought to have been checking the water for the cow or pulling any little weeds that might have come up around the tomato sets during the night. He might be angry enough to tell her she couldn't go to graduation. He might even tell her she couldn't go to school today to sit for her final examinations, and if she didn't take them, the school might fail her and she'd be forever without her eighth-grade diploma. Terrified as she was of what Butcher might say, she felt a flash of anger at herself for not having thought through the possibilities. She should have left the dress alone until evening.

Butcher looked past her and out the window at the empty clotheslines. Bertie couldn't remember a time when he'd broken a hard stare at her, and the change made her more nervous.

"You finish all your chores?" He was looking toward her again, but somehow not quite at her.

"Almost, sir," she said, struggling to relax her throat enough to get a breath. "I'm going now, just as soon as I change my dress. I had to make sure it fit."

Still he stood in the doorway, watching her. Did he expect her to take it off then and there?

Bertie took a step toward the door. "I'll be right out, sir. Soon as I change."

"How long's that program Saturday?"

She didn't dare go any closer. He might see her trembling. "The ceremony's at three," she said. "At the church. There's a light supper after. And after that . . ." How could such a cold stare burn a hole in her? She should just give up the party, not even mention it, come right home after she got her diploma. No hair ribbon. No dance with Wallace on the lawn. But Wallace would understand, wouldn't he? She was almost sure he would.

"After that," Bertie began again, but suddenly Mabel appeared behind Butcher.

"Daddy," she said, touching his arm lightly, "your breakfast's ready. Will chicken be all right for supper?"

Daddy, Bertie thought. She loved her sister but despised her for calling him that.

Butcher turned his head slightly toward Mabel, then looked down at his arm, where her fingers still rested. Without looking up, he spoke in Bertie's direction: "Saturday, you be in by eight-thirty. Not a minute later."

He walked off to the kitchen, Mabel calling after him, "I'll be right there, Daddy."

With a quick look behind her, Mabel slipped inside the bedroom and closed the door. "Let me help you with the back buttons."

Bertie turned toward the mirror. "Why do you call him that?"

Instead of answering, Mabel took the brush from the dresser and drew it through Bertie's hair in long, firm strokes. "It fits just right," Mabel said. "The dress. Like it was made for you." She smiled over Bertie's shoulder at their paired reflections. "Just look how beautiful you are."

Bertie closed her eyes, enjoying the way her scalp tingled with every stroke of the brush. After Mama died, it was the way Mabel — fourteen then, the same age Bertie was now — had stilled Bertie's sobbing. That, and spending hours with her on their shared bed, looking at pictures in the stereopticon, just like they'd done with Mama, long before Jim Butcher spent a few weeks of rough charm on her, drawing her out of her widow's loneliness, persuading her that, without a man, she'd surely lose the little patch of land left to her, along with the only security she had for her girls.

In the months after Mama's passing, they'd hear Butcher round the back of the house, throwing rocks or dried-up corncobs, sticks of kindling or empty bottles — whatever he could find — at the side of the barn, raging at the sky, calling God a filthy bastard for breaking his promise. Sometimes, to cover up the sound, Mabel would read out loud to Bertie, or they'd sing songs Mama had liked, but always, before long, they'd get out the photo cards Mama had collected since she was a girl, and Mabel would fit them, one at a time, into the clamps on the stereopticon.

Bertie's favorite was "The Mother's Tender Kiss," from a set Mama had been given a year or two before she married their father. Dated 1905, it showed a wedding party against what seemed a wall of huge blossoms, even a ceiling, like a cave of lilies. Everyone in the photo — the women in their layers of lace and the men in their slim black suits — looked toward the bride, almost obscured by her mother, who leaned in for a final kiss before her daughter became a wife. When Bertie was very small, she thought the picture was of her parents' wedding, and even though she knew now it wasn't true, in her mind, that's just how it had been: a day of flowers, of lovely women and handsome men, all happy and loving each other.

"Mabel," Bertie said now, placing her hand over the brush and taking it from her sister. "What'll I do when you get married?"

"Who says I'm getting married?"

"It's bound to happen. Boys like you."

With her quick and gentle hands, Mabel separated Bertie's hair into three sections and started braiding it. "That's not for me," she said. "So don't you worry about it."

"Do you still think about Freddy?"

All last year, Bertie had been terrified that Mabel would leave her to marry Freddy Porter. It seemed then that everywhere she went people had something to say about how Mabel Fischer ought to snap up her chance before it got away from her. Freddy had an uncle who owned a furniture store in Louisville, and it was said he was planning to get Freddy started in the business. Of course the older girls were jealous — the girls that used to be Mabel's friends before she had to leave school — saying the only reason Freddy liked her at all was for her looks, but Bertie knew that wasn't true. Maybe she hadn't seen it then, but now, when she remembered, she could see that Freddy had looked at Mabel the way Wallace sometimes looked at her. Suddenly, now that it seemed possible *she* might be the one to get married, the one to leave her sister alone with a hateful man, Bertie was ashamed that she hadn't really been sorry — sorry in her heart — when Butcher ran Freddy off. The idea of being left behind with her stepfather had been so terrible that she had refused even to ask herself if Mabel's heart might be broken.

"Did you like him very much?" Bertie asked. "Freddy?"

Mabel finished the braid and held the end secure in her hand. "I did," she said. "But it doesn't matter now. Should I pin this up, or would you like me to tie it?"

"I have something." Carefully, so as not to

27

pull the braid from Mabel's hand, Bertie bent to open the bottom drawer again. The unfurled ribbon was in easy reach. "Will this work?"

"It's more the length for braiding in," Mabel said, "but I can fix it some way."

"No, just pin it," Bertie said, stroking the ribbon. "I want to save this for something special." She was surprised, when she looked at Mabel's reflection, to see her sister smiling at her.

"That's the one Wallace bought for you, isn't it?"

Bertie flushed with the discovery, and for a moment all she could think of was how ugly the pink chiffon looked on her now, with her change of color. "How did you . . ."

Mabel laughed. "Did you forget the store's on the way home from school? I've seen you two going past for months — since October at least." She wrapped an arm across her sister's chest and pressed her cheek over the very spot Wallace kissed. "I'm happy for you, Bertie," she said. "I like Wallace."

Quickly, Mabel fastened up the braid in a loop, then picked up the brush, sweeping it through her own hair in rough, short strokes. Meeting Bertie's eyes in the mirror, Mabel tipped her head toward the closed bedroom door and whispered, "You mustn't

let on to *him*, though. He wouldn't like it."
She laid the brush on the dresser. "I'd better get in there before he hollers. And you'd
better get changed or you won't finish your
chores in time to get to school."

With her everyday dress on, the looped
braid was too fancy — people would laugh,
say she was putting on airs — so Bertie
plucked out the pins and shook her hair
loose, tying it back from her face with piece
of twine. What was it Wallace saw in her?
She was so plain, she might as well have
been invisible.

Around the house, that was the best way
to be. If not for Mabel, she might have run
away a dozen times over, but her sister
always smoothed things, seeming to know
the way to talk to calm Butcher down. Then,
late at night, after they had heard him go
down the hall to bed, Mabel would relight
the lamp and get out the stereopticon.
They'd take turns with it, spreading the
cards across the rug.

Mabel might hold out a view of downtown
San Francisco or New Orleans or Chicago
and say, "Let's you and me go there."

And Bertie would gaze at the gray city and
try to imagine herself there. She couldn't —
she'd never been out of Juniper. "What
about money?" she would say. "He expects

me to go to work soon as school's out."

Mabel would smile — always a smile shadowed with secrets, but a shadow that stilled Bertie's worries, as if the things she didn't know were what kept her safe. "Whenever he sends me to the store," Mabel told her once, "I keep back a nickel or a dime — whatever I think he won't notice. That I save. I'll work extra when I can, like I've been doing for your commencement dress. By the time you finish high school, there'll be enough to get us out of Juniper, to get us started somewhere else."

There was plenty of money in Butcher's strongbox, the one he kept back of the low cabinet behind the whiskey bottles. Surely Mabel knew about that. Or maybe she didn't. Bertie hadn't known about it for long — only since she'd stepped around the corner early one morning last winter while he was loading up his pockets for his trip to the bootlegger. He didn't see her, but she saw him put the box back in its hiding place.

Just a week or two ago, while studying a view of New York, Mabel had again said, "We'll go there. You and me. Someday."

"Oh, Mabel, let's go now." She could surprise Mabel with the money. Make up some story about how she'd earned it. Or about how Mama had hidden it away for them. A gift. "Let's go right after graduation. I can work, too." Bertie had meant it when she said it, caught up in the idea of getting away from Jim Butcher, meant it until she remembered Wallace. Leaving Juniper would mean leaving Wallace, and she didn't want to do that.

"One of us should finish school." Mabel squeezed Bertie's hand. "For Mama's sake. Besides, right now I don't have enough to get you or me to the other side of town. When we go, we need to get at least as far as Indianapolis — the bigger the city and the farther away the better." She stretched back across the bed and gazed at the ceiling. "When you start a new life, everything has to be different."

Bertie took another quick look in the mirror, then picked up her books so she could go on to school straight from the barn, right after she'd turned the horse out into the little pasture and cleaned the stall. She knew some of the others talked behind her back, gossiping about her clothes and her dirty shoes, but what did it matter if Wallace didn't mind?

She stepped into the hall, just in time to hear Mabel saying, as sweetly as you please, "Another cup of coffee, Daddy?"

She wanted to love Mabel — did love her — but at times like this Bertie wondered if it was possible to love someone you couldn't understand, someone who could do something so terrible. Mostly, she was sure Mabel hated Butcher as much as she did, but Mabel would never admit it, not even when she and Bertie were alone. Sometimes Bertie thought she heard a sneer in Mabel's voice when she said *Daddy.* But even if that was true, saying it at all was still an insult to their father — the father Mabel, being five years older, remembered far better than Bertie could. Bertie hadn't started school yet when he'd been called up for the war. There'd been only a couple of letters after he left home, which Mabel, like Mama before her, kept in the blanket chest along with the telegram saying he'd died of influenza a week before he was to ship out to France.

Mabel remembered him so well she could still tell stories about his teaching her to look under the leaves when hunting blackberries, and about the eagle-shaped swing he'd made for her one summer. He'd slung the swing's rope over a thick limb of the maple tree in the front yard and said, "Now you can fly as high and far as you want. Far as you can think."

How Mabel could remember all that and *still* call Jim Butcher Daddy, Bertie couldn't accept — wouldn't forgive — no matter how good a sister Mabel was to her. She would tell her so — today, right now. She'd stand in the kitchen door and throw an angry look at Mabel. So what if Butcher saw it?

But the moment she was in the doorway, seeing Butcher hunched over the table, leaning on his thick arms, strong as iron chain, Bertie lost her nerve. Then, as if she sensed Bertie watching them, Mabel looked up suddenly, her eyes wide, almost terrified, and with a quick jerk of her head she told Bertie to be on her way.

With Mabel's look, Bertie forgot about Butcher, and her courage returned. The signal annoyed her. And besides that, she was hungry. She would march right in and cut a slice of bread for her breakfast, take a piece of cheese to carry for her lunch.

She took one step. Mabel lifted her hand as if to say *Stop!* her eyes now wider still, diving up and down between Bertie and Jim Butcher. Those eyes pleaded, as Mabel shook her head violently. *Now.* She was telling Bertie. *For God's sake, go now.*

There'd never been such a crowd in the sanctuary of the Emmanuel Baptist Church, not even on Easter Sunday. Every pew was full and the people who couldn't get seats lined the walls and clumped in the aisles. The graduates sat hip-to-hip in the first two rows. Bertie stood up again and turned around to scan the congregation, ignoring Irma Henderson, who was tugging on her wrist and telling her to sit down. "They're about to start, Bertie. Please!" Irma pulled harder. Bertie stayed on her feet.

They had to be there. But no matter how hard she looked, forcing herself to go face by face, she couldn't see them anywhere — not Mabel or Wallace. It was possible they had slipped in while she was sitting down, but surely they would wave from wherever they were if they saw her. Over and over she ran her gaze through every row and into every corner, but they just weren't there.

At the edge of the stage, old Miss Callahan sat down at the piano and began playing the melody of "We Gather Together" while her first-grade students filed into the choir loft to prepare to sing. Bertie had learned the hymn herself at that age, baffled by most of the words: *The wicked oppressing now cease from distressing* — what could that mean? How she used to stumble over that odd way of phrasing: *And pray that thou still our defender wilt be.* Now, as she stood with the rest of the congregation to join in, the words slipped easily from her mouth. Had she ever really listened to them, even after she had learned their meaning?

Just the idea of gathering together made her want to cry. What might she have done that would make Mabel and Wallace desert her this way? People were sure to notice. Everyone else in her class had at least one parent present, plus grandparents, brothers, sisters, cousins — and here she was with no one who cared enough to come.

While the principal stood in the preacher's place and gave a speech about stepping off the train in Juniper as a young teacher in 1900, Bertie crumpled a handful of chiffon in her fist. She saw now how foolish the dress was — much too pale a color for her, and too like the ancient peach-colored silk that silly spinster Miss Callahan always wore when she sang at weddings. Had Mabel thought the same thing when she helped her pick it out? Had her own sister set her up to be mocked?

She didn't want to believe these things about Mabel, but how could she not? Her sister couldn't be trusted. Time after time, Mabel had urged her to cooperate with Jim Butcher — and just look at the way she played up to him, speaking softly and keeping her eyes lowered, smiling from time to time, and even touching him gently now and again. This whole last week had been worse than ever, seeming almost like Mabel was inviting Butcher to court her. Not once since Monday, when she'd tried on the dress, had Mabel come to brush out Bertie's hair or to sit on the bed to look through the stereopticon or talk about school or ask about Wallace.

And what about Wallace? That same afternoon, Monday, he wasn't on the stoop waiting for her after school. Instead, Henry Layman was there in his place, saying Wallace wouldn't be able to turn up for the rest of the week. When Bertie had asked the reason, Henry just shrugged: "That's all he said."

None of it made any sense — or at least none Bertie wanted to accept.

I like Wallace. That's what Mabel had said.

No one had been more surprised than Bertie when Wallace started paying attention to her. Not that he was the best-looking boy in town — he was barely an inch taller than she was, dark blond hair always in a tumble, and sturdy as a stump from hard work, with dozens of small scrapes and scars to show for it — but just about everybody said he was one of the nicest boys there was, and, more important, good-hearted and responsible.

Wallace was so much older than she was, too, just a year behind Mabel, and even though Bertie would marry him tomorrow if he asked, she'd worried that when he was ready he might decide she was too young. Not long ago she'd heard a couple of boys laughing behind her back, saying if a fellow thought he needed a Fischer girl enough to stand up to the trouble that came with Butcher, he'd be crazy to go for Bertie over Mabel.

She didn't want to set the last piece of the puzzle into place. It just fell in on its own.

Two days ago, knowing Wallace wasn't going to be waiting for her, Bertie had walked into town to get some thread that would match her dress, just in case a button came off or a seam broke at the last minute. Mabel was supposed to be working until 5:30 at Kendall's, but she was standing with Wallace under the awning of the hardware store, tucked as far back as they could be behind a display of washtubs. Wallace had hold of both her hands and leaned his head close to hers. Mabel was nodding, looking nervous, but there wasn't any question they were agreeing on something. Then Wallace drew Mabel into his arms and held her, her head nestling against his neck, his hand on her hair.

What are you doing? Bertie had called to them from her heart, the words stopping in her throat. *What are you doing?* A firm pair of hands — she never knew whose — settled on her shoulders to urge her back onto the walk and out of the street.

"Bertie, what are you doing?" Irma's whisper stung her ear. "They've called your name." Irma pushed her forward, nudged her up the steps and across the stage, then grabbed her elbow to keep her from turning in the wrong direction as they stepped back onto the floor.

When the ceremony was over, Bertie let Irma lead her to the church hall with the rest of the graduates. She wandered through the buffet line, spooning food onto her plate, but after a few minutes she left it untouched on the corner table where she'd gone to be out of everyone else's way.

The church bell was just chiming five when she pushed past the Anderson clan, who were celebrating the graduation of their twin sons. She was nearly to the door when she heard her name called out over the Andersons' laughing chatter. "Bertie! Bertie, wait!" She turned toward the young man's voice. Wallace had come. She was sure it was Wallace. When he found his way through the crowd to clasp her hands, she would scold him — just a little, not too much — for being late. "Bertie!" she heard again.

It wasn't Wallace at all. She could see Henry Layman trying to get to her. He was waving something over his head — a piece of paper, maybe — and calling out for her to stay put for a minute.

So Henry had been sent as messenger again. It was a dirty trick. Yellow, it was. If Wallace wanted to tell her something, if he was going to tell her he liked Mabel better, then he could do it to her face. And Bertie would see to it Mabel looked her in the eye, too. She wasn't about to listen to any made-up excuses they'd fed to poor Henry.

Bertie shook her head at Henry, still struggling his way through the crowd. She turned on her heel and went out the door.

There wasn't a soul on the street, just a couple of dogs tumbling in play on the parsonage lawn. The sun, so bright this morning, had faded behind heavy ash-colored clouds and the air simmered with the feeling of coming rain.

She'd give anything to think of somewhere to go besides back to the house, but she wanted out of this ridiculous dress and out of everyone's sight. Pretty soon, it would be all around town about Mabel and Wallace

— off somewhere together on Bertie's special day, laughing at her.

Would it be possible, if she worked, to live on her own? She was pretty sure Butcher wouldn't make a fuss, even about losing a hand around the place, and she didn't care if Mabel did. She'd heard Nellie Perkins was looking for a girl for the boardinghouse to do some scrubbing and to help the cook. If she could get her room and board for the main part of her pay, then she wouldn't need but a few dollars a month for other things. She wouldn't even have to wait for morning. If she hurried back, she could get changed into a clean housedress and get everything settled with Mrs. Perkins before dark.

In spite of the blister rubbing at the back of her right heel, Bertie picked up her walk to a trot and then to a full run as she approached the corner where, for months, Wallace had said good-bye with a kiss. When she turned onto her road, dusty from too little spring rain, she stopped in front of the Mitchell place to catch her breath and pinched at the damp chiffon to shake it away from her body.

"Bertie, come on in here." Mrs. Mitchell was standing on her porch, wiping her hands on her apron.

"I'm just going home, ma'am," Bertie said, starting on her way again.

Mrs. Mitchell rushed down the steps and out to the gate. Everything about her was atremble, even her red-rimmed eyes. She fumbled with the latch. "No, honey, please," she said, reaching over the gate, trying to grab Bertie's wrist. "You come in and let me give you some lemonade."

Bertie protested again, said she was in a hurry, but, having freed the latch, Mrs. Mitchell came out of the gate, took hold of Bertie's shoulders and steered her onto the front walk, through the house, and into the kitchen. "You need to stay here for now," she said. "There's some trouble at your place. So you just wait here till it passes."

"What kind of trouble?"

No amount of questions could get Mrs. Mitchell to tell her what was going on. She wouldn't do anything but shake her head and chip off more ice to drop into Bertie's glass, but at last the woman looked out the window at the dark clouds. "I need to get those clothes off the line. You just stay here, Bertie, and pour yourself some more lemonade."

This was her chance. The instant the back screen door banged behind Mrs. Mitchell, Bertie was out of her chair and pushing through the front door. It seemed like all the women on their road had been put on watch for her, calling from their porches or waving dish towels out their kitchen windows, but she ran past them. Whatever this trouble was, it must be the reason Mabel and Wallace hadn't come to the graduation. The fear of it made Bertie's head swim, and she felt a rush of shame for having thought they could betray her.

She stopped short at the end of the chicken-wire fence that marked their land.

Five or six men were gathered outside the barn. One of the doors was partly open.

Everything was quiet — no sound from the chickens or from the songbirds that usually swooped in to feed before a storm. Nothing but the shaking of the leaves.

Bertie recognized Mr. Mitchell and some other men who lived nearby, but a couple of them were strangers to her. They were standing in a crooked row, staring in at something they could all see through the open door, so none of them saw her until she'd walked right in amongst them.

"Whoa, Bertie!" Mr. Mitchell grabbed her just like his wife had done and swung her away from the barn and toward the house. "You go stay up on the porch. I'll take you on to my place in a minute."

"What's happening?" Bertie asked. None of the men would answer her. They wouldn't even look at her.

Everything was odd.

Somebody had tied the cow to the fence rail, right in the place where a slat was missing, so the cow could reach through to nibble at the little cornstalks, just ankle-high.

The plow was out in the middle of the patch Butcher had said this morning he was going to plant with more beans, but the mare was unhitched, wandering around through the cucumbers.

And every now and then, when the wind kicked up, Bertie could hear a muffled banging, as if the back screen door had been left unhooked.

Another man Bertie didn't know stepped out of the barn. Even from her place on the porch, she could make out the shape of his badge. The sheriff. He took off his hat and stopped in the yard to talk to Mr. Mitchell, looking up once or twice to glance over at her. Mr. Mitchell shook his head and walked slowly back toward the barn.

The other man came toward Bertie and sat down on the top step beside her. "Bertie Fischer? That short for Alberta?"

She nodded. The sheriff reached out to

43

take her hand. She started to pull it away, then thought better of it.

"I asked the men there to keep you out of the barn," he said. His hand was warm. Strong and sad. "Your stepdaddy's hanged hisself. They're just cutting him down now."

"Where's my sister?"

The rain started in small spatters, and the sheriff looked up for a moment, as if he might read the answer in the clouds. "Looks like she's run off," he said. He reached in his pocket and held out a bit of crumpled paper to Bertie. "There's a couple of empty whiskey bottles up in the loft. Neighbors said Butcher was a drinker?" He looked at her for confirmation he obviously didn't need. "Found this right near him," he said, nodding toward the note. "I figure he had it in his hand when he swung off, and then dropped it when . . ."

Bertie took the paper from the sheriff and smoothed it open on her knee. Just four words, not addressed to anybody. It was Mabel's writing. *Gone away with Wallace.* An *M* for her name, the way she signed all her notes.

Two:
DEPARTURE

June 1927
Juniper, Kentucky

MABEL

"Wait!" Mabel pulled hard on Wallace's hand.

"We'll miss the train!"

Already the whistle for the approaching 4:18 had sounded, and from behind the line of juniper trees, Mabel could see a few people gathered in front of the station. By now, Bertie would be sitting in the church with her diploma in her lap, waiting for the principal to finish his address on the importance of discipline and initiative so she could shove through the crowd of other people's relatives to look for Mabel and Wallace. What would be the expression on Bertie's face as it dawned on her she'd been left alone? Confusion or fear? Betrayal? Despair? Mabel pushed the image away. She

45

couldn't look at it. She wouldn't.

"Mabel, we have to go now," Wallace said. "Now — or we have to go back." His chambray shirt stuck in dark damp patches to his chest, and his hair, soaked with sweat from their run, was the color of soiled straw. A few hayseeds clung to his neck, the reason she had stopped him. Mabel picked them off and held them out for him to see before shaking them from her fingers. Without a word, she took his hand again and they turned toward the station.

Mabel kept her eyes down while Wallace paid for the tickets, but still she could feel the stares from people already on the train and from the four or five others standing around, all of them, she supposed, wondering about this rumpled and dirty pair without any luggage between them. She wanted to look up, to see if anyone they knew might be watching them, but she didn't dare. And then Wallace's arm was around her shoulders, and he was guiding her into the car, past the cluster of passengers at the front, settling her by a window near the back, sitting beside her, drawing her head to his chest.

"It was the only way," Mabel said. "Wasn't it?" With another blow of the whistle, the train lurched away. When they got to Louisville, they would disappear in the crowd, get their tickets for Chicago, and leave another for Bertie.

Wallace's voice creaked like an old spring. "Was it?"

Not once before had he hinted at doubt. Mabel lifted her head and looked at him. If he'd noticed her movement, he gave no sign of it. His eyes were fixed on something she couldn't see, a scene playing out silently in his own mind. This is how it would be. She and Wallace would travel through the night and into another day, locked separately inside their questions. This is how it would be for the next two days, until the three of them were together again, safely in Chicago, when she could tell Bertie everything.

But how could she? How could Mabel tell Bertie even as much as she had told Wallace, which wasn't all? Could her sister bear it? Just five days ago, she and Wallace had been so certain. So short a time ago as last Monday, they had agreed there was nothing else to be done. Now for every decision that had seemed inevitable, Mabel could think of three or four more she might have made. She might have found a way — made up some excuse — to send Bertie on ahead of them. But what would Jim Butcher have believed? What could Mabel have said that wouldn't have set off questions, that wouldn't have pricked his rage? Or she and Wallace might have hurried to meet Bertie at the graduation party, and they all could have left together, on the late train. But, no, it would have been too risky to delay, too dangerous for Bertie to travel with them. Or she might just have waited — waited to see if there was any other answer. But what then? What would another month, another week, another day have cost her sister?

It was the way Butcher had looked at Bertie. Even from the back, as Mabel stepped into the hallway to tell him his breakfast was ready, she could see it in how he was leaning into the room, the way his head tilted, the way his hand pulsed on the knob.

There was no decision then, only instinct. A light touch on his arm. A smile. A question about supper. Enough to break the spell, but for how long?

Years ago, when Butcher had looked at her like that, Mabel had been alone, no one to interpret for her, too innocent, like Bertie was now, to know what it meant. Just like Bertie, she'd been standing before the mirror in a pretty dress, one from Mama's trousseau, altered to fit — rich green shantung for her first Christmas dance. When

Butcher's eyes narrowed to a dark stare, Mabel hurried to explain it was Mama's dress, one packed away the day she got the telegram saying her soldier husband had died of influenza. Still Butcher stared, and, heart banging, Mabel asked him if he minded her wearing Mama's dress. He shook his head. "It's right you should have her things. Suits you," he said, smiling, so she believed him. And when she came home that night, out of the dark cold after the dance, Bertie already in bed, he'd been so kind to her.

He'd built a fire and had made a pot of tea, leaving it on the hearth to keep it hot. She didn't need to tell him how she liked it, with just half a spoon of sugar. Her hands were icy from the walk home, and when he passed her the cup, she was grateful for its warmth.

"Was your mother showed me how to make a pot of tea right," he said. "Used to boil it like coffee till it was so bitter you had to stir in a whole sugar bowl."

"It's good," Mabel said. "Just like Mama's." That wasn't true. It was thick with tea leaves and he had let it steep too long by the fire, but the gesture had been thoughtful.

He asked her about the dance then, sup-

Mama's stereopticon, the clamp full with cards. "Sit down," he said, motioning to the bed. "I know how you like looking through this thing. Some pictures here you've never seen before." He sat beside her and handed her the viewer. Mabel pressed it to her forehead, gasping at what she saw. The card was tinted, dozens of colors deepening the scene, and the lovely women, pinked with life, seemed so close she could touch them.

There were five women, three standing on richly carpeted steps, one leaning against what looked like a marble column, and the other sitting on the tile beside a large square bath, all of them draped in lush silks — rose, teal, saffron, emerald, bronze. On their heads they wore matching turbans, some of them decorated with peacock feathers. Behind the women were long windows with tops like upside-down tulips, and through the windows, blue, like blossoms of sky. Palm fronds peeked out from the edges of the scene, and a large gold urn and flat bowl sat beside the bath.

"Wonderful," Mabel said. "Is it in Turkey? Bertie will love this." She looked at her stepfather. "May I show her tomorrow?"

"There's no hurry," he said. "Look again." He'd removed the first picture. Two of the women on the steps had opened the silk draping at the top, exposing their breasts. The tints of their flesh, the detail of their nipples, the depth of the optical trick made those round breasts as real as Mabel's own. Before she could speak, Butcher pulled aside that picture, and now the first three women had completely removed their top draperies. One was reaching forward to untie another's skirt. The woman beside the column had moved to join the one beside the bath. They had both disrobed entirely and now sat gazing intently at each other's nakedness. One extended her hand as if to caress her companion's breast.

A flick of Butcher's hand, and now all the women were naked, their silks lying in shimmering heaps. Some had gotten in the bath, though they stood to show off their bodies. One pair sat on the floor, facing each other, their legs entwined.

Mabel threw the viewer aside and sprang up, but Butcher caught her by her waist and pulled her down onto the bed. "Prettiest girl," he said, and pressed his mouth hard against hers. His throat swallowed her scream and his hard chest absorbed her struggles. He held her down with the weight of his body, and when he released the kiss, he clamped one hand across her mouth and the other across her throat. "Not a sound, now." He pressed her throat harder. "Not a sound. This stays between us. Wouldn't take a bit of trouble to kill that sister of yours."

Both terror and ignorance had kept her from screaming again. Mabel knew little then of what happened between men and women, and so when she lay there while he tugged her party dress off her shoulders and over her hips, unlaced her corset and rolled down her stockings, she thought he was just going to look at her, perhaps beat her. Anything else was beyond her conceiving, so, when he turned her over on the bed and jammed her face into the wool blanket, she couldn't comprehend what he was doing, imagining he must have sprouted claws to dig within her and tear out her insides. She'd seen him disembowel a deer once and thought now he must be disemboweling her.

He'd been less cruel to the deer. He'd killed it first.

In the dawn light, she was astonished to wake up, to find herself alive. In his bed. In his arms. Her hip bones felt as if they'd been torn from the rest of her body, perhaps broken, and there was such a burning inside her, she thought he must have driven in a lighted candle to sear her with the melted wax. But she was strangely clean, too. The soft scent of lavender rose from her skin, and she was wearing one of her mother's linen nightdresses.

Though it was agony, she rolled to her side, trying to slip out of the bed without waking Butcher, but his arms tightened around her. His breath on her neck, he nuzzled against her. "Little wife," he said. "In this room, you're my little wife."

"Oh, no, no." Hot tears flowed down Mabel's cheeks. Again she tried to pull herself free.

"In this room, I said." Butcher clasped his fingers like a vise around her jaw and forced her to look at him. "Everyplace else, you're my little girl." Nothing, not even coal, was blacker than his eyes. "Say it. Say 'Yes, Daddy.' " Mabel twisted away, but he jerked her back, holding even tighter now. "Say it!"

"Yes, Daddy."

"Like you mean it."

She closed her eyes and tried to swallow, tried to recall her father's face. What came to her was Bertie's face — little Bertie, still sleeping, she prayed, two rooms away — Bertie's face and Butcher's words from last night. Two long breaths. Another swallow. A whisper. "Yes. Daddy."

Against the train windows, rain clattered like giant handfuls of thrown gravel. Beside her, Wallace sat with his head back, hands shuttering his eyes. Mabel looked across the aisle, out the opposite windows. North, beyond the river, shafts of lightning pierced the black clouds.

When they got to Chicago, Wallace would go out to find a place for them to stay while Mabel waited in the station for Bertie's train. Bertie was sure to be tired, upset, confused — angry and afraid — and the first days would be hard, harder even than the days after Mama died, but once Bertie was with them, when they could hold her hands and touch her cheek while they explained all, Bertie would understand, and she would forgive them.

The rocking of the train slowed as it approached a station, small, in need of painting — so like Juniper's. A few seats away, a couple and two children stood up, collecting bags and cardboard cases.

Wallace took his hands from his eyes. "Louisville?"

"No," Mabel said. "One of the little towns. I don't know which." There were three or four such stops — she didn't remember. She'd been on the train to Louisville only once — a special treat, Butcher had insisted, for her sixteenth birthday. That day he took her first to

Stewart's, made her parade and twist before him in each of the half-dozen dresses the saleswoman had selected before he chose one made all of white lace. After that, they lunched in the tearoom, where the waiters gathered to share their best wishes, setting before her a small cake decorated with fresh rosebuds.

Outside the store, Mabel turned back the way they had come, toward the train station, but Butcher linked her arm in his and led her down Fourth Street, around the corner, blocks and blocks away from the bright stores, onto a street with signless, smoky brick buildings. He knocked at a shabby green door, immediately answered by a whiskered man in his shirtsleeves who pointed to a corner half-covered by a thin curtain and said, "Put her back there. I'm all set up."

His courtly manner gone now, Butcher shoved the Stewart's box into Mabel's arms. "Change into this. Everything."

She pressed as far back into the corner as she could and set the box on the floor. Beneath the dress lay silk underclothes, white silk stockings, and white slippers embroidered with ivory and silver thread. Glancing from behind the curtain, she saw the men with their backs to her, leaning over a table, talking, so she slipped out of her dress and tossed it over the curtain rod to give her more cover. Shivering against the cold sting of the silk, she stepped into the lace dress.

"Mabel! Hurry it up."

When she came out from behind the curtain, Butcher snatched her hand and pulled her to him. "Told you she was a beauty," he said, and kissed her hard, his tongue wedging her lips open, then he lifted her in his arms and carried her into another room where there was a swing placed before a backdrop painted to suggest a summer garden. Butcher set her on the swing and gestured toward the other man, now standing behind a camera. "Do everything just as he tells you."

Five days ago, seeing the way Butcher had looked at Bertie in her graduation dress, Mabel had gone to Wallace and told him how her stepfather, since the Christmas before she turned fifteen, had come sometimes once, sometimes nearly every night in a week to force her from the bed she shared with her sister and into his. She told how his whispered threats about Bertie had taught her to keep silent, had schooled her in concealment. But she hadn't told Wallace about the pictures.

They were stereo portraits, a series in the tradition of the Turkish women, twelve views in all, which for years to come Butcher would make her look at while he slid his hands under her nightgown, rough fingers pressing every curve of her body.

There were two copies of the first photograph — one given to Bertie to support the story Mabel was instructed to tell of her splendid birthday visit to the city. In that one, she sat demurely on the swing, her shining hair spread across her shoulders. View by view, her clothes fell away, first the dress, then the chemise, the tap pants, the corselet, the stockings. For the last six, she was entirely naked, ordered to lie on the swing, to arch her back, to spread her legs.

"Ready for the last," the whiskered man said, then told Mabel to kneel on the seat.

She would get through it, she told herself. She would. Just one more. She closed her eyes, took a deep breath, tried to separate herself from her body. The swing creaked.

Butcher, naked, a black mask over his eyes, sat beside her.

"Lean over, girl," said the man behind the camera.

Butcher wrapped his hand around the back of her neck to push her head down, letting go only when her face was inches from his thighs, her long dark hair pooling in his lap.

She jerked upright at the screaming of the whistle, echoed by the conductor's final warning of departure: "Tucker's Creek to Louisville. All aboard!"

Mabel sprang to her feet. "We have to go back!"

Wallace caught her hand. "Mabel, the train's moving."

She stumbled across his legs and fell head-first into the aisle. Righting herself, she crawled a few feet forward. "Stop!" she cried, her face wild.

With the help of another man, Wallace lifted her up and got her back to their seat. All through the car, passengers stared and pointed, murmuring their concern and ir-ritation.

Wallace held her tightly, but still Mabel trembled. "Next stop," she said. "We have to turn back at the next stop."

"We can't." Wallace rocked her, his voice a singsong. "We can't."

"We can wait for Bertie at the station. We'll all go on the late train."

"Sweetheart," Wallace said. "We can't. You know we can't."

"In Louisville, then. We'll meet her train in Louisville."

"Mabel . . ."

"*Please,* Wallace."

Though he touched his fingers to her lips to urge her to stay quiet, Mabel couldn't stop the tears. "She mustn't . . . She can't go back to the house. What if she goes back to the house?"

"But you told her not to," Wallace said. "In your note. Didn't you?"

Mabel wailed. "It won't work. It won't work. Something will go wrong. She's sure to want some of her things. The stereopticon. We could go back for that — just for that."

"We'll find her one in Chicago."

"You don't understand!" Mabel struggled to get out of the seat again, but Wallace pulled her to him, holding her head against his chest.

"Mabel, Mabel," Wallace whispered, stroking her hair. "It's too late, too late."

Yes. Too late. There was no going back now.

THREE:
THE LETTER

November 1933
Newman, Indiana

BERTIE

Not a drop spilled for once. The rusted threads of the cap scraped when Bertie twisted it back onto the lamp. She ought not to use any kerosene this time of day, she knew, but there wasn't enough light coming through the window and her fingers were too cold to cut the cabbage. Hans would fuss about it, but she'd just have to remind him how he was always telling her they had to save where they could on the light bill. He'd come right back and say kerosene cost money, too, but then he'd go sit at the table and wait for supper and not offer another word about it. She'd keep the lamp going only until she had the fire blazing in the stove.

Her stomach flopped inside her when she

thought of the smell that would soon fill the house — like a mildewed wool coat of Mabel's she'd once found in the old barn, only heated up to spread the stink. If she had the salt to spare, she'd shred a couple of heads and pack a crock for sauerkraut. But no, even if she did have the salt, it took weeks to ferment the cabbage . . . and then if it spoiled partway through, all that food — wasted. And if the kraut did take, what would they eat in the meantime?

At least Alma was asleep. She'd dropped right off as soon as Bertie had set her in the rocking chair, bundled in one of her daddy's sweaters. Bertie was glad for it. That child had gotten so she cried every time she saw a head of cabbage, choking on her tears, not able to say just what upset her, but Bertie knew, even if Alma didn't exactly. It was the way her small belly filled with gas after she ate it. Four-year-old bellies weren't made to eat cabbage nearly every day — nor grown bellies, either, for that matter, but that's how it was. Every week for months, when Hans carried in the grocery box — two or three heads of cabbage. And then one day, suddenly, it would be potatoes and they'd feel like Christmas had come, until more months passed with potatoes and potatoes, each week a little softer and more shriveled. After that there might not be any vegetables at all, except the canned tomatoes and the dried beans. The only thing that was sure about what came in the grocery box was that it would never be enough and the last day or two of every week, first she and then Hans would go without so Alma could have a little something.

She gathered up the chopped cabbage and dropped it in the pot then slid her palm across the counter to make sure she didn't miss any little pieces. Mama used to sprinkle a little caraway in if she had it, or some cracked pepper. That small yellow onion, chopped fine, might be nice on top for a change. Bertie wiped her hands dry and scraped the knife clean on the edge of the pot, ready to peel the onion — she'd save the leavings to drop into a broth — then stopped herself just before she made the cut. Hans would need that onion tomorrow, sliced onto the last of the bread. If she used it tonight for flavor, she'd have to send Hans out to work without a lunch, and that wouldn't be right.

At least he had work. Most of the other women she knew couldn't say the same about their men. From one day to the next, Hans never knew what he'd be doing — unloading trucks, digging ditches, clearing brush, laying bricks. When Bill Crother had to shut down the mill, he'd turned off close to a hundred men, keeping just a dozen to make up his work crew — even Hans with his bad leg. Somehow, for the last two years, Mr. Crother had managed to find work for them steady, waiting at the empty mill every morning at six to carry them off to wherever they were needed, sometimes moving them three or four times in a single day. He'd stay right with them, Hans told her, working alongside them, then put in hours longer asking around to find another day's work. There were plenty of folks needing help who couldn't pay for it — even in trade — but good as Mr. Crother was, he put his men first and wouldn't take any charity work. He did his best to hand each of them a few dollars every week, but mostly he paid in groceries because he could stretch the money better that way. Now that winter was coming on, Bertie hoped the coal company would use the crew regular again, since they paid in coal. Each man got a shovelful for every full load sold — on a good day that might be five or six — and at the end of the day, they could divide up the flakes left behind in the truck bed. It didn't leave them any extra, but most days last winter they'd had some to warm up the house of an evening, enough to take the chill off before they tucked Alma into the bed between them.

Just like she'd promised herself, Bertie snuffed the lamp now that the cabbage was stewing. Nothing to do but let it cook and to wait for Hans to come home to dish it up. She'd grown up thinking of her family as poor, but it had never been like this. They didn't have much at Christmas, and until her hips and bosom had spread out bigger than Mabel's, she'd worn her sister's hand-me-down dresses. They'd learned not to waste food or anything else, and at school, though it did make the teacher mad, they used up every bit of space on their paper and wrote new compositions on the backs of ones that had already been marked. But now she knew what it really meant to be poor. She could think of a hundred things to do — like stitch up the seam in Alma's blue dress, but how could she? What was she to do, unravel a seam from one of her own to get a length of thread? Her dresses were all so old, any thread she'd get would break in the pulling. She'd clean the windows if she had a few drops of vinegar. Or she would mend the chair seat that had broken through if she had any cane on hand. She'd at least wash her hair so she'd look a little nicer when Hans got home, if she could spare the soap. *If, if, if* — that's what these years had done to them.

There was a banging at the back door, enough to rattle the window. Bertie glanced at Alma, still asleep in the rocker, and stepped into the hall to look. Alice Conrad. She came at least once a week, asking Bertie for some sugar or extra yeast or a little wedge of bacon — always something Bertie either didn't have or couldn't spare — every time making a point about how her husband had lost his job when the mill closed. There were three or four others like Alice who lived nearby, women bitter that Hans had been kept on when their husbands weren't.

Bertie had overheard them talking one day when she passed them on the corner, on her way down to the riverbank with Alma to watch the barges pass. "Bill Crother's brother died of the polio, you know," said one. The others nodded, and it was Alice who said what the rest were thinking. "Just pity, then. Why else keep a cripple when there's plenty of strong-legged men to do the work?"

Bertie wished now she'd said to them what had come into her head: *Crother's kept him 'cause he's the best one down there. Never missed a day of work, and there isn't anybody can lift more.* But she hadn't said it. Instead, she'd clamped her lips tight and shoved past them, dragging Alma behind her. If she had said it, they wouldn't have believed her and would have just turned their noses up and walked away, but maybe then they wouldn't keep coming over asking for things, trying to make her feel bad. Not that she did. Why should she? But she did hate the sight of every one of them.

"Afternoon, Bertie." Alice turned the knob and stepped inside without being asked. "Cooked cabbage?" She walked over to the stove and lifted the lid on the pot. "My little Harry just loves cabbage. Specially with corned beef. I can't think when the last time was we had some."

Again, Bertie held her tongue. Only last week she'd seen Alice coming out of the relief office with an order of groceries, and there was a tin of corned beef peeking right out of the top. Ever since President Roosevelt had taken over, all those men who'd been let go from the mill — between the grocery orders and the checks — were doing about as well as they were. It hardly paid for Hans to wear himself out with working. All he had to do was put in as disabled, but he would have died before he quit and went on the relief.

"Would you have a cup of flour to spare?" Alice asked.

"Used the last for the bread yesterday," Bertie said. It was a lie, but it might just as easy be the truth.

"It's Sue's birthday, you see." Sue was Alma's age. "And if I just had a little more flour, I could make her a cake. I've been saving the sugar for months." Alice had something in her hand, a piece of paper, and she kept running her fingers along the edge of it, over and over.

"I wasn't able to do a cake for Alma's last birthday." Instead of closing the door, Bertie opened it wider and said to Alice, "A child that age is really too little to know any different."

Alice pulled out a chair and sat down, tapping the paper she was holding on the table. "That wind sure is cold, Bertie. But nice you're able to have the house good and warm."

Nothing to do but shut the door and go on over to the table. She wouldn't sit down, though. Standing beside Alice, Bertie could see what she had in her hand. An envelope. The same pale yellow, the same blue ink. It had gone to Alice's box by mistake and now here was Alice, come to pry.

"What's that you've got there?" Bertie asked.

"Well, I swear," said Alice. "I think I must have left my head right behind me on the pillow this morning." She laughed at her own joke, and Bertie did her best to force a smile. "This came to my house. It looks like it might be for you." She held it up before her face, as if to read it for the first time. "But really I don't see how it can be. Those people at the post office have got you mixed up with somebody named Alberta Fischer."

Bertie didn't have to see the address on the envelope to know how it was written: *Miss Alberta Fischer, General Delivery, Juniper, Kentucky.* The return address was someplace in Chicago. Mabel never put her name on it, just a single *M,* but even without that, Bertie would have known who it was from. She could always pick out Mabel's handwriting, as delicate and pretty as she was. Up above the original address, somebody at the Juniper post office would have printed *Mrs. Imogene Jorgensen, 738 Clark Street, Newman, Indiana.* She wished she could take back the note she had scribbled to the Juniper postmaster right after she was married, telling him how to send on any mail that might come to her. He must have thought it an odd thing for her to do, since she'd never had a letter in her life, but right away he sent out an envelope that had been sitting with the dead letters for four or five months, paying extra out of his own pocket for the postman to bring it straight out to the house. She'd even had to sign for it.

"I was Fischer before I was married," she said to Alice. "And there's some who've always called me Alberta." She held out her hand for the letter.

"This one's come a long way," Alice said, pretending again like she hadn't spent a long while studying the envelope's details before she ever stepped out of her house. "Postmark says Chicago, Illinois. You got family in Chicago?"

"Now I think of it, Alice, I believe I did save back a little flour. You said you needed a cup?"

"Two cups would be better."

Getting up from the table, Alice scraped her chair across the floor, and Bertie pointed at Alma sleeping in the rocker. She opened the cabinet door just enough to reach in and get the flour canister. No reason to let Alice see what else was inside. She could have put the flour into a sack, but instead she scooped it up in two coffee cups, so Alice would have to put the letter down.

"I thank you for bringing the mail by,"

Bertie said, leading Alice back to the door. "Hope your cake turns out."

Alice turned to look at her over the cups of flour. "I'll be anxious to hear all about your letter."

"Bye," Bertie said, closing the door just a little too fast so Alice had to quick-step out of the way.

Back in the kitchen, she closed off the hall door to keep the heat in, then sat down at the table and picked up the envelope. Most folks looked forward to letters, but like all the ones that had found her before in Newman, this wasn't the one she wanted.

Hans had stood up and looked solemn when that first letter came, like it was some important telegram, and she'd made up a story quick, showing him how it had been forwarded. She told him it was nothing but a letter from her grandmother's sister, who didn't write too often, then she folded it into her apron pocket so he'd forget about it. When she and Hans were getting to know each other, she had told him that because she shared her mother's name, Imogene, the family had all called her by her middle name, Alberta — Bertie for short. It had surprised her how easily the lie had come, once she made it up, and how it felt almost true, right from the start. As far as Hans was concerned, her given name was Imogene Alberta Fischer and she had just passed her twenty-sixth birthday instead of her twenty-first. When she'd left Juniper behind her, she'd taken her mother's Christian name and her sister's age and told everyone she was an only child whose parents had both died of the flu in '18, taken in by the preacher of the Baptist Church until she was old enough to earn her keep. There was a piece of truth in all of it. Daddy had died of the flu, and after Jim Butcher hanged himself, the preacher did take her in until Nellie Perkins was ready to have her at the boardinghouse. Bertie wished now that she'd decided to take her mother's full maiden name, Imogene East, when she was on the train out of Juniper, the greasy dollars from Jim Butcher's strongbox in her pocket, but then there had still been a little part of her that wanted to leave a trail in case Wallace took a notion to follow it.

Odd how even that first letter had the same address as this one, not directed to the old house. Maybe Mabel had somehow heard the news about Jim Butcher. Or maybe she just figured with her gone, Bertie wouldn't stay there. Well, she was right about that. A sour burn pricked the back of

Bertie's throat. Time and again she'd tried to work out some other reason for Mabel to leave her like she did. But in the end it didn't matter. That's what she'd done. And that's how she'd shown herself for what she really was.

Every time a new letter came — this one made the eighth or ninth — Bertie prayed it would be the last, but Mabel wasn't one to give up. Lucky thing that after the first, all the rest had come with the regular post while Hans was at work. But now Bertie had Alice Conrad to worry about, with her big mouth. No knowing who she might tell. At least she hadn't opened it — the seal was still tight — but Alice could sure start the questions going if she wanted to.

Well, the letters had to stop. But how to do that without writing back?

The day after that first letter had come, after Hans had gone to work, Bertie had almost opened it, hoping for some news about Wallace, but she couldn't bring herself to read anything Mabel had to say. There was nothing to say. Nothing but lies. Even an apology would leave too bitter a taste — not that she believed Mabel would ever apologize.

"Mother." Alma was scooting her way out of the rocker, pale cheeks drawn in, thin brown curls sticking all over her head, her daddy's faded green cardigan slipping off her shoulder, not looking any better for her nap. When Alma was born, she was plump as a dumpling and Bertie had worried the girl would tend to heavy like herself — well, like she used to be — but now she couldn't imagine her daughter as anything but rickety. She didn't even seem to want things, not like a four-year-old should, and Bertie reckoned this was because Alma had learned wanting didn't do a bit of good. Even now she knew the child wasn't calling for her so much as just letting her know she was awake again.

"Come on over here." Bertie sat down at the table and pulled Alma onto her lap, folding the sleeves of the sweater up around her daughter's tiny wrists. "Let's count things." Alma lifted her arms to wind them around her mother's neck, but Bertie caught her hands and pushed her arms back down, then twisted the child around again to face the table. She spread her own hands flat and said, "Count," and Alma touched each of her mother's fingers, calling off the numbers without energy. "Now the buttons," Bertie said, leaning back to reach to the low shelf for the old tobacco can, filled with buttons from clothes long gone. She dropped a handful onto the table to keep Alma busy.

"Flower," Alma said, rolling between her fingers a small, carved silver button.

"Rose," said Bertie, taking the button from her daughter. "A rose is a kind of flower." She handed Alma a tortoiseshell button and pointed out the different colors, then lifted Alma into another chair and stood up. "Find me two more like that," she said, and while Alma sorted, Bertie slipped the rose button into her pocket. She ought not to have kept them, and she really ought to go through the button tin to find the other one and just throw them out — but then, it seemed wrong to waste them. They'd look pretty on a dress for Alma when she got a little older. Besides, no one in Newman, not even Hans, knew anything about that pink dress except that she'd worn it when they married in the judge's office.

Not too long ago, out of the blue, Hans had asked about the dress. "You never wear it," he said.

"Nothing to wear it to." She shoved her fist deep into the bread dough she was working on the counter. "It's too fancy for church."

"We got an anniversary coming up. You could wear it then."

"Can't," she said. "I gave it away in a church drive a while back. It never did fit right." She was afraid to turn to look at his face, so she lifted the dough with both hands and flipped it over. It sounded like a slap, coming down. She wouldn't have thought Hans would remember that dress. Every now and again he would shake her up with some tenderhearted feeling she didn't think he had. She sure couldn't tell him the truth — that she'd cut that dress to pieces the day after they were married.

The wedding hadn't been anything like what she used to dream of, though life before Hans had been so long ago, she was finding it harder all the time remembering what her dreams had been. More than anything before or since, she'd wanted to marry Wallace. That much she knew. There wouldn't have been the money for a grand wedding, of course, but they would have been married in the Emmanuel Baptist Church in front of everybody they knew, and when they kissed, everyone would have teared up, seeing such love.

And afterwards? What was it she had wanted afterwards? They'd talked of children, lots of children, and Bertie had seen herself wiping small faces, had seen Wallace laughing beneath a tumble of little bodies

76

on snowy mornings, had imagined year after year cupping a new tiny hand in hers to show just how far to poke a bean seed into the ground.

Storybook notions of a foolish girl, those were. Even so, she would have liked to be able to say she loved Hans, that in six years she had come to love him, but she didn't think that was true, not unless the warm, solid feeling she had for him was love. It was respect, she thought. And appreciation. But love? She'd loved Wallace, had felt a tingling and leaping inside her, and even now when she thought about him for more than a minute or two, that feeling came back.

Of course she wasn't sure Hans loved her either. He'd never said he did. He hadn't even courted her, really. He was already one of the customers at the restaurant when she was hired on to wait tables, and at first she steered clear because she thought he was one of those men who played with girls' feelings. He was always laughing and teasing with the waitresses and asking young women who came in by themselves or in pairs to sit down and let him buy them pie and coffee, but then Bertie started noticing how, when those same girls came in later and Hans was there, they'd nod or wave at him real quick, then look away. If he'd treated them badly, they would have pretended not to see him or they would have walked out. None of it made any sense — not until she saw him get up one day to pay his ticket. Not a minute before, Bertie had heard the girl who had sat down at his table agree to go to the pictures with him, but as soon as he stood up, she was falling all over herself to make up some excuse about just remembering a promise to help her mother. Hans had nodded, offered her his hand to shake, and then waited for her to scurry out the door before he moved painfully in his leg-swinging limp toward the cash register. Bertie felt so bad for him that the next day when he was in for lunch, she scooped up an extra-big helping of mashed potatoes for him, and before she knew it they were talking. She wasn't allowed to sit down with him while she worked her shift, but when he asked her to the pictures, she said yes right off.

He was friendly and kind, but there had never been anything romantic between them. That first evening, when he walked her ever so slowly home after the pictures, she'd reeled off her lie about being nineteen, which was probably the main reason he asked to marry her just a few weeks later.

He was twenty-four — a whole ten years older than she was, if she had confessed to her right age — and ready to settle down. He'd made no secret of that. All his brothers and sisters, older and younger, had married — there were ten of them, counting Hans — and because he was the one left without a family, it had fallen to him to look after his parents, but they were gone now. She noticed he got fidgety whenever the picture at the theater was a love story, and when he told her how his own parents' marriage had been arranged before they came over from Denmark, she understood he hadn't come up thinking that people had to love each other to be married, only that they needed to stick together and help each other along once they were. He'd managed to save a bit of money, he told her, and when he finally did say, "I'd like to marry you if you'll have me," he added right away, "I'll buy you a house, and you can stop working. I'd like us to have four or five children, but I'll accept whatever the Lord brings."

She had almost told him about Wallace then, and Mabel, too, but she couldn't think of how to say it. You had to really trust someone with your heart to tell them how your sister had betrayed you and bewitched your boyfriend into running off with her.

Then if she told about that, she'd wind up telling him about Jim Butcher and all the talk about how it was Mabel's fault he'd killed himself. She'd heard how the women whispered all through the wake.

"Fool he might have been. A drinker. But she threw that boy in his face, sure as I'm sitting here. Her sister's beau."

"Hard to believe that nice Hansford boy could be taken in like that."

"It's the nice ones don't have any strength against a tramp. Her mama hadn't been dead a year when she started making over that poor man, turning his head — we could all see it, Emily, you the same as the rest of us. I expect deep down Jim Butcher felt so bad over it, he lost his mind, couldn't see it was the best thing for that girl to run off."

"Too bad she had to pull Wallace along with her, though. Hurt her sister like that. And I've never seen anybody take on like his mother has these last couple of days."

If the chatter of gossips had been the worst of it, in time Bertie might have found a way to tell Hans, but it wasn't. A few days after her stepfather was buried, she told Mrs. Small, the preacher's wife, that she wanted to go back to the house for her things. Reverend and Mrs. Small insisted on going, too.

"You go on and sort through your dresser, honey," Mrs. Small said. "The Reverend and I will go into Jim's room to look around for anything that might have belonged to your mama."

"If you see the stereopticon, I want that."

In her room, Bertie hurried to unload her dresser drawers and her closet into the washtub Mrs. Small had brought with her, but there was something else she was after. She left the filled washtub on the bed and stepped quietly into the hall. The Smalls were talking low, more gossip, but with their special tone of sorrow. Nobody else, Bertie was pretty sure, knew where Butcher had kept his money, and she wasn't about to let those men from the auction house put it in their pockets when they hunted through what was left. It wouldn't take a minute to slip into the kitchen and reach behind the whiskey bottles for the strongbox. Then there was a wild shriek, so near that Bertie, thinking she'd been caught, knocked a bottle to the floor and had to leap out of the way to keep the liquor from splashing her feet. In an instant, the wad of bills was in her pocket and she was back in the hall, following the sound of hysterical sobs coming from Butcher's room.

Reverend Small was lifting his wife from

the floor into the hard chair where Butcher used to sit to put on his shoes.

"What happened?"

Reverend Small's head snapped up, his face white, his eyes streaming. Bertie stopped where she was.

The Reverend knelt beside his wife, clasping her hands in his. When he began to pray, Bertie bowed her head. That's when she saw the stereopticon lying on the floor near the bed, a scattering of photo cards around it. One card lay closer to the door, close enough for Bertie to reach with her toe, while the Smalls clung to each other, eyes closed. In an instant she recognized the swing and garden background of Mabel's birthday portrait, but she didn't understand the rest. Not at first. A figure of a woman sitting on the swing, wearing nothing but a white half-corset and stockings, her legs spread wide to display thick hair darker than the long locks that draped her shoulders. Her head was tilted down, as if she were trying to hide her face. Bertie didn't have to pick up the card to see that it was Mabel.

How could she tell Hans about that? What, she wondered, would this nice man think of her if he knew she had a sister who could show herself like that? And what would he think of her if she told him that even though she thought Mabel was a tramp, worse than Jezebel, she was still glad Jim Butcher was dead? He might fear for what bad seed she could pass on to his children, and then he would take back his offer, and her chance to live in peace and to stop struggling on her own would be gone.

Of course he'd kept things from her, too. He hadn't told her that he thought whatever belonged to him belonged to everyone else in his family. She'd worn herself out that first spring and summer after they were married, digging up the ground behind and alongside the house, planting corn, beans, peppers, cucumbers, tomatoes — even onions and some dill. And when the harvest started coming in, she worked from early in the morning until way past dark, putting up quart jar after quart jar. She was just carrying the last of the beans down to the cellar when Hans came walking in with three of his sisters, each one of them carrying a crate. He marched them down to the cellar and waved his hand around at the full shelves. "Take whatever you want," he said.

To this day he had never understood why she was mad. That evening she'd yelled and cried, telling him and telling him it wasn't right he should give away her hard work like that, but he just said, "That's how we do things in my family" and "We would have never got through all that ourselves." She'd made up her mind then and there he wasn't going to do it again. When spring came, she didn't plant a garden, and she packed up all the empty mason jars and sold them to a woman down the street.

He hadn't told her about the whiskey, either. She couldn't abide drinking, even if he did get it legal instead of from a bootlegger like Jim Butcher always did. There wasn't a thing she hated to do more than cry, but she just couldn't help it when, right after bringing her back from the judge's office and showing her around her new house, he pulled one of those flat bottles out of the kitchen cabinet and poured himself a drink.

"It's for my leg," he said, but she kept on crying.

"I hear men make all kinds of excuses for it."

"Really, Bertie," he said. "The doctor wrote up an order for it. My leg aches so at night, it helps me sleep." He tried to put his arms around her, but she pulled away and ran into the bedroom. He had enough sense not to follow her right then. She could hear him rummaging around in the drawers in the kitchen. When he did come in, he tapped her softly on the shoulder and held out a raggedy piece of paper. There was a doctor's name printed on it, and a note she couldn't read except for the word *whiskey.*

She had to accept then that maybe the doctor did prescribe the whiskey like medicine, but it wasn't until things got so bad and the mill closed and Hans was bringing in less money every week that she saw how he hurt without it. Prescription or no prescription, they couldn't afford it, and night after night, he walked the floor, in too much pain to settle down. Deep inside, though, she couldn't help feeling glad that there wasn't any whiskey in the house.

Now that the president had gone back on Prohibition, it didn't matter so much that they didn't have a lot of money. With liquor being legal again, it wasn't so high, and it seemed like it was everywhere. On those nights when Hans got into bed and climbed on top of her, she had to hold her breath to keep from being sick when he breathed that nasty sweet smell into her face. It was worse the times he'd get impatient and not wait to see if one drink would quiet the pain. When that happened, she'd leave Hans at the kitchen table, pouring one drink after another, and she'd dig herself down into the covers, wrap her arm around Alma, and pretend to be asleep when he finally came to bed.

Knowing how much she hated drinking men, because of Butcher, Wallace had sworn to her he would never take a drop. There was so much Wallace knew about her — more even than she'd ever told Mabel, especially things about Mabel, like how Bertie felt ugly standing next to her and how she was jealous of how smart and quick Mabel was. She'd even told him how she hated Mabel sometimes, like when she'd make up to Butcher the way she did. How could a person who knew so much about her run off like that? Mabel had made him somehow; Bertie didn't doubt that. But every spell wore off in time, didn't it? Why hadn't he written to her to explain? Why hadn't he come looking for her?

Bertie sat down again at the table and poured out a new pile of buttons for Alma, sorting through them quickly to find the other rose. It was there. She snatched it up before Alma saw it and slid it into her pocket with the other one. She picked up the letter again and got up to stir the cabbage and turn down the fire.

Wallace wasn't going to write. The time had come to bury him, to bury it all. Bertie lifted the lid to the firebox, reached into her pocket, and tossed in one of the buttons. It popped in the fire, clattering against the walls of the box. Startled, she dropped the other back into her pocket — she'd find another way to get rid of it. For a moment, she held the letter high over the flame, feeling the envelope growing crisp in her hand, but she didn't drop it in.

Turning away from the stove, she opened the catchall drawer next to the sink and worked her fingers through a mix of old nails, pieces of broken dishes, and lengths of twine until she found a pencil. It was dull, so she scraped away at it with a knife, whittling a point. She would make the letters stop, once and for all. She wiped the counter dry before she laid the letter down and then dragged the pencil, blackening out the name and address the Juniper postmaster had written in. When she was satisfied that nothing about her Newman identity could be read, she sharpened the pencil again. *Deceased,* she wrote, drawing a line from the word and circling her name, her old name. *Deceased,* she wrote again at the bottom, along with the words *Return to Sender.*

FOUR:
LIKE SHIRLEY

January 1937
Newman, Indiana

ALMA

"Eggs, milk, soda crackers. Eggs, milk, soda crackers." At first Alma had said the list again and again so she would remember it when she got to the store, but now she chanted it and squeezed at the dollar inside her mitten to help keep her mind off the cold. It wasn't working. The sky was as dark as smudgy pencil and snow had begun to mix in with the rain. Her cap was already soaked, the damp cold beginning to seep through her coat.

When she'd gotten to school this morning, the teachers were standing outside telling everyone to go back home right away. Alma could see for herself that the river had risen enough to cover the school yard, and when she passed a cluster of older girls, she heard one of them say the water had gotten into the basement and that the principal was afraid the whole building would wash away. A boy in Alma's class, Ricky Creech, jumped all around the girls, tugging at their scarves and hats, chirping, "No school! Flood's gonna get the school! No school!" The girls looked at him soberly and the tallest one pushed him away and called him a silly, stupid child.

Alma did go straight home, just like her teacher said to, but Mother made her go back out again when Alma told her there weren't any soda crackers to go with her tea. "Better get some things while we can," Mother said, taking a dollar from the baking powder can and handing it to Alma.

"Will they send Daddy home, too?" Alma asked, but Mother just grunted and said her back was still aching from the baby and she needed to lie down again.

Mother was mad at Daddy for going out with the men this morning. They'd come early in a big truck, knocking on doors up and down the street, looking for volunteers to come fill sandbags, build rowboats, and do anything else that was needed.

Alma had followed Daddy onto the back porch and wedged into the corner where the dust mop leaned. Mother came out while Daddy was sitting on a bucket, pulling on his rubbers, and said, "Who are these men?"

"I don't know, Bertie, just men from the town. Everybody that's able has to pitch in."

Mother stood right in front of the outside door, arms crossed and resting on the mound of the baby. "And who's going to pay you for that work? That's what I want to know. Who?"

Daddy shook his head. "I've got to go."

"You tell them you can't go on account of your crippled leg. You know you can't hardly walk when it's cold like this."

Daddy fastened the buttons on his rubbers and stood up. He reached out and tried to take Mother's hand, but she stuffed it down tighter behind the crook of her arm. "I'll be back before the water gets too high," Daddy said. He was trying to use his patient voice, but Alma could hear the way it frayed out around the edges, just a little, like static on the radio. She was used to the sour sound of Mother's voice, all turned in on itself, like it didn't really want to come out, but Daddy didn't get angry so much. "You'll need to take care of things here," he said to Mother. "Put up high what you can and pack a bag. Might have to leave in a hurry."

He held out his arms for Alma and lifted her up for a kiss. "You mind your mother, now. Do what she tells you." Alma tightened her arms around his neck and held on, nuzzling her face in his coat collar. It was still wet from last night, chilled and mildewy at once. He'd be so cold if he went out in a wet coat, and she wanted to say so and beg him to stay, but Daddy didn't hold with fussing and he might lose his temper if she cried.

Daddy rubbed her back then tugged gently at her arm. "Have to go, sweetie." He lowered her to her feet and faced Mother, insisting without any words that she move aside and let him pass.

Alma followed her mother back into the kitchen. Mother sat at the table and put her head down. Alma stood beside her quietly, waiting to be told what to do, but Mother stayed still. Alma didn't think she was crying, but she reached out to touch her mother's shoulder, just in case, because that's what Alma always wished people would do when she was sad.

Mother jerked upright with the touch but didn't turn her head to look at Alma. "You'd better go on to school."

"Daddy said I should help you."

"Daddy said for you to mind. Go on to

91

school."

So she had gone to school, only to be turned around again. When she came back in the house, Mother was on the stepstool in the kitchen, making room on the highest shelf in the cabinet for the things she kept under the counter, but she wasn't hurrying.

"There's water all around the school," Alma said. "Teacher said we shouldn't come back till it says so on the radio."

Mother grasped the lowest shelf of the open cabinet to steady herself while she got off the stepstool. She closed her eyes, rolled her head round and round, and rubbed at her back. "I'm going to lie down for a while," she said. "Be a good girl and fix me a cup of tea to settle my stomach. And bring me some soda crackers with it."

Alma was afraid of the stove, the hiss of gas and how you had to hold the lit match out to get the flame. You never could tell how far it would jump out at you, like a fiery snake. But Daddy had told her to mind and Mother had used her "Don't-sass-me" voice, so she had no choice. She filled the kettle and pressed the lid down until it snapped tight, then set it on the burner. Her hand trembled as she held the match out while she eased on the knob. Gas sputtered at her before catching and swirling into a short flame. The fire was too low to get the water boiling, so she reached to turn up the gas, but before she could, the flame flashed out to lick at the sides of the kettle and then with a gasp shrank to a flicker. Alma backed away from the stove. The flame kept changing size — she'd never seen that happen before. She was too scared to leave the kitchen to tell Mother about it, so she waited, calling out that the tea was almost ready every time Mother shouted for her to hurry up.

When at last the kettle began to whistle, Alma flipped off the gas and leaned back against the counter for a minute. She took a deep breath and held it to steady the heavy kettle while she poured hot water into the waiting cup, then took the squashy tea bag from the saucer where it rested. Mother had taught her not to be wasteful and to use every tea bag for two days. And she was to count the dips of the bag — three crisp dunks — so the tea wouldn't be too strong.

All the way to the bedroom, she took baby steps, trying not to slosh any of the hot tea onto her hands or, worse, onto the floor. Mother was sitting up in the bed, eyes closed, so Alma set the cup on the bedside table and started to tiptoe out.

"Is that the tea?" said Mother, opening

93

her eyes. She patted the place beside her. "Thank you, doll. Come on up here while I drink it."

When her mother spoke sweetly like this, Alma could almost forget the other times. For as long as she could remember, she'd tried to work out what made Mother angry and what made her kind, but there just didn't seem any way to really tell, since something that made her happy one day might make her mad the next. Daddy said it was just that Mother felt bad right now, that sometimes waiting for babies to come could make a woman sick, but Mother and Daddy had talked about the baby only since the end of last summer, and Alma could remember plenty of times before that when Mother was snappish.

And there had been a long time when the leaves were orange and red, about the time Mother's belly had started to get round, when Mother had acted mostly happy. One day when Alma got home from school, Daddy was dancing Mother around the living room in his jerky step and Mother was laughing. Then when Mother saw her standing in the doorway, she danced over alone and swooped Alma up into her arms and swished and turned back towards Daddy. On the radio an orchestra was playing the tune for "Blue Moon" and Daddy was swaying along with the music, tapping with his bad foot, singing made-up words of his own that didn't quite go with the rhythm: "Crother's Mill is open again . . . money comin' in . . . Bertie's gettin' a gas stove . . . blue moon."

"Tea's good," Mother said, taking a loud sip. "Get me some crackers, sugar."

"There's no more," Alma said, and Mother's mouth turned down the tiniest bit. Then she had set the cup back on the table and swung her legs over the edge of the bed. "We better go see what else we need."

Alma snuggled her face down further in her scarf, trying to find a dry spot, and chanted the list again: "Eggs, milk, soda crackers." She tried to imagine Daddy building a rowboat. When she thought of him filling sandbags, she worried about the sand going down into his rubbers and into his shoes, scratching at his feet. Her own feet inside her rubbers were suddenly so cold she could barely feel her toes, and looking down, she cried out. Water was rushing around her, just like the water had in a creek she'd waded in last summer. But this wasn't a creek, it was Market Street. She was almost to the store, just another block. Mother would be upset if she came home without the groceries, so she sloshed on. By the time she reached Gibson's, the water was lapping at her ankles. The store was closed. She pounded at the door and waited, but nobody came.

Further down the street, closer to the river, the water seemed to be gushing up and pouring toward her, as if it were coming after her. She turned for home, but in the short time on Gibson's stoop, the water had come up higher, too deep now for her to run like she wanted to, and anytime she tried, her feet threatened to slip from under her. She walked and walked, her legs weak, tired out from having to push through the dirty river. It wasn't quite so high and fast when she got to Beeler Street, but still it swooshed over the round toes of her rubbers. At the end of Clark Street, which had only been rain-wet when she left the house, she did begin to run, even though she couldn't feel her feet and the water here splashed with every step, up her legs and over tops of her boots.

Panting, she pushed onto the back porch, letting the screen door bang behind her. "Mother! Mother!"

Alma saw the way her mother's mouth tightened at her empty arms and at the dirty tracks she'd made. "The river, Mother. The store was closed."

Mother pulled the curtain aside and looked out at the street. "Go turn on the radio," she said. "Then go get your corduroy pants, your warm sweater, your good dress, and a couple changes of underwear and lay them on my bed. And one toy — just one, mind."

Alma already knew what she was going to take, not a toy at all. It had rained and rained for almost two weeks, and on Tuesday, her teacher had told the class that the river was rising fast and there might be a flood if the rain didn't stop. "Think about what's most precious to you besides your family," she said, and they all had to stand up and describe what they would take if they could have only one thing. Alma said she would choose her china doll, and the teacher had smiled, but Alma knew what she would really take was her Shirley Temple scrapbook.

On the front, it looked like Shirley in her bright yellow dress was stepping out of the giant green book to smile at everybody. Alma kept her best school projects inside, plus a picture of Daddy, and a story from an old newspaper about a baby that was stolen away. Daddy had given it to her and said the baby's father was famous and flew airplanes and that she should keep the story because it was something important that happened during her lifetime, even if she couldn't remember it. She'd pasted it in to please Daddy, but she didn't like thinking about a stolen baby. She did like the picture she'd colored of the Indian mother. After making that at school, she'd brought it home and pasted it in the scrapbook, and then, on her own, she drew a little baby on a piece of white paper and cut it out like a paper doll. She knew where Mother saved sheets of brown paper from grocery parcels, so, while Mother was busy hanging laundry out, Alma sneaked to take a piece. She cut a big shaky circle, dotted the center with paste, and pressed it on the page beside the Indian mother. When it was dry, she folded up the bottom of the circle and the two sides, then tucked the baby in. In Mother's sewing box, she found a threaded needle, and she punched this down into one of the side flaps, leaving a long end of thread, then punched the needle up through the other flap, cut the thread and tied a bow to keep the papoose nicely snug. She liked being able to slide the baby out to lay it in the mother's arms for a little while, then put it back in the pouch to keep it safe.

She also had a picture of Myrna Loy, cut

from a magazine Daddy had found on a bench outside the drugstore. In the picture, Myrna Loy was wearing a frothy apron and holding out a beautiful platter with a big roasted turkey ringed with apples and roses. Underneath the picture, it said "The glamorous Miss Loy is a star in the kitchen as well as on the silver screen."

The best thing in her scrapbook was a card with two pictures, side by side, of a dark-haired girl on a swing. The girl was wearing a pretty dress of white lace, and though she wasn't smiling, she was even more beautiful than Myrna Loy. Alma didn't understand why the pictures looked just alike, and she didn't know who the girl was, but sometimes when she looked hard, she thought it might be a picture of her mother. No matter how much she wanted to, she couldn't ask Mother about it, since she'd stolen the picture from the family Bible — way in the back in the Book of Revelation that nobody ever read. If she wanted to know about it, she'd have to put it back in the Bible and pretend to find it again, but she was afraid if she did, Mother might take it away and hide it someplace Alma could never find it.

"Are you getting those things?" Mother called. "Hurry, Alma!"

Alma lay on the floor and reached far under the bed to pull her scrapbook out. In her dresser, she had two warm sweaters, but one of them, the green one, really belonged to Daddy. She took that one out for him and imagined herself wearing it over her own if she had to set out to rescue him. She could see herself in the rowboat, standing at the front, directing the grown-ups where to go and keeping them calm by being cheerful, like Shirley Temple always was. If in the confusion Daddy got arrested, like Shirley's daddy in *The Littlest Rebel,* Alma would put on her good dress and go see the president to get him out of jail, just like Shirley did. That picture was her favorite. In most of the others Daddy had taken her to see, the children's parents had somehow got lost. When she and Daddy left the theater, Alma was always sure to smile and tell him how she liked the picture, but later in bed, she would push her face into the pillow and cry for those poor lonely children.

"Alma, come now!"

Alma took a long look around her room and then stacked and carried her things back to her mother's room. Mother was folding a dress and putting it in an open case beside a pair of shoes. Next to the case, the Bible lay on a pile of other clothes waiting to be packed. Mother held out her arms for Alma's bundle. She didn't notice Daddy's green sweater, but she held up the scrapbook and said, "Are you sure this is what you want? Everything that's left behind might get ruined." Alma imagined the river surging into their house, filling up the gas stove, floating the kitchen table, pouring into her room, drowning her dolls, her toy monkey. A tear ran down her cheek like a tiny river.

"Alma?"

She nodded. "It's for remembering."

Mother looked at her for a moment, her mouth turned up in just one corner, then she laid the folded dress and the scrapbook in the bottom of the case.

When she was finished, Mother closed the suitcase and carried it into the front room, then sat down in the big chair and closed her eyes. Alma went to the window to look out again. The rain was coming down harder than ever. Across the street, the water had come up halfway on the tires of the car Mrs. Mialback left parked in front of her house for her son to drive on Wednesdays when he came to take her shopping. When Alma pressed her face against the window and squinted, she thought she could see Mrs. Mialback at a second-story window.

Their own house had just one floor on top of the basement. On the radio, the music had stopped and there was nothing but people calling up crying and giving their addresses, asking for someone to come after them. They didn't have a phone at their house, but Alma didn't worry. Daddy would come for them. He'd said he would.

The hall clock chimed another hour passing, and then another. The river had come up over their front yard and the first step into the house was almost covered. Alma stood out on the front porch, leaning over the railing, trying to count the odd things that drifted past in the street — a couple of wooden chairs, a man's hat, three tires, a dead cat, six or seven big cans of peas, and many more things she couldn't recognize. Somewhere, behind and beneath her she heard what sounded like a giant faucet left to run.

Mother flung open the door. "It's in the basement!" Her eyes were red-rimmed and wide open and she snatched Alma into her arms and pulled her into the house.

"Daddy will be here soon," Alma said, trying her best to sound sure the way Shirley always did. Mother paced around the room, holding up her belly with one hand and rubbing at her eyes with the other.

Another hour passed and the water covered the next step. Just one more before it was on the porch. Across the street, Mrs. Mialback was leaning out of her upstairs window, screaming. Her dog was barking along with her, but he was a little dog and Alma couldn't see him.

Mother whirled around to glare at the window and covered her ears. "What good does she think that's gonna do!" Mother picked up Daddy's red glass ashtray, the one that sat by his chair, and threw it against the wall. Alma ducked down behind the couch and curled into a ball. She didn't want to cry. She didn't. Daddy would be there any minute, and he would want to see how brave she had been.

When Alma peeked up over the back of the couch, Mother was gone, but she could hear her rattling around in the kitchen. Mrs. Mialback was still screaming, but now Alma could hear her words clearly: "Over here! Up here!"

Yes, there was a rowboat coming down the street. She couldn't quite make it out from the window, but when she ran out onto the porch, there it was. Alma jumped up and down, waving her arms, then ran back inside the house. "Daddy's coming!"

She and Mother wound their wool scarves

around their necks and hurried into their coats. Mother carried the suitcase out to the porch and they both shouted and waved. There were two men standing in the boat and two others sitting and rowing. A woman and three children sat around them.

Across the street, Mrs. Mialback leaned out her window to wave at the men, then she snapped down the window. A moment later, she was standing in her coat on her porch, her little white dog in her arms.

When the boat got closer, one of the standing men waved right at Alma. Alma called, "Daddy! Daddy!" The men looked at each other.

The rowers guided the boat right up to the edge of their porch and one of the men jumped out onto the flooded steps. Alma didn't know him. She looked at the faces of the other men, who nodded at her and motioned for her to come onboard. Daddy wasn't there.

"Anybody else in the house, ma'am?" the first man said to Mother.

Mother shook her head, handed him the suitcase, and then pushed Alma forward to be lifted into the boat. Another man jumped out to help lift Mother into the boat, and then the rowers worked to turn it around to cross to Mrs. Mialback.

When Mrs. Mialback reached out to hand her dog to one of the men, Mother tried to stand up. "I'm not going in a boat with any filthy dog!"

"Mrs. Jorgensen," said Mrs. Mialback, "he's a gentle dog. I'll hold him tight so he won't bother you."

Mother looked up at the man who had lifted Alma into the boat. "You will not take that dog! It's people that have to be worried about now."

Alma wanted to say something, but Mother was so angry, she was afraid. Fritz was a nice little dog and he minded whatever Mrs. Mialback said. He could even stand on his hind legs and spin in a circle like a dog in the circus.

"I won't have it. I won't have it," Mother kept saying. "You will not put a dirty dog in with me and my child!" She put her hand on her belly, and Alma heard one of the men whisper to another about women who were expecting.

Mrs. Mialback stepped back on her porch and held Fritz close to her. She looked icily at Mother and then said to the men, "Will you send another boat for me, please? If you can?"

The men looked at Mother and shook their heads, then nodded at Mrs. Mialback.

As the boat moved away, down towards Beeler Street, Alma watched Mrs. Mialback and Fritz getting smaller and smaller on their porch.

It seemed like they were in the boat a long time. They stopped at some houses further down the street and picked up Mrs. Peters and her children and then shaky old Mr. Nash and his sister. The boat was full now, but people shouted at them from windows, begging them to stop. They rowed past a few other boats, all full, and each time Alma tried hard to see Daddy, but he wasn't there. Just after they passed the sign for Pearl Street, one of the men said everybody would have to get out and wade toward Hill Street, where there were trucks waiting for them.

The men who had been rowing the boat jumped out to help them all onto the flooded street. The water was up to Alma's knees and so cold it took her breath. For a moment she thought she might sink into it, but then she felt the strong grasp of her mother's hand. They walked in the direction the men pointed and when they got to a place where the river was down around her ankles, Alma looked back to see the men rowing down Pearl Street — to get Mrs. Mialback and Fritz, she hoped.

With every block they walked, there was less and less water, and it seemed strange when they got to Hill Street that it was almost dry. There were more people there than Alma had ever seen, and the terrible noise of people crying and shouting, of truck motors rumbling, and of men sawing boards and pounding nails. Lined up in front of the Catholic church, twenty or thirty men were building boats. They all looked the same in their dark wet coats, their hats pulled down over their eyes, but Alma scanned for Daddy.

Mother tugged at her hand. "Come on." Ahead of them, a nun was holding a writing pad and taking down people's names and then telling them to climb up into the trucks. While they waited, three or four trucks pulled away, the beds so full that everyone was standing, pressed up against each other.

Now Mother was dragging her to one of the trucks, past the men who were working on the boats. Alma looked and looked, and then she saw one of the black-coated men limp over to a pile of lumber. She yanked her hand from her mother's and ran. "Daddy! Daddy!"

It was Daddy, and when she got to him,

he caught her in his arms but didn't pick her up.

"We're going on the truck," Alma said. "Come on. I packed you a sweater."

Daddy grabbed her hard by the shoulders and looked in her face. He wasn't smiling. "You go right now," he said. "I have to stay here. Stay close to your mother."

Alma looked behind her. Mother had followed and she looked mad. "Don't you ever run from me like that again!" Mother's hand came down hard across Alma's cheek and she grabbed Alma roughly by the arm. "You want us to miss that truck?"

Alma's face stung and she could feel it growing red and hot and wet with tears she couldn't stop. She looked at Daddy. He looked upset with her too. "Go on, now," he said, swatting her bottom. "Go on."

A big man picked her up and carried her off toward the rumbling truck. She twisted in the man's arms, first trying to get away and then struggling to look over his shoulder so she could at least wave good-bye to Daddy, but he was lost again in the crowd of dark-coated men. Other arms grabbed her as she was lifted onto the truck, and soon she couldn't see anything except the bodies pressed against her. On the street, someone was shouting for them to push in

108

tighter, make more room. There were so many people that no one could fall, even when the truck jostled away. Around her, everybody chattered, everyone except Mother, who stared up at the gray sky, but no one seemed to know where they were headed.

FIVE:
THE POSE

April 1943
Chicago, Illinois

MABEL

It was obvious to Mabel that the girl wanted
to keep her coppery hair pinned up in a
twist — that she probably really wanted to
cut it short like all the other girls — but her
father insisted that she let it fall around her
shoulders. "Hair is a woman's glory, Daisy,"
he said. "Yours especially." Lock after lock,
he lifted her glory at the ends, as if picking
up water, each fine strand draining from his
fingers to settle like a gleaming waterfall,
from which she, the river's nymph, peered
out.

If you could discount the girl's expression, she was as lovely and untroubled as a
Renoir child, but Mabel could not discount
it. She knew what it meant — the mouth
and cheeks soft in calculated placidity, eyes

110

outwardly shimmering with naïveté but focused on something deep inside — something knowing, solid, and true. Mabel had worn it herself. The girl, Daisy, was perhaps twelve, a little younger than Mabel was when she had mastered the pose.

"See there," said Daisy's father, Emerson Harker, who stepped back to admire his work. "Ask Miss Fischer if you don't believe me. This makes a better picture. Miss Fischer?"

Mabel started at his question and looked away from Daisy toward him. "There's no formula for a good photograph, Mr. Harker." The smooth dark gloss of Daisy's hair against the nubbly white lace bodice, the contrasts heightened in developing, would certainly enrich the portrait, but she wasn't going to tell Harker that.

Mabel stepped behind the camera, looking up occasionally to ask Daisy to tilt her head or resettle her hand. For each change, the girl had to be asked only once, for she struck every new position exactly right the first time.

When she was finished, Mabel said, "I'd like to get some unposed shots of Daisy, too. Maybe at home?" Harker stared hard at her. Trying to read her, Mabel thought, size her up. "At your convenience, of course," she said, offering her best professional smile. "It's a specialty of mine." She swept her hand around to direct his attention to the photographs on the studio walls, subject groupings, mostly of soldiers and their families, mixing formal portraits with more natural moments. "No extra charge," Mabel said. "The session fee covers an hour or two in a more informal setting." That was a lie. "Anywhere you feel most yourself — your house, the park, a church —" Mabel pretended not to notice the sharpness in Harker's eyes. "Your choice."

When Harker turned his look to Daisy, Mabel watched her too, but she was a careful girl, so cooperative, her expression as serene as before.

Arms crossed, Harker took floor-pounding steps from one group of photos to the next, staring at them as though they had given offense. "You're not going to hang her on your walls," he said. "I don't need any of these hopped-up boys coming round my girl, trying to lure her into trouble just 'cause they're going off to the war. Plenty of V-girls around for that."

Mabel kept her tone casual as she switched off the fill lights, stealing another glance at Daisy. "I don't put up anything without the client's permission," she said. "And even then, I don't tell anybody who's in the picture." She went to where Harker was standing and pointed at the photo showing a dozing young marine stretched out on the ivy-patterned sofa in his mother's living room, his uniform rumpled, his infant son asleep on his chest. "If he doesn't come back," Mabel said, "this is the picture his wife will cherish. Even more than their wedding portrait." She nodded to the wedding photo — the groom, not a soldier yet, standing awkwardly straight, his bride, head to toe in lace, looking out from her veil with wide eyes, both struggling to look grown-up and dignified, both failing. "Startling how young, she is, isn't it?" Harker's head snapped toward her. Mabel nodded again toward the photo. "The bride."

Perhaps she had said too much, but Mabel was determined to go on, to show Harker he couldn't rattle her. She pointed to another photo, one of the marine and his parents around the kitchen table, laughing and spooning up large bites of blackberry cobbler. "I could take shots of you with Daisy while you're here," she said, "but if you'll let me take both, I think you'll like the home photos better."

Harker rubbed hard at his forehead with his fingertips. He turned his head to look again at Daisy, still sitting on the stool in front of the backdrop. He would not look at Mabel. "Saturday afternoon," he said, "around two. No more than an hour." He took a small notebook from his pocket, wrote out his address and phone number, and handed it to her. "Ring up when you're on your way."

Just like Paul used to, Mabel kept the studio closed until noon on Thursdays so the morning was free for making prints. The first week she worked there, she had asked him, "Why Thursday?" He said it was because Thursday was the slowest day and mornings were slower than afternoons and he liked having the break just before the busy time on Friday and Saturday, but Mabel had never seen the truth of that. Even before those long Depression years, there hadn't been any busy time to speak of, and they'd kept the studio going by taking postcard photos and stringing for the *Chicago Tribune*. Any morning would have done as well as another, but she soon discovered how important regularity was to Paul, how he looked forward to the quiet, there alone in the glow of the red light, and then to the sunlight that met him when he was ready to come out again. Though now she often had to stay late to make prints after hours, Mabel had kept with Paul's schedule, treating her Thursday mornings as inviolable.

She swished the print in the first tray with the tongs and watched the outline of Daisy Harker's face bloom. Behind Mabel dangled strips of negatives, dozens more ghost images of Daisy. Having a few prints to take with her on Saturday would help persuade Harker to let her go on with the session if he balked. On the shelf above her were rolls and rolls of still-undeveloped film capturing other girls who had come to sit for portraits to send off with their boyfriends bound for war, and still more rolls of the men, the boys, who were going — all of them desperate to record a time that was already gone, to have something more tangible than the slippery images of memory.

The war had brought Mabel more business than she could handle on her own. To fit in the extra session at Emerson Harker's, she'd had to reschedule two other sittings — but Paul would have done the same. Still, it seemed unfair of fate that Paul should miss the boom time, a chance finally to have enough money to live decently without scraping, but Mabel was glad, too, that he hadn't lived to see the new war. His gas-scalded lungs had filled with fluid and carried him off two months before Pearl Harbor.

Paul had told her once it was his five months in France that had turned him into a photographer. Not that he had wanted to record the agony in the Marne. "No," he'd said, "I decided then and there I wanted to be in control of what I saw." She had liked that idea of control, but when she'd started taking photos herself, she saw quickly that the most beautiful pictures — the most beautiful because they were the truest — came of spontaneity, not posing. She had gladly traded in hope of control when she realized the camera had given her something she'd craved even more: invisibility. Behind that black box, she disappeared, becoming the observer who could not be observed. She wanted no photos of herself and had never allowed Paul to take another after the first, the one she exchanged for a job.

Crazy how he'd taken her in like that, right off the street — more than fifteen years now — a thin girl in a dirty coat who'd never even touched a camera. She'd spent most of the three days after Wallace disappeared wandering around Union Station, answering every boarding call to search for him in the crowd. Finally, after she'd taken

116

to sleeping on a bench beneath the arching skylight in the Great Hall, the manager came with a couple of guards and told her vagrants weren't allowed and that she'd have to leave. "I'm just looking for my family," she said. "I have a room." The manager didn't believe her, just humored her by saying, "Then you'd best go back there and get some sleep."

She'd been telling the truth about the room, but by the time she was forced out of the terminal, it was as good as lost because she wouldn't be able to pay the week's rent. There was no point in even showing her face at the grocery, since Mrs. Winniver had reminded her every day she'd worked there that plenty of others would like to have her job. Working for Mrs. Winniver had been like stepping round a bobcat for twelve hours a day, and Mabel would have quit except that the bruised apples, scuffed carrots, limp greens, and sprouting potatoes she got to take home with her pay on Mondays were mostly what she and Wallace lived on, saving everything they could trying to bring Bertie to them.

But Bertie hadn't come.

That first day in Chicago, Mabel had survived the long hours of waiting for Bertie's train by imagining their embrace —

how she would notice the strong breadth of Bertie's back, how she would breathe in the sweet smell of her sweat and marvel at the softness of her hair, as if at once she were holding her sister in her arms for the first and the last time.

Wallace had returned just before the train was due. He carried apples in his pockets — three lovely apples to celebrate his having found a large room for them, clean and cheap, rented by a landlady willing to believe his story that they were all siblings, doing their best to stay together now that their father had died.

They stood for a long time after the train had departed, looking up and down the platform and all through the station, trying to persuade themselves that Bertie had gotten off and was waiting for them on a bench in a dark corner somewhere. "She probably missed the connection in Louisville," Wallace said at last. "You know how that train's always late getting into Juniper."

"Is it?" Mabel had never known it to be — for years she had used the faint whistle of the 10:45 coming into the station as her signal to mark her page, lay her book aside, put out her light, and kiss her sister's dreaming cheek — but she wanted to believe Wallace. "Yes," she said. "That must be it."

Wallace shrugged. "Let's go find out the schedule from Louisville."

They'd gone back to their room to sleep, but they hadn't slept at all, fearing they would miss the first train, due just before six o'clock. Bertie wasn't on that train. Or the next. She wasn't on any of them — this they knew for certain, because for the next four days, one or both of them met every train that came out of Louisville, Indianapolis, and every other possible connecting stop between Juniper and Chicago.

They had no money then to send for another ticket, so they wrote to her: *Darling B — We will send train fare with instructions by July 15. We'll meet you at the station and will explain everything. Forgive us. Stay quiet. Love M & W.* No return address, in case anyone in Juniper was looking for them, sent to Bertie at General Delivery.

In July, they sent the money and waited for the train. In August, they sent more money and waited again for the train, and so on in September, October, and November, always with the clearest instructions they could give: *Take the 8:35 out of Louisville to Chicago on the 19th* — or whatever day they had singled out.

Though she could see Wallace dissolving by degrees, Mabel refused to give up hope.

119

One or more of the letters might have been lost, she told herself, or the money stolen. It might not occur to Bertie to check with the post office at first, but after a while it would — or the postmaster would ask around until he found her — and there the letters would be, waiting for her, and if she'd missed the latest date, she would understand that in another month, another letter would come and she would take the train then. Mabel was so sure that they would all be together again by Christmas that, without telling Wallace, she had put back a little money to buy some cherry cordials, Bertie's favorite. In January, she would see to it that Bertie started back in school, and then when Bertie graduated, the first high school graduate in the family, if Bertie and Wallace still felt the same — and why wouldn't they? — they'd be married.

Imagining sitting by a fire with Bertie and Wallace's children at her feet, listening as she read to them the books their mother had read to her and Bertie — *The Secret Garden, Idylls of the King, A Girl of the Limberlost* — had pulled Mabel through all the hard days since June, but now what did she have? In their letters, they had said only as much as they dared — that Wallace still loved Bertie, that there was nothing but friendship between him and Mabel — but Bertie would not forgive them; her failure to come had made that clear. And understanding this, Wallace had left.

At first, Mabel didn't realize he had gone. She'd come back to their little room around 6:30, as usual, ready to heat up a mix of vegetables for their supper before Wallace headed out for work. She thought he must have gone in early, taken half the day janitor's shift, as he sometimes did for a little extra money, but when the next morning came and Wallace didn't return, she knew. He'd taken his coat, but his spare shirt still hung on the peg beside his bed. The pencil that had been in his pocket when they caught the train from Juniper was on the washstand. Beside it, overlooked the night before, lay his room key. Nothing else — no note, not even a fragment started and thrown away. Nothing except the memory of how Wallace had seemed a little smaller every time he came by the store from the station, his hair stringy and wet from melting snow, to say Bertie once again hadn't gotten off the train. That, and the memory of those terrifying times Mabel would wake in the early-hour dark to hear Wallace weeping on the other side of the screen, calling for Bertie and moaning, "Lord, forgive me."

That morning, Mabel had picked her way around icy snowdrifts, looking for Wallace everywhere they'd ever gone together or apart in Chicago, tracing over and over her route to the grocery and his to the office building he swept and mopped every night, describing him to anyone who would stop long enough to listen. Finally, exhausted and chilled through, she settled in at the train station. For a while she had let herself hope that Wallace had taken the risk of sneaking back into Juniper to fetch Bertie himself, but if that had been his plan, he would surely have taken his clean shirt and left her a note saying what he'd done. If he'd gone anywhere at all, with or without Bertie, to start another new life, he would have told her. Wouldn't he? By the third day, Mabel had given up praying for everything except some sign that Wallace was safe, even if he chose to be alone. But there was no sign.

Evicted from the depot, she wandered up one street and down another, winding through town, paying no attention to where she was going, looking in shop windows, seeing nothing. That's what she was doing when Paul spotted her and came out of the studio, pulling a dusty brown cardigan over his dingy white shirt, wanting to take her picture. "Please," he said. "You're so pretty

— so pretty and so sad all at once."

The very idea of standing again before a photographer paralyzed her even as she longed to run. "I don't like to have my picture taken," she said, eyeing the big, grinning, red-faced man before her. He was old enough to be her father. Old enough to be Jim Butcher. But not like either of them. Not being like Butcher would have been enough. This man didn't have her true father's quiet ease, though he didn't seem to mean her any harm. Still, she wasn't sure she could trust her instincts. "Why do you want a picture of me?"

"Nice samples are good for business," he said. "Customer comes in, sees a photograph of a pretty girl, he thinks, This fella's mighty good." He laughed, pushing his single lock of hair back from his forehead, and then the laugh became a cough that shook his shoulders. He turned away a little and covered his mouth with a handkerchief pulled from his pocket. Then, when the fit was over, he turned back to her and picked up as if it had never happened. "It's easy, see? I take a picture of you — even if it's nothing special — it'll still be sweet to look at, and I get some of the credit for what God made."

She liked him in spite of herself, but she

didn't let on to him, not then. "No," she said. "You can get somebody else." She took a step away, right into the path of a woman loaded down with Christmas shopping. When she had mumbled her apologies and the woman had pushed on, Mabel looked back over her shoulder at Paul. "Besides, I don't have the money to pay you."

"Free. Free," he said. "You'd be doing me a favor." The whole time he talked, he hadn't taken a single step toward her, as if he knew she might bolt if he did. He'd even calmed his vibrant hands by clasping them behind his back. "Just come in and have a look," he said. "See what I do."

He was obviously proud of the photographs he showed her, some framed on the walls, some in big albums, but they looked a little stiff to her, as if the subjects were enduring the process, even the ones who were smiling. The studio itself was a mess — spent flashbulbs rolling around on the floor, prints scattered across every flat surface, cloths dropped here and there, two or three plates with bits of dried cheese and bread crumbs. A photograph of her wasn't what he needed.

What she needed was a place to anchor her while she kept searching, kept trying to gather her little family back in. "I'll trade you," she said. "I let you take my picture to put up and you give me a job keeping this place clean. I'm good with hair, too, so I can help you get people ready for their pictures."

"Done!" He flung out his hand for a shake. She was startled by her own boldness, stunned and suspicious that he had so easily agreed to her silly bargain. He even gave her a few dollars, an advance on her first week's pay, so she could make the rent on her room. Walking back there against the bitter wind, she had begun to wonder if, seeing her need, Paul had somehow set the whole thing up, tossing about a quick mess, just so he could give her a job. To this day, she still wondered. Far-fetched, maybe, but not impossible; indeed, the longer she knew him, the more likely it seemed.

Paul had the power to see even the subtlest signs of a person in trouble, and he had the gift of being able to give without appearing to. The woman who ran the bakery next door would sometimes find that the heavy bags of flour had been lifted onto her storeroom shelves while she was out front paying for the delivery. A messenger boy who'd half-ridden, half-carried his bicycle into town to get his punctured tire repaired might come out of the shop and find a dollar woven into a wheel spoke. Their own customers, always the ones who had long saved for the luxury of a special photograph, would often come back after paying to mention some miscalculation on their bill, and Paul would jovially tap his head and say, "My mistake!" and when they would promise to pay him the rest when they could, he would wave them off and say, "No! No! Paul Connolly pays for his own mistakes!"

At one time or another, nearly everyone in the neighborhood had told Paul their greatest sadness — because he let them tell their stories in their own time and way. It was nearly two years before Mabel told him about Wallace, calling him her brother, and several months more before she told him about Bertie and how she and Wallace had written and written — how she had written since — and never gotten an answer. To tell him about Bertie, she had to identify Wallace rightly, not as her brother, but as Bertie's beau. When she did, she didn't confess to having lied before, just went on as though she were mentioning Wallace for the first time. Paul's eyebrows didn't even flicker in question. He never asked why she'd left Juniper, why she couldn't simply go back and talk to Bertie, and for that, she loved him.

While Mabel became an expert at eluding Paul's sneaky efforts to photograph her, she was pleased at how she'd managed to catch him unawares perhaps a dozen times in as many years, a quick snap of the shutter as she pretended to test the light or rewind a roll. She'd saved all those negatives in secret, concealing them in the cabinet under the name M. Brownlow, recalling Oliver Twist's rescuer. When Paul died, she printed every one of the negatives, unwilling to give up a single view of her friend, and hung all but one in the darkroom, where, in the dim light, it would seem that he was still there, watching over her shoulder, guiding her. Her favorite, she hung in the studio, behind the counter. Paul would have scoffed and snatched it from the wall, saying no one wanted to look at such an ugly bloated old man, but she defied his memory on this and kept the portrait up because his laughing face — with his mounded cheeks, bad teeth and squinting eyes — was glorious.

One by one, as she finished them, she clipped the prints of Daisy, ten in all, to the line to dry, then shut off the red light, stepped out of the darkroom, and pulled up the shades on the front windows to let in the late-morning light. Sitting backwards on the bus stop bench in front of the shop, staring in at her, was Daisy Harker.

Mabel turned the lock on the door and stepped out to the sidewalk. "Hi," she said. "Have you come for your photos? They won't be ready for a couple of days. I was planning to bring them with me on Saturday."

Daisy said nothing, just stood up, walked nearer to Mabel, and studied the yellow words *Photographic Studio* on the window, tracing the letters with her finger. "Can I come in?"

Mabel stood aside to let Daisy pass. "No school today?"

Daisy walked around the studio, hands behind her back, strolling from one grouping of photos to the next. She hadn't looked at them when she was in with her father. "Sometimes I don't go," she said.

"What do you do those days?" Mabel closed the door, but she didn't turn the sign around to OPEN.

"Library," Daisy said.

Mabel settled herself on the stool behind the counter. "I used to do that myself," she said. "Not skip school. I wasn't able to finish school, but sometimes I'd make up a reason why I needed to leave work early, or I'd tell my stepfather that I had to work late. Half an hour here, half an hour there. I still

128

don't know how I managed to read as many books as I did." Daisy was looking at her now, focused and intent. She almost nodded. Mabel added, "But never enough."

When Daisy turned again to look at the photos, Mabel smiled to see her hair pulled up in a clumsy twist. "Your hair's pretty that way," she said. "I can help you fix it so the ends don't come down." She got off the stool and motioned for Daisy to take it.

While Daisy pulled out the pins, Mabel set the dressing tray on the counter. Loose, Daisy's hair fell halfway down her back. Mabel drew the brush through in short, shallow strokes to find the tangles, which she picked out gently with her fingers.

"Why'd you quit school?" Daisy asked. She sat very still while Mabel worked, just like Bertie used to.

"I didn't, exactly. When I finished eighth grade, I had to go to work." She didn't mention Jim Butcher. "We were poor."

"Who's in that picture?" Without moving her head the least bit, Daisy pointed over her shoulder to the wall behind Mabel.

"That's Paul," she said. "This was his studio. He taught me to use a camera."

"He looks nice," Daisy said. "I looked at him the whole time the other day." She was quiet for a moment. "I don't like having my picture taken."

Mabel gathered Daisy's hair in her hands, smoothing it into a silky rope. "Neither do I," she said. "And neither did Paul. But photos are for other people. Isn't there a picture of somebody you have that you wouldn't give up?"

"I wish I had one of my mother."

"Nobody ever took her picture?"

Daisy straightened on the stool, her back like marble. "All burned."

Mabel fished through the dressing tray for pins and held out a few for Daisy to see. "These will hold better." She started the twist and said, "I wish I had pictures of my parents, and especially of my sister."

"I used to think I'd like to have a sister," Daisy said, "but I don't anymore. Does yours live here?"

"No." Mabel lined her lips with hairpins to avoid saying more. For all she knew, Bertie might live in Chicago, or anywhere else. Or she might not live at all. When the letter marked *Deceased* had come back to her, she'd locked herself in her room for two days, cycling in and out of weeping, answering the door only at Paul's urgent pounding and pleas to let him give her some soup. When she let him in, he didn't pry, just sat quietly with her, patting her shoulder occasionally, seeing to it that she survived.

When she was calmer, she rubbed an eraser at the heavy pencil marks obscuring everything on the envelope but Bertie's name, which she herself had written, and the words *Deceased* and *Return to Sender,* which at times struck her that Bertie had written, but after years of separation, she couldn't be sure this was Bertie's writing. Pressing away the black, blowing away the eraser fragments, she struggled to think of something else, but only two ideas, equally upsetting, rocked in her head: Bertie was dead; or Bertie wanted Mabel to think she was.

Whoever had obliterated the writing on the envelope had done it with such fervor that much of the paper had come off with the lead. She could make out that someone had forwarded the letter, but of that address, there were only fragments — a house number with a 3 in it, a few letters from the name of the city, and a ghostly *I* for the state — Iowa? Indiana? Illinois? No trace she could follow.

"So he didn't like to have his picture made?" She'd almost forgotten Daisy, and that they'd been talking about Paul.

"Oh, no," said Mabel, pushing in the first pin. "I had to sneak up on him."

"Is that what you're going to do to me?"

Mabel laughed. "Hardly sneaking. When I come on Saturday, you'll know why I'm there." Daisy's head tilted forward, just a bit. "Have I made this too tight?"

Daisy shook her head.

"Don't you want me to come, Daisy?"

The girl turned suddenly, the motion pulling her hair free from Mabel's hands, unfurling the twist. Her eyes were urgent, the rims softly red, glistening with small tears. "I do. Say you will. Please." Daisy's hands wrapped around hers, pressing her fingers tight. "Please."

Paul might have been standing right behind her, his sturdy kindness urging her to listen, to see. Mabel looked at Daisy, as if with his eyes. "Of course I will," she said. "Of course I will."

On Saturday, Mabel locked the studio nearly three-quarters of an hour before she needed to. The prints she'd made of Daisy were still in the darkroom cabinet, in an envelope marked only *D*. Boarding the bus, her feet barely touched the three steps up, as if her hurrying would make the driver go faster. She'd memorized the address but clutched the slip of paper Harker had given her, glancing at it over and over, mentally reciting the route so she wouldn't miss the stop. She was on the corner, just half a block from Daisy's father's walk-up, by 1:20.

She hesitated a moment before she rang the bell, shifting the handle of her camera bag into her left hand, wondering idly about the red door flanked by concrete planters filled with daffodils. Harker was sure to answer and be angry that she was early, that she hadn't phoned first. She would apologize for not calling, say she'd simply left early for fear of being late, but still he might turn her away. If he did, she wouldn't know anything more than she knew now — not for certain. But if he let her in, and if she saw something — what would she do then?

Her eyes burned in the afternoon light. She'd barely slept since Thursday, lying in the dark, picking apart every detail she could remember about the day Daisy and Harker were in the studio, and about how different Daisy had been when she came in on her own. Maybe she was wrong. She wanted to be wrong. There could be all sorts of reasons for Daisy's behavior, all sorts. Except Mabel couldn't think of any. Still, there wasn't any proof. Daisy hadn't said a word. But then, Mabel knew very well that particular silence. What she couldn't close out of her mind were the images she hadn't caught with her camera: the barest flicker of a smile, that secretly triumphant expression of ownership Emerson Harker had let slip while he fanned Daisy's hair over her shoulders — that, and what she had seen, or thought she had seen, reflected in the camera lens when she turned her back to adjust a light: Harker bending to kiss Daisy on her forehead, on the tip of her nose, on her lips — holding that kiss for one second, two, three, four.

Still no one answered the door. Should she ring again? Mabel leaned in and tried to listen, but she heard nothing except the street noise around her. She knocked lightly. In the window to her right, a curtain twitched. And then came the tumbling of a lock and Daisy stood in the open doorway. She was pale. A smear of hot-red lipstick sliced her cheek. Her white blouse puffed open where a button was missing, the snapped thread still in place, the ends waving from the cotton like frayed arms. Daisy pushed back some locks of hair that were matted to her neck, revealing pinkish bruises, like crushed roses. "He's gone for cigarettes," she said. "He'll be back any minute."

"Which way?"

Daisy pointed up the street. Her cuff was torn.

Mabel held out her hand. "Do you want to come with me?"

Daisy's hand snapped into hers like a mate. With her other, she slammed the door, and they ran back the way Mabel had come, down the street, around the corner, block after block, ignoring the curious shouts of playing children. Mabel spotted a cab, hailed it, and they breathlessly tumbled in. "Union Station," Mabel said, and minutes later when the driver turned to say the fare, Mabel shoved a bill at him, tossed her camera bag onto the sidewalk and pulled Daisy out behind her. People coming out of the station grumbled about courtesy and the wrong door as Mabel and Daisy knocked into them. They pushed their way toward the ticket windows, and only then did they stop, panting, to study the time-tables.

"Does it matter where?" Mabel asked. Daisy shook her head. The big clock read 1:42. The train bound for Indianapolis left at 1:55. Just then, the boarding call crackled from the loudspeaker. At the nearest window, Mabel paid for their tickets and they hurried to the platform. Daisy started toward the open door of the car, but Mabel stopped her. She stroked a lock of hair, damp with sweat, from Daisy's eyes and held the girl's face in her hands. "Are you sure? Really sure? We do this, we can't come back."

Daisy nodded. "You know, don't you?" Those shining eyes Mabel had noticed that first day in the studio, those eyes that had seemed to divine a place inside Daisy herself, now penetrated Mabel's heart. "It happened to you."

"Yes," Mabel said, and took the girl, that brave girl, into her arms and held her tightly. "Never again, Daisy. Not ever."

Daisy drew back, holding on to Mabel's hands. She looked around at the scurrying crowd. The patina of studied calm slid from her face in favor of righteous resolve. "Did you change your name when you ran away?"

"I thought about it," Mabel said. "But there was a part of me that hoped to be found."

"I've already been found."

Daisy flung her arms around Mabel's waist and Mabel squeezed her hard. Gently releasing the embrace to slip out of her jacket, Mabel held it open to Daisy. "Here," she said. "Wear this." She wiped the lipstick from Daisy's face with a handkerchief and kissed the girl's damp cheek. "Better get on."

Not until they were settled in their seats, Daisy nestled against her, weeping quietly, not until the train had rocked and rattled its way out of the station, out of the city, across the Indiana border, did Mabel allow her own tears to spill over. For a long while, she sat stroking Daisy's hair, saying nothing. At last, Daisy sat up, her eyes red but dry. "Let's make a new name," she said. "A name that means us."

Mabel wiped away her own tears. "Any ideas?"

Daisy smiled — such a beautiful smile. "Who do you miss most? From before?"

In fifteen years she hadn't said the name out loud to anyone but Paul. Now she looked out the window, remembering how she and Wallace, on another train, had silently watched Juniper slip away. Mabel felt Daisy's cool fingertips on her chin, softly turning her away from the past.

"Who?" Daisy persisted. "What one person would you have with you if you could?"

"My sister." Mabel's knotted throat released as she said it. "Bertie."

"I'd want my mother," Daisy said. "Her name was Ella."

"Ella." Mabel kissed Daisy's forehead and

hugged her close. "That's lovely."

Holding her hand flat before her like a sheet of paper, Daisy scribbled across it with her finger. "El . . . Elber . . . Bertel . . . Bertelle." She looked up at Mabel, her face a sunrise. "Bertelle," she said. "We'll be the Bertelles."

Daisy leapt to her feet and twirled in the small space before Mabel, her eyes full of fun. Placing a hand on the window to steady herself, she struck the pose of a sophisticate. "How do you do?" she said, extending her free hand to Mabel. "My name is Daisy Bertelle."

"So happy to make your acquaintance, Miss Bertelle," said Mabel, and, joining her hand with Daisy's, she drew it to her cheek, kissed it, and held her arms open to her daughter.

Six:
Independence Day

July 1947
Newman, Indiana

ALMA

In the front seat, Mother was making a show of fanning herself with a road map she'd taken from the glove compartment, snapping it up and down, up and down, with short strokes that didn't stir much air. "Bertie, just crack the window a little," Daddy said, but Mother ignored him.

Alma leaned forward, forced to shout over the roar of wind from Rainey's open window. "She doesn't want to muss her hair, Daddy." Alma glanced at her little sister to see if she'd taken the hint. Rainey was sprawled on the seat, pretending to be in a faint, her long hair whipping out the window, which she'd insisted on putting all the way down. By the time they got to Mr. and Mrs. Crisp's house, Rainey's hair would be positively filthy. Child or no, Rainey oughtn't be allowed to behave this way, Alma thought, and, besides that, it simply wasn't fair that Mother didn't come to the defense of *her* hair the way she'd done for Mother's. Alma was grateful she'd had the foresight to wear a light scarf, and she did have her compact mirror and comb, but it was still possible that one of the Crisps would see her before she had the chance to correct the damage. Mostly, she was afraid of Gordon's mother's response, for Mrs. Crisp always looked just like she'd stepped out of the hairdresser's chair. But perhaps this afternoon Alma could win back any lost favor by asking Mrs. Crisp to share her secrets for looking fresh.

Mother sighed loudly and turned her face toward Daddy, her lips pressed tightly together. "I still say it's the boy that ought to come to the girl's on holidays." She stared hard at Daddy to make clear she expected him to answer. "Any holiday."

Daddy said nothing. There was nothing to say. When Alma had told him about the invitation, he'd said it was fine with him, only that she needed to get driving directions from Gordon, since he'd never been in that part of town. Mother was still furious that Alma hadn't come to her about the invitation first, and ever since, she had been taking it out on Daddy. "Well, if we don't get home in time to get the sparklers out for her," Mother said, cocking her head to indicate Rainey, "then it'll be your job to hush her up."

That was enough to rouse Rainey from her faint. She could work up tears faster than anybody Alma had ever seen. *"Daddy,"* Rainey whined and sputtered. "You *prom-ised!"*

While Daddy tried to soothe her, saying if they couldn't do the sparklers tonight they'd do them tomorrow, Alma just shook her head. Spoiled. Spoiled. Much as she hated to think it, that was Daddy's fault. Well, Mother's, too, for allowing it. One thing was sure: No child of hers would ever behave in such a way. She'd done her best these last several years to give Mother suggestions about how to get Rainey to mind, but it never did any good. It seemed like every month there was an article in *The Ladies' Home Journal* or *Good Housekeeping* about how to correct a naughty child, but even when Alma showed her mother the clippings — advice from real experts — she waved them away and said, "You just wait 'til you have one of your own, and then we'll see," as if having a child was some kind of divine

punishment for all one's accumulated foolishness.

Indeed, they would see. Already, just from
the articles she'd saved, Alma had practically an entire housekeeping and child-care
encyclopedia, and she was proud at how
usefully she'd organized it: a gold scrapbook
for decorating, brown for cooking, green for
gardening, white for cleaning, blue for child
care, and red for first aid and home safety.
Other girls she knew wasted their pocket
money on movie magazines, but long before
she'd even had an idea of whom she might
marry, Alma had been planning her life as a
young bride. She had Mrs. Murchison to
thank for that — and she had the heavens
and the flood to thank for Mrs. Murchison.

After that long journey from Newman,
first drenched and cold on the big truck,
then stifled in the boxcar of a train with
other people escaping the flood, entering
the Murchisons' living room in Greenwood
had been like entering a palace. Even now,
every once in a while, Alma heard Mother
complain to someone about how that Murchison woman had left them standing for
ages on cotton rugs she'd spread out to
protect her fancy carpet from their dirty
shoes, saying how they were welcome in her
home but, Mother said, never offering her a

seat, "And me with my back aching, big as a cow." Alma, though, had not minded at all. It would have broken her heart to get a speck of dirt on that luscious blue carpet with the golden swirls, or on the lovely furniture upholstered in rich shades of velvet.

What Alma remembered most about those first few days was that she was happier than she ought to have been. They didn't know where Daddy was or what had become of their house, and Mother mostly stayed in her room, moaning quietly, sometimes from the baby and sometimes about her sofa or her new stove. Alma was careful not to show her happiness, smiling only when thanking Mrs. Murchison for a cup of hot chocolate or Mr. Murchison for offering her part of his newspaper to look at, but inside she was warm with pleasure. Mother didn't fuss at her openly like she did at home, and Mrs. Murchison let Alma help polish the furniture, but instead of snatching away the cloth and saying she was doing it wrong like Mother would have, Mrs. Murchison showed her the right way. At night, Mrs. Murchison tucked her into a bed dressed with smooth sheets that had been kept in a drawer with a lavender sachet. Every morning on his way to work, Mr. Murchison stopped to send a telegram to Daddy, telling him where they were, and every evening on his way back, he stopped to inquire for a reply.

After nearly two weeks, the reply finally came: Daddy was fine; he was living in a tent city, sharing a tent with a couple of other men, spending his days cleaning up Newman. He thanked the Murchisons for taking in his family and promised to get there to collect them as soon as he could. Mrs. Murchison made a lemon cake to celebrate, and after dinner she gave Alma the telegram, along with a new pair of scissors and a bottle of paste, suggesting she save it in her Shirley Temple scrapbook with newspaper articles about the flood. The Murchisons were rich enough to take papers from Louisville, Indianapolis, and Chicago, so it didn't take long for Alma to fill nearly a third of the book. Seeing that, Mrs. Murchison said, "I think you have enough of those flood pictures now, dear," and brought her a stack of old magazines. "You cut out anything you'd like. Perhaps you would enjoy picking out the things you'd like to have in your new house." Alma smiled at that, and over the next several weeks, she had decorated her fantasy house ten times over, always going to Mrs. Murchison to ask advice on color, and whether it was appropriate to paper the walls with a floral if your furniture was in a patterned chintz.

She forgot about Daddy's promise to come, and she nearly forgot about Mother, who now seemed like nothing more than a strange, reclusive neighbor. They'd been at the Murchisons' a little over three weeks when, one bright Saturday afternoon, Mrs. Murchison drove Alma into Indianapolis — the Murchisons had their own car, which gleamed like fresh buttermilk — and there they shopped for a new dress for Alma while Mr. Murchison stayed behind in Greenwood to talk to Mother. That dress was the prettiest she'd ever owned, soft yellow organdy sprinkled all over with tiny embroidered pink roses. When they got back, she ran to show it to Mother, who looked at the dress for only a second, then turned her face to the wall and said, "Don't be getting used to such things."

"Alma, come in here for a moment," Mr. Murchison called from the living room. He held out his hands for her to come and stand before him while he sat in his chair. "I've had a letter from your father," he said. "We've decided it's best for you and your mother to stay here until he can get your house ready for you. The baby will come anytime now and it would be too hard on your mother not to be in a proper house. You'll go to school here and finish out the year." Alma forgot herself in her joy and flung her arms around Mr. Murchison's neck. He patted her back awkwardly, saying, "You're a good girl not to cry," then unlocked her grasp and went to join his wife in the kitchen.

At school Alma said nothing about the flood and pretended that she was the Murchisons' niece, who had come from Boston to stay with them for the spring, and possibly forever. Secretly, she liked imagining that the Murchisons were her true parents, and she had to pinch herself sometimes to keep from calling them Mother and Daddy. Alma barely saw her mother at all — she was in bed for the last few weeks before the baby came and for the next week after — and Alma thought so little about Daddy that when Mr. Murchison brought him in from the train station the day he came up to see the baby, she almost didn't recognize him. He picked her up and hugged her against his smelly old shirt, calling her his "brave Alma girl," but then he set her down and spent most of the rest of his visit cooing at the baby, carrying her when she fussed, rocking her to sleep with his funny hobbling walk. Alma thought the baby ought to be called Ernestine, after Mrs. Murchison, but Daddy insisted on calling her Rainey. She didn't remember Mother voting.

Ten years had passed since Daddy had taken her and Mother and the baby back to Newman, far away from the Murchisons' beautiful house, but Alma still corresponded regularly with her friend. Mrs. Murchison often included in her letters helpful hints she had learned at her club meetings, and during the war, when so much was scarce, she always wrote beneath her signature the saying, Practicality need not come at the sacrifice of beauty. Alma had liked that so much she'd made a sampler of it, spending an entire Saturday measuring and lightly sketching out the words with dressmaker's chalk on a small piece of linen she'd found in Mother's sewing basket, devoting nearly a week of afternoons to embroidering it. At the time, she had wanted to add a border of flowers to frame the words, but she was afraid of getting the petals uneven and spoiling the sampler. Now she was glad she hadn't tried, having come to see the sampler as more elegant for its simplicity.

"Alma, read me the last couple of directions on there." Daddy was reaching back over the seat with the slip of ivory paper on which Gordon had written the instructions, perfectly neatly. "I'm on Mymosaw now," he said.

"*Mim-O-sa*, Daddy."

"That some kind of Jap tree?"

Alma pressed her hand to her forehead and took a deep breath. "It's two more streets to a left on Dogwood," she said, "and then it's the next right onto Plum. They're number five hundred."

Alma leaned back in the seat and opened her purse to get her mirror. Just as Daddy made the turn onto Plum, Rainey pushed the grimy sole of her shoe against Alma's skirt. Alma flung the foot away from her, which sent Rainey tumbling onto the floor, yowling.

"You children hush up back there," Mother said.

Children. Honestly, it was too much to bear, but snapping back would only convince Mother she was right, so Alma kept quiet. Now that she and Gordon were as good as engaged, Alma's plan was to spend as much of the next year as possible with the Crisps. Next summer, when he'd finished medical school, they would marry, and even if they had to stay in the area for

Gordon's residency, they could make their home across the river in Louisville and she could see as little of her family as she liked. And after that, who knew where they might end up — Savannah, Chicago, Philadelphia, maybe even Boston.

Daddy turned the car into the drive for number 500. When Alma saw the red-white-and-blue silk bunting draped between the Doric columns on the Crisps' entry porch and heard her mother say only, "Well," she forgot about her hair and longed to reverse time, back to when Gordon had told her of his parents' invitation. Then, she had thought only of how she wanted to show Mother and Daddy the kind of life she would someday have, but now, she could see how foolish that had been. How could she ever have considered mixing her parents with Gordon's? Mrs. Crisp set even her everyday table with china and linen napkins. She used a gravy boat. Crystal candy dishes were artfully placed on the perfectly waxed surfaces of her mahogany occasional tables. The Crisps' radio was concealed in a fine console cabinet, not standing garishly in the open on top of an old water-puckered veneer dresser, its frayed cord dangling. And what would happen when her family, who had never eaten any fish that wasn't fried, were presented with Mrs. Crisp's signature summer luncheon of cold salmon and tomato aspic? She should have lied to Gordon and said her parents couldn't come and then done everything she could to keep the Crisps and her family apart until the wedding. The afternoon would be one humiliation after another. Daddy would treat the table service as if it were their own chipped dishes and dingy red-and-white-checked towels from Woolworth's while he told stories about the happenings at Crother's Mill. Mother would say nothing except a few thank-yous through tightlipped smiles and act as though she were being asked to eat a beating heart from diamond dishes. Rainey would throw her hand over her face, crying "Ugh!" and refuse to eat anything until she saw the aspic, which she would dive into, mistaking it for cherry gelatin.

Perspiration broke out across Alma's face as she walked ahead of her parents toward the door. It was too late now to turn back. In the middle of the walk, she had to stop and hold her handkerchief to her lips for a moment until a wave of sickness passed. Surely Gordon had warned his parents that the Jorgensens, Alma excepted, were backward and vulgar, but it was one thing to hear of it and quite another to see it. The

Crisps liked her well enough, she believed, but she feared they might also be urging Gordon to look around a bit — he could certainly do better. She longed to turn and plead with her family not to embarrass her, but Rainey would start making hideous faces, Mother would go sit in the car, and Daddy would shake his head and gaze at her, his eyes full of unfathomable hurt. There was nothing to do but breathe an earnest prayer to God to preserve her dignity, then ring the bell and wait.

SEVEN:
EXPECTING

Christmas 1953
Newman, Indiana

BERTIE

Bertie settled an ornament made to look like a basket of daisies on a back branch and pinched the wire hook to make it hold. What on earth daisies had to do with Christmas, she didn't know, but the piece was from a set Hans had bought years ago, a whole summer garden in tissue-thin glass — daisies, irises, roses, violets, lilies. Seemed like that man was forever buying ornaments.

Picking one of the six angels out of the box — "sugar angels," the girls called them, because their little white gowns sparkled — she tried to find a place where it would show. The angel wasn't but an inch high, too small even for this little tree, but Hans and the girls would notice if she left it off. Foolishness, it was. She liked Christmas as well as anybody, but it didn't make a lick of sense to spend money on something that would be on the trash heap in a week. Even this piddling tree had cost four dollars. The man at the Lions Club stand must have thought he was being real cute when he said they charged fifty cents a foot, "But they all start with two-fifty for the trunk!" He was wearing a Santa Claus hat, as if that justified robbery.

"It's for charity," Hans said, but that wasn't why he was standing there, his face nearly buried in a big spruce, trying to hide that he was laughing with the salesman.

Laughing at her.

If she hadn't insisted on going with him, he'd have come back with a tree that touched the ceiling. She was still upset with how, right in front of that man in the hat, Hans had argued that an eight-foot tree cost only a couple of dollars more than a three-foot tree, forcing her to remind him they needed to put away as much as they could, what with Alma's baby coming. Hans would never admit it, but the truth was that a little tree sitting on a table was much prettier than one that took up half the floor. It wasn't her fault if some of the ornaments had to go back to the attic.

Bertie heard the car and looked out the

window. Hans and Rainey were together in the front seat, smiling and jabbering over something. When they got inside and saw she'd started on the tree, they wouldn't like it, but that was just too bad. She had too much to do to stay up half the night decorating just so Rainey could have a minute's pleasure seeing the tree for the first time on Christmas morning. That was the way Hans liked to do things, and it was all right when the girls were children, but Rainey was as good as grown now. Besides, Alma and Gordon would expect the tree to be up when they got in.

Rainey was giggling when she pushed open the door. She clutched a Woolworth's sack in one arm. Hans limped in behind her, hugging two more stuffed bags against his chest. Bertie had sent him to the grocery for sage.

"What's all this, then?" she said. An ornament shaped like a bunch of grapes dangled from her fingers.

Hans passed her, set the bags down on the dining room table, and started pulling out package after package of lights — blue, green, red, white. "Half price," he said, like it made any difference. "There's two extra strings for the tree." He looked back at her over his shoulder and noticed then that

Bertie had already started the trimming. She hadn't put on any lights. "The rest are for outside," Hans said. "I start now, I can have 'em up before Alma gets here."

"And just how do think you're going to do that? You're telling me you're going to start climbing around on the roof in this cold?"

Rainey shook the packages out of her bag now and started sorting the lights by color. "I'll help, Daddy."

"You stay off that ladder," Hans said. "But you can watch and help me keep 'em even."

"Where's my sage?" Bertie held out her hand, not really expecting him to put anything in it. "I can't make my dressing without the sage."

"Not *sage* dressing!" cried Rainey. "I don't like sage."

Hans rooted in the bottom of one of the bags and brought out a smaller one, torn and wrinkled. He handed it to Bertie.

She pulled out the tin to make sure he'd picked up the right thing. When those two got together, it seemed like Hans forgot everything she said. She was sure she had Rainey to thank for the extra stop at the Woolworth's and all that money wasted on the lights, and now there'd be the expense of burning them. *Sage Leaves* was written in red on the tin. "It's Alma's favorite," Bertie said, turning toward the kitchen. "You two can finish up that tree yourselves. I have work to do."

She'd laid out the bread to dry yesterday, so now she gathered up the slices and started breaking them into the big mixing bowl. On the stove, the turkey neck and giblets had been simmering all morning, and the kitchen smelled of good strong broth. When the bread was done, she set out the onions and celery to chop. Hans passed under the window with the ladder and a moment later she heard the sound of it banging up against the house, followed by Hans' thumping, lopsided climbing. He was singing — not even a proper carol, but the piece they'd done in church on Sunday, something about Emmanuel coming to help Israel, which they pronounced *ISS-rye-elle* when they sang. That was Dorothy Ansen's doing. She'd gone to some college and studied music, and ever since she'd joined the First Baptist Church, it was thought too plain for the choir just to sing the hymns, kind of leading everybody else along. Now every week they had to learn special music, which kept Hans out practicing Wednesday nights way past nine o'clock, and then he'd come home singing and not be able to settle down. Dorothy Ansen might be able to sleep in, but Hans had to be up at 5:00 A.M., and Bertie had to be up even earlier to get his breakfast.

Hans did have a nice voice, soothing and deep. When she was a girl, Bertie had liked it when he sang "Side by Side" to her, walking back from the movies. He would lean in close, crooning in her ear about how the two of them would travel down the road together, helping each other along the way, no matter what kind of trouble or sadness might come. After they were married, he still sang it to her every once in a while, especially through the Depression, but it was never the same. It wasn't until one night, late, when Hans had gotten up to tend Rainey, that Bertie realized he'd stopped singing to her altogether, just to her — probably a year or more — and after that, the only time she heard their song was when he creaked across the floor, singing to the baby in his arms. She'd heard Rainey humming that tune, so Hans must still sing it to her special, like when they were out in the car together.

Hans always told people it pleased him to sing for the glory of God, but sometimes Bertie had the feeling it wasn't just the Lord he was singing for. On Sundays, the women quieted down and gave him all their attention whenever he had a solo. They ought to be ashamed to stare at him like that, with her sitting right there in the back of the church. Finally she'd had enough and stopped going to the service, tending the nursery instead, listening to the choir over the intercom. She'd hoped Hans would get the idea — say something, ask her back — but he didn't.

He stood up straighter around those women and cocked his smile, laughing and joking with them, telling funny stories. If they weren't too young, twenty-five or more, they didn't seem to mind about his bad leg. For years now, Bertie had had to force a smile when they would come up just to tell her how lucky she was to have such a wonderful husband. Dorothy Ansen, blond, slim, red-lipped, had raved about him. "He really could have been a professional singer, Mrs. Jorgensen," she said, "if his voice had been trained." It was a silly thing to say about a voice, Bertie thought, but she knew the woman was just throwing around her learning, trying to cover up that she fancied Hans. She made that clear enough by giving him a main part in the special music nearly every week.

Hans had never said so, but it was Bertie's

belief that Dorothy Ansen was behind his wanting to take up with that traveling singing group, the Gospel Wind, that had come for Revival last year. Everybody talked about how good they were, but she never heard them because she was too busy with the babies. The way Hans told it, three of the singers walked up to him after they heard his solo, asking him to replace their baritone, who was retiring and moving down to Florida. Hans was so proud when he came to tell her, his eyes glowing like she'd never seen them, even brighter than when the girls were born, but she'd had to put her foot down. She couldn't manage with him traveling just about every weekend, she told him. The house and the yard would fall to pieces if he ran off and left her. He couldn't expect her to do everything. He never said anything more about it after that, but he did once leave the church bulletin beside the radio, folded open to an announcement about how the Gospel Wind was going to make a record.

Hans was singing a different song now — "Good Christian Men, Rejoice," it sounded like — somehow managing to keep time in spite of the uneven pounding of the hammer and the tapping of the light strings against the house as he pulled them up.

Rainey was singing along with him. Her voice wasn't nearly as good, and Bertie was sure Rainey knew it, but that child would do anything she thought would get her daddy's attention. Shameful. She was too old to be making up to Hans the way she did, laughing at everything he said, smiling too much, twitching her skirts, changing her ways to whatever she thought would please him.

Just like Mabel used to do. "Yes, Daddy," she'd say. "Thank you, Daddy." *Daddy.*

More than once, Bertie had had to clench her fists and breathe deep to get hold of her anger at Rainey for causing her to think of Mabel. Sometimes she'd have to close herself in the bathroom until it passed. More than twenty-five years, and she was still torn up about it. There'd been a time or two when she'd almost told Hans about Mabel, but then she'd look at him close, knowing that though he would never say it to another soul, he thought she was hard, cold. What would he say, then, about all those letters that got forwarded — letters she never answered, never even opened? How would she explain about how the letters found her? She'd have to tell him about taking her mother's name, and then he'd want to know what for and why she'd even

160

left Juniper, and then in time he'd come around to wanting to know why she'd sent the Juniper postmaster her married name and address if she wasn't going to answer any letters. No way to untangle all those mixed-up lies without telling him about Wallace, and that wouldn't do.

She couldn't remember now how long ago she'd given up hoping to hear from Wallace. He must be dead, long dead; otherwise, in time he would have seen his mistake and come looking for her. That pale green hair ribbon he'd given her — it was a Christmas present — still lay, almost like new, inside one of Mama's silk gloves, tucked in a plain gray box, way back in the cupboard up above the hall closet, the one she had to get up on a chair to reach. Besides a few dresses and the family Bible with Mabel's picture inside it, the ribbon and the glove were the only things she'd brought with her from Juniper, and the only things she'd really been afraid of losing when the flood came. She'd saved the Bible from the rising water because she thought Hans would expect it, but the picture had been lost years before. It didn't matter. She didn't know why she'd brought Mabel's portrait from Juniper in the first place, shoving it into the Bible as an afterthought. But Wallace's ribbon and

Mama's glove — on the day of the flood, she'd packed them before anything else, while Alma was getting her own things, then kept them safe all those months she'd had to stay with that Murchison woman in Greenwood, carried them back to the house on Clark Street and then to this one, all without anybody else ever knowing about them.

Bertie tucked her head down and wiped her cheek against her shoulder. That onion was making the tears run, but she kept on chopping because Alma liked a lot of onion in her dressing. She could hardly wait to get hold of her grandbaby. The first time she said that, right after Alma called to say she was expecting in June, Hans had looked at her funny, his mouth hanging open. Bertie couldn't see a way to make him understand. She'd been so young when Alma came, not quite sixteen — another truth Hans didn't know — and then with Rainey it had been all that upset with the flood, living with a snooty woman, trying to take care of the baby and Alma too, and then having to get the house back together without any money to do it with. Until she started working Sundays in the church nursery, she hadn't known herself what a comfort a baby could be, all quiet and warm, snuggled up against her bosom, trusting her to take care of it. Loving her.

Alma would have an easier time of it. She was twenty-four, plenty old enough for a first baby. She had a doctor husband, enough money, and a nice little house, but even so she'd be scared being alone with the baby all day — all new mothers were — so Bertie had made up her mind that Hans would have to drive her up to Ohio as soon as the baby came, and she'd stay for two or three months, helping out until Alma got on her feet, longer if Alma wanted.

Bertie covered the dressing, shoving the bowl far back in the refrigerator so it wouldn't get knocked around, then sat down at the table to pick out the walnuts Hans had cracked for her earlier. Black-walnut fudge. Another of Alma's favorites. She hadn't made it in years.

From outside, she could still hear Hans and Rainey's muffled singing, but she didn't listen closely enough to catch the tunes. When she finished with the walnuts and looked up, she was surprised to see it was getting dark. Soon, she'd need to get out what was left of the roast from last night's supper and heat it up.

Alma and Gordon were probably at the Crisps by now. They were odd, the Crisps, having their Christmas on Christmas Eve, but it was just as well, since she'd never had to put up a fight with them over where the kids would spend Christmas Day. It meant they got in a little later than Bertie would have liked, going on to ten o'clock sometimes, but as long as they were there for Christmas breakfast, she could accept it. She'd picked up a box of Cream of Wheat special, because if Alma took after her, she wouldn't be able to stomach the eggs in the morning.

Outside, the singing had stopped, but she could hear Rainey chirping and cheering, and a moment later the girl was clattering in the door and hollering, "Come see! Come see!" Rainey stopped short in the kitchen and stood breathless, impatient. *"Mother."*

"Your daddy's going to be hungry and so will you be," Bertie said, "so just give me a minute." She scooped up the walnuts, wiped her hands, then got the kettle with the roast out of the refrigerator and set it going on the stove.

Rainey had already gone back outside and was standing with her arm linked through her father's when Bertie came down the steps. "Come way out in the yard," Rainey said, waving for Bertie to follow. When she was nearly to the maple tree, Bertie turned.

How ever could there have been so many lights in those boxes? Hans had lined the white lights, now glowing like tiny squashed moons, all along the lower edge of the roof, and then he'd run the red and green side by side up the sharp edges, right to the chimney. Her stomach lurched — Hans might have fallen — but the feeling faded instantly into a warm delight, as if the lights were inside her. Hans had saved the blue bulbs to trace the porch roof and posts, making a soft, sleepy, embracing glow. Bertie looked and looked. She wasn't in her own yard; this wasn't her house, but some strange, wonderful, glittering place where her big, aproned body burned away, and she, released, drifted into that gleaming color.

"Aren't you glad Daddy bought so many?"

Bertie stared at Rainey for a moment, struggling to understand who she was and why she was speaking.

"Didn't he do a good job?" Rainey said, leaving Bertie's side to hug Hans.

Bertie looked again at the house.

Yes, it was pretty.

She rubbed her arms against the cold. When the light bill came, Hans wouldn't be so pleased with himself. "Y'all come in for supper now," she said, heading back toward the house. "I've got more to do after I clean everything up."

After supper, Rainey and Hans worked on the tree, humming along with the radio. When Bertie finished the dishes, she cooked the fudge, beating it with slow, quiet strokes so she could hear *Christmas with the Mormon Tabernacle Choir,* coming into their living room, all the way from Salt Lake City, Utah. She sent Rainey to bed at ten o'clock, and at eleven she turned off the radio and told Hans she would wait up for Alma and Gordon. She ignored the moan he gave when he got up from his chair. His hip ached him most nights, but he was sure to feel the pain of his hours on the roof for the rest of the winter.

Bertie turned on the lamp beside her chair and picked up *Reader's Digest,* but her eyes were too heavy to follow the words. She would have liked to go on to bed — she had to be up early to put the turkey on — and she would be more comfortable if she changed into her nightgown and housecoat and got her hairnet on, but she'd be embarrassed for Gordon to see her in such a state.

It was selfish of the Crisps to keep the kids out so late, but they were the kind that had to have everything their way, and just so. She worried some that Alma might have a bad time of it, since Gordon was just like them, but Alma had made up her mind to marry into that family, so there wasn't a thing Bertie could do about it except to go up and help with the baby and, here and there, urge Alma to take up for herself more.

The sound of the key tumbling the lock startled Bertie from a doze, and for a moment, she couldn't think what was happening. Alma and Gordon were just coming through the door, whispering to each other as they set their suitcases on the floor.

"You ought not to have waited up, Mother," Alma said.

Bertie stood up and smoothed her dress. "You must have got to Gordon's parents' late."

"No, no," said Gordon. "We made it by four." He picked up the suitcases and pushed past Bertie. "Same room?' He didn't wait for an answer.

"So," Bertie said, giving Alma a quick kiss on the cheek — hardly a cheek at all, so dry and taut. "Did you have a nice dinner?"

Alma plucked at the fingers of her gloves, nodding.

"What did you have?"

Alma laid her gloves — such fine leather,

they might be silk — beside the radio and loosened her scarf. "Roast duckling with an orange glaze," she said. "And a little salad."

"That's all?"

"It was plenty, Mother, really."

"You're not eating enough." The girl was so thin, a little twist could snap her in two. "Let me get you something," Bertie said. "Come into the kitchen."

Alma slipped off her coat and laid it carefully across Hans's chair. "I'll drink a cup of tea," she said, "but I can make it. Why don't you go to bed?"

"I'll get the tea," Bertie said. She picked up Alma's things to take to the hall closet. "Get your nightgown on and come in when you're ready."

The kitchen light blinded her when she flipped it on, and she knocked into a chair that Rainey hadn't pushed back up to the table. She put the teakettle on the stove and then pressed a finger to the block of fudge. It had set up just right, so she cut along the lines she had marked and settled the pieces into a tin lined with waxed paper — all but four, which she arranged on a plate for Alma.

Alma slipped up behind her and reached into the cabinet for a cup and saucer. "Please, Mother," she said. "I can do that. I know you'll be up early." She hadn't changed into her nightclothes. Under the bright kitchen light, she looked even thinner. She'd always been too skinny, but since she'd taken up with Gordon, she'd gotten even scrawnier, and the last few times Alma had visited, Bertie noticed she mostly just pushed the food around on her plate.

Bertie blamed Gordon's mother. That woman was nothing but a bundle of sticks. The time or two Bertie had met her, Mrs. Crisp complained, on the one hand, that she had to send every stitch of clothing she bought to the seamstress, since she could never find anything small enough, and, on the other, she chattered about what hard work it was to keep trim. Bertie had noticed too how Mrs. Crisp soaked up compliments on the fancy meals she fixed but never took a bite of anything. That must be where Alma had gotten it.

Well, she just wouldn't wait until June to go up. She'd pack some things and go with Alma and Gordon day after tomorrow, when they drove back to Ohio. She could do the cooking and look after Alma. Hans and Rainey would just have to see to themselves.

Bertie followed Alma to the table and set the plate of fudge in front of her. "Did you bring a warm-enough nightgown? I can get you another blanket for the bed."

"I'll be fine, Mother."

"You eat that fudge, now. It's the kind you like."

Alma picked up a piece and sucked on the end of it, then put it back on the plate.

"Doesn't that taste good to you?"

"It's delicious, Mother. Thank you. I've had enough."

Bertie smacked her hands on the table. "This has got to stop! Now's not the time to be worrying yourself about getting too fat or listening to any of that nonsense from you know who. The doctor will want you to put on thirty or forty pounds — you just ask him."

Alma stared into her cup. "He said twenty or twenty-five."

"Well, then," Bertie said, nudging the plate of fudge toward Alma. "This will make a good start. And tomorrow, you be sure to fill up your plate and eat everything."

Alma still didn't touch the fudge.

"How about some crackers?" Bertie said. "Or a piece of toast?"

Alma took a sip of tea and then pushed the cup away. "Nothing, thank you."

"Is it the cooking smells that upset your stomach?"

Alma stood up and took her tea to the sink and poured it out. She rinsed the cup and set it on the drainboard.

Bertie stayed at the table. "I'll go back home with you on Saturday," she said. "I'll do the cooking until you feel like you can be in the kitchen without being sick."

"It's not necessary, Mother."

"Alma, you have got to eat. If you won't see to it, I will. You have to put on weight so the baby's good and strong."

Soft, glassy clinks stirred from where Alma was standing, her back to Bertie. She was putting away the supper dishes. When that was done, she wiped the counter and re-folded all the kitchen towels on the bars. At last she came back to the table and stood behind the chair, gripping the back. "There is no baby, Mother."

Bertie felt like all her insides squeezed up and drained right out her feet. For a few seconds, Alma, and even the kitchen itself, drained away, too. Bertie pressed at her throat to stop the words from sliding off with everything else. "When?"

Alma looked at the calendar tacked on the side of the refrigerator. "About three weeks." Her voice was a little weak perhaps, but steady. How could she be so calm? Bertie wanted to get up, to put her arms around her daughter, but that cool voice froze her in her seat.

"You didn't call," Bertie began, and then her throat closed up. She could see herself sitting on Alma's bed, holding her and rocking her like a child, telling her everything would be all right. She could see it all, even though it had never happened, not ever.

"There was nothing to be done," Alma said. "Nothing you could do. Mrs. Weigel was very kind." Mrs. Weigel was the wife of the foot doctor Gordon had gone to Ohio to work with. Not family. "She stayed with me the first afternoon I was back from the hospital, and then she and a couple of women from her church came over the next day to do the cleaning for me and to make dinner for Gordon."

Bertie stared at Alma, trying to see something of herself, something of Hans, in this composed stranger who stood so straight and spoke so primly. Her head was pounding. Hans would blame her. He would never say it, but he would blame her somehow.

Alma went on as though she were telling a story about nothing worse than dropping a bag of groceries. "And then Mrs. Murchison — you remember Mrs. Murchison, Mother. She drove over from Greenwood and stayed until last Tuesday." Bertie saw her daugh-

172

ter's lips quiver. Alma pressed her fingers to her mouth and closed her eyes for a moment before she spoke again. "She and Gordon get on so well. He says he's never seen the house so clean. And she left me with several recipes for things Gordon especially likes."

Bertie's head still throbbed, but her insides had settled back into their usual places. She could see Alma clearly now.

"I know Daddy will be disappointed." Alma released the chair and took a step back. "Thank you for the tea, Mother," she said, "I think we'd both best get to bed." She paused only for a second before turning toward the doorway. "I'll see you in the morning."

EIGHT:
THE RIVER

April 1954
Juniper, Kentucky

MABEL

No one knew how the fire had started. At least no one Mabel and Daisy stopped to talk to — a few bent, hollow people they saw picking through the smoldering remains of houses, barns, toolsheds. "It'd be down to the woods somewheres," one man had told them. He didn't look up from his work, just kept knocking the soot off one thing and another, sometimes choosing a still-unrecognizable item to drop in a metal bucket beside him. "It's always the woods."

A woman in a faded housecoat printed all over with blue hydrangeas — what she'd been wearing when she saw the fire coming over the ridge toward the house four mornings before — offered another theory. "Started at the lumber mill, I'd say. All them

174

saws they got down there's so old. Old wiring. Just waiting for a fire. And here with this bad drought. You think folks'd be more careful."

Someone else suggested the fire must have started at the high school, since there was nothing left of it. "Kids, you know. Fooling with chemicals maybe. Too scared to speak up." One or two others blamed the power company for not tending soon enough to a wire that had come down in the rainless thunderstorm that hit the night before all of Juniper had flung its belongings into anything with wheels — cars, pony carts, wagons — and run for their lives.

Most people agreed with the first man: The fire had likely started deep in the woods that surrounded Juniper and that for generations had kept the sawyers employed — probably a third of the men in the town — but they had different notions about how. Campers from up north who didn't know about the drought, a lit cigarette tossed from a passing car with paper cups or hamburger wrappings. Or it could be arson, some said — maybe out of pure meanness, maybe for work. One man shook his head when he said to Mabel, "But you wouldn't know about that, not being from around here." He shook his head again and returned to his sifting.

Back in the car, Daisy pushed open a wing, then thought better of it when a breeze carried a few cinders through the small window. "Why didn't you tell him?"

"What for?" Mabel said, hearing an edginess in her voice that took her by surprise. "I don't know him. Why open up a round of questions about my past with some stranger who's just lost his?" She could feel Daisy looking at her, feel her daughter's mind weighing whether to ask another question or let the matter drop.

Daisy took another route. "What did he mean about arson for work?"

"When there's a bad fire," Mabel said, "a real wildfire, the Forest Service can't get people here quick enough, so they count on local men to help, and they pay them something. And then there's plenty of building work after."

Daisy stared out the window at ash heap after ash heap. Except for an occasional brick wall still half-standing, or a warped woodstove, it would have been hard to identify the heaps as former houses. "Not much point if somebody did do that," she said. "It doesn't look like there's anything to rebuild. The town's all but gone."

Mabel drove on slowly, watching the road

for debris, trying to find her feelings about what had become of Juniper. All around, the blackened remains of trees poked up from the ground, giants' matchsticks, charred, splintered, broken. Daisy noticed them, too. "How is it they can still stand?"

Even after such a long time gone, Mabel had thought she would be able to find her way around pretty easily, but the fire had changed everything. In some places it was even hard to tell whether she was driving down one of the remaining dirt roads or just a path cut by fire. One moment, she chided herself for not having come back sooner — at least to find out anything she could about what had become of Bertie, or whether anyone had ever heard again from Wallace. Then the next, she told herself that her questions could only raise others — questions that, even if she answered them, wouldn't change a thing for anybody. There wasn't any reason but hope to make her imagine she could find a trace of Bertie, especially now. In spite of the one letter that had come back to her, the one out of the dozens she had sent since 1927, she didn't believe Bertie was dead. She would feel that in her heart, wouldn't she? And after all, it was remarkably easy to disappear. No one knew that better than she did.

"That's the church," Mabel said, stopping the Chevy and pointing at a gray mound of tumbled stone. "The Emmanuel Baptist Church. I recognize the cross." The cross had stood out front, beside the footpath. When Mabel was eleven or twelve, there had been a ceremony to erect it, and she remembered how odd it had looked to her, this black iron cross not quite six feet high, seeming like a scrawny man holding out his arms, guarding the property. She hadn't ever been able to stop thinking of it that way, and now she felt a tightening in her throat, seeing the sad, skinny man, his left arm painfully twisted, leaning against the pile of river rocks that had once been the church's front wall.

Mabel got out of the car, and Daisy followed. Together they stood before the ruined church. "Mama and Daddy were married there," Mabel said. "And Bertie and I were baptized by Reverend Small. Not here. In the river." She clasped her hands against her chest and smiled faintly. "Well, I was baptized twice. When it was Bertie's turn, she was scared of the preacher dunking her under, so I went with her."

"You mean you went first to show her not to be afraid?"

"No, I mean I really went with her. I got

behind her, wrapped my arms around her, folded her hands in mine and hugged them against her chest, so when the preacher got hold of us, he held my back and our four hands. Everybody was cheering when we came back up."

It was her last happy memory of church. Not long after that, Mama had married Jim Butcher and stopped going to services. Mabel and Bertie had gone for a time, and the church women had done their duty when Mama died, but Mabel had felt their stares after that, stares that burned her naked, making her feel ashamed that they might know what was going on in Jim Butcher's house, making her feel not only that they knew but that they blamed her for it.

"So you know where you are now," said Daisy.

Mabel pointed to her left. "The school was over there," she said, seeing now what the man in the soot-streaked flannel shirt had told her earlier — nothing left. "And down that way," she said, pointing toward the right, "was the main corner. Turn left and go down a block and you'd get to town, all the stores. Turn right to pass the rich people's houses. After a few blocks, the sidewalks turned to paving stones, then gravel, then dirt. We lived on the dirt."

"No difference now," said Daisy. She continued to look toward the corner for a moment, then turned back to the car.

Mabel took her hand. "Let's walk for a while. Do you mind?" She opened the rear door of the car and leaned in over the seat, emerging with her camera hanging from a strap around her neck, her pockets bulging with rolls of film. Officially, Mabel was in Juniper as a photographer for the *Indianapolis Star*, though it had taken some persuading to get her editor to give her the time to come down. She'd barged into Jonas's office while he was setting out his lunch.

"What do our readers care about a fire in some little town in Kentucky nobody ever heard of?" He held a fat corned beef sandwich in one hand while he tried to flatten the waxed paper wrapping into a makeshift tray on his desk. "So?" He looked at Mabel over the tops of his glasses. "Make your case."

While Jonas dismantled his sandwich and painted the top slice of bread with mustard, Mabel argued that the *Star*'s circulation reached out toward the areas in Indiana surrounded by forest. "The pictures can go with a story reminding people how fast a forest fire can move," she said, seeing her editor wasn't biting. "I can interview some expert," Mabel sputtered. "In prevention. Or get the fire chief to talk about planning an escape route." A child could have punctured her ridiculous argument.

Jonas rubbed at the back of his neck, pretending to consider the idea, even tossing out a name or two, but now Mabel knew he had made up his mind to let her go. She had noticed him listening from his doorway a little while earlier when Lannie picked up the story about Juniper off the wire and used it as a chance to mock again what he called Mabel's "Bourbon drawl." They all knew she was from Kentucky, but none of them, not even Jonas, knew her connection to Juniper — not until now, anyway. "Three days," Jonas said. "No more."

She thanked him and pulled the door shut behind her, avoiding the eyes of her fellow journalists as she hurried through the clutter of desks and out the door. Though it shamed her even more to think of it, Mabel had been prepared, if Jonas had refused her, to remind him that in the nearly ten years she'd worked for the paper she hadn't ever made a request for a particular assignment. She was ready to point out, too, that she'd had more of her photographs picked up by the AP than anyone else on the staff, that she had won three awards, the first of them for shooting the baking contest at the state fair — an assignment everyone had laughed at — given for her photo of Mrs. Jefferson Twichell cradling her blue ribbon like a child, a moment the awards committee had praised as evidence of Mabel's "instinct for the intimacy of human joy."

From the café on the corner, Mabel called Daisy at the bank and said, "I need you to go with me. I can't do it alone."

Daisy agreed without hesitating, and, so far, Mabel hadn't asked her what little lies she'd had to tell to get the time off, whether she would have a job when they returned to Indianapolis on Thursday. Had she asked, Daisy would have said, "What does it matter what I told them? If they fire me, I'll find something else."

Mabel marveled at Daisy's ease in herself, the way she seemed sure of what mattered and what didn't. Daisy had had half a dozen jobs since high school, leaving them one after the other when the work collided with rehearsal schedules for the playhouse. Some of Mabel's acquaintances had let her know they thought Mabel was too indulgent, that Daisy was too old to be allowed to quit a job over something as frivolous as saying lines on a stage, but even if the role was a tiny one, Daisy gave her whole self to it. Only a petty person wouldn't admire that.

Early this morning, Daisy had been up and dressed long before Mabel, her small suitcase by the door, ready to follow wherever her mother led her. Not until they had crossed the border into Kentucky did Daisy ask, "What do you hope to find, Mamabel?"

"I don't know, sweetheart," Mabel said, and that was the truth. But at the same time, she was conscious of an entirely different truth. She wanted to find some sign of Bertie and Wallace, yes, but there was something more she couldn't quite name. What was it? Peace? Certainty? Absolution?

There had been times — not frequent, but intense — when Mabel wanted to tell Daisy everything. But she knew she never would. From the beginning, they were fused by pain that would remain unspoken, experience they would never describe for each other. Both of them had lost the people they'd loved most in the world. Both of them had been used by men they'd had to call "father."

Though Daisy had never said so, Mabel knew from the way her daughter couldn't stand anything binding her waist or wrists — how she had to have even the sheets left untucked at the foot of the bed — that at times Harker had tied her. And through the wailing nightmares, when Daisy fought off her blankets, pleading to her familiar incubus not to force her mouth open, not to choke her with his vile flesh, Mabel learned some of the details of what her darling girl had endured.

In the early years, Mabel had feared what she herself might dream, what Daisy might learn from the words replayed in a nightmare, but once, when talking over Daisy's terrors, Daisy had said, "You never talk, Mama. You cry. Only tears. No sound."

They both carried with them their private hells, doing their best, as Paul had taught her, to think on freedom and kindness. Long before there was Daisy, one day when Mabel and Paul had been sitting quietly at a table, going over the monthly accounts, she had put her hand over his and said, "If you ever want to talk about the war, I'll do my best to understand." Gently he'd lifted her hand from his and drawn his own away. He sat there for a long time, staring into lonely air. In time, he turned his wet eyes to meet hers. "You can't understand. Only someone else who was there. And then, when you meet him, what connects you, what makes you trust each other, is knowing the same thing. You don't talk. There's no reason to talk. He knows what you know. And that's enough. Because it has to be."

Tears sprang to her eyes. She knew now why she had never told Paul about Jim Butcher, knew why she hadn't even been able to tell Paul the reason she wouldn't let him photograph her. She, too, had a battlefield in her past, different from Paul's. A place and time that had brought her to do things she could never have done, and couldn't have answered for, in ordinary life.

Even so, though she shared a kind of old soldier's past with Daisy, Mabel feared what her daughter would think of her if she ever learned the whole story. There wasn't a way to tell about it directly, not in a way that would encompass the truth. Talking could only unlock what Mabel knew she had to keep caged.

When Daisy was still in high school, she had brought home a copy of *The Strange Case of Dr. Jekyll and Mr. Hyde*. For her required essay on the book, Daisy decided to discuss the damage Hollywood had done to Stevenson's tale, pointing out the foolishness of an added love story just so Spencer Tracy could make love to Ingrid Bergman. It had been a couple of years since Mabel and Daisy had seen the picture together one winter matinee, and, as ever, Mabel had delighted at Daisy's precise recall of film scenes — clearly the actress in her — so Mabel had borrowed the book. How it had haunted her, revealing why she, why Paul and so many of his fellow soldiers, buried the darkness within. In the story, the hale and hearty Dr. Lanyon, after witnessing Hyde's retransformation into Jekyll, dissolves to a wraith. Once a great lover of life, once a believer in knowledge as a good in itself, the dying doctor says to a visiting friend, "I sometimes think if we knew all, we should be more glad to get away."

Paul had told her once that he'd thought of suicide, going so far as to walk out onto the Michigan Avenue Bridge one April day, wearing his heavy wool coat. "That and boots," he said. "I worried it wasn't enough of a drop. I thought the extra weight would pull me under pretty fast."

"What stopped you?" she had asked.

Paul finished putting away the equipment he'd been cleaning and walked to the street window of the studio. The late-morning sun had settled on the bench in front, and a couple of women sat together, packages between them, their faces turned to the warmth. Some people glanced at Paul as they passed, a few with smiles, but most didn't notice him, lost in their own business.

"They'd just finished the esplanade," he said at last, continuing to look at the passersby. "Not the friezes." He looked now at Mabel. "But you know that."

She nodded and took a few steps toward her friend. They had gone together to the unveiling. It was the first day he'd trusted her to roam with one of the cameras, free of his advice, and, later, when they studied the drying negatives, he'd put an arm around her and said, "You have an eye."

Mabel touched Paul's shoulder and asked again, "What stopped you?"

"I don't know exactly." He turned from the window and sat down at the worktable, his head in his hands. "I remember thinking about all the people out on the esplanade, like it was a holiday. I knew I'd have to wait until it was dark. I didn't want any kids to see me jump. So I waited, just watching. After a while I took off my coat, bundled it up, and sat down on it. I watched some more. Around sunset, when I looked at my watch, I saw I'd already waited six or seven hours, and I thought, Okay, I've lived six hours more than I thought I would. I could see myself living another ten or twelve, to get through the night. Next morning, I thought about going to the bridge again, early, before everybody turned out for work, but I figured I'd give it a try to live through the afternoon. Just to see. After that, I kept on deciding, five or six hours at a time, then a day, a day and a night, until I realized I wasn't having to decide anymore. I was just living."

So many times, in the years between losing Bertie and gaining Daisy, Mabel had repeated Paul's words in her mind. Just a few hours more. A half a day. Only one more day. And in that way, she had decided to live.

Without Mabel's realizing it, she and Daisy had passed the main corner and were now turning down one of the streets in what had once been Juniper's three-block downtown. What few buildings there had been of brick now remained as charred shells, while the smaller wooden buildings had vanished. Mabel stopped, raised her camera, and started shooting. Suddenly, a stout woman emerged from behind one of the blackened brick walls, waving her arms, shouting, "Just what do you think you're doing? Who are you? Stop that right now!"

The woman, her gray hair flecked with ash and pulling from her bun, now stood red-faced in front of Mabel, yanking at the camera strap.

Mabel lowered the camera but kept a firm grip on it, protecting the lens with her cupped hand.

The woman released the strap and took a step back. She stared at Mabel hard, studying her face, as if trying to imagine it in another time.

Daisy said, "Sorry, ma'am. We don't mean any harm."

The woman ignored her, cocked her head, and narrowed her eyes at Mabel. "I know you."

Mabel looked away, then down at the camera as she fumbled in her pocket for the lens cap. Her hands were trembling. She tried to think what to do, but it was as if her mind had struck a wall. She knew this woman. Mrs. Kendall. Her old boss.

Mabel pretended to search her other pocket for her press identification. "Must have left it in the car, or pulled it out with something," she muttered. "So sorry." She shook out her hair so that it fell across one eye and now glanced quickly between Mrs. Kendall and the rubble around them. "My name's Bertelle. I'm a photographer for the *Indianapolis Star.*"

"Indianapolis."

"That's right." Mabel offered her hand,

hoping the woman would look at that rather than at her face. It didn't work.

"Bertelle," said Mrs. Kendall. "Bertelle. What were you before that? Before you were married?"

"I've never married," said Mabel. She didn't know how she'd explain if Mrs. Kendall demanded to know who Daisy was.

"What's your first name?"

A sudden wind kicked up the ash, forcing them all to cover their eyes for a moment. "I'm sorry," Mabel said when the wind settled to a breeze, "I see we're bothering you. What was this part of town before the fire?"

A look of doubt flashed through Mrs. Kendall's eyes, and she answered the way she might have answered a true stranger. "Businesses and such," she said. "That was my store over there." She pointed, and Mabel looked toward the pile that had once been Kendall's Dry Goods, hoping her eyes suggested curiosity and sympathy.

"Any idea how far the fire line goes?" *The crisis has passed,* Mabel thought. She was all journalist now, and Mrs. Kendall apparently had decided she'd been mistaken.

"Down by the river, about two miles out," Mrs. Kendall said, pointing the way Mabel knew so well. "Didn't get to the cemetery."

190

"Sorry again to have troubled you," Mabel said, turning and motioning for Daisy to follow. "Good luck to you."

Behind her, Mrs. Kendall snorted at the ill-placed goodwill, but at least they'd gotten away from her.

Mabel walked quickly up the street, moving faster as she approached the corner. Behind her, Daisy called, "Slow down. Mama! Mama, stop!" Mabel didn't stop until she'd reached the car. While stowing her camera in its bag, she felt Daisy pulling on her arm.

"Look at me, Mama."

Mabel turned toward her daughter but couldn't look at her. She leaned against the car, swept her hair out of her eyes, and stared at the fire-tortured cross propped against what was left of the church.

"That woman knew you," Daisy said. "And I think you knew her, too."

Mabel nodded.

Daisy's voice strained between annoyance and compassion. "What are we doing here, Mama? You could have asked that woman if she knew anything about Bertie. Isn't that what you want? To know something?"

Mabel lifted her eyes to her daughter's pleading face and turned away. She felt Daisy's warmth beside her, felt the girl's slender arm slipping around her waist, drawing her close. Daisy was the taller one now, even without high heels.

"Tell me, Mama-bel. What do you want?"

Mabel pressed her head against Daisy's, then eased out of the embrace. "I don't know," she said. "Really, I don't." She couldn't bear Daisy's look of exasperation and quickly raised a hand against whatever question she might ask next. "I want to drive some more. Down to the river."

Year after year, so many years ago, sometimes braving the cold water as early as Easter, Mabel and every other kid who lived close enough to the Laurel River to make it on foot or on bicycle had splashed and swum and floated in the cove. Everyone except Bertie, who was afraid of the water. Mabel had coaxed every way she could think of, trying to get Bertie to tell her why she was afraid, but her little sister would twist away from her and run high onto the bank, crying, "I just am. Leave me alone!"

Wallace was nearly always there, clowning but careful. Even after all this time, Mabel could tick off five or six names of younger children Wallace had taught to swim. Once in a while some kid's older brother or sister would try to show them a frog kick or how to swim just under the surface, but they always came back to Wallace and his legendary patience. Mabel herself had seen him at work — arms held steady under a little boy's back, singing out words of encouragement for as long as it took for the boy to feel he could manage a backstroke. He, too, had tried to persuade seven-year-old Bertie, eight-year-old Bertie, nine-year-old Bertie to let him teach her, but Bertie always refused. He'd stay for a time on the bank with her, skipping rocks downstream from the swimmers, so she wouldn't feel left out.

When Mabel steered the car around the final bend, she saw that Mrs. Kendall had been right. The fire had rolled right up to the river and died. On the fire side of the bank, everything was burned down to the water, and bits of trees bobbed in the current, but on the other bank, it was still spring. Looking west of the swimmer's cove, squinting in the sunlight, Mabel could see where the jagged far edge of the fire had been, just this side of the bridge, not a hundred yards from the cemetery.

Without a word, she got out of the car and started on her way there. Daisy followed a few steps behind.

It was a well-kept cemetery. While she looked around to get her bearings, Mabel wondered idly who did the mowing and trimming — the Freemasons, perhaps. Then, as if she had been here only last week to refresh the flowers on her mother's grave, she walked straight to the familiar plots. There was her father: *Albert Fisher, 1889–1918*. Beside him, because on her deathbed she'd demanded it and because Mabel had fought for it, calling on the doctor as witness to final wishes, was her mother: *Imogene Fischer Butcher, 1890–1922*. Though Jim Butcher had protested, there was another stone, shaped like a tiny pillow, next to Mama's, etched with the words:

CHARLES
STILLBORN SON
1922

For the whole time Mama was pregnant, Butcher had bragged to everyone that he was going to name the boy James, after himself, but when Dr. Moseley came in and told Butcher the baby was dead and that his wife would likely die within the hour, Butcher made him write *Charles* on the certificate, saying, "Not going to waste my name on a dead son."

"That's my father," Mabel said when Daisy stopped beside her. "And Mama and the baby."

"I saw some pretty wildflowers down by the river," Daisy said. "I'll go pick some and bring them back for you."

Mabel waited beside her parents' graves until she saw Daisy dip out of sight; then she moved up and down the rows restlessly. There were names she recognized, people from church, a near neighbor and his wife. There was Naomi Linder, who had been three or four years ahead of her in school.

No sign of Bertie, even accounting for a married name. No Albertas at all that she could see, except the one for Alberta Gunther, one of the oldest graves in the cemetery, a small weather-pocked stone marked *1842*. The idea that someone with her own name lay in the ground had troubled young Bertie, and she wouldn't answer to Alberta after that, not for anything — not until Butcher gave her no choice.

Mabel found him at the northern edge, where the town had traditionally buried the ones unclaimed by family. The marker was a slate, sunk now into the ground and barely visible: *James Butcher, d. 1927*.

Under her feet he lay.

In a pine box, most likely, rotted by the damp ground.

Under her feet.

She stomped once. Twice.

And then her feet were pounding the ground. Pounding so hard she felt the strike through her whole body. Pounding as if her rage could drive the bastard deeper into Hell. Pounding. Pounding. Pounding. For her mother. For Bertie. For herself.

For all that he had cost them and for the price she would pay and pay and pay.

Mabel stopped, her strength spent. But for her wheezing breaths, there was no sound. The birds had flown. The unscathed leaves hung silently in the unmoving air. Waiting.

She scrubbed at her eyes with her palms, furious at the tears. The sun was lower now, and moving in its glare, she saw Daisy back at Mama's grave, arms full of flowers. She started toward her daughter, wandering aimlessly through the stones, seeing but not registering the names carved in them. There was a granite bench she didn't remember. She dropped onto it, exhausted, grateful. She could rest here a moment, under the linden tree that stretched its limbs overhead. From the bench, she could see Daisy, nearer now but still further than Mabel could yet carry herself, looking every inch a devoted granddaughter, brushing dirt from the headstones with her fingertips, taking great care arranging the flowers.

Watching her daughter, Mabel stroked her fingers along the front edge of the bench. Something was carved there. A vine of roses? She leaned forward to get a better look, and when she did, she saw the back of the bench chiseled with three-inch-high letters: *HANSFORD.*

All around her lay Hansfords. The elders who had passed when she was a child. A four-year-old daughter, Wallace's sister, from scarlet fever. His father, Gregory. His mother Margaret, just three years ago.

And there, between them, was his stone:

BELOVED SON
WALLACE ARTHUR HANSFORD
LOST IN THE LAUREL RIVER
1909–1927

Mabel stood up, but her legs gave way, as if they were nothing but pillars of sand. She was on her knees, arms clutching her ribs, near to shattering from the howl that rose from her, that unfurled like a rope to pull Daisy to her.

Then Daisy was beside her, holding her tightly, rocking her, cooing, "Mama, oh, Mama."

She felt her daughter's arms, heard her daughter's voice, but their comfort was as the comfort of a cave, a protective hollow for one's lonely terror.

She should have followed him. Should have followed him. All those years ago, hard as she had tried not to, she had known that Wallace would go nowhere but back to Juniper. She should have followed him. Should have faced with him whatever had to be faced.

Mabel stared past the stones, past the new grass and the wildflowers Daisy had let tumble. She stared past Daisy, past the present, into the past, and saw what she had never seen.

A frigid December day. Early-morning sleet. Wallace standing in his sodden coat at Union Station, scanning the passengers coming off the Louisville train, straining for a glimpse of Bertie. It was too much, not finding her, not finding her as he had not found her so many times before.

He pushed his hand in his pocket, counted the fare, and stepped onto the next train south. He heard nothing, would let himself hear nothing, until the conductor called "Louisville." There, silently, he stepped onto another train, slid into a dirty corner, and leaned his head against the window to wait for Juniper.

He would have made it before Mabel

finished work that day, would have stepped off the train, turned away from the town, passing the small farmhouses glowing with supper lights. He would have walked through the winter mud until he came to the river, just to the place where the current was fastest. He would have stood there until dusk became darkness, tossing stones he couldn't see. Then, from the memory the body holds in itself, he would have climbed to the highest point on the bank and looked out over the river, trying to see into the darkness, calling Bertie's name. And then he would have taken one last step. Into the air. Into the black water.

NINE:
THE BURGER CHEF

Summer and Fall 1956
Newman, Indiana

RAINEY

June

No one was going to stop her; she'd made up her mind about that. Rainey fastened the waistband on her skirt — a leafy-green check, just right, she thought, with her sleeveless white blouse. She couldn't risk stepping out in the hall to the full-length mirror, so she tilted the one on her dresser as far as it would go and climbed on her desk chair to try to see how her flats looked with the skirt. High heels would have been better, but it was at least a two-mile walk to State Street, so these would have to do. The green scallop along the sock cuffs was a nice touch. Hopping down from the chair, she admired the way the skirt ballooned around her, and for a moment Rainey wished she were daring enough to wear it without the petticoat, like Sally sometimes did.

If not for Sally, she might have given up her plan weeks ago. "Do you want a life or not?" her friend demanded whenever Rainey said she didn't know if she could go through with it. All spring before graduation, and during the two months since, she'd watched an eight-man crew knock down what was left of Carson's Feed Store, clear the lot, lay a new foundation, and raise the pitched-roof shape of the new Burger Chef. Last week, the sign had gone up, and she'd taken a walk down there, specially, to smile up at the mustached chef rising like a chimney out of the red kite-frame border. A black crossbar declaring HAMBURGERS anchored the kite at the center and seemed to keep it and the happy chef hovering safely just above the ground. She hadn't seen the sign lit up yet, but Sally, who had stopped at a Burger Chef on a trip to Indianapolis, had told her every part of it seemed to float in the night sky, glowing white, orange, green, red, and gold.

Rainey had stood for a long time on the other side of the street, studying the chef's face, almost praying to him, really. A shiver of fear mingled with delight rushed up her spine as she thought of what her parents would say to that.

A job, she had mentally urged the chef. *Please, a job.*

A job meant money. Money meant she could enroll in September in the bookkeeping course at the junior college right along with Sally. And the course meant that soon, in just a year or two, she could have a nice job in an office in a city like Louisville or Indianapolis, a little apartment for herself or a bigger one to share with Sally, a closet full of beautiful clothes, a dresser drawer for nothing but gloves, and maybe even a car of her own.

She leaned over the dresser and looked in the mirror, seeing, instead of her own face, the familiar chef smiling back at her. Silently, she mouthed the words *I'm counting on you. My only hope.* It was the sort of corny thing people said to each other on *Love of Life* or *The Secret Storm,* which her mother — icy glass of cherry No-Cal in hand — devoted herself to every afternoon, but the words seemed appropriate at this moment. To get out of Newman, she needed to be able to wave her very own bankbook at Mother like a sword. Unlike Alma, she didn't have a former local boy like Gordon Crisp coming back on schedule from his first year of practice in podiatry to marry her. Everybody knew Mother couldn't abide the Crisps and didn't much like Gordon, but that hadn't stopped her from throwing Alma's success in Rainey's face. It had gotten worse when no one asked Rainey to her junior prom, unbearable when she again had no date for her senior prom. And then, when Alma showed up with Gordon a day early for Rainey's graduation and announced she was expecting — that's when Rainey had decided absolutely that she was going to listen to Sally.

Rainey had waited for nearly two weeks after her graduation to tell her parents her plans to take classes at the Anderson County Junior College come fall, just so it wouldn't look like she was trying to steal Alma's thunder, much as she wanted to get back at Alma for stealing hers. Resistance — even an outright battle — she expected from her mother, but it took her up short when even Daddy answered with a tight, almost practiced phrase that snapped, like closing a book: "That's not for you."

"Foolishness," her mother had added before Rainey could ask Daddy what he meant. Mother had just plowed on with, "Are you forgetting how you had to repeat the third grade? And then it took that nice Miss Lewis all that extra work so you could pass your history class that one year."

"But, Mother, I was sick . . ." Rainey began. Why was it that she was the only one who ever seemed to remember that? Chicken pox, mumps, German measles, and a polio scare all in the same year, and then those two months in bed with a broken leg her first year of high school.

But neither one of them was listening. Mother said, "Come mash these potatoes, now," and Daddy was already doing the word jumble in the paper, and Rainey couldn't find a way to bring the subject up again with him.

Close as they were, she couldn't ever be quite sure where Daddy stood on anything, except that he loved her, but it was his manner of loving that confused her most. She knew he wanted the best for her, but what was that, and how did he know? Did it have anything to do with what she wanted for herself, with what she thought would make her happy? Did it even leave room for her to figure out what that was?

As for talking with her mother about it, well, she might as well have said she wanted to work her way to China on a fishing boat. Girls got married: That's as far Mother's imagination went, though she never suggested how Rainey might manage it. Apparently, she believed that if Rainey just stayed busy for a few years with housework, eventually a boy she knew from school or church would grow up enough to get a job selling insurance and buy her a house in town.

Well, she wasn't going to wait around for some nameless, faceless boy who decided he wanted her just because he was ready to settle down and she was all that was left. One last look in the mirror, a flick of the comb to right a wispy brown curl above her ear, a swish of rosy lipstick, and she was ready.

The dining room clock chimed nine times. She'd planned everything well. It was a little warm for mid-June, but even with walking slowly to keep from raising a sweat, she could easily make it to the Burger Chef by ten o'clock. The manager wasn't due with applications until 10:30, so if there weren't many people in line outside, she could walk another half block down to the library to freshen up in the restroom and rinse her mouth with a sip of cold water from the fountain.

Taking a deep breath, and then another, Rainey tucked a fresh handkerchief, her comb, and lipstick into her clutch bag, opened her bedroom door, and stepped into the hallway as lightly as she could. The sweet smell of strawberries thickening into jam carried through the house on the steam drifting from the kitchen. Her mother had been determined to teach her the whole process, from cleaning and stemming the berries to labeling the jars, so Rainey had been forced last night to whine and act the brat a little to assure her chance this morning of slipping out of the house. A well-timed "*Da-a*-dy," at the dinner table had led him to say, "Bertie, let her be for now." And though her mother had tightened her lips and said, "It's time she learned," they all three knew the matter was settled. Her father had schooled his wife and daughters to understand that while family disputes at any time were never desirable, at the dinner table, they were intolerable. What they also knew, in spite of the family show of pride in Alma, was that Rainey was her father's favorite and that, in small things anyway, he would give in to her. Once the job was in hand, she was sure she could bring her father around to her side about college. After all, if what he wanted was for her to find a nice man to take care of her, she could meet a better class of men working in some professional office. And Daddy's support alone would silence Mother.

Five steps took Rainey from her bedroom

to the hall doorway. Another three steps into the dining room and she could peek quickly into the kitchen. If a batch of jam was cooking, her mother had to be at the stove, stirring and checking for signs of gelling, which meant she would be in the nook beyond the sink, out of sight from the dining room. To her relief, Rainey could hear her mother in the kitchen, half-humming, half-muttering, but could not see her, so she backed through the dining room into the living room and to the door, taking care to turn the knob silently, to pull the door not quite to, and to catch the screen door on the porch before it could bang shut. In another moment, she was turning the corner onto Locust Avenue, on her way, free.

When she got to the Burger Chef, no one was waiting at all, and even though it still wasn't 10:30, a man in a white shirt with a red bow tie waved her inside from one of the tables in the dining area. "Looking for a job?" he asked. She nodded and took his hand while he introduced himself as Mr. Buchanan, the manager. Smiling in the empty-eyed way of ticket takers at the fair, he asked her if she'd finished high school — *yes* — if she had any work experience — *no, unless he counted working concessions at basketball games* (he did) — and if she was

207

planning to get married anytime soon. Next thing she knew, he'd shoved some papers across the table for her to fill out, then pointed behind the counter and told her she could go back there and dig in the boxes until she found two uniforms in her size. After that, he said, the crew manager, Millie — a fiftyish woman Rainey recognized as a waitress from the Blue Goose Diner — would show her how to work the grill and assemble sandwiches.

Before Rainey knew it, her skin was coated with a thin film of grease and sweat, and it was four o'clock. She was to report for training again at nine o'clock tomorrow morning, and so on for the rest of the week, and then on the Monday after, the restaurant would open and she'd work an alternating shift of days and nights. She didn't say anything to Mr. Buchanan about the bookkeeping course, figuring by the time September came she'd be such a valuable employee that he would let her get all her hours in on nights and weekends.

At home, the first wave she had to flail against was over how she'd been gone all day without even a word to her mother. "What do you mean, doing a thing like that? You've been brought up better!" Right then, Daddy came in from work, so Mother shouted more loudly to make sure that before he had even reached the kitchen he not only heard her fury but understood the reason for it. "Slipped out the door like a thief, with nary a word! And with me there in that hot kitchen, working to put up those strawberries before they spoiled. You ever think what might have happened if I'd slipped hauling that big canner full of jars off the stove? There I'd be on the floor, burned and dying and calling out for a girl that doesn't care a straw for a soul but herself!"

Rainey stood still, eyes lowered, as she had been taught by countless bare-handed whippings to do. She pressed her lips into a practiced expression of shame, which served now to stop a smile from taking over, for she knew that, more than anything, her father hated her mother's hysterical rants. Daddy pulled out a chair and sat down at the kitchen table, propped up his elbows, cupped his forehead in his palms and waited for Mother to wear herself out, which she did in a minute or two.

For a moment, everyone was silent — Daddy still with his head in his hands, Mother poised in front of the refrigerator with a spoon raised and drawn back like a mallet, and Rainey leaning into the wall, but not slumping as if she didn't care.

Mother spoke first. "What are we going to do with this girl?"

Rainey straightened up, gathered a wad of her skirt in her hand, and waited for her father to look at her. When he did, he asked almost casually, with no hint of accusation or disappointment, "So where did you go?"

"I walked up to the new Burger Chef to see about getting a job," she said. "I was the first one there."

He smiled a little at that, but not enough that her mother could see. "You get it?"

Rainey nodded, still not risking a smile. "I've been training all day."

Daddy arched back in his chair and reached up with one hand to massage his neck, then twisted his head back and forth and from side to side until a tiny dull snap signaled a vertebra sliding back into place. He took a pack of Marlboros from his shirt pocket and rooted behind the butter dish and the napkin holder for his lighter. A shaft of sunlight coming through the window of the back door, just behind him, caught a few specks of sawdust in his oiled hair and made them sparkle. He tapped a cigarette out of the pack, lit it, and then, after four full drags, said, "You know you'll have to get yourself there and back."

"Sure, Daddy."

He knocked a long ash into the chipped saucer he used for an ashtray and stubbed out the flame gently so he could finish the cigarette later. "All right, then." He looked at Rainey and then at Mother, who had put down the spoon and was now clenching and unclenching her fists at her sides. "No harm in it I can see." He got up and started out of the kitchen. Rainey stopped him long enough to kiss his cheek and whisper, "Thank you, Daddy," when he passed. He squeezed her hand, two times quick.

He hadn't even asked what she wanted to do with the money. Marveling at how easy it had been, she turned to leave, having forgotten about her mother, thinking now only of stripping off her oily clothes and getting a quick bath before dinner.

"You — Rainey Jean Jorgensen," said Mother, resetting a pot lid a little more loudly than necessary. "You won't last the summer."

July

What Rainey liked best about her job was scooping up the freshly drained and salted fries and shaking them into the little paper envelopes. She liked the busy times, too, when she felt quick and efficient, smiling a

211

bright welcome at a customer, punching the keys on the cash register, and moving back and forth behind the counter, arranging the order on a tray or settling it into a carryout sack she opened with a snap.

Tuesday nights were usually slow, especially after eight o'clock, so there wasn't much to do except wipe up the tables, refill the straws and napkins, or — tonight — sneak glances at the stocky boy in the front booth. He'd finished his third burger more than an hour ago, and since then he'd sat with his legs stretched out along the bench, tapping the table, watching her. If he'd ever been in before, she hadn't noticed him, but now, with no one in the restaurant except herself and the new hire, Cindy, who was busy cleaning the grill in the kitchen, Rainey couldn't help it. He was maybe twenty or twenty-one. Not much to look at — short, at most a couple or three inches taller than she was, with eyebrows and eyelashes so pale there seemed to be none, leaving only the purplish rims underneath to bring attention to his light blue eyes. But his hair was interesting — thick, curled in red-gold locks, like the hair she imagined on boys in fairy tales, and when Rainey concentrated on this, she began to like him.

Back in the kitchen, she checked Cindy's

work on the grill and, noticing a car pulling into the lot, said, "Looks like your mother's here. You go on. I'll finish up."

Rainey wiped the edges of the grill, which Cindy had missed, checked the clock, washed her hands, and started back to the front to tell the boy in the booth that it was closing time. Just as she came out of the kitchen through the swinging door, he stepped in front of her. "Give you a ride home?" He was smiling.

Rainey's nerves skipped under her skin. Who was this bold young man? Of course she would say no — but she wanted to say yes. And why not? What was the harm? It was less than a ten-minute drive, after all. Only — Sally was probably already on her way.

"Thanks," Rainey said, taking a step back, "but my ride will be here in a minute." She started toward the door, as if to show him out, then smiled at him. "I hope you'll come again."

"I'm Carl," he said, stepping in her way once more, playfully, like a suitor in a Hollywood musical. "Maybe you can call whoever's coming for you? Tell them not to come?"

"I guess I could," Rainey said, lowering her eyes. There was a fleck of dried mustard on her uniform. She scratched it away with her fingernail. "But I'm sure she's already left."

Carl leaned in closer to her. "Try," he crooned.

Rainey shook her head. "It won't do any good," she said, her words buoyed on a nervous laugh. "But okay. Don't say I didn't warn you." Rainey dialed Sally's number, and listening to it ring, she flushed under Carl's steady stare and hoped he would feel how much she wanted him to come back, maybe ask her on a date.

"Hello?"

Rainey was so startled at the sound of her friend's voice, she coughed, choked back a hiccup, but managed to stammer, "Sally? I'm glad I caught you."

"Met a guy?" Sally asked.

"How did you know?"

"Had to happen some time." She could imagine Sally smiling in her world-wise way. "Have a good time."

A few minutes later, when Carl ignored Rainey's directions to turn onto Maple Street, she kept quiet, grinning in the dark, glowing in wonder over how marvelous things seemed always to happen by chance. Carl drove to the baseball field, dark for hours now after the evening's Little League game. He parked the car behind the bleachers and they sat and talked. He told her he was studying to be an engineer and that he was working through the summer for a building contractor.

"My father works at Crother's Mill," Rainey said. "Thirty years last winter. They gave him a nice watch. And a plaque." She glanced at Carl's hands, poised on the steering wheel and lit by the moon. They were far too smooth for a construction worker. Why should he tell such a funny lie? she wondered. Was he trying to impress her? She was about to ask him, when suddenly his hands were off the wheel, pressing against her back and pulling her to him. After that, all she could think about was the kissing — one, two, three, and then so many and so long she didn't care about counting anymore.

At last he released her and said, "I guess I'd better take you home. You have some excuse to give your folks?"

When they got to her street, Rainey pointed out the house, but Carl didn't pull in the drive. She was just about to invite him in when he reached across her and opened the door. "See you tomorrow," he said, as if they'd already made plans.

It was a little frightening to so abruptly

find herself standing alone in the middle of the street, watching Carl drive away, trying to understand what had happened, but when she closed her eyes and thought again of the heat from Carl's skin against her own, the sweet oniony taste of his mouth, all her fears sizzled away inside delight. This was just like a romance in a story — sudden and intense — nothing parents would understand. Certainly not her parents. Not now. Carl was exactly right to drive off the way he did. All great passions began as thrilling secrets — and this was hers.

Rainey managed to keep Carl a secret by telling Daddy that Mr. Buchanan had decided she was experienced enough with closing the Burger Chef to total the day's sales and balance the books, instead of leaving it for him to do before opening the next morning. "He says it'll be great practice for my bookkeeping course — put me ahead of the other students," she said, "but it means I'll have to work an hour later, maybe a little more. Sally will still pick me up." Once she was sure Daddy believed her, she told the same lie to her mother, and Rainey was free to think about Carl.

Now, back at the ball field, on their fourth night together, Carl led her from the car to the side of the bleachers and leaned her against one of the supporting posts. His first kisses were light, but soon they grew harder, deeper, and then he was pulling her under the bleachers. Kissing her again, he twisted her in his arms so her back was to him. While he sucked at her neck — how she loved his mouth on her neck! — he reached for her hands, placed them on the edge of one of the seat planks, and wrapped his arm around her like a sash. With his other hand, he worked her skirt up to her waist and pulled down her panties. There was just the briefest sear of pain when he pressed himself into her — like a smooth round stone, yet hot and damp — but, oh, she liked it, how much she liked it, when he tightened his other arm around her and rocked and swayed like a solo dancer, as if he were the back and she were the front of the same body.

"You only met him last week!" Sally was so flustered she knocked Skimble off her lap. The skinny black tom hissed and batted their ankles. The friends were sitting together on the porch swing, Rainey's parents just inside, watching *Gunsmoke*. "Let's go out to the stoop," Sally whispered. When they were settled, Sally leaned in close. "Are you sure, Rainey? Are you sure that's what happened? I mean, you've never. . . . have you?"

Her friend's seriousness seemed so silly that Rainey laughed. How could she have done it before when she didn't even know there was such a thing to do until it happened? But what difference did it make? Now she knew why the girls in high school used to giggle with excitement whenever they had a date. This was why they couldn't concentrate in English class on Monday mornings, why they always asked for extra time on their homework.

"Did he force you? Did you fight him? You're not thinking you're in love with him?" Sally's questions fired so quickly, Rainey couldn't keep up with them.

Fight him? What a ridiculous thing to ask. Why should she? "It's okay," she said, reaching over to pat Sally's arm.

How could Rainey explain she'd just done what seemed easy and natural, like how when she was eight she suddenly found the balance on her roller skates, one second clumsy and the next — flight. And no, she wasn't in love with Carl — at least she didn't think so. Not yet. It was the experience she adored, a feeling so wonderful she couldn't even imagine it when it wasn't happening. "Why are you so upset about this?" she asked Sally. "You date all the time."

"I don't do *that* all the time! I don't do that *ever*."

"But why not?" Rainey said. "I've seen you kiss Ben lots of times."

Sally stared at her, mouth open. "Oh, come on, Rainey. You know that's not the same."

"Well, okay," Rainey said, "it's not the same as kissing, but it's not that much different. It's nice."

Sally stood up and put her hands over her face. "Did he tell you that? Is he the one that said it wasn't any big deal?"

As a matter of fact, all Carl had said was that he'd dated lots of other girls before her, so Rainey just assumed he knew what people did on dates, but she thought better of saying that to Sally.

"Look," said Sally, "I know you don't get along so well with your mother, but you should listen to her on this." She leaned down to hug Rainey. "I've got to go home now. See the guy if you want to, but don't do that anymore."

That Sally. She'd always seemed so wise before, so how strange it was that she didn't understand about this. And what did she mean about listening to what Mother had

219

told her? Mother had never talked to her at all about boys, except to say Rainey didn't need to have anything to do with them until it was time to marry. The few times she'd tried to ask about what it was like to be married, her mother had said, "Like everything else — some good, some bad. You'll find out by doing. No point talking about it."

Well, this settled it. She just wouldn't say anything more about Carl to Sally, not for now — and definitely no good could come of mentioning him to her parents. Probably they'd make her quit her job, and she wasn't about to take that chance. So she would keep quiet — just for the time being — until she could be sure where things were going.

October

What a summer it had been. First job. First boyfriend. First — everything, really, and so wonderful — because she could finally see, really see, what her life might be. Rainey set a bundle of napkins on a clean tray and carried it from table to table, tucking the thick stacks into the holders, looking up every now and then to see how the new hire, Dennis, was getting along with the inventory. How quickly things changed.

By the beginning of August, she had already outlasted the three girls who started the same week she did, as well as two of their replacements, which made her, Rainey Jorgensen, the senior employee — aside from Millie and Mr. Buchanan himself. Then Mr. Buchanan promoted her to night manager. And at the end of the month, when she enrolled for her classes at Anderson County Junior College, he told her that when she was finished with her program, he could recommend her for a job with the company headquarters in Indianapolis if she wanted it. Imagine that — *her*. In Indianapolis. A real chance to do just what she'd dreamed of. With her own job secure, she and Sally could take an apartment and get along fine until Sally could find something, too.

These days, between her classes and her work schedule, Rainey was busy every minute, but she loved it all — the feeling of responsibility that came with training the new employees, like Dennis; the challenge of her schoolwork, even though it was hard; the excitement of meeting other young people like herself, people with goals. People like Richard, a boy in her economics class, who was going into banking.

People very different from Carl. Finally, after they'd been together for a month or so, he told her he had never been to college,

221

had never even thought about becoming an engineer. He wasn't working construction, either, which she'd known all along. Instead, what little time he referred to as "working" was spent running errands for a friend of his who fixed cars out of a home garage. The lies hadn't mattered to Rainey back then — then, from the time she got up in the morning, she had watched the clock, figuring up every few minutes how much longer before she would be with Carl, feeling his heart thumping against her back. All day long, and then with Carl at the ball field at night, her heart would sing, *This is love, this is love,* but now her days were filled by sitting in her classes at the junior college, smiling back at the boys who were smiling at her — Richard among them — and she forgot about Carl entirely for hours at a time. Like this morning — when Richard asked her if she wanted to go see Elizabeth Taylor in *Giant* at the Grand a week from this Saturday, she'd said yes without a single thought to Carl.

She wished now that he was coming to pick her up after work tonight like he usually did, just so she could go ahead and break up with him, but he'd told her he would busy every night this week, helping to overhaul an engine. Rainey didn't really believe him — and if she had confessed all her feelings to Sally, her friend would have told her to pick up the phone and get it over with — but that didn't seem fair. After all, Carl was her first love, and even though she knew the romance was over, she still had a warm feeling for him, and he deserved better than getting dumped over the telephone. She'd see him soon enough — probably the first of next week — and in the meantime she'd enjoy her Saturday date with Richard.

Rainey filled the last of the napkin holders and then collected the mustard and ketchup bottles for refilling. Fifteen minutes to closing. Daddy would be here soon. Sally had a night job of her own now and couldn't pick her up, so it was a relief to Rainey, when she was forced to ask Daddy to give her a ride, that she could tell the truth — Sally was working. But soon Carl would be out of her life, and she could stop lying altogether. She planned to tell everyone — even Mother — about Richard, right from the start.

Rainey walked back to the kitchen to check Dennis's inventory, pointing out that he'd forgotten to count the condiments and paper supplies in the storage closet. While he finished that, she shut down the fryer and scrubbed the grill, then locked the door and cashed out the register.

She had just stepped outside when Daddy pulled up. "Don't wait in the dark alone, Rainey," he scolded. "Wait inside until you see me."

"Yes, Daddy." She slid onto the seat and pulled the door shut, then turned a little to smile at his profile, outlined in dim flashes by the occasional passing car. She could hear the crackle from his shirt pocket as he fumbled for a cigarette, so she pushed in the knob on the dashboard lighter to get it ready for him.

He smoked without talking the rest of the way home. When he shut off the engine, he reached for Rainey's hand and squeezed it twice, but instead of releasing it like he usually did, he held on.

He took another drag on his cigarette, held the smoke for a long time, then blew it out, as if with his last breath. "Your mother says you've been having dizzy spells."

Rainey laughed and leaned through the darkness to kiss his cheek. "Oh, Daddy, it's nothing. It's only happened a couple of times when I didn't eat any breakfast."

He didn't turn toward her at all, just stared out the front windshield, the end of his cigarette glowing bright, then dim, bright, then dim. He let go of her hand, rolled his window down a couple of inches, tossed the cigarette onto the driveway, and lit another. "Your mother's taking you to see Dr. Wolfe in the morning," he said at last. "You're not to argue about it. The cab's coming at nine-fifteen, so you be ready by nine."

He pushed his door open, dropped the second cigarette beside the first, and ground them into the gravel with his heel. Rainey stayed in her seat, watching her father limp up the steps to the house. She would do what he asked, of course, but what a nuisance. She'd hoped to have a chance to talk to Richard after class tomorrow, but she could look for him in the cafeteria on Wednesday.

Three days later, on Friday, Mother blocked the front door to keep Rainey from going to work. "I've called that Mr. Buchanan and told him you won't be coming back anymore," she said.

"Mother!" Rainey tried to push past her. "What are you talking about? Is this about the ride?" Her mother stood as firm as a tank in the door. "Please, Mother. Let me go. I told you I had that all worked out. Daddy won't have to come get me after this week." She tried to read her mother's face

— only anger and resolve. Not the reason for it. Rainey stepped back, took a deep breath, and tried again. "Please. *Please*, Mother. I'm going to be late. We can talk about it tonight — whatever it is."

"You go back to your room right now and take off that uniform," Mother said. "There's not to be another word about it. Not 'til your daddy gets home."

Rainey knew better than to keep battling when her mother was like this. She thought about waiting for her to go back into the kitchen, then slipping through the basement door — she could get down the steps and out the back before Mother could catch her — but a sneak escape would only make things worse. She'd just have to wait until Daddy got home to straighten everything out — a little over an hour — and then she could go on to work and explain to Mr. Buchanan that her mother had had some kind of crazy fit. She would go back to her room, she decided, but she wouldn't take off her uniform. That would save time when Daddy finished telling Mother to stop her fussing.

Rainey expected her to start on Daddy the minute he got home, but she zipped her lip and waited all the way through supper — didn't even say anything about how Rainey was still wearing her uniform.

Then, right at the table, over the dirty dishes, Mother said it: "This girl's pregnant. Dr. Wolfe called this morning."

For a whole minute, there wasn't a sound in the room except the pendulum swinging back and forth inside the cabinet of the wall clock. They'd all stopped breathing. Then, without looking at Rainey or her mother, Daddy pushed up from the table, his arms shaking under his small weight. He might have been ninety. Slowly and painfully, he limped into the living room to his chair, his keys jangling in his pocket with every swing of his bad leg.

Rainey sat still, stunned, while Mother gathered up the dishes. *Pregnant.* How? How could she be?

The question had barely formed in her head when she realized the answer. Things Sally and other girls had said through the years converged with some drawings remembered from her junior biology book to make her at once ashamed of her own stupidity and angry at Mother for not having explained the simple facts. This was why Sally had been shocked when Rainey told her what happened on the baseball field with Carl; this was why Sally had told her to stop.

Her gushing tears couldn't cool her burning cheeks. She looked toward Daddy, but he just sat in his chair, staring toward the dark screen of the television. In the kitchen, Mother was running steaming water into the sink and dropping the dishes in, one by one. Rainey ran into her room, slammed the door and flung herself on the bed, wailing as she had never done before. When at last she was quiet, she slid to the floor, her back against the bed, and hugged a pillow to her chest. Soon, soon, Daddy would come in as he always did, take her hand, squeeze it two times quick, and tell her everything was going to be all right.

The room grew dark, but Daddy did not come. Rainey turned on the lamp beside her bed so that, when he passed her door, he would be able to see she was still up. He didn't come.

After a while, Rainey heard the sound of the television, but she couldn't quite make out what the show was. She looked at her alarm clock. Just past eight o'clock — time for *The Life of Riley.* It was Daddy's favorite. Hers, too. They used to watch it every week, until she started working nights. Together they would laugh at Riley's clumsiness, raise their eyebrows at him when his wife, Peg, did, and they'd sing out his signature phrase along with him — *What a revoltin' develop-*

ment this is — right on the beat, while Mother would sit in her chair, doing her crochet, shaking her head and muttering about how an actor good enough to play Babe Ruth just like he was the real thing oughtn't waste his time making such a silly program.

In the morning, Rainey heard Daddy stirring around in his room, getting ready for work. She heard him and Mother talking in the kitchen — just a word or two here and there — and then the sound of the car starting and the crunching rattle of the gravel under the tires. It was nearly noon when Mother finally tapped on the door and said, "Your daddy's coming home early to drive you over to the college to quit. You need to be dressed and ready to go at three-thirty."

Daddy didn't say a word when Rainey got in the car. She wanted to say something, but all she could think of was that she was glad that nobody she knew took classes so late in the afternoon, and she was pretty sure he wouldn't appreciate hearing about that.

Daddy didn't offer to go in with her. She took the shortest way she knew to the office. "I have to leave school," she said to the woman behind the window, but she'd said it so softly, she had to repeat it twice. The withdrawal form looked so much like the admission form she'd filled out just two months ago, Rainey nearly lost control, but she managed to keep pressing out her details with the pen — name, age, address — right up until she got to the line that said "Reason for Withdrawal." She stared at it so long, the woman finally called to her, "Do you need some help, honey?" and so Rainey scribbled, "Moving." She supposed it was true. Mother wouldn't let her stay in the house now — not even if Daddy insisted.

Daddy started the car the instant Rainey closed the door. Instead of turning for home, he drove through town and out past the county line, not seeming to be going anywhere. It wasn't like him at all; he didn't like to drive. After a long, silent time, he looped toward town again and finally turned down the road to the high school, where he stopped the car in the parking lot. She'd never seen Daddy full out cry, but she thought he might now, his eyes were so wet. He dug his handkerchief out of his pocket and blew his nose.

"Do you love him?" he asked.

Who? she almost said, but she caught herself in time.

"If you love him and you want to marry him, whoever he is, I'll see it gets done,"

Daddy said. "If you don't, then we'll manage."

He didn't say how they would manage.

"You have to tell me the truth now, Rainey." He looked at her, tears rolling down his cheeks. "Do you love him?"

Did he want her to say yes? Would everything be all right then — would Daddy think that made everything all right? Would he stop looking at her that way, all the little pieces of his heart swimming in his eyes?

She *had* loved Carl — had been *in love* with him. She remembered now hearing people talk about how the *in love* feeling went away after a time, and then there was just ordinary love, love without the churning stomach and the giggles inside every breath. Ordinary love — not much of a feeling at all, just something you knew was there.

"Yes, Daddy," she said. "Yes, I do." And when she said it, her love rushed back to her, not quite as strong as it once was, but she could feel it.

Daddy took her hand and squeezed it. Two times quick. Everything was going to be all right.

TEN:
ICE

September 1964
McAllister, Ohio

ALMA

Alma refilled the canapé tray, refreshing the parsley edge and counting out equal numbers of sandwiches — watercress, herbed butter, egg and anchovy, deviled chicken — framing these with shrimp puffs and angels on horseback. She consulted the colored sketch she'd made days ago, having precisely measured the finished size of the sandwiches, and, satisfied that she had replenished the tray to its original glory, she set it on the counter behind her and reached for the sketch of hors d'oeuvres. This morning, when Gordon noticed the sketches, he said drawing food was a waste of time, but they had been her salvation. Her husband's preliminary list of tidbits for the party — including a large order for crudités, cheese,

232

crackers, nuts, and olives — was overwhelming. The drawings had helped calm Alma, making her confident that she could manage the grand party Gordon expected. Besides — along with her shopping list and her schedule for washing, cutting, cooking, and storing — the sketches would slip right into her notebook for entertaining, and if she made a few modifications, she could use this menu again.

Alma was proud of what she'd done, proud that Gordon had allowed her to recognize she could do it without the hired help she'd asked for — a sweet girl she'd met at the grocery who waitressed at Raquel's, the only restaurant in town where the staff understood it was proper to serve from the left. Or so she'd been told. Alma had never been to Raquel's, having to stay home to look after Milton — Gordon didn't approve of sitters — but Gordon had occasionally been invited to dine there with the Powells.

Yes, she thought, gazing at the pleasing array of colors and shapes on the tray — *yes,* she'd done all this herself. Mother couldn't have done it — not that she would ever have occasion to give such a party. No, had Mother been here, she couldn't even have helped. She would have screwed up her mouth in mockery to cover that she didn't know what a canapé was, or how it was different from an hors d'oeuvre. Mother wouldn't have been able to stock a praiseworthy bar that assured every guest would have precisely the cocktail he or she preferred.

Alma picked up the canapé tray and pushed carefully through the swinging door into the living room. The guests, only a few of whom Alma had met, were clustered in threes and fours, talking, smoking, gesturing with their cocktails. Alma glided from group to group, offering the tray, hoping at least to be able to catch someone's eye long enough to smile warmly, introduce herself, and perhaps toss off a witty remark, but they were all so engaged in their conversations, they didn't notice her, only the tray.

"Shouldn't we ask the O'Connors?" she had said to Gordon last Tuesday evening while she addressed the invitations from the list he'd given her. "Or the Ketchums?"

Gordon was watching *The Man from U.N.C.L.E.* "This is a different crowd," he said, not turning his eyes from the television.

Alma certainly knew that. Bruce Powell held some important office in the Chamber of Commerce, and most of the other men on the list were city officials, but she still couldn't see why their coming should preclude inviting their usual guests — Gordon's acquaintances from the Kiwanis Club and hers from the Ladies Auxiliary. "But surely some of the men know Jack O'Connor," she said. "Wasn't he treasurer of Kiwanis once?"

"These fellows are Rotarians," Gordon said. When Alma asked what difference it made which civic club they belonged to, Gordon folded the paper roughly, rolled his eyes at her, and said she knew nothing about economics. She supposed she didn't, really — at least not more than she had come to understand while running a household budget — but he still hadn't answered her question. His desire to impress these men and their wives couldn't just be for the sake of business. After all, since he had completed the purchase of Dr. Weigel's practice, he was the only podiatrist in McAllister — indeed, the only podiatrist in a hundred miles — so it wasn't a question of building up his clientele. Perhaps he was thinking of running for City Council, but she couldn't imagine how he could make the time for that.

Having made one circuit of the room, Alma set the canapé tray on the buffet and nudged a few cucumber lilies and radish roses into a more appealing arrangement.

Now perhaps she could mix herself a Tom Collins and join the party for a few minutes before checking the food again.

She felt a light pressure on her arm and looked up to see a fiftyish woman with frosted blond hair smiling at her. "Such a nice party," the woman said. "You're Gordon's wife, aren't you, dear? I'm Claudine Powell."

Alma offered her hand, but Mrs. Powell suddenly turned to nod toward Gordon at the bar and said, "When he was round to dinner last week, Gordon told us all about the new kitchen. You must show it off to everyone."

"Of course, any time you like," Alma said, wishing she had an excuse to say no. Gordon gave her one. From his post behind the bar, he was jiggling the empty ice bucket.

"Please excuse me," she said to Mrs. Powell. "My husband needs me."

As Alma took the ice bucket from Gordon, she remarked that she had just met Claudine Powell.

"You've got to keep up with the ice, you know," Gordon said. "How do you expect me to mix drinks without ice?"

Alma nodded and turned to go back to the kitchen.

"I'll need more crushed ice when you get

back with that," Gordon said, loudly enough that a few of the men near the bar stopped talking and looked at her.

Alma took the bowl of ice from the freezer and tapped it with an ice pick to separate the cubes. After she'd filled the bucket, she emptied four more ice trays into the bowl, returned it to the freezer, and ran water to refill the trays. She wished she'd thought to say to Claudine Powell that Gordon ought to be the one to conduct the tour of the new kitchen, since it had been remodeled according to his plan, not hers.

Alma had wanted a range — not a wall oven and a cooktop with the immense awkward vent hanging over it like some giant wide-mouthed vacuum tube, poised to swallow her up. And she had wanted everything in pink and yellow, all soft and bright. Along with her old friend Mrs. Murchison, who'd come to stay for a week last spring, Alma had spent hours every day sorting through magazine photographs, advertising brochures, and color samples, designing the kitchen she had dreamt of since childhood — butter yellow appliances set off by pink-and-yellow tile accented in aqua. But Gordon and his mother, who had come in especially from Newman two months ago to give her opinion, had insisted that aqua appliances were more elegant, and that red-and-black tile up the wall and, in larger blocks, on the floor would be most tasteful.

Gordon and his mother had chosen dim accent lighting, too, to set off various aspects of the kitchen they believed most attractive. One of these was the display of crystal on open shelves. Alma had suggested the pieces would be safer but still visible in a windowed cabinet, but Gordon had shaken his head in annoyance, saying open shelves commanded attention. Certainly they demanded attention — twice already in the three weeks since the renovation was complete, Alma had had to wash and hand-dry that spectacular glass to keep it sparkling.

Sometimes she caught herself looking at the pretty yellow refrigerator in the brochure, but she could see now, of course, that Gordon and his mother had been right about the aqua. Alma still hadn't warmed to the tile floor, though, thinking it looked like some absurd, nightmarishly large chessboard.

Claudine Powell pushed through the kitchen door and said, "Well, here you are." She took the ice bucket from Alma's hands. "Now, you just put that down and come enjoy the party."

Alma tugged at the rim of the bucket. "Gordon needs the ice."

With a wry smile, Claudine shook her head. "Gordon, Gordon." She pushed the door partly open with one hand and, rather too loudly, Alma thought, called out, "Bruce!" A slim, balding man in a gray suit appeared, and Claudine said, "Bruce, this is Alma. Isn't she pretty?" Bruce said hello and then was suddenly holding the bucket Claudine had thrust into his hands. "Take this to Gordon," she said.

Claudine strolled to the center of the kitchen and turned around slowly, taking it all in. She pointed at the rotisserie. "I suppose Gordon likes leg of lamb."

"Two or three times a month," Alma said.

"Well, he doesn't have to clean that contraption, does he?"

"It's not so very difficult to clean," Alma said. That wasn't true at all, but she wasn't sure she liked Mrs. Powell's tone, as though she and Alma were co-conspirators.

The older woman laid one hand lightly on the refrigerator door. "This is Gordon's doing, isn't it? The scheme? No woman I know would want all these dark colors."

"Gordon's mother likes them," Alma said, but Mrs. Powell went on as though she hadn't heard her.

"Hurts your eyes to look at that checker-board."

Alma got the bowl of ice out of the freezer again to load the ice crusher, checking to be sure it was set on *Fine.* Gordon was particular about his ice. When she looked up from her cranking, she saw Mrs. Powell had the food sketches in her hands.

"Did you do these?"

Alma nodded. "It was silly, I know, but I needed to see what everything looked like first to be sure the food would fit my serving pieces."

"It's nice work," Claudine said. "Looks like something you'd see in a cookbook." She put the sketches down and patted Alma on the arm. "I'll leave you alone, dear. I know it's hard to be hostess. Next time, think about hiring a girl to help you for the evening."

Alma dumped the first load of crushed ice into the large bowl she would take out to Gordon and then put another load in the crusher. She looked at the sketches again, seeing, she thought, a little of what Claudine Powell had seen. Surely it was ridiculous for her to feel so pleased with the woman's compliment, which was probably really nothing more than casual politeness, but Alma felt a rush of warmth in her cheeks.

Earlier in the evening, when she'd made her first round with the hors d'oeuvres, she had noticed Milton, looking so handsome and grown up in the blue suit his father had chosen for his birthday, holding an Old Fashioned glass half-filled with orange juice, clearly thinking himself the equal of the two men who laughed at his third-grade jokes. She wanted to do a watercolor portrait of him while traces of the adored infant remained in his face, to capture him before he tumbled over the edge into puberty.

Surely in another year or two he would be able to sit still for a portrait. Last year when Alma had tried it, Milton became impatient, complaining he wanted to work on his science experiment — he was calculating how long it took various insects to die after being sealed in jars with a cotton pad soaked in alcohol. When she tried to assure him that she needed only another fifteen minutes and went to settle a cushion behind his back to make him more comfortable, he had slapped her hard across the face.

Mixed with the shock of the strike, Alma had felt a sudden, intense longing for Daddy, who in an instant would have snatched Milton by the collar and laid him across his knee for a whipping. Alma had been too stunned to do anything herself, even to speak, and Milton ran off toward his room, singing some song he'd learned on the radio, while she got up to get a cold cloth to hold against her stinging cheek. The boy had hit her so hard he'd left a red mark, but it was easily concealed with an extra layer of foundation.

Gordon had told her when they married — and she had agreed — that when the time came to have child, he would handle the discipline, and so Alma waited without a word through the afternoon, through Gordon's two after-work scotch and sodas, and then through dinner, until Gordon had sent Milton to his room to do homework.

She had sat down on the edge of the ottoman, facing Gordon. Very quietly and very calmly, she had said, "Dear, our Milton has misbehaved."

Gordon folded the newspaper in his lap, reached to get a cigarette out of the engraved silver case on the side table. He tapped the end of the cigarette five times against the gleaming walnut surface, picked up the lighter, and, finding it empty, clapped it back down. He looked past Alma and held his hand out, which she understood to mean that he expected her to get up, cross the room, get the lighter they kept on the mantel, and return it to him. She did this, and he flipped the top, spun the wheel with a hard flick of his thumb, lit his cigarette, put down the lighter, and took two long drags. Now he looked her unwaveringly in the eye and said, "Well?"

When she explained what had happened, Gordon tipped his head back and laughed.

Laughed and laughed.

She thought he might never stop.

When at last, still laughing, he looked at her again, he took no notice of the tears that had spilled from her eyes in spite of her resolve not to cry. "That boy knows his own mind," he said, tapping a dangling ash from his cigarette. "That'll teach you to listen to him when he says he's tired of sitting around."

"You're not going to punish him," Alma said, so softly she wasn't sure she'd said it at all.

"For what?" Gordon seemed almost angry now. At her. "Why should I punish him for being annoyed that you were wasting time he wanted for studying? You ought to be glad he's so serious about science." He stubbed out the cigarette, unfolded his paper, and said nothing more.

At the time, she'd felt wounded by both

her son and husband, and she'd spent the rest of the evening crying in the bedroom, wondering if either of them would come in to stroke her shoulders. But after a time, she came to see that Gordon was right. Yes, she was truly blessed to have such a son, who, still so young, already knew he was going to be a doctor — a surgeon, perhaps — and who didn't have time to sit for portraits while his mother taught herself to paint. No, she wouldn't ask him again. If she wanted to paint him, she could do it from a photograph. Or she could paint the tree in the backyard.

Life was the way you looked at it, she reminded herself. Truly, it was. There had been a time, a year — almost two — after Gordon decided against their having another child, when Alma had nursed a heavy sadness, but at last she had come to see Gordon's view: the expense — of time, money, and attention — could only be drawn against Milton's account — and that wouldn't do. "Nearly thirty thousand dollars to bring up one just to age seventeen," Gordon had told her, quoting a report he had read in one of his magazines, "and that doesn't include college. Or medical school."

How fortunate she was to have such a good provider for a husband, a man who calculated these things. A man thoughtful enough to arrange for her to have a new kitchen with a dishwasher, a garbage disposal, and even a trash compactor. A man who was sensible and practical when it came to handling their fine, ambitious son.

Yes, she was lucky. That was clearest to her when she thought of what her life might have been, given what she'd come from.

Just look at the mess Rainey had made of her life — embarrassing the whole family by having to get married, and then, just when she was beginning to get settled, she'd run off with that little girl of hers — without any explanation to anyone — and filed for divorce. And the worst of it — not more than a year later, there was Rainey, pregnant again, this time by some man she refused to name. Shameful. Those girls of hers, Lynn and Grace, were certain to grow up half wild, no standards at all. Alma felt sorry for them. She felt sorry for Mother and Daddy, too, for the humiliation they must have had to face at church, but when she thought about how they had always indulged Rainey — or at least how Daddy always had — her sympathy waned. Probably Mother had resisted, at first, but then gave in, Alma supposed, when Daddy put his foot down on behalf of his favorite. Yes, she could see that

Daddy might have forced Mother into agreeing to have Rainey back, but even so, that was no excuse for the way Mother doted on Rainey's girls, while she was only polite to Milton.

Well, Alma was out of all that and glad for it. She could bear visiting her parents in Newman once or twice a year, and the rest of the time she could enjoy the prestige of being a doctor's wife — and perhaps, in time, the wife of a city councilman.

Alma checked her reflection in the broad side of a crystal pitcher on Gordon's open shelves, tucked a few strands of hair back into place, picked up the bowl of crushed ice, and pushed through the door to join her guests.

Eleven:
Letting Go

June 1965
Newman, Indiana

RAINEY

Lynn's cries punctured Rainey's sleep.

"No! Daddy! Don't let go! Daddy! Daddy!"

Rainey stumbled across the room to her daughter's bed. Still asleep, Lynn thrashed, not screaming now, but seeming desperate to. Her lips were pressed tightly and her face was turning red, as if she were holding her breath.

Mother appeared in the doorway, her face white, her housecoat only halfway on. Daddy limped in behind her, still dressed from the day, his clothes rumpled from the couch. Neither of them had taken time to put on their glasses. They stood at the foot of the bed while Rainey hugged Lynn to her chest, rocked her, and rubbed her back, murmuring, "Breathe, baby. Lynn, breathe.

247

You're okay. You're okay."

Last night, when Carl had brought Lynn home — hours later than he was due — he did not say why she was dressed only in a man's large T-shirt, but, as he laid her in her bed, he explained the square of gauze over the girl's eye by saying she'd slipped on the dock. She'd been running too fast, he said, and banged her head into a post. He'd taken her to the emergency room — there didn't seem any point in calling about it, not after the doctor said she would be all right, not since they were already so late. All she needed was a couple of stitches, a tetanus shot. *An accident,* Carl said. *Could have happened to anyone* — and though she hated to, Rainey had to admit it was true. Lynn was always running too fast, falling down, and might as easily have cut her head on their own front stoop. What had frightened Rainey most was how groggy Lynn was so many hours after the fall. For several minutes, Rainey had patted her daughter's cheek and rubbed her hands, and finally Lynn had roused, opening her eyes for a moment before falling again into a deep sleep. *They gave her something for the pain,* Carl told them, *because of the stitches* — but after Carl was gone, they had looked at one another, she and Mother and Daddy, as if each was waiting for one of the others to say they didn't believe him, not quite.

From her bed in the corner, Grace began to cry, and it was only then that any of them noticed the three-year-old was awake, sitting bolt upright, her eyes wide and streaming with tears.

"You come on with me," Mother said, lifting Grace into her arms. "You can sit with your grandpa on the porch."

Grace sniffled and rubbed at her eyes, then laid her head on her grandmother's shoulder. "Can I chase lightning bugs?"

"They've all gone to bed, sugar," Mother said. "But you can listen for the whip-poorwills and whistle back to them, like Grandpa taught you."

"Will Grandpa sing?" Grace asked.

Daddy nodded. "You take her on out, Bertie," he said. "I'll be along in a minute."

Lynn's body had at last relaxed into stillness, and she breathed steadily again, but Rainey continued to rock her. She looked up at her father, and then, feeling her tears coming, turned her head away. "What am I going to do, Daddy? I can't . . ." There were too many ways to end that sentence, all rushing at her at once. *I can't let him keep taking her. I can't stop him. I can't protect her. I can't not protect her.*

249

Daddy reached for Rainey's hand, gave it two quick squeezes, and hobbled back toward the front of the house. She knew he wanted to help, knew he would give everything he had to help, but he didn't know any more than she did about what to do, where to start. Even Mother had been trying her best, being kinder to Rainey these last few months, ever since Carl had turned up again, insisting on having his visits with Lynn — a right, the lawyer had told Rainey, that was still legally Carl's, despite his never having exercised it before. No one, it seemed, could untangle the mess she'd made.

Rainey eased her daughter back onto the bed and tidied the sheets as best she could. In the dim light that filtered from the hallway, she could see Lynn's face — a face now twisted and creased with worry, the face of an old woman, not of a child barely eight.

This, too, was her fault — all the scars of her mistakes, written on her little girl's forehead.

No good could come of wishing backwards, she knew, but sometimes her mind would slip off before she could catch it — wishing she'd never taken up Carl's first offer to drive her home, wishing she'd never met him, wishing even that she had never gotten her job at the Burger Chef. When those thoughts came, she pushed hard at them, driving them down again, for to wish away Carl would be to wish away Lynn, and Rainey didn't want that. But if one day she rubbed a lamp and a genie appeared before her, she knew exactly what she would ask — to go back to that night in the car with Daddy when she told him she wanted to marry Carl. If she were granted that wish, Rainey would grab her silly nineteen-year-old self and shake some sense into her, stop her from saying "Yes," stop her from declaring to Daddy — and to herself — that she was in love when she wasn't.

Though she had long forgotten how it had felt to love Carl — she supposed she had, for a few weeks that summer — she did remember how it had felt to be nearly four months pregnant, standing beside him in the judge's office, dreaming of their future, seeing herself slipping her fingers through his hair, long after it had gone silver. What a strange sensation, remembering how at the time she had thought the day a happy one, and yet also remembering how it had really been, just as if she were two different people with two different experiences of the same hour.

Carl had been late. He'd arrived with his mother, a pruny woman with home-dyed hair the color of withered marigolds, who, when she entered, looked away and refused to return Rainey's greeting. Mother had talked all the way downtown in the car about the disgrace, but once they'd stepped inside the City-County Building, she'd hushed up, answering any question, when she was forced to, with a gesture or a step forward. Daddy had driven more slowly than usual, not once looking up at Rainey in the rearview mirror to roll his eyes at something her mother had said, and when they walked across the parking lot, Rainey had had to grasp his arm to steady him.

After the wedding, nothing was like she'd ever imagined it would be. There was no cute little apartment with flowered curtains, no afternoons fixing herself up while the dinner cooked, no romantic evenings curled together in an armchair, talking about what their baby might be like. There was his parents' ramshackle farm lined with tumbledown fences, nasty chickens and pigs rutting up the yard, big red dogs that Carl's father bred for fights, snarling and hurling themselves at the pen day and night, and for the newlyweds a tiny damp room in the basement filled with greasy car parts and racing magazines. Never in her life had Rainey believed it was possible to miss Newman, but she did. Siler was less than an hour across the state line, but it might as well have been on the far coast of Hell.

In Siler, nobody ordered Rainey to do the cooking, the scrubbing up, or the laundry, but she saw right away that if she didn't do it, it wouldn't get done — and for the most part, when she was in her last month and couldn't be on her feet long, it didn't. It was just the same when it came to Carl's finding a job. From one day to the next, he didn't turn a hand toward it, and it wore Rainey out to be the only one who seemed to think he ought to be looking, so just as soon as she could after the baby came — several weeks sooner than the doctor would have liked — she hitched a ride into town and found a job clerking at the drugstore. When she got back, she told Carl he had to teach her to drive.

It knotted her stomach to leave Lynn behind in that house, but working was the only way she could see for getting them out. Every day when Rainey got back, she was sure to find Lynn screaming with hunger and lying in a foul wet diaper, but after she got her cleaned up and soothed, she whispered to her baby, promising that soon,

soon, she would take her away.

For eight months, Rainey saved every penny of her pay, and then, one day on her lunch hour, without a word to Carl, she rented a small house in town and called a woman about sitting for Lynn during working hours. Before leaving the drugstore that evening, she filled the car with empty boxes from the stockroom, and as soon as she got back to the farm and tended to Lynn, she started throwing all their things — hers and Lynn's — into the cartons. When she was finished, she set three or four empty boxes on the bed and went out to the old barn where Carl was messing with one of the half-dozen cars that would never run again, told him the address of the house and said he could come with them, but if he didn't have a job within two weeks, he'd have to go.

Three days — three glorious days — she and Lynn had the house to themselves. When Carl showed up, he'd already gotten a job selling furniture. He'd bathed and shaved, had bought some new clothes, and while he still couldn't be called handsome, he looked nice enough to introduce as her husband. At first, she thought maybe it was going to be okay with them, because he seemed as happy as she was about being away from the farm, but soon he was ignoring Lynn like before and treating Rainey like she had the brains of a caterpillar, calling her stupid and mocking the idea that she could ever have been a bookkeeper when she had trouble balancing the checkbook, making a dunce cap for her out of a sheet of newspaper when she forgot to put a new bag in the sweeper after taking out the full one.

She was unhappy, but what was there to do but make the best of it? She couldn't think past that thought then. He was her husband, simple as that, so she had to find a way to live with him. It wasn't as if they spent all that much time together. Most nights, after he swallowed his supper, he'd leave again and stay out until past midnight. After a while, Rainey didn't even wake up when he fell into bed beside her. In the morning, just before she headed out the door with Lynn, she'd nudge Carl and tell him the coffee was ready and that he had to be at work in an hour.

If the drugstore hadn't flooded, they might have gone on like that for years without her knowing what Carl really was. A pipe had burst in the employees' restroom, but no one had realized it until a customer waved a bottle of Vicks Formula

44 above his head and shouted that he was nearly ankle-deep in water. The manager shooed all the customers out and locked the door, and the employees waded through the stockroom, trying to find a shutoff valve. When at last the water was stopped, someone called a plumber, and the manager told them all to go home and not to come back to work until he called in a day or two.

Rainey's first thought had been the money, how she and Carl couldn't afford to lose any of her pay, so to save the couple of dollars that would have gone to the sitter for the afternoon's work, she stopped on her way home to pick up the baby. Lynn was cranky, having been woken from her nap, and Rainey was so busy trying to settle her, she didn't notice, when she parked in front of the house, that Carl's El Dorado was three or four spaces further up.

She was hoping to get Lynn back to sleep, and she was glad, once she was home, that she could lie down with her daughter and maybe get a little nap herself. She set Lynn on the living room floor, handed her a teddy bear, tossed her purse onto the couch, kicked off her wet shoes, and went to turn down the covers.

And there was Carl, wearing nothing except the white shirt he'd put on that morning, feet on the floor, chest on the bed.

And the naked man curled over him, thrusting — all Rainey could think of in that first paralyzed instant was that he had blond hair, a beard, and she didn't know him.

Behind her, Lynn called, "Mommy!" and Rainey swung round, ran back to the living room, scooped up her child, and didn't look back.

What she had seen in the bedroom flashed in her head over and over like a slide stuck in a projector, and each time, she took in new details: Carl's shorts — the ones flecked with the tiny brown shields — clinging to the edge of the mattress; one of the pair of pictures with the finches and the ferns knocked almost sideways on the wall behind the bed; the alarm clock on the nightstand facedown; an open jar of Vaseline tipped over on her pillow. She looked and looked, not understanding what she saw or what it meant any more than if her baby had transformed into a hissing cobra before her eyes: incomprehensible, horrible.

She had no recollection of getting Lynn into the car, or of picking up the exit for the expressway on the other end of town, or even of having decided where she was going. One minute she had stood frozen in the doorway of her bedroom in Siler and the next, four hours later, she was in the doorway of Sally's apartment in Indianapolis, Lynn shivering in her arms, yowling, her red corduroy pants soaked through with urine.

"Rainey, your shoes," Sally said while Rainey shook her head, saying, "I was afraid to stop," as if that explained why she wore none and why her stockings were splotched with black, pilled and torn around the toes. She still had on her blue smock from the drugstore, the sleeves and shoulders streaked with makeup from where she had scrubbed away her tears as she drove.

With the help of half a bottle of wine, Rainey finally choked out the scene to Sally, but it was Sally who had to explain its meaning, because Rainey couldn't fathom how men could do such things. The next day, carrying a purse stuffed fat with tissues and wearing a borrowed dress, she'd found a job and, a couple of hours later, a divorce lawyer. She'd tried then to arrange it so Carl couldn't get near Lynn, but because she couldn't bring herself to tell the lawyer what had really happened, there wasn't anything he could present as grounds to deny regular visitation.

That was another mistake, piled on a great wobbly stack of them, but at the time, it didn't seem to matter. As bad as her three years with Carl had been, the solution appeared to roll right out before her, a kind of red carpet reward for having made it through. When she told Carl she wouldn't be asking for any money, he told her he wouldn't challenge the divorce. When she told him the Chevy wouldn't hold up to driving Lynn down to Siler every two weeks, he told her he didn't want to waste his weekends coming to Indianapolis. That first Christmas after she left, when she took Lynn back to Newman to see Mother and Daddy, Rainey had held her breath whenever the phone rang or a car passed the house, but she never heard or saw a sign of Carl. Plainly, he had made up his mind to forget all about Lynn, so Rainey made up her mind that Lynn would forget him too. Rainey never mentioned his name, never showed Lynn any pictures of Carl or told her any stories about him — and it worked. It wasn't until Lynn started kindergarten that she even began to notice that other children had two parents, and when at last she asked where her daddy was, Rainey told her daughter that her father was a bad man who had never loved them or wanted them. "You won't ever have to know him, sweetie," Rainey said, certain Carl would never be anything more than her own private, sickening memory.

It had all worked better than she could have hoped, and even though she and Mother argued and fussed, even though her paycheck was always spent weeks before it was earned, Rainey told herself she was lucky — right up until five or six months ago, when Carl had called the house, saying he wanted to start having Lynn with him every other weekend. Things had changed, he told her. He'd gotten himself a good job with the county, working for the road department. In another year or two, he'd probably be a supervisor — or so he claimed. Since he didn't know if he would marry again — Rainey snorted at this, but Carl ignored her — Lynn would probably be the only child he would ever have, and ever since his mother had died, his father had been asking about Lynn, saying how he wanted to know her. Rainey told him to go to hell and slammed the phone down — she couldn't imagine how he'd found out they were in Newman again — and when he didn't call back, she let herself believe the crisis was over, but a few days later, she got a letter from a lawyer, saying that if Rainey didn't abide by the original visitation agreement, Carl would take her back to court. In the letter, there was even a day and a time set for when Carl expected to pick Lynn up for her first visit.

Right away, Daddy called somebody from church who gave him the name of a lawyer, Mr. Prather, and Rainey took an afternoon off work to go see him, but he told her there was nothing he could do. Even if they could manage to get Carl's parental rights rescinded — "And there's not much hope of that," Mr. Prather said — it would take time. Months at the very least, possibly years. And so Rainey had made herself tell him about Carl and the other man — everything she had seen in the bedroom. When she began to cry, the lawyer came around his desk to sit beside her and offered her his handkerchief.

"I'm so awfully sorry," he said, shaking his head in disgust. "A nice young woman like you, churchgoing family." While Rainey wept out her fears, Mr. Prather agreed that it would be a terrible thing indeed to let her child be exposed to that perversion. "But," he said, "I can't build a case on what you've told me — only one incident, so long ago. It would be your word against his." It wasn't enough, he said. She had to let Lynn go.

What agony it was, that first day Carl came for Lynn. Having neither seen him nor even heard of him for nearly five years, Lynn squalled in terror, begged not to be made to go, and tried to pull away from him as he led her to the car. For the next thirty hours, Rainey paced the house and smoked, praying to whoever might be listening that Carl would realize that Lynn hated him — that she would always hate him — and he would give up this farce of being a father. Lynn was still in hysterics when Carl brought her home, and Rainey believed her prayer had been answered. But two weeks later, Carl came again, and though Lynn fought him, she did so with less intensity. After a while, there were no tears at all, and not so long after that, Lynn began to smile, even laugh, as the time to go with her father approached. In the last couple of months, beginning days before Carl was due, Lynn would chatter excitedly about the places he had promised to take her, snapping *"No!"* at Grace when she asked if she might go too, and the moment Lynn saw his car pull in the drive, she'd be out the door, squealing, "Daddy!"

Carl kept Lynn charmed with movie tickets and new toys and days at the fair — things Rainey could rarely afford. He was buying her baby, plain and simple, and there wasn't a thing she could do about it.

"Is she staying quiet?" Mother came in with the big mixing bowl, which she set on the floor by Lynn's bed. "This water's good and cool." She wrung out the washcloth that had been soaking in the bottom of the bowl and handed it to Rainey.

Lightly, so as not to wake Lynn, Rainey wiped the shining sweat from the girl's face. "Where's Grace?" she asked, handing the washcloth back to her mother.

"With Hans. On the porch." She passed the freshly wrung cloth back to Rainey. "Poor little thing was so tired, she dropped off first thing. They're stretched out together in the lounge chair — but your daddy's awake." After another two or three passes of the washcloth, Mother drew in a long, whistling breath. More than any other, that sound pricked Rainey's nerves to attention.

"Just tell me — once and for all," her mother began.

"Oh, please, Mother. Not this. Not tonight." She couldn't bear another of her mother's determined explorations — not now — testing every little opening that might trip Rainey into blurting out the name of Grace's father.

"It's not that," her mother said. "I just want to know — I think you owe it to me and your daddy to tell us — if one of these days some other buzzard's going to turn up wanting to take Grace from us."

Rainey pressed the damp cloth to her own throat, then turned it to the cool side and held it at the back of her neck. "No, Mother," she said. "No. Never."

"How can you be sure? That's what you said about the first one — he'd never come back."

"It's not the same, Mother. You just have to believe me."

Almost from the moment Rainey had met Marshall, she had resolved not to tell her mother about him. She just couldn't face all those hours on the telephone, with Mother wanting to know if she had learned anything at all, lecturing her on what a poor judge of men she was, reminding her that she was a divorced woman with a child and that she had to be careful not to give people anything to talk about and twist against her. So nobody knew about Marshall, not really. At four, Lynn had loved his attention, and though she had cried a little when Rainey explained that Marshall had to go away, her memories of him faded quickly. Sally, sworn to secrecy, knew about Marshall, of course, knew that he was Grace's father, but the sweet recollection of their time together was Rainey's alone.

"Rainey, we're none of us strong enough to go through this again," said Mother. "I'm asking you — what makes you sure?"

"Because he doesn't know about her. I wasn't with him long. He never knew I was pregnant." Now that she'd said it, Rainey was relieved. Her mother would no doubt think her the worst of tramps, but what did it matter? She went on: "And I didn't try to find him to tell him because I knew he wouldn't answer to it if he did know" — this was a lie, but a lie that would surely put an end to her mother's questions — "so he won't ever come. Grace is mine. *Ours,*" she added to appease her mother, all the while thinking, But Marshall is mine. Only mine.

No other time in her life was so free of regret — three lovely months, if she counted from the Saturday night when she'd tripped over Marshall while he knelt in front of the row of mailboxes, trying to open a package with a nail clipper. She'd been carrying a paper grocery sack filled with garbage, looking side to side, watching her step as she came down the stairs from her apartment, never expecting someone might be on the floor right in front of her. She'd managed to catch herself when her shins banged into him, but the bag had catapulted from her arms, scattering coffee grounds, carrot ends, cereal boxes, and cigarette butts across the black-and-white linoleum on its way to the umbrella stand, where it burst on impact.

Silently, the young man — she'd never seen him before — had put down the nail clipper, pushed his package against the wall, and started sweeping coffee grounds with the edge of his hand onto an open *National Geographic.* Rainey watched, amazed at how much he was able to get up without a cloth. And she would never have thought, as he did, to take an empty cornflakes box and tap the grounds off the magazine into it. He had torn off the edge of another box and was starting to use it to sweep up the cigarette butts when Rainey finally said, "Oh, please. Don't do that. I'll get a broom and another bag," and hurried up the stairs.

When she got back, he was standing waiting for her, and she was startled to see how short he was. Kneeling, he'd given the impression of height somehow, in spite of his narrow shoulders and small head — not at all the kind of man she had dreamed would rescue her.

He held out the remains of the bag, folded together like a wonton, into which he had gathered and compacted all the trash, and he placed this carefully inside the fresh bag Rainey held open. Taking the bag from her and nodding to the entry door, he said, "If you'll open that . . ." and then he lifted the lid on one of the cans just outside and dropped the bag in.

"Thank you so much," Rainey said. "Sorry about your magazine. Did I hurt you when I ran into you?"

"Fine, fine," he said — in answer to what, she didn't know. He seemed confused, looking back and forth between the package on the floor and his dirty hands, which he kept trying not to put in his pockets.

"Let me get that for you," Rainey said.

"No, that's fine," he said. "I'll get it later."

How strange he seemed, skittery. She wondered if he was nervous about the box, which was a thought that made her suddenly nervous. "Well, then," she said, turning back to the steps, reminding herself to walk slowly, casually, and then to bolt the apartment door the moment she closed it. "Really, thanks for your help," she said, looking over her shoulder toward him but avoiding his eyes.

"It's just —" he said. "It's just — well, you see my hands are filthy and my keys are in my pocket, and . . ."

Rainey stared at him, breathing hard. Was he suggesting she reach into his pocket, fish out the keys? She thought of Lynn asleep

267

and alone upstairs. Sally wouldn't be back from her date for hours.

The man reddened a little. "I'm sorry. I've only just had these pants dry-cleaned and I need them Tuesday." He held his hands out like a child might. "Could I come in just for a moment and wash my hands?"

"Sure," Rainey said, though she was not at all sure, her voice cracking in proof. "We're just to the right of the landing." Inside the apartment, she pointed to the bathroom and he went in. She leaned against the door frame, watching him carefully, trying to pretend she wasn't. "So what's in the package?" She congratulated herself on how conversational the question sounded.

"Potsherds."

"Potsherds," she repeated.

"Is this one okay?" he asked, pointing to a hand towel, and she nodded. "I'd left them — the potsherds — with my parents for safekeeping. I'm going for a teaching assistantship — for graduate school — and I need them for a presentation I have to give. At IU. They're in Arizona," he said. "My parents. That's where I found the sherds — on some property they'd just bought near Flagstaff. I asked them to give me a year to dig before they started building. They're good like that, my parents. My father just retired."

Rainey hadn't imagined he could talk so much — not that she really understood what he was talking about. "So you have an interview on Tuesday?"

"Yes. Tuesday." He was relaxed and smiling now. "Would you like to see them? The sherds?"

"I would," she said, forgetting all about her fear, now trying to conjure up a picture of what she was going to see. From the door of the apartment, she watched him retrieve his package, handing him a pair of scissors when he returned. "I thought maybe you were a Communist." She laughed.

"No," he said. "An archaeologist."

Across her kitchen table, he spread the fragments of clay vessels — unimaginably old — some pieces so small, they might have been dust, others large enough to suggest the curve where a hand had once rested. He talked on and on, practicing his presentation, she supposed, and while he did, Rainey thought what an inadequate word *clay* was to embrace what lay before her — the reds, browns, grays, and ecrus. Each time she picked up a piece to hold it in the light, Marshall showed her how to see what she would never have noticed on her own

— a faint residue of paint, or the eroded remainder of an etched design, now no more than a scratch, fine as a hair. *Earth,* she thought. Here was *earth,* in all its meanings.

A long while later, when Marshall had packed away the sherds again and got up to leave, she told him about Lynn, let him peek in at the child asleep in her bed, and asked him to come to dinner the next night. The night after that, when he invited Rainey out to celebrate his interview in advance, he'd made sure to choose a place they could all go, where Lynn would be as welcome as they were.

From the start, Marshall was more natural with Lynn than she was, able to keep the girl cheerful while Rainey cooked or got changed. He stocked his car with coloring books and inexpensive toys and taught Lynn how to play I Spy.

It was weeks before they kissed, but when at last it happened — Rainey had had to lean in close and lift her face to him to let him know it was all right — his lips touched hers so completely, so tenderly, she wept. He drew back then, his eyes full of concern, and she had smiled, shaken her head, and pulled him to her. Making love — those wonderful, wonderful weeks — he looked into her eyes, stroked her cheek, her hair, her neck, kissed her, said her name.

Mistakes, mistakes, her mother would say. If Rainey dared to tell her about Marshall, Mother would say Rainey's every choice had been bad: a mistake to speak to him, a mistake to go out with him, a mistake to go to bed with him, and a mistake to let him go. Strange, wasn't it, and exasperating, how people could be so certain they were using exactly the right word to describe something, when really they were using exactly the wrong word. Grace herself — her beautiful, sweet-hearted Grace: If people knew the truth about her birth, they would whisper to each other that Grace was "a mistake."

Rainey had no intention of letting that happen. Thankfully, it hadn't been difficult to keep the secret. Within just a few weeks of returning to Newman with the girls, she realized that everyone outside the family simply assumed Grace was Carl's child. Mother and Daddy had been too embarrassed to tell anyone about her divorce when it happened, and so now the neighbors and people at church were divided, when they gossiped about whether Rainey had left Carl or Carl had left her. Of course, she'd had to tell the lawyer, Mr. Prather, that Carl wasn't

Grace's father, but on hearing this, Mr. Prather had once again shaken his head sadly, making clear he thought it was perfectly understandable that Rainey, after her terrible shock, would have been vulnerable to the charms of a normal man. He certainly wasn't going to tell anyone.

So all Rainey had to do was stay quiet — she was good at that. And her silence would be a protective shield around Grace, who would grow up believing what it was natural for her to believe — that she and Lynn shared the same father: an absent father, but the same.

But Rainey hadn't reckoned on Carl's coming back. Though she hadn't lied about Grace — he couldn't charge her with that — she had let a lie be believed. What would he do if he found out? She couldn't think about that — not now.

Rainey passed the cloth again to her mother for another rinse in the cool water and laid her hand on Lynn's neck. The child still seemed overheated from the violence of her nightmare, so Rainey folded down first the summer bedspread and then the top sheet. With the refreshed cloth, she wiped her daughter's bare legs, and as she did, Lynn began to stir.

"Are you waking up, baby?"

Lynn's eyes fluttered open, then winced closed again as she moaned.

Mother now knelt beside the bed and gently stroked the girl's hair. "What's the matter, honey? Are you hurting? Tell Grandma where."

"It hurts." A tear rolled down Lynn's cheek. "It hurts."

"You banged your head pretty hard," Rainey said. "It probably will hurt for a while, but I can get you an aspirin." She started to get up.

"Mom!" Lynn's cry was followed by a sharp intake of breath and a flow of tears.

Rainey sat down again and took Lynn's hand. "Is it just your head, baby? Please. Try to tell me where you hurt so I can help you. Is it your tummy?"

"All over," Lynn wept. "My middle. My arms."

"Turn on the light, will you, Mother?" Rainey shielded Lynn's eyes from the sudden brightness. "Now, let's have a look at you," she said, lifting the T-shirt.

From her chest to her navel, a pale yellow-brown band girdled Lynn's body. In other places, especially under each arm and along her ribs, she was pocked with deeper, purple bruises, like fingerprints.

"Mother! Come see!"

"Oh, Rainey! She couldn't have gotten all this from just falling."

Rainey drew the T-shirt down again and stroked her daughter's cheek. "How did you hurt your head, Lynn? Can you tell me?"

"On the post."

"When you fell on the dock?"

"When I was in the water."

"In the water? In the lake?" Suddenly Rainey remembered the white canvas shorts and the sleeveless seersucker blouse. They were strangely damp, wrapped in a towel, stuffed into the top of Lynn's bag. She'd remarked on it to Mother, wondering if Lynn had been playing in a sprinkler.

Rainey began to shake. "Why were you in the lake?" Lynn had never learned to swim. She had told Carl over and over that Lynn didn't know how to swim, that he had to promise not even to let her go wading by herself.

"Lynn, why were you in the lake?" Rainey asked again, her voice too sharp.

Lynn turned her face into the pillow, weeping pitifully.

"Honey . . . honey," Rainey soothed. "I'm not upset with you. Just tell me, please. How did you get in the lake? Did you fall?"

Lynn sniffed and choked. "Daddy let go."

Rainey felt herself falling, as if she were

dropping under the water, but then she felt a firm arm winding through hers. Mother was holding her up.

"Sweetie." Rainey pressed her throat to stop her own rising tears. "What do you mean, he let go? When you slipped on the dock? Was he trying to catch you?"

Lynn shook her head fiercely, clamped her eyes shut, and wailed, "He said I was a rotten girl. He was swinging me. . . . *Too high, Daddy! No! Daddy! Don't let go!*"

With their trembling hands, Rainey and her mother petted Lynn until her sobs carried her back into sleep. For a few moments longer, they sat together on the bed, silent. At last, Mother stood up and switched off the light. Rainey watched as she found the washcloth, put it back into the bowl, picked up the bowl, and set it down again.

"In the morning," Mother said, softly, slowly, "I'll stay home with Grace, and your daddy will drive you and Lynn over to see Dr. Wolfe. You tell him to call that hospital doctor to find out everything he can." She placed her hand on Rainey's shoulder. "And then we'll all go back to see that lawyer — that Mr. Prather."

Rainey put her face in her hands.

"You're not to worry about the money," Mother said, kneeling beside her. "You're not to worry about that." She took Rainey in her arms and rocked her, back and forth, back and forth. "You hear me?" Mother said. "You're not to worry. We'll be all right. Our girls will be all right."

Twelve:
Breaking

November 1965
Newman, Indiana

LYNN

When astronauts were out in space, they floated around like dandelion fluff. That was because in space there wasn't any gravity. She had learned that at school. Gravity was what held you down on Earth and what made an apple fall and bruise when you let go of it. Gravity came from below and it didn't hurt at all, except when it helped pull you down if you tripped on the playground. Try as she might, though, Lynn couldn't think whether she had ever learned the name of what it was that pressed you down from the top. What was the heavy heavy thing that pushed down all over her, that pushed so strongly even on her face that she couldn't lift her head up? She wanted to move her arms, to raise them and feel

277

with her fingers what might be on top of her, but it was even harder to move her arms than the rest of her. If she really tried, she could scoot her bottom a little this way and that, and, even though they were caught in something hot and scratchy, she could twist her feet toward and away from each other. She could wiggle her fingers, but not her wrists or her elbows, not even a little. Sometimes when she opened her eyes to try to see what it was on top of her, she saw only yellow light, but it seemed too high to be touching her, and it hurt her eyes. Other times, it was dark, except for a dim light off to one side. When she heard what sounded like voices nearby, she tried to ask someone to help her get out from under, but even her voice seemed trapped.

Now, her eyes were open again. It was dark above her. Somewhere down past her feet, there was a blue glow that seemed to breathe, in an uneven way, sometimes slow, like it was asleep, and sometimes short and fast, like it had been running and was out of breath. She found she was able to raise her head now, just a little, so she tipped up toward the blue light and saw what looked like big gray turtles bobbing through the air, surrounded by darker gray leaves that looked almost as big as the turtles. She'd never seen a turtle float in the air, and she wanted to watch, but her head got too heavy and dropped back down. In the lake, when she was underneath, a turtle had paddled above her. She had wanted to push her arm up through the water to grab the turtle's flipper so it could pull her along, but the turtle was too fast and the water was too heavy. It wasn't fair that everything else seemed light and free. She didn't expect to be able to fly or even to float on the air, and in her mind she told God so. She just wanted to be able to raise up and look around. She wanted to be able to rub at her eyes, which itched with tears. She wanted to blow her nose.

A man's voice seemed to come from the same place the turtles floated in the trees: *Today U.S. soldiers fell under heavy fire while raiding a village south of Da Nang said to be sympathetic to a band of Vietcong guerrillas that has terrorized troops in that region in recent months.*

"Please turn that off, Mother."

Lynn understood that. It had been a woman's voice.

"She's asleep." Another woman's voice.

"She doesn't need to see that if she wakes up," said the first voice. "There's not to be anything on that might upset her. That's what the doctor said."

"Well, I can't sit here in the dark without the television. If you want it turned off, then I have to have a light so I can crochet."

Grandma Bertie crocheted. In the daytime, when she watched her programs. The gleaming silver hook flashed through the bright yarn while Grandma talked to the people on the television, warning Lisa not to open the door because some strange man who had come to Oakdale was watching her from the bushes, or telling Bob to be careful and to check the medicine in the needle because another doctor was trying to get him to make a mistake so the man in charge of the hospital would see to it Bob's license was taken away and that he would never again practice medicine.

"You know it's costing a dollar and a half a day for us to have that TV."

"I told you I'd pay for it, Rainey," Grandma said. Lynn was sure now it was Grandma Bertie talking. "There's nothing in my programs gonna upset her. She likes watching them with me when she's home from school."

"Fine. Watch those in the morning. But do you have to have the news on now?"

"I'm waiting for *Gunsmoke*. The girls like Festus."

Lynn could hear her mother sigh the way she did sometimes, with a whispered *I swear* buried inside it, but she didn't say anything else to Grandma Bertie.

Lynn still felt like something was on top of her, but now that she knew Grandma and Mother were there, she wasn't so scared. The way they talked, they could see her, and if they could see her, soon they would see whatever it was that covered her and take it away. But she might have to wait for them to get Grandpa Hans and some other people to help, since it was so heavy.

It was getting a little easier to keep her eyes open, and, even though it was dark, if she looked really hard when the light from the television flashed brighter, she could see that above her there was a ceiling, and in the ceiling there was one of those big lights like they had at school, the ones that held the long white tubes. If someone flipped the switch, the light would shine right in her eyes. She could turn her head a little to the side, and when she did, she could see the edges of what looked like a pillow, though it was hard and rough against her cheek, not at all like the one she had at home. So she must be in bed. A strange bed with a kind of silvery fence around it, like a crib but not cheerful. She was very hot and she now could see there were lots of white blankets on top of her, but there must be something more than that. Maybe under the blankets.

"Hey, sweetie." That was her mother's voice. She couldn't make out a face, but the familiar shape of Mother's puffed-up hair leaned over her, and she caught the sticky alcohol smell of hair spray and the minty smell of cigarettes mixed up with the other, sweeter mint that came from the red-and-white candies Mother rattled in her mouth when she wasn't smoking.

"I want to get up." Lynn was surprised at the sound of her own voice. She hadn't even had to try to force the words out.

"I expect she needs the pot," Grandma said.

"No," Lynn said. "I want to sit up. My nose itches." She felt her mother's hard, polished nails scratching at her nose, too hard and in the wrong spot. "I want to do it," she said.

Mother stopped scratching. "You have to lie still," she said. "That's what the doctor says."

On television one time, Lynn had seen a man in pajamas sitting in a wheelchair. Another man was talking to him about the wheelchair and the man in the pajamas was saying that he'd have to use it for the rest of his life because of shrapnel in his spine. *Lie still.* That's what the man in the pajamas said the doctors kept telling him. "Six months of nothing but laying flat on my back," the man said. "I was plenty glad to get into the chair."

Her daddy had told her that shrapnel was what was left over after a bullet or a hand grenade, which was a little bomb, exploded. The spine was the back. If your spine was hurt, you couldn't walk anymore. Her back hurt, when she thought about it.

"Sure, I'd rather walk," the man in the pajamas had said. "Even back to Nam." And then he had said, "Well, maybe not."

Lynn remembered now, too, that there was a war in a place called Vietnam, a place that the teacher had shown them on the map. It bulged out underneath China and touched what was called the South China Sea, even though it looked like the same water as the Pacific Ocean, which touched California. She could find Vietnam if she had a map, but she didn't really understand where it was. On television every night, Walter Cronkite looked out at the people in their living rooms with his kind face, and in his warm, gravelly voice he talked about Vietnam. Then there would be pictures from Vietnam and different newsmen talking.

283

The newsmen were dressed like soldiers, but you could tell them apart because the newsmen held microphones. The people who lived in Vietnam, the ones who weren't soldiers, wore clothes like pajamas all the time, like the man in the wheelchair, but they wore them even if they weren't sick, and some of them wore funny hats that looked like sinking haystacks. On the news every night and in Grandma Bertie's *Life* magazine every week, there were pictures of soldiers — some of them sitting and talking while they smoked cigarettes, some of them riding in helicopters, some of them walking through the woods, carrying rifles, some of them leaning against trees or lying in tall grass with shiny black splotches on their arms, legs or faces. Lynn knew the black splotches were blood, and that if they had a color television at home, the splotches would be red. Sometimes the splotches were so big you couldn't see where the face had been at all. Those soldiers couldn't get up. When somebody was shot on *Gunsmoke*, they didn't get up either. There weren't any splotches then, but that was because *Gunsmoke* was make-believe TV. The news was true and the dead men were really dead. Lynn understood that, but Grace couldn't. She was still too little.

Lynn tried again to pull herself up. "Do I have shrapnel in my back?"

Her mother straightened up and looked over to where Grandma Bertie was sitting. "Shrapnel? Where'd you get an idea like that? You don't even know what that is."

It was making her tired to talk, so Lynn didn't try to correct her mother. "Will I have a wheelchair?"

Grandma was beside the bed now, squeezing Lynn's foot through the covers. "You'll ride in one when you go for your tests."

"Will I have to have it forever?"

Mother tucked the covers around her tighter. Too tight. "Why are you being so silly? Of course not."

"Why can't I get up?"

"I've told you all about that, baby," Mother said, her voice sharp around the edges. Lynn knew she mustn't ask anymore. "The doctor has said you have to rest." Mother leaned down and kissed her lightly on the forehead. Lynn could feel the smear of lipstick and wanted to wipe it away, but even though it didn't seem so much now that something was pressing on top of her — she couldn't *see* anything — she still couldn't move her arms.

"Grandma's going to stay with you," Mother said. "I'll be here in the morning —

probably way before you're even awake. Then I'm going to take Grandma home so she can get ready for church, and I'll come right back and stay with you all day. You start thinking about any of your books or your games you want, and Grandma will call to tell me."

Mother's heels clicked away like gunfire.

"There now," Grandma said, patting at Lynn's heavy arm. "You want to see what's going on with Festus? He'll be on in a little bit. I might could raise the bed up some, so you can see the television."

"I'm hot," Lynn said.

"You have to keep warm, now."

"I'm hot."

Grandma looked at her for a moment and shook her head, but then she pulled back the top blanket. There were still too many covers, too much weight. "More," Lynn said.

"Let's see how this does." Grandma smoothed the blanket over the end of the bed. "It'll take a minute or two for you to cool down."

"Where's Grandpa?"

"He's home with Grace. They'll come in to see you after church tomorrow."

Lynn wanted to ask if Grandpa would come on his own just to see her special, without Grace tagging along to hog up everybody's laughs and proud smiles, but she couldn't work out how to say it without making her grandmother wag her finger and tell her not to be so selfish.

"Now," Grandma said, "if the doctor says it's okay for you to have it, I'll send your grandpa out to get you some chicken from Colonel Sanders. You and your sister can eat it here on the bed, like a picnic. Wouldn't you like that?"

Lynn closed her eyes and swallowed hard. Her throat was dry and her nose still itched. It was hard making Grandma understand. "Where am I?"

Grandma's eyes and mouth opened wide. "Well, you know where you are. We've been here since yesterday."

Lynn couldn't remember yesterday.

"It's the hospital, sugar."

"Is Bob here?" Lynn asked.

"Bob?"

In her head, Lynn could see Bob's dark hair and the way he always smiled with his mouth closed, but then his picture swam away and she saw, only for a second, a bald man in black robes sitting behind a shining wooden wall that was taller than she was. Bob had another name. What was it? "Dr. Hughes," Lynn said, suddenly remembering

Bob wasn't a real person. Her cheeks burned. Grandma would think she was stupid.

Grandma laughed. "That's a television hospital," she said. "This is a real hospital. Remember how we came to see Mrs. Davis here one time?"

She remembered Mrs. Davis — the tiny lady from church who had a bunch of violets on her hat. Mrs. Davis carried butterscotch in her purse and every Sunday she gave Lynn two pieces — one for her and one for Grace — but Grace didn't know about that, since Lynn always ate them both. When Mrs. Davis got sick, Grandma had made Lynn and Grace come to the hospital with her. Then one Sunday, the preacher said Mrs. Davis had passed away.

"Am I going to pass away?" Lynn asked. She knew that meant *die,* but Grandma always said it the other way.

"Good Lord, what notions you children get!" Grandma looked up to the ceiling, clenching her fists, whispering, "Give me strength." Grandma stood like that for a long time, sucking in breath and whooshing it out, sucking it in and whooshing it out. Finally, she leaned down close to Lynn and said, "Now, you don't need to talk like this around your mother. She's mighty upset

already." Grandma fiddled with the covers and pulled down another one over the foot of the bed. "You remember when we went to the courthouse — that was Thursday. Well, you took on awful bad when the judge talked to you — kicking and screaming so, we couldn't get you settled down. Your grandpa had to help your mother get you outside." Grandma shook her head. "What's a big girl like you doing carrying on like that? You got so worked up, you made yourself sick, and we had to come on over here. So you can get some rest."

While Grandma talked, Lynn closed her eyes. She saw the bald man again, leaning down toward her where she sat in a high, hard chair, crying, trying her best to stand up in the chair so she could make the judge hear what she was saying, but her black Sunday shoes were slick on the bottom and they kept sliding across the polished wood and catching in her skirt. "No," she was saying to the judge, but he just kept on talking. "No," she said louder, but he didn't pay her any mind. "No!" she screamed, and then she was crying and slamming her fists. *"No! No! No!"* And then the judge was banging a hammer on the desk and Mother was grabbing her around the waist, pulling her out of the big chair, and somebody — it must

have been Grandpa — tried to hold her feet.

Daddy was there. Daddy was there and his face was red and wet and he was reaching out his arms toward her. She was reaching out to him, too, but the harder she reached, the further away she got. She screamed for him, screamed and screamed, and then somebody smacked her hard and splashed water in her face and she thought for a second she was in the lake again. Hot sweaty hands held her wrists and ankles and Mother leaned down across her, crying, "It's all right, baby. It's all right. You're safe now. You don't ever have to go with him again."

Now Grandma was stroking her hair and saying, "There, there, sugar." The stroking felt nice, and Lynn could feel herself relaxing the way Daddy's big yellow dog, Mr. Goldwater, did when she massaged his velvet ears.

Since she was being quiet and good, not screaming like before, maybe Grandma would let her talk some, let her ask about some things, like why she couldn't get her arms loose to push herself up, but she wanted more to talk about Daddy.

"I want Daddy," she said.

Grandma stopped stroking Lynn's hair, leaned all the way over the bed, and took

her hard by the shoulders. "Don't you be saying things like that. Don't you upset your mother talking like that. You need to get it through your head that man's a good-for-nothing."

Lynn started to cry. "I want Daddy. Where's my daddy?"

"Listen to me, girl." Grandma was so close, Lynn could smell her cinnamon gum. "The judge decided it's not safe for you to go back there anymore. And — that man, he's to stay away from our house. You won't see him again. He's lost his rights to you."

Rights. What did that mean? For days and days after she had gone into the lake, she lay in her bed, listening to Mother talking in the living room to Grandma and Grandpa, or to someone on the telephone, and she kept saying, "He nearly drowned my little girl. I have to get his rights stopped." After that, the next time Daddy came to get her to take her to the farm, Mother held her tight in the kitchen while Grandpa went to the door to make Daddy go away. It happened like that three times in a row, and since then, whenever Daddy was due, Mother told Lynn he had gone away and wouldn't be coming for her.

And then the other morning, Grandma came to get her up and helped her put on her Sunday dress instead of a school dress and told her they were going into town to the courthouse. "Grandpa's already in the car, so you better scoot," she said. Somebody knocked on the front door and Grandma said, "That'll be Hazel." Hazel was Mrs. Wyler, their next-door neighbor.

Lynn waited until she could hear Grandma opening the door for Mrs. Wyler, and then she took her shoes and sat in the hall beside the doorway so she could hear what they were saying. "I don't know how long we'll be. Grace oughtn't to be any trouble, so long as she's got her beads and things to play with. I'll come after her soon as we get back."

"We're all praying for you," said Mrs. Wyler.

"Well, then pray the judge sees that man's not fit to be around any child." Grandma said good-bye to Mrs. Wyler, closed the door, then called out, "Lynn, c'mon now!"

Always before, Lynn had liked the courthouse. Last spring, her class had taken a bus there, and while they stood on the stone steps, the teacher explained the columns were called Ionic. At school, when she'd first watched the filmstrip about Greek buildings, Lynn had decided she liked Corinthian columns best, but when she was able to stand right next to the courthouse columns with their scroll caps, she liked them better than the flowery Corinthians.

This time, when she walked into the courthouse between Grandma and Grandpa, she was too nervous to notice the columns. No matter how much she asked, nobody would tell her why they had come. On the school trip, her class had gone into an empty courtroom and pretended to have a trial. She was the judge. This time, when Grandpa opened the courtroom door, Lynn could see there were people inside, including Mother, but when she tried to follow Grandpa, her grandmother held her back and pulled her over to a hard bench. "We'll wait," she said.

They waited so long, Lynn's bottom hurt, but Grandma wouldn't let her take her book down on the floor so she could stretch out on her stomach. "You'll muss your dress," Grandma said. About the time Nancy Drew started worrying that something had happened to keep her father from joining her at the haunted mansion like they'd planned, Lynn heard her mother crying. Nobody else she knew cried like Mother, all stopped up and choking, holding her hand over her mouth like she was trying to stuff the sadness back in. Then Mother opened the door, her eyes puffy and her hands shaking, and said, "They're ready for you now."

Grandma pushed her forward and Lynn went in. All the way at the end of the room, there was a bald man in black robes sitting behind the judge's high desk, just as she had done. He wasn't smiling, but he seemed friendly. He was motioning for her to come toward him. Beside the tall desk was a heavy wooden chair, the witness chair, and a man in a gray uniform was patting the arm of the chair, showing her she was to get in it. She passed between the two tables where in their play court Joey Beasley and Tim Jackson had sat, pretending to be lawyers. When she climbed up in the chair, she first looked past the tables to the benches, lined up like pews in church, and saw there weren't so many people after all. Grandma and Grandpa sat together on a bench way in the back, and then, further up, on the other side, she saw Grandpa Dieter, Daddy's daddy. She smiled and waved because she hadn't seen him since the day at the lake, and he gave a little wave back and then looked down at his lap. Next to Grandpa Dieter was Daddy's friend Vernon — in her head she had named him "Bear" because of the black hair that covered his arms and legs, and even his chest and his back. Vernon didn't look at her.

Daddy was sitting at the table on the right, beside a man she didn't know. When Daddy looked up at her, his eyes were sad but his mouth was tight, like he was angry. Mother was sitting at the table on the left with another strange man, her eyes still puffy, her mouth a sharp slice of bloodred. Nobody smiled back at Lynn, and she felt her own smile slide away like candle wax.

"There now," Grandma said, patting Lynn's leg through the blankets. "That's a good girl to stay quiet."

Lynn was still too hot, but she didn't say anything to Grandma. She was trying hard to remember, but all she could get were quick flashes — one picture she just barely had time to see, and then another, like slides clicking past in a dark classroom.

The bald judge leaning toward her and asking her name.

The bald judge asking her, "What were you doing before your father threw you in the lake?"

The bald judge smacking his gavel down so hard she had to cover her ears. Him saying, "Calm down, child. Tell me the truth, now."

The bald judge, his face like a red balloon, smacking the gavel down over and over and yelling, "Order! Order! Sit down, girl! Sit down!" Not letting her tell the truth.

The bald, sweaty-faced judge standing, pointing at her mother, saying, "Take this child out now!"

After that, a swirl of voices and faces, hands on her and then not, like she was being sucked up in a tornado, like Dorothy Gale from Kansas. No one would believe her. No one would listen to her. That was like Dorothy, too, except no beautiful witch in a shimmery dress came to quiet everyone down so Lynn could tell her story.

"We were playing," she tried to tell the judge. Grandpa Dieter was grilling hot dogs. Vernon was sitting at the end of the dock, fishing. He always came with them when they went fishing. She was playing hide-and-seek with Daddy, and when he found her curled in the soft needles under a giant Christmas tree, veiled, she thought, under the low branches, she scrambled out and ran from him, squealing, toward the dock.

"That's slippery, Lynn!" Daddy panted out. "Lynney, *STOP!*"

But she was too giggly and ran on. She did slide a little on the dock, and her foot scraped a nail. She started to cry, but the pain didn't last more than a second. It vanished when Daddy scooped her up. He shook her a little and said, "You have to mind," and then they were both laughing and he held her tightly under her arms and swung her from side to side. "So, you want to be a rotten girl?" he said. "You know what happens to rotten girls?" He swung her high to the right and even higher to the left. She was scared. She yelled, "Too high, Daddy! No! Daddy! Don't let go!" But Daddy was still laughing. He didn't hear her. He swung her higher still, laughing. "Rotten girls go in the lake!" And he let go.

She could remember a big smack, then darkness, then a second when she opened her eyes and saw the turtle paddle over her head. Then she was cold and there were people shouting at her and something pushing on her chest and something wet on her mouth and she choked and the air inside stung so much she opened her eyes and saw a big black bear on top of her. After that, she didn't remember anything else until she woke up in her own bed, with Mother wiping her legs with a cold washrag.

"Festus is coming on," Grandma said, fussing with the covers again. "I'll raise up the bed so you can see."

While Grandma rooted around for the switch, Lynn thought about how her Sunday school teacher once told her she could catch more flies with honey than with vinegar, so she concentrated on making her voice sweet. "Please, Grandma," she said. "Can't I call Daddy?"

"Don't start working yourself up again," Grandma said.

Lynn felt her eyes getting wet. She mustn't cry. She mustn't cry. "Please," she said, "I won't say anything to Mother. Please, Grandma. Let me call Daddy?"

Grandma's voice was vinegar. "I've told you and told you, child. You're to forget about that man."

There was a little buzz and Lynn felt the bed raising her head and shoulders up. Now she could just see the outline of a telephone on a table past the foot of the bed. Beside the telephone was a vase with a single white rose, glowing blue from the light of the television, which hung from the wall above.

Lynn didn't care now how sour her voice sounded. "I'm gonna call him! You can't stop me." She couldn't remember Daddy's telephone number, but she knew she could dial zero. The operator would help her. She struggled to pull herself out of the bed, but her arms and legs were stuck. She pulled and pulled, so hard she was starting to lose her breath. Grandma was scurrying around the side of the bed, saying, "Stop that!

Lynn, settle down right now!"

Lynn lurched forward as far as she could. The pillow slipped to the middle of her back, and the last of the covers dropped from her shoulders to her lap. Thick straps were pulled tight across her arms, and now that she saw them, she could feel the same straps across her legs. "Let me go! Let me go!" she screamed. "I want Daddy! Let me go!"

From somewhere outside her she heard Grandma calling for help. The white form of a nurse appeared, her shoes squeaking across the floor. The nurse would help her. "Please let me go," Lynn whimpered. "Please."

"I'm going to put you back down, honey," the nurse said, and the bed grumbled its way flat again. "Just a little stick."

It wasn't a little stick at all, and Lynn tried to roll away from it, but the straps stopped her. She tried to think about how she could get away. Maybe like Houdini. But she couldn't think how to begin. If only Daddy knew where she was. If only Daddy would come for her.

The heaviness settled over her, pushing, pushing. Pushing her down like before. Down and down, under the water.

THIRTEEN:
UPHEAVAL

February 1966
Indianapolis, Indiana

MABEL

Once again, Vietnam had made the cover of *Life*. A pair of soldiers in a trench — one, in spite of the great dirty bandage covering his eyes, looked up at the sky, perhaps hoping for a helicopter, while on his leg he cradled the other soldier, whose wounded head was mummy-wrapped, with only a triangle of face left free.

Though it was much too cold, especially since she hadn't put on a coat when she stepped outside to get the mail, Mabel sat down on the porch swing and opened the magazine. Inside, there were five more full spreads of photographs. She studied them, trembling. Though none of the faces was familiar to her, every one of them called up the faces of her boys — the seventy-two soldiers she had photographed in the last three months.

The project had come to her one day on her lunch hour, when she was on her way into Fleming & Sons to pick up some stockings. A display of official military portraits filled the store's front window, lined up by the dozens, as if in regiments. By design, the portraits all looked the same — crisp uniform, rigid posture, staring, absent eyes. And terrifying youth — they all had that in common. But there was nothing, not so much as a wrinkle of a lip, to say that *this* boy is not the same as that one, or that one, or that one. Seeing the photographs, Mabel forgot entirely about the stockings and walked straight back to the desk she shared with three other photographers at the *Indianapolis Star.* A few moments later, she had scratched out an advertisement offering a free photo session to any serviceman with orders for Vietnam, in exchange for his agreement to let her photograph him once more when his tour of duty had ended. She had meant the ad to run in ten consecutive issues, but by the third day, she was so overwhelmed with calls, she canceled it. Since then, word of mouth had taken care of the rest.

"Mama!" Daisy called from the kitchen.

"What do you want to do with all these jars on the top shelf?"

Mabel sighed and went back into the house. The whole idea of this move — an idea Daisy and Barry had cooked up, apparently when they were on their honeymoon — was to make Mabel's life easier, get her into a place small enough to keep clean, a place with an efficient kitchen, where everything was in easy reach, a place where she didn't have to face stairs when she wanted to get into her studio and darkroom. So what if her knee gave out a little? she argued. Using the stairs was probably the only thing that had kept the knee from locking up altogether. Besides, she was settled. She liked her neighbors, and the people who worked at the small local grocery all greeted her by name. But then, after Daisy and Barry had shown Mabel the house they'd found for her, two blocks from their own, pointing out how the spare bedroom and bath could easily be converted for her work, her daughter had clinched the deal by saying, "You don't want to have to come all the way across town every time you want to hold your grandchild, do you?" Before Mabel knew it, she was nodding agreement through her tears and the house was bought.

"Daisy, get down from there!" Mabel dropped the mail on the kitchen table and lifted her hands to urge Daisy off the chair she was standing on. She had set all the jars on the counter and was now stretching to reach the far corners of the shelf with a cloth.

"Let Barry do that," Mabel said. "You're nearly five months. You're liable to fall."

When Daisy turned to look at her mother, her gaze shifted to the copy of *Life,* which had landed faceup on the table. "I'll get down if you promise me you won't look at that magazine. You know how upset you get." Daisy did not approve of Mabel's project, and each time she saw a new set of photographs, she said, "Please be careful, Mama. Don't get too involved with these guys. Think how terrible it will be for you if you find out any of them have been —"

"You can't protect yourself from loss," Mabel said. "You know that as well as anybody." Still, she understood what Daisy was really afraid of. In the last twelve years, ever since her breakdown in the Juniper cemetery, Mabel had fought through three or four bouts of depression — weeks at a time, when she was incapable of pulling out from under black despair. The last one had been set off in late summer by a report on the news showing American soldiers burning a village in Vietnam. Mabel couldn't take her eyes off the television — the flames, the smoke, and the masses of terrified people, Morley Safer talking through it all. For days afterward, she refused to miss the news, read every newspaper and magazine story about that terrible act, haunted by the way Safer had put the fire in context: "A man lives with his family on ancestral land. His parents are buried nearby." And as if she had seen it all, Mabel imagined those people, suddenly homeless, displaced from families, wandering in desperate search of one another. As a girl, she had believed she would live out her life in Juniper, tending the graves of her parents, and one day marry and have children who would tend her grave. Before long, though she knew she should be concentrating her sympathy on those poor Vietnamese, her mind locked on Juniper and the way it was when she had last seen it — nothing but charred shells of places she had known — and then her mind slipped to why she had gone there, and how she had failed. The next morning, she just couldn't get up, though Daisy called her and called her and finally came in to lean over the bed, saying, "Mama-bel. Please. *Please, Mama.*" Mabel could see the pain of it in her daughter's eyes — another round — but she just couldn't help it.

At the time, Daisy had just begun rehearsals to play Nora in *A Doll's House,* so their darling Nick, whose talents made him the staple of the playhouse's musical-theater productions, moved in to see Mabel through her bad time, as he had done so often before. No natural son could have loved her more than Nick did. She'd been so happy over the friendship that had burst into being when, barely out of high school, Daisy and Nick met in summer stock, but Mabel had never expected she would be the beneficiary of Nick's seemingly endless store of devoted affection.

"C'mon, give me your hand," Mabel now said to Daisy, but her daughter waved off the help, steadying herself with one hand on the back of the chair and the other braced on the counter.

"See there," Mabel said, noting Daisy's bright red cheeks, "you've gotten yourself overheated."

"Well, it's hot. What's the thermostat set on?"

Mabel rolled her eyes, and when she caught Daisy doing the same, they both laughed. Not once in all the years they'd been together had they ever agreed on temperature: Daisy was always too hot, and Mabel was always too cold.

Mabel took a clean dish towel from the stack waiting to be packed, ran it under cold water and dabbed Daisy's face with it. "The doctor said you have to be careful. It's not usual to have a first baby so old."

"I just saw him on Monday," Daisy said, "and he told me he wished his eighteen-year-old mothers-to-be were all as healthy as I am." She rinsed the towel under the faucet and wrung it out. "Do you hear me? Healthier than girls half my age."

"Still," Mabel said, dragging the chair back to its place at the table, "even healthy people can fall off chairs. If there's any more climbing to do, let Barry do it."

"What am I being elected for now?" Barry came in, arms full of empty boxes.

"You," Daisy said, kissing him over the boxes and taking them from him, "are just in time to take another load to the car." She pointed to one of the packed boxes and said, "I'll be right behind you with another one."

"Not too heavy," Mabel said, but Daisy told her she worried too much, and then picked up a box marked *Plates*.

Mabel still missed having Daisy in the house. She wasn't sure she would ever get used to living alone — she hadn't liked it before, those years in Indianapolis, and really for most of them, it felt like she wasn't alone. Up until Paul died, she'd spent nearly all her time with him in the studio, going back to her rented room only to sleep. After Chicago, in their early years together, Mabel had savored Daisy's company, expecting that someday her girl would move out on her own, get married, and then Daisy started high school — a beautiful copper-haired girl who attracted the notice of boys but wouldn't let any of them near her. When she finished school, Daisy put all her energy into acting, working part-time and taking whatever roles she could get, until finally — the same year as Nick — she was asked to join the repertory theater as a resident player. Over the years, Daisy had rebuffed and ignored dozens of admirers, and so naturally Mabel had come to accept that her daughter, like she, wanted nothing to do with men and would always remain single. She could see herself going on and on with Daisy — and with Nick, who did like men but was terrified of being found out. A misfit bachelor trio, they were, content with one another. But then last summer, Nick met Ted, who wouldn't let him hide, and only a few weeks later, Daisy unaccountably allowed a balding, thick-waisted insurance salesman to come into her dressing room to present her with an immense bouquet of pink roses. That was Barry. By the first of October, after a four-day engagement, they were married, on-stage, not ten minutes after the curtain had come down on the final ovation for Daisy's last performance in *A Doll's House.*

What a happy night that had been. After everyone pitched in to clear the set — the cast, crew, a few dozen friends, and Ted, of course — they all danced, swirling in ever-changing and varied pairs against a back-drop of ornate nineteenth-century wall-paper. Mabel grew faint as the playhouse's young lighting director twirled her across the floor, but Nick cut in and saved her, dancing her backstage to the brocade sofa, where she accepted the handkerchief he pulled from his pocket. "Now, this is just a breather, Belle," he said, fanning her with a playbill. "Daisy will miss you if you're gone too long." From the wings, they watched Daisy laughing with her head back as she and Barry danced. Daisy could glide across a floor like vapor, but it pleased Mabel to see how her daughter matched herself to Barry's gluey steps, as if being in his arms was the surest thing she'd ever known.

Such joyous upheavals — a new son-in-law, Daisy expecting, and Nick beginning to trust love at last — but at times Mabel still felt like her house had been picked up, shaken, and set back down again, nothing really broken this time but a few things fractured, everything out of order.

Perhaps this was one of the reasons, one of so many, why she wanted to fill as much of her time as she could with her soldiers. In this work, there was order and purpose — and it was important work, she believed, even if she couldn't say just how. When Daisy had held her hands and said, "Why? Why do you want to do this?" Mabel could only think of something her mother had said long ago, about Jim Butcher's time in France: "Terrible things he saw over there. Things nobody should ever see. Having to do things nobody should ever have to do."

She showed Daisy some photographs she'd clipped from newspapers and magazines — some of villages turned to ash; some of weak, blindfolded prisoners, of skeletally thin Vietnamese lying dead; others of American soldiers wet, muddy, exhausted, bleeding — and she tried to explain the question she was struggling to answer for herself: Were such terrible things — terrible things like killing, like having no choice but to kill — carved like ghostly scars into the face, perhaps only to be seen in those fleeting instants between the expressions one prepared for the world? In those instants only the camera could catch, Mabel wanted to find the truth about who those boys were before Vietnam — and after, the truth of who they had become.

Mabel sat down at the table and opened the magazine again. No devastated villages this time, but plenty of broken young men, overcome by shelling and rifle fire, doing their best to carry their wounded brethren to safety, patch them up, and keep them alive until help dropped from the sky.

Long ago, a month, maybe two, after Daisy had somehow gotten her home from Juniper, Mabel surfaced from a tranquilizer haze to remember Wallace's grave and to gasp at the pain of her exploded heart. Nick was there, and he rose from the chair where he'd been reading to kneel by the bed and stroke her hair. She cried for a long time — it was spring and the sun was still up when she woke, but it was dark before she could hear anything her friend said to her.

"I'll take you back, Belle — to Juniper — if you want to go." And then Nick told her that he'd gone there himself, on his own. Daisy had told him everything she knew, and so, armed with names and dates, he'd borrowed a car and gone in search of Bertie.

What he found was a dead village. Though a few people still picked through the rubble, no one lived in Juniper anymore, and no one, Nick was told, ever planned to live there again. The young families had left first, dispersing to neighboring towns where the parents could get their children back into school. Soon, the older ones followed, and people who had lived for generations in Juniper put down new roots in Wilton, Paint Rock, and Tucker's Creek. So Nick had gone to these places, too, asking everyone he could find if they remembered a couple of girls named Fischer or a boy called Wallace Hansford.

"There is something —" Nick said, and Mabel held her breath while he told her he'd spoken to an old friend of Wallace's — Henry Layman. "He said Wallace asked him to give Bertie a letter, and so he went to look for her at the church. He said she seemed upset, and she wouldn't wait for him when he called to her — just ran out the door. He saw her a few days later, at the funeral — he said your stepfather hanged himself. By then, he told me, it was all over town about how you and Wallace had run off together. He said he figured all that was in the letter was some kind of good-bye or explanation and that giving it to Bertie after all she'd been through would be like rubbing salt in a sore, so he threw it away. He never saw her again after that."

Mabel shook violently and she clenched Nick's hands until her knuckles were white.

"It's possible," Nick said, "really — I think it's possible that there's somebody around there who knows where she is, or at least where she was headed when she left. When you're stronger, I can take you back there — me and Daisy — and we'll keep looking, together."

"No." The small word croaked from Mabel's throat. "No. No." Tears burned like acid on her cheeks. "It wouldn't be right."

She told Nick about the letters she and Wallace had sent, about the letters she had sent for years after Wallace had gone, and about the one that had come back to her in Chicago — *Deceased.* "I think," Mabel said, "I think — but I don't know — that Bertie wrote that herself." She knew then, finally knew it as a truth she still wanted to deny: After what she had done, she had no right to tread whatever new ground Bertie might have cleared for herself, no right to cause her to grieve Wallace anew, and no right to stand before her sister and torture her with a plea to forgive.

Mabel slid her hand across the open page of *Life* and looked at the broken men lying prostrate in a watery field of cane. Some damage could never be undone. One could only try to stand, take another's arm, and stagger on.

"Mama! Mama, come quick!"

She leapt up at Daisy's cry and ran toward the front room. "What is it? Honey! Are you hurt?"

Daisy was leaning on Barry, her arms wrapped around his neck, and she was dragging him around in a clumsy little dance. Barry looked over Daisy's shoulder at Mabel, his face overspread with jubilation.

"Mama!" Daisy broke from the dance and held her hand out for Mabel. "Give me your hand! Give me your hand!" She pressed Mabel's palm into her small round belly. "It moved. The baby moved! Press here. Harder. Can you feel it?"

Mabel pressed, trying to hold still while Daisy laughed and kissed her, while Barry laughed and kissed her, trying in spite of her own laughter to hold her palm firm and steady, waiting for the next tremor.

FOURTEEN:
PRISONER

March 1973
Newman, Indiana

GRACE

In the attic, on a windy day, Grace always imagined the house might fall. The cold air sliced through the vents, sucking at the roof, and the windowpanes jiggled in their frames. Particular as he was about keeping up with repairs, Grandpa never seemed to notice that only specks of paint remained on the strips of wood dividing the glass. Even last spring when he had laid blankets of pink fiberglass between the rafters and pounded in planks for a floor to give them more room to stack boxes of cast-off toys and clothes, he'd left the windows alone. Grace was glad. Except for in summer, when it was too hot to breathe, the attic was her favorite place, and the windows, hazy with years of grime, made it seem abandoned, more hers for the claiming.

In spite of the grime and frost, the windows gave her a good view of the snow, pushed by the wind into powdery hills. Hour by hour since early morning, whenever Grandma said into the telephone how in all her born days she'd never seen a March snow like this, her estimate of how much had fallen had grown by an inch or two, despite the snowfall's having ended before dawn. It was hard to tell how deep the snow would have been if it had lain flat and still, but from the attic, Grace could see what she could not see: the washtub Grandma kept turned over beside the grape arbor, just in case she had to get the clothes off the line in a hurry — gone; the maple tree, twenty-nine inches high when Grandpa planted it for her tenth birthday last May — buried; the green-painted swing set — the crosspiece of each A-frame seeming to sit on the snow, like a frozen snake.

She would like to put on her warmest clothes and go outside to play, maybe tunnel out a little cave where she could sit for a while all alone in the quiet, but Grandma would say, "You'll catch your death and the ambulance won't be able to get to us through this mess." Grandma would tell Grace she might fall, that the snow might collapse on top of her. "And how would I ever get you out — saying I could even find you?"

When it was warned the snow might fall for days, Grandpa had packed up the car and driven to Crother's Mill to stay with other men at Bill Junior's. When he called to say he'd made it, he said the road was so slick it had taken him almost two hours to drive the eight miles. Mother's boss, Patrick, had picked her up yesterday morning in his jeep, having arranged to give her a room at the Galloway Inn so the two of them could trade off in twelve-hour shifts at the reception desk. Grace had thought about calling Mother at the motel to ask if she could go outside, but she knew Mother would snap that she was busy, and Grandma would be mad that Grace had gone behind her. The first thing Lynn did when she heard about the snow was to get on the phone and talk her friend Elsie Myers into getting her parents to let Lynn stay with them while school was canceled. That had made Grandma mad, too, when she found out about it, but before anybody in the house knew the plan, Lynn had called Patrick to ask him to drop her off at Elsie's on the way to the motel. When Patrick got there, he picked up Mother's suitcase and said to

Lynn, "All set, Lynn-dee-Lou?" Mother's face turned red and her mouth went tight, and so did Grandma's — but neither of them would speak out in front of company, which Lynn well knew.

Except for not being allowed to enjoy the snow, Grace didn't mind being at home just with Grandma. She liked the peace of having the bedroom to herself, instead of having to share with Mother and Lynn, and if she asked nicely, like she had this afternoon, she could probably get Grandma's permission to come up to the attic every day or two.

"I want to look for some old coloring books and crayons," she'd said, "in case the TV goes out. Maybe some puzzles."

"Aren't you a little old for that?" Grandma pulled a saucepan from the cabinet beside the stove and set it on the counter.

"I'm tired of reading," Grace said. "Lynn took all the good books with her."

"All right, then." Grandma spooned cocoa powder and sugar into the pan. "Reach me the milk, Grace," she said. "Don't stay too long and get yourself frozen. Look in the boxes alongside the chimney. And careful not to bang your head."

She would get the coloring books and puzzles, but the real reason Grace had come to the attic was to find a safe place for her POW bracelet. For the last week, ever since she and Lynn had watched their POWs getting off the plane that had brought them from Hanoi, Lynn had been after her to send her bracelet back.

"I'm sending mine," Lynn said, and a moment after the reporter identified the slim, straight figure coming down the roll-up stairs as Lt. Col. Conrad John Lewis, just promoted to colonel, Lynn had her bracelet off. "I'm getting an MIA next."

A few minutes later, Capt. Mark P. Stevens, now Major Stevens, stepped off the plane, smiling and waving. The reporter said the major had gotten home just in time to celebrate his thirty-fourth birthday. Grace wished she could be there — wherever there would be for him — to hug him after he blew out the candles. She would have seen to it that his cake was simple and plain, no pastel scallops and icing roses.

"That's it!" said Lynn, grabbing at Grace's bracelet. "Hand it over and I'll mail it."

"No."

"That's the way it works." Lynn rolled her eyes. "You can write a letter if you want, but the bracelets are supposed to go back to the men to let them know we remembered them."

Grace pulled her wrist to her chest and cradled the bracelet with her other hand. For two years she had worn it, never taking it off — even facing up to her teachers, who wanted her to leave it in her desk at recess, explaining to them how she had to wear it always, like a wedding ring, at least until she knew her captain was safe. Well, now he was safe, and Grace felt the joy of that far down in her belly, but she had come to love Capt. Mark P. Stevens, USAF, 9-9-66, and wanted to keep him. Wasn't that remembering?

So she had lied to Lynn, said she had written a letter and had taken it to church on Sunday to ask Reverend Mike, the youth minister, to check it for mistakes. "He's going to mail it for me in a church envelope," she told her sister. She wouldn't put it past Lynn to ask Reverend Mike about it, but Grace would worry about that when it happened, after she'd hidden the captain somewhere Lynn would never find him.

But where would that be? Lynn didn't come up to the attic much — at least Grace didn't think she did — but Lynn was a big snoop, so the boxes marked *Grace* wouldn't do. None of the boxes, really — or even the handsized space in the back corner of the old sofa, under the cushion — not inside anything that somebody could carry off. She poked around the chimney to see if there might be a loose brick, but even if there had been, she couldn't count on Grandpa not to patch it up sometime and seal Capt. Mark P. Stevens inside, a prisoner again.

At last she thought of it. There was one plank in the new floor, along the front of the house, that didn't quite butt up to the old floor. When Grandpa had cut the lumber last spring, he told her how he'd measured and measured so there wouldn't be any waste. He knew he'd be short an inch and a half on the last plank — not worth buying more wood for, not for an attic — and so he'd planned to leave the gap in the spot where the roof was pitched steep, where no one was liable to walk, and where cold air from the window and corner wouldn't seep through. He'd shown Grace where the space was, then pulled a heavy box on top of it, grinned and tapped his forehead with his finger: "Horse sense."

So as not to make extra noise Grandma might wonder about, Grace crawled under the hanging clothes, around the crib, and then stood up to tiptoe past the dress form Grandma never used when she sewed. She walked the last few feet on her knees and then pushed her whole weight into the box that sat over the gap. When the space showed again, she sat for a moment with her back against the box, stroking the engraving on the bracelet, still on her wrist. If it weren't for Lynn, she could keep her captain near, if not on her wrist, then in her jewelry box, but there was no way to do that without fighting, and if either Grandma or Mother heard Grace and Lynn arguing, they'd make up their minds on the spot about what was to be done, and Grace couldn't risk their telling her she had to send the bracelet away like Lynn said. They might as easily tell Lynn to hush up and let Grace keep it if she wanted to, but there was no knowing for sure what they'd decide.

At least this way she could come up once in a while and hold the bracelet and remember, and years from now, when she was eighteen, she could come take it back for good, even wear it again, and nobody could tell her what to do. If her Captain Stevens could survive more than six years in a prison camp in Vietnam, she could wait to have back her token of him. And inside her mind, she wouldn't have to wait at all. She could think about him as much as she liked, think how — even if she knew it wasn't true — he might be her father, how she would run across the front yard to him and jump in his strong arms, how he would swing her around and then gently set her on her feet again. Together, they would walk hand in hand to the kitchen, where Mother would turn and laugh in surprise and kiss Captain Stevens and hold out one arm to each of them to gather them to her in a hug.

But why couldn't he be her father? Things like that happened in books and movies all the time — people getting lost from each other and finding their way back again. Maybe Captain Stevens had changed his name and so Mother wouldn't realize who he was until she saw him on the news.

It was Lynn's fault Grace thought about these things, thought about them until she was sick to her stomach. Grace was only four or five when she started looking into men's faces, trying to see something of her own. That was a year or so after Lynn had come home from the hospital. One night, while Mother was working the late shift, Lynn was lying in her bunk, forcing Grace to listen to her plan to write a letter to her father — their father, Grace believed — a letter saying how much she missed him. Lynn said she would send the letter as soon as she could find out his address. "Then," her sister said, "he'll come and take me away."

Grace couldn't remember now why she'd said it — perhaps Mother had scolded her for something earlier that day — but she'd said to Lynn, "Maybe I'll go with Daddy, too."

"He's not *your* father," Lynn said. "He told me. He's *mine.* No one else's." Then Lynn had hissed at her through the dark, just like a snake, "*You're* the reason Mother sent him away. Daddy told me. Mother thought she was going to get the other man to marry her, but he ran off. He didn't want you. *Nobody* wanted you."

Grace looked down once more at Captain Stevens's name. "I love you," she said, then took off the bracelet, kissed it, and slipped it into the gap, tucking it just under the lip of the plank, resting it on the pillowy insulation.

She'd shoved the box so far under where the ceiling slanted, she couldn't get behind it to push it back, and it was too heavy to pull, so she would have to empty it, at least partway. The box wasn't taped shut, just the flaps folded over each other, and when she pulled them loose, a moth flew toward her face. On top, there was a green button-up sweater, like the kind Grandpa wore around the house in the winter, sprinkled over with holes where moths had been munching. She laid the sweater on the floor and pulled out five or six McCall's patterns, obviously used but the pieces refolded neatly inside the envelopes. The pictures on the envelopes showed aprons trimmed with ruffles and lace, and soft, drapey dresses with swishy skirts, matched with white gloves and hats touched up with netting and flowers. Except for women in the movies she watched with Grandma, and the ones interviewed at the Kentucky Derby about their grand hats made specially for the day, the only women Grace had seen wearing hats and gloves were a couple of the very old ladies at church, but instead of elegant high heels, those ladies wore what Lynn had mocked as "sensible shoes." Next, Grace pulled out a book all about making slipcovers, and then another about curtains, and underneath these, stacks of *Good Housekeeping* and *The Ladies' Home Journal* from the 1940s. Under the magazines lay what Grace at first thought was a record album cover. On the front, six- or seven-year-old Shirley Temple, in a short yellow dress, seemed to be trying to sneak out from some giant's scrapbook. An open jar of paste, half as tall as Shirley, sat in front of the book, as if the unseen giant might at any moment pluck the brush from the jar, snatch up Shirley, and paste her inside forever.

"Grace!" Down below, Grandma rapped on the frame of the open attic door. "You been up there too long now. Come on down. The hot chocolate's ready."

"Just a second, Grandma." Grace pushed the nearly empty box over the gap in the floor and rushed to put everything back inside except the scrapbook. Lucky she knew just where she'd stored her old coloring books, so she was able to grab several, plus the candy tin full of crayons, and stack them up on the scrapbook before she started down the steps. Grandma was waiting just outside the door.

"What's that you got?" Grandma tapped at Shirley Temple, who, Grace now saw, was also on the back in the same picture.

"This was underneath the coloring books," Grace said. "Is it okay if I look at it?"

"That's your aunt Alma's. She was crazy for Shirley Temple. So was your mother."

Grace knew this. Among the things Mother treasured, which neither she nor Lynn had ever been allowed to touch, was a cobalt blue juice glass, a ghostly image of Shirley Temple's head smiling out the front. For Mother's sake, Grace had tried to like Shirley's movies — and she did like it when

Shirley danced with Bill Robinson or Buddy Ebsen — but it made her mad that all lost or orphaned Shirley ever had to do to get a father was to want one. That had never worked for Grace.

Grandma put a firm hand on Grace's shoulder, steering her toward the kitchen. "Come on in and lay it on the table so we can see it."

The kitchen was warm and smelled thickly and wonderfully of the hash Grandma was making for them with the last of Sunday's roast beef. It was Grace's second-favorite meal, after the roast beef itself. Tiny whiffs of hot chocolate tucked themselves between the waves of the meat, carrots, and potatoes.

Grandma set two brimming mugs on the table, three marshmallows melting in each, and pulled two chairs close together. Grace smiled when Grandma turned the scrap-book on its front so she could open it from the back. Nobody in the family besides them looked at books that way.

"That's a queer thing to paste in a book." Grandma ran her fingers across tinted draw-ings, cut from old magazines, of living rooms decorated in soft pinks and yellows. On the next page there were funny ads for appliances — one showing a couple in evening dress, a Persian cat at their feet, looking inside a refrigerator held open by a man in a tuxedo, the caption declaring "Plus-Powered Kelvinator Cuts the Cost of Better Living." Another ad proclaimed the "Streamlined Beauty" of a boxy stove.

Grandma turned another page. "Well, look a' here," she said. "That's a picture of the '37 flood. Probably took that from an airplane, or maybe the fire tower." The ink was faded on the dingy newsprint, making the scene look foggy, more eerie. Right in the center, a church steeple pointed like a rocket at the stormy sky, while, for what must have been miles and miles, houses that looked a lot like theirs seemed to float on the rims of their pitched roofs.

"Your aunt Alma must have started keeping this when she was seven or eight, I guess," Grandma said. "I was carrying your mother when the flood came."

Back and back they paged. Aunt Alma, younger then than Grace was now, had pasted in a picture of men in police uniforms and hard hats sorting through hills of canned food to pack in boxes for relief stations; one of a child squalling in his mother's arms while a dark-haired doctor gave him a shot for typhoid; another of people elbow-to-elbow among cots at a shelter; and several more of people being helped into rowboats in the flooded streets.

"See that?" Grandma said. "Me and your aunt Alma rode in one of those. Your grandpa went off early in the morning to help build them."

Grace pointed to one picture that showed a woman and a little girl, each holding a frightened cat. She thought of her own cats, Smokey and BoBo, and tried to think of how she would manage to save them in a flood. She'd worried all night about them out in the snow, hoping they'd found a warm place before it got too deep, maybe through the hole Grandpa had cut for them in the shed door; Grandma wouldn't allow them in the house.

Now Grandma laid her finger on the picture, almost like she wanted to stroke and soothe one of those terrified cats. "There was this lady on our street," she said. "Mrs. Mialback, I think her name was. She was all set to get into our boat with her little white dog, but —" Grandma turned over the page quickly. "But — some woman — she made a fuss about the dog. Wouldn't let it in the boat." Grandma pressed at the deep V lines between her eyes. "I never did know if she got out okay — I mean Mrs. Mialback. She wasn't there when your grandpa moved us back in the house, and none of the ones that did come back to the street seemed to know what became of her. Used to be a nice place she had, but nobody ever came to fix it. They tore it down the summer Grandpa bought this house."

"I wouldn't ever leave Smokey and BoBo to drown," Grace said.

Grandma shook her head but didn't answer. She turned the pages back to the flood pictures they'd already looked at. "Won't be a flood here," she said. "When I was laying in the bed waiting on your mother to be born, I made up my mind I wasn't going to let your grandpa rest until he'd moved us to higher ground. And I didn't."

Grandma lifted the open scrapbook to catch the light coming through the window in the back door. Something slipped out, like a long postcard, dropping on its edge to the table and then onto the floor. Grace pushed out her chair and got on the floor to get it.

"Grace, get up," Grandma said. "What are you doing down there?"

Grace picked up the card, yellowed around the edges. It wasn't a postcard. The back had some writing across it, the name of a photographic studio in Louisville, and a date, 1924. On the front were two identical-looking pictures of a pretty dark-haired girl who looked about Lynn's age — fifteen or sixteen. She wore an old-fashioned white lace dress and sat, unsmiling, on a swing.

Grace clutched the card and pushed up from the floor. "Why would somebody want two of the same picture? Is this like our school pictures, where you get a sheet and cut them all apart?"

"What is that?" Grandma reached out her hand.

"It fell out." Grace held the card for her grandmother to see. "Says it was made in Louisville. She's pretty."

Grandma closed her eyes, her face white, and for a moment Grace thought Grandma was going to faint. "Mabel," she said.

"Mabel?"

"My sister."

"You have a sister? Where is she?"

Grandma's white face became red and her eyes opened, fierce. "Clear away all this foolishness." She stood up, the card still in her hand, looking off somewhere beyond Grace. "Take this book back up to where you found it. I've got to get the table set for supper."

It was only 2:30. "There's just us tonight, Grandma."

"If the snow clears, we might have a houseful!"

Grace tried to move, but she was as frozen as if she'd been buried under the drifted snow. It would be days before the plows would get to them.

"Grace, I told you to put this up. Now!"

Grace grabbed the scrapbook from the table and ran through the house and up the attic stairs, taking no care to watch her step. She dropped the scrapbook onto the floor and flung herself on the old sofa, sobbing. The cushion smelled of mice, and she imagined her tears seeping through the upholstery, dampening their soft gray heads. The mice could suck the tear-soaked stuffing, quenching their thirst without having to suffer the cold. But no, tears were salt, and could only make the mice more thirsty.

When she could cry no more, she sat up on the sofa. The scrapbook lay open and twisted on the floor, the spine broken. She knelt beside it, doing her best to tuck the brittle pages back into place. When she was finished, she hugged the book to her chest and returned to the box that now sat under the slant of the ceiling. She shivered with cold and thought longingly of the hot chocolate left behind on the table, the marshmallows melted into foam, probably too cool to warm her now. Remembering the green sweater, she pulled it out of the box and wrapped herself in it. She would stay here awhile, warming herself in Grandpa's moth-eaten wool, slipping her fingers into the gap of the floor, with Capt. Mark P. Stevens just beyond her reach, waiting until Grandma remembered her and called her back down.

FIFTEEN:
HANGING ROCK ROAD

October 1978
Siler, Kentucky

LYNN

"I think I recognize that store!" Lynn pointed out the window as the car breezed past a deep-porched frame house with a weathered, hand-painted sign identifying it as Odell Anderson's Grocery.

Derek glanced up in the rearview mirror to get a look at it. "How much further, you think?" he asked. "I'm getting low on gas and it doesn't look to me like we're going to find any stations out here." He had wanted to stop for gas an hour ago, near Newman, but Lynn wouldn't let him. It would be just her luck, she told him, that they'd pull into the Shell station and there Mother would be, gassing up the Nova. Lynn had scrunched down as the express-way carried them past town, afraid that

333

someone in a passing car would recognize her and word would get back to Mother.

It couldn't be long now. Though she had memorized the directions days ago, Lynn looked again at Aunt Alma's letter, folded down to show only the words *With warmest wishes, Alma* and the directions to Daddy's last known address. "How many miles have we come since the last turn? It says we're to go left on Hanging Rock Road after eight and a half miles."

"Just keep your eyes peeled for a gas station," Derek said.

"I think that's where we used to stop to get bait."

"Where? Who?"

"That store back there. Daddy and me — and a friend of his, I think." She felt a flash of pain in her chest. "Sometimes. On the way to the lake."

She remembered coming out of the summer heat into the damp, musty cool of the store, where she could stand beneath the slow-turning ceiling fan and sip an Orange Crush. She'd liked the thick bologna the owner cut for their sandwiches, and the way he'd keep moving his tobacco-stained finger back from the cut edge of the big bologna roll until she said *When.* What she didn't like was how he'd fold up the bologna slices in white paper, then turn right around to a cooler behind him and scoop up a handful of night crawlers into a paper cup he'd taken from beside the soda fountain. And she didn't like it later at the lake when Daddy would pull a fat worm out of the cup and wave it in her face, black soil still clinging to it in tiny clumps. But he was only teasing her.

"There's one," Derek said, and Lynn saw ahead of them another hand-painted sign in front of a whitewashed block building: BOBBY'S GARAGE. GAS. OIL. LAST CHANCE BEER.

"Is that some local brand, do you think? Last Chance Beer?"

Lynn felt too edgy to try to decide whether Derek was serious or making a joke. "Siler's in a dry county," she said. "Just over the line."

Derek steered the car into the station and a man in a blue shirt smeared with black grease met them at the pump. "Fill up?" Derek nodded and asked about a restroom. The man motioned toward the block building.

"Think I ought to get some of that Last Chance Beer?" Derek asked Lynn, unbuckling his seat belt. Then he turned to speak to the man out the open window. "How about a pay phone?" The man nodded and Derek said what he'd said at every stop since they'd left Lynn's dorm. "You think you better call?"

"I'm going to the restroom," she said. "I need to stretch my legs."

When she had shown Aunt Alma's letter to her roommates, Michelle and Julie, they had both told her she ought to call, or at least write to Daddy first. "What if he's not there?" Julie said.

"Five hours is a pretty long drive to find out somebody's gone on vacation or moved," Michelle added, though neither said what all of them, including Lynn, were thinking: What if he didn't want to see her?

Aunt Alma had provided a telephone number, and in the ten days since the letter had come, Lynn had gone three or four times to the hall phone booth, staring at the black receiver. She couldn't very well reverse the charges like she did when she called home, so she'd have to be ready with a huge supply of coins to keep feeding the pay phone. She'd gone so far as changing a ten — her spending money for the rest of the month — but once she was in the phone booth, new doubts washed over her. If she got lucky enough for him to be home when the phone rang, would forty quarters be enough to convince him it was really her? Thirteen years was a long time, nearly two-thirds of her life. And even if she could persuade him of her identity, would there be enough quarters in all the world to stay on the line long enough to get him to agree to let her come to Siler? Best to take her chances, she decided. Just go there and face him. It was much harder to turn someone away than it was to hang up the phone or rip up a letter. Wasn't it?

The restroom was surprisingly clean, though badly in need of paint. There were rusty stains in the toilet bowl and around the sink drain, and the mirror was pocked all over in places, its silvering dingy. Lynn leaned in to see how much her fear showed on her face.

"Your coloring is the same," Aunt Alma had said. The same chalk white skin that turned splotchy in the sun, the same frost blue eyes and red-blond hair. Lynn wondered if his hair, like hers, curled tight in the rain. Last spring, when she'd come home for break, so proud of her new feathered cut, Mother had sneered and said, "*Farrah Fawcett* hair? Is that allowed for revolutionaries?"

Aunt Alma told her, "His face is square, too, like yours. But your nose is your mother's." Her nose had always been the part of her face Lynn liked the least.

Last month, on an impulse, Lynn had hitched a weekend ride with Michelle, whose family lived just forty minutes away from Aunt Alma and Uncle Gordon's house in McAllister. She covered herself by first calling home to tell her mother that she wouldn't be in the dorm during phone hours. "It'll probably be an all-nighter in the library," she said. "I have a paper due in American history." Before calling, she had practiced reciting her excuse, but suddenly it didn't seem enough, so she added, "And early Saturday morning I'm going with some people in my class — the professor's going, too — to picket the building site for the nuclear plant. We'll probably be there all day, and then I'm off to the library again." They were half-truths — not that she minded lying to her mother. After all, she was sure Mother had lied to her plenty. There *was* a no-nukes rally that day that some of her friends were going to, and ordinarily she would have gone, but there might not be another chance for a ride for a long time. And she *did* have a paper due — in a week.

When Alma opened the door, Lynn said to her aunt's astonished face, "I want to find my father. Mother won't help me. Will you?"

Alma laid a cold, thin hand on her shoulder and said, "I've always thought it was wrong the way your mother handled all that. Rainey's so emotional — always overreacting."

Lynn agreed. Who wouldn't? When Lynn was fourteen or fifteen, upset over a low grade on an English essay — a low grade she knew was unfair — Grandma Bertie had responded to her tears by saying, "Settle down, or you'll make yourself sick. You're so like your mother — every little thing gets you worked up." Those words had pulled her up short, just like reins on a runaway horse, and from that moment Lynn had resolved to mistrust emotion. After all, crying over the grade in front of her teacher had done no good. The next day, she'd taken her paper in and quietly explained the reasoning behind her argument, admitting that the presentation was flawed, one or two points having been left out. The teacher had let her rewrite the paper and the grade was raised to an A, proof to Lynn that it was the mind that mattered — cool logic to arrange facts into reason.

"What did you think of him, Aunt Alma?" Lynn asked, sitting down in one of the stiff high-backed chairs, upholstered in what looked like ivory satin.

Alma drew her lips into a tight pucker. "It doesn't matter what I thought of him." She turned to the end table and began straightening an already straight stack of the three most recent issues of *The Ladies' Home Journal.*

"Please."

Alma fluffed a pillow, then picked up a crystal dish filled with translucent pink candies and held it out to Lynn. "They're flavored with rose hips," she said. Lynn forced a smile and shook her head.

"I can't really offer an opinion." Alma replaced the candy dish on its doily. "I met him only once or twice before your mother carried you off to Indianapolis. She never would tell anyone why."

Lynn knew only the irrational fragments of that story, her mother's words: "Something terrible happened. I had to get you away. Nobody could have made me leave my baby in that house for another minute." If Lynn asked, "But why? What was the terrible thing?" Mother would either start sobbing or shouting. At other times, Lynn would ask why she couldn't see her father, or at least be in touch, and Mother would try to justify the severing of his visiting rights by saying, "He never even tried to see you — not for five years."

"But then he did ask," Lynn would say; "I know he did." She'd seen the letter from Daddy's lawyer. Determined to find out what had happened — she must have been about twelve then — she had twisted Grace's hair, threatening her little sister and forcing her to keep watch while Lynn climbed on a chair to reach the big brown envelope Mother kept on the high shelf of the closet, all the way at the back. The letter was in the envelope, along with a lot of other legal papers, but Lynn didn't tell her mother she'd read it. "Grandma told me," she said.

This fired her mother's anger and she made Lynn look her in the eye. "It was all about hurting me, getting back at me. Don't you ever imagine it had anything to do with you. He never cared for anybody but himself."

But those weekends — those few months, years ago — Lynn had felt cared for, loved. She had been happy then, glowing under her father's attention, nobody around to say *Isn't Grace pretty. Isn't Grace sweet. Look at what Grace made. Why can't you be quiet and mind like Grace?* — no Grace around at all to claim a share and be put ahead of her.

Exhilarating, it was, that time with Daddy — like being at a circus, where even if something scared you, it was part of the pleasure. Daddy liked running down hills, carrying her on his shoulders. He taught her to play football, showing her how to fall by tackling her to the ground. In the car, heading into curves, he would push the gas to the floor, shouting that he was A. J. Foyt, going for the win.

Lynn knew, even if nobody else believed her, that it had been an accident — her going into the lake. Or, if not an accident exactly, then a moment of fun gone wrong. Daddy hadn't meant to hurt her, but nevertheless, the whole family — Mother, Grandma, and Grandpa — blamed him. And ever since then, Lynn had felt them all watching her, though they pretended not to. Yet there they were, always, calculating her moods, whispering to one another about her time in the hospital, studying her for signs of a relapse of what they called her "nervous breakdown." "It's all still there in the nightmares, the way she cries," one of them might say. "That man throwing her in the lake."

It was true that when she was small, Lynn would yank awake, drenched in sweat and arms weak from flailing, but she wasn't dreaming of Daddy — not in the way they all believed. She remembered no recurrent nightmare except the one she still sometimes had, even now — fighting and twisting as she was carried out of the courtroom, screaming over her mother's shoulder, reaching out her arms to her receding father, who was reaching out to her. Daddy was clear enough in the dream, face red and wet with grief and fury, but when she woke, she couldn't call up the image, not even of how he had looked when she was a child. If there had ever been any pictures of him at their house, they had long ago been destroyed. Once, Daddy had given her a photo to keep. She was standing in front of a Ferris wheel, Daddy with his arm around her, and another man, big and dark, on the other side. The big man was holding up two fingers behind her head for devil's horns. When Daddy gave her the photograph, she wrapped it in a handkerchief and slipped it inside the zippered pocket of the yellow purse she'd gotten to carry with her Easter dress, but when she thought to look for it again, months after she came back from the hospital, the handkerchief was there, but not the photo.

She missed a lot of school that year — the whole winter — and spent her days on the couch, watching *As the World Turns* and *The Guiding Light* with Grandma. In all that time, no one told her what had happened after she'd been carried from the courtroom. All anyone ever said about Daddy was that the judge had decided he couldn't see her anymore. No one told her why that was. No one told her why Daddy didn't call or write or send her presents.

Lynn leaned in toward the mirror again and checked her makeup. Her eye shadow was too heavy, she decided, and her lipstick was too dark, making her look years older. She wetted a paper towel and wiped off as much color as she could, then went back to the car. Derek was leaning against the gas pump, talking with the attendant while he washed the windows.

When they were on their way again, Derek said, "We're on the right track. The guy back there said it's not more than another seven or eight miles."

Lynn stared out the window, trying to persuade herself she recognized the landscape. Here the leaves were just beginning to turn, some around the edges, others spotted with orange and red. The green of the maples was fading into yellow and the leaves were almost translucent in the afternoon sun. Back at school, the ground was already thick with sweet-smelling brown leaves that swirled in the air with the lightest breeze. On their drive south, mile by mile, the trees had gotten greener, as if the wheels of the car had turned back the season.

"He knows your dad," Derek said.

"Who?"

"The gas station guy."

A rope squeezed at her heart. "You didn't tell him who I was?"

"Of course not. I just asked about the address." Derek looked in the rearview mirror more than necessary and slid his hands up and down along the wheel. Clearly, he had something else to tell her.

"What did he say? Did you find out what he does or anything like that?"

"He used to do some kind of work on the roads — that's what the guy said — but then he got run out of that job. A long time ago."

"Run out? What do you mean? Why?"

Derek slowed for a curve, steering stiffly, as if he'd never taken one before. "Sounds like he's doing okay, though — financially. The guy said he sold a lot of land a few years back to a developer — after his dad died. But he kept the old homeplace. He lives alone there now — except for some dogs."

"Tell me what he said. About the job."

"Probably the same exaggerated nonsense you've heard at home." Derek cut his eyes at her, so like the way her family did when they were afraid to tell her something. "It's just talk, Lynn. Even if I told you, you wouldn't mind about it — you're too open-minded for that."

"Derek —"

"All right," he said. "The guy called him 'an old fag' — your dad."

"Oh!" Lynn choked on a hot burst of tears.

"Lynn, I'm sorry. I shouldn't have used that word," Derek said. "But it doesn't bother you, does it? You don't care if he's gay. Do you?"

Lynn noticed a quaver in Derek's voice. Did it matter to him? And if it did, should that matter to her?

"Lynn? Are you okay?"

"Yes!" she snapped. "Of course I am." She pressed furiously at her eyes. "I don't know." Derek was asking her how she felt, but what did it matter what she felt? She knew what she believed: Nothing was important but thought — reason. Just look at all the times she had stood up against classmates, and even professors, attacking them for their absurd prejudices. And last

346

year, even though she'd never been to California, she made signs and sat for a whole day with five others in front of the student union in support of Harvey Milk's campaign. So why was she upset? It was nonsense.

When Derek had said the word — *fag* — she remembered not her father, but that other man — the big one. Had she heard him say that word, or heard someone say it about him? Bear, she used to call him — but not to his face. He had a goofy sense of humor, and he'd always been friendly to her, bringing her into his jokes, but she'd never liked him. Whenever she visited, it seemed he was there, too. Always — when she wanted to have Daddy to herself.

Lynn saw the sign for Hanging Rock Road. "I've changed my mind," she said. "I want to go back."

Derek made the turn, then slowed the car almost to a stop, keeping his eyes anxiously on the rearview mirror. "I've put almost three hundred miles on my car," he said. "My chemistry reports are going to be late. You're doing this."

Lynn let her tears go.

"Christ," Derek said, almost too quietly for her to hear. Almost.

She was fond of Derek, and there were

times — mostly when they were in the backseat of his car or squashed together in her bunk — when she thought she might like to marry him, and he was a sweetheart to bring her all this way, but right now, when she really needed him, he was like a mole on concrete — blundering and helpless.

Up ahead on the right, there was a gravel turnaround. Derek drove there, stopped the car, and turned off the ignition. He reached over to Lynn and laid his arm awkwardly across her shoulders. He tried to pull her to him, but the steering wheel and the gearshift were in the way.

Lynn sat back in her seat and dug a package of tissues from her purse. She dabbed at her eyes and blew her nose and hoped at least Derek would not say *Pull yourself together.*

Derek laid his head back and stretched his long body as far as the seat would allow. He rolled down the window and tapped an irregular rhythm on the steering wheel. "Look," he said, "let's just go on like we planned. I'll go with you to the door. I'll explain why we're here if you want me to. Okay?"

Derek turned Lynn's face toward him. So gently, as if he were touching a day-old kitten, he stroked her cheek. "Okay?" He smiled, his eyes raised in hope.

Lynn took his hand in hers and kissed it. "Okay," she said, and Derek started the car.

Just as the directions indicated, the farm appeared on the left as they came out of a sharp S-curve. Grandpa Dieter's farm — or what was left of it. On the ridge behind were new houses, cheap, close together, and all alike. But the old house was the same, except for now being a soft dull blue instead of white. And there was a chicken house she didn't remember, surrounded by a high rail fence with chicken wire filling in the gaps between the rails. At the sound of the car, two chickens that had been perched on the little tin roof flew clucking down into the yard, stirring the other chickens into a flurry of flapping wings.

The commotion among the chickens set the dogs to barking. They were big red dogs, skinny but strong — three of them. Lynn was grateful to see they were in a chain-link pen, a padlock on the gate. When she and Derek got out of the car, the dogs lined up side by side, dropped their heads level with their backs, and growled low — a deep, steady, terrifying sound.

Lynn laid her hand in Derek's waiting palm — it was solid and dry, strong — and let him lead her up the front walk and onto the porch. There was no doorbell, so he opened the screen door, knocked hard, waited, knocked again, and let the screen close.

The door swung open. Standing on the other side of the dark screen was a blocky man in his mid-forties, a head taller than Lynn, with a square face and reddish hair.

"You two lost?" He sounded irritable, even angry, as if they'd interrupted something. He stepped out onto the porch so suddenly Lynn and Derek had to jump back out of the way. The man went to the corner of the porch nearest the pen where the dogs were still growling, more loudly now. He pounded on the side of the house and barked, "Quiet!" The dogs fell silent and dropped to the ground, heads between their front paws but eyes wide and alert.

The man turned back to them, arms crossed. "What is it?"

Lynn felt herself go pale. Her throat was so tight she involuntarily lifted her hand to it as if to tear away whatever was choking her. "I . . ."

"Mr. Brandt?" Derek said. "Are you Carl Brandt?"

The man acknowledged with a slight nod, eying them with suspicion.

Derek quickly introduced himself, then

put his arm around Lynn. "This is Lynn," he said. "Your daughter. She's been wanting to find you for a long time, but her mother wouldn't allow it."

"Rainey," the man said bitterly.

"That's right," Derek said. "Rainey Brandt. This is Lynn."

Lynn could think only of how grateful she was for Derek's arm around her, keeping her steady, keeping her from running. How good he was. She would marry him today if he asked her.

When the man before her stepped into the sunlight pooling at the center of the porch, Lynn recognized his frost blue eyes. "Daddy," she said.

The man came closer, testing each step, as if the floor might dissolve under his feet.

"Daddy. It's *me*."

"Lynney?"

There it was, right before her, so close she could see a multitude of tiny lines — the sad, loving face of her dreams.

"Yes, Daddy."

She held out her arms as in the dream and closed her eyes, struggling to trap the image of him, like a saint's portrait inside a knight's shield.

"Lynney Lou?"

Suddenly his arms were around her,

351

squeezing her so tightly her sobs clogged inside her ribs. She pressed her arms against his back, imagining herself small again, so small she nearly disappeared against his broad chest, imagining all that had happened going backward, undoing itself — her nightmare cries, gone, for there was no nightmare. The weeks in the hospital, gone. The courtroom, gone. Everyone except the two of them, gone. Everything gone — until she was back with him on the lake, hiding under the giant Christmas tree, popping out, laughing as he chased her, him scooping her up and swinging her, laughing. Swinging her, laughing with her. And this time — *this time* — he wouldn't let go.

SIXTEEN: TURNINGS

March 1979
Newman, Indiana

RAINEY

Rainey opened the door to the bedroom without knocking. In spite of the midday sun that poured through the window and flooded the desk, Grace was bent under the blazing lamp, curling long strips of gold wire into tiny, tedious spirals with a pair of needle-nose pliers. Rainey couldn't see the point of it — Grace would ruin her eyes and her small, pretty hands — but she had to admit that when Grace linked several dozen variously sized spirals to make a bracelet or necklace, the creation was lovely. There was a word for it, a word that sounded like the tinkling of high notes on a piano — *filigree.*

Instead of putting up posters of rock stars or photographs of friends like other girls,

Grace had covered the walls on her side of the room with panels of velvet-covered corkboard — glistening emerald, ruby, amethyst — on which she displayed an ever-changing arrangement of elaborate jewelry. Grace sold enough pieces at school to buy more supplies, but her grades this term — except for her art class — weren't very good. Rainey had been meaning to talk with her about that — the grades. Grace needed to bring them up if she was going to get into college. That was another thing they needed to talk about — Grace's frivolous plan to study art instead of something sensible like computers — but it would have to wait. Rainey had other things on her mind.

"Grace," Rainey said, standing behind her daughter's chair.

"Mmm?" Grace didn't look up from her work. She was completing a very delicate link, more complicated than what she'd done before, or at least it seemed so to Rainey. Grace had curled the wire on both ends, toward the middle, creating two large spirals in the center, each doubling back and looping out toward the ends into smaller spirals — like two treble clefs on their backs, touching toes.

Grace showed no sign of stopping, so

Rainey said, "Put that down, please. I want to talk to you."

Grace set her tools on top of the sketch she'd made of the finished piece and folded her hands on the desk. Rainey leaned in to look at the sketch — grand enough for royalty, very impractical for any modern young woman. She wouldn't be able to sell that one, not even for prom.

"Grace!" With two rigid fingers, Rainey tapped smartly on her daughter's shoulder, and at last the girl switched off the lamp and scooted her chair in a half turn toward the center of the room.

Preambles made Rainey impatient, especially when she had something serious to say, so she sat down on the edge of the bed and faced Grace with a hard stare. "I want you to tell me everything you know about your sister."

A flicker of a satiric smile nudged the corners of Grace's lips. Rainey wasn't going to take that nonsense. "You know what I'm talking about," she said sharply.

Grace opened her mouth, then closed it and rubbed at the depressions the wire had made in the pads of her fingers.

"It's no good trying to lie for her," Rainey said. It was this point that made her especially angry. Grace and Lynn had never been close, Lynn lording it over Grace all her life, trying to make her feel stupid, just as she did with everyone else, so Grace's loyalty ought not to be with her sister, but with her mother.

Rainey pressed. "I know she's been sneaking away from college to see —" She couldn't bring herself to say *her father.* She started to say *that asshole,* but she'd noticed the word made Grace fold inward. Rainey went on: "— to see that *thing* known as my ex-husband." Her shudder of disgust was partly real, partly exaggerated to show Grace how upset she was at Lynn's betrayal.

"Did Lynn tell you that?"

"You know perfectly well she did not."

"How could I know?" Grace shrugged and looked at Rainey as if to ask another question — one Rainey didn't want to answer. Grace would ask, *What makes you so sure Lynn even knows where he is?* and Rainey didn't want to say that one day last week, when Lynn was home on spring break, she had read Lynn's journal straight through while Lynn was out with friends.

She had learned a great many things about her elder daughter — for one, just how much time Lynn spent running around to scream about rights: rights for women, rights for the Haitian boat people, rights for trees and for the ozone layer, rights to be safe from nuclear power. Rainey had learned, too, that Lynn was sleeping with her boyfriend — that Derek, who sneered when he said, "Yes, Mrs. Brandt," or "No, Mrs. Brandt," so full of his own importance. And she had learned that somehow, some way, Alma — her own sister — had had a hand in Lynn's sneaking. Everyone, it seemed, had turned against her.

"Lynn didn't tell me," Rainey said, proud of how calmly she spoke but still wanting Grace to know she was angry. "Of course you didn't, either. Never mind how I know. I do, and you're going to tell me what you know about it."

Grace tucked a stray, stringy brown lock back up into the headband that held her hair out of her eyes while she worked. She said nothing.

"Grace. Tell me. How long has she been sneaking around? How does she get down there?"

Grace stalled, rubbing at the back of her neck, looking up to the ceiling, down, to the side. When at last she leveled her gaze at Rainey, there was a flash of defiance. "I don't know if it counts as sneaking."

"Well, what else would you call it, I'd like to know?" Rainey's voice grew shrill. "She's gotten down there somehow, time after time. Without a word to me — lying to me outright. Making up stories about where she's been."

Grace's clear stare chilled Rainey. "You think she needs your permission? To see her father?"

Rainey began to shake. She clutched at the bedspread, trying to compose herself. "The judge ordered . . ."

"Lynn's over twenty-one, Mother."

"She wasn't twenty-one when all this started." Rainey could feel her argument, so carefully imagined, slipping out of her grasp.

"Yes, she was," Grace said.

"So you *do* know when she went the first time!" Rainey stood up and turned her back on Grace. She couldn't look at her, not right now. "What does age have to do with it anyway? Is that a license to lie?" She tried to trace the pattern of a chained collar pinned on the wall before her, but it eluded her, breaking its rhythm every time she thought she'd unlocked its secret. Then she saw it: the wire twined like overgrown rose vines, but there were no blossoms — only a tangle of thorns. "He's hypnotized her, hasn't he? Making big promises about sending her to law school?" That was all over Lynn's journal, too. Pages of it. Rainey could feel Grace, behind her, measuring her words.

"I really don't think this is any of my business, Mother. Or yours."

Rainey wheeled around, arms crossed, the collar forgotten. "Anything your sister does that affects this family is my business. Like sneaking."

"And what would you have done if she had told you?"

"I would have stopped her!" How dare her own child question her like this? She should walk out of the room, come back when she had regained her calm, but she plunged on. "I'd have pulled her out of school if I had to. Kept her here until she swore never to go again. I would have protected her."

"From what?" Grace picked up the link she'd just made and turned it in her fingers. "You would have made her a prisoner? For how long?"

"No! Stop twisting my words." Rainey could feel the tears pushing at her eyes. "You learned that from your sister." She pressed her fingertips against her closed lids. "He's just going to build her up, make her think he's going to pay all the bills, and then he'll pull it all out from under her. It's a trick. Don't you see?"

"And why would he do that, Mother? What would he get out of it?"

"He wants to hurt her again! He wants to get at me." She reached for Grace's hand. "Please, help me. *Help me.* Help me make her understand what a liar he is — he's a *snake,* Grace."

Turning her chair back to the desk, Grace said quietly, "You think she'll listen? You've already given it a lifetime — two lifetimes. Three, if you count yours."

Rainey grabbed Grace's shoulders, trying to pull her around again. "What's that supposed to mean?"

Grace twisted from Rainey's grasp, propped her elbows on the desk, and let her head drop wearily into her waiting hands. "For as long as I can remember — for as long as Lynn can remember — you've run him down. Looking for every chance to insult him, telling us how horrible he is."

"He was. *He is.*"

Grace laid her head on the desk and closed her eyes. How sweet she looked that way. Innocent. Until now, Rainey hadn't realized how cruel her younger daughter could be — how secretive she was, how stealthily she could cut, like the thorns of a rose.

Eyes still closed, Grace said, "So why not

tell us what it was that made him so awful? So we could decide for ourselves."

"Grace — have you been going down there, too? Don't lie to me. Have you? What's he been promising you?"

Grace sat up, shaking her head. "Why would I go, Mother?"

Rainey backed away and sat down on the bed again. "All I ever wanted was to keep you girls safe." She was losing her battle against her tears. "Safe from all the bad things in life, from knowing. . . ." She dug a wadded Kleenex from her pocket and blew her nose.

"Safe from what?" Grace turned to stare out the window. "What exactly?" The sun had gone behind the clouds and the bare branches waved in the rising wind, as if struggling to touch. "Don't you think it hurts to be without a father?"

Rainey found another Kleenex and blew her nose again. "Your grandpa is the best father anyone could want."

Grace glared at her. "You don't get it, do you? Of course we love Grandpa. But he's your father, not ours." She picked up the spiral link and flung it at the window. "Why do you expect us not to want one?"

Rainey held her head erect. "I expect you to trust me. To show me some respect." She dabbed a remaining tear from her cheek. "There were a lot of things I wanted," she said. "Things I never got. Things I gave up for the two of you. I think that deserves something."

"You can't make somebody else pay for what you lost," Grace said. "Or you shouldn't, anyway. Lynn just wants to find out for herself. If the man's the mess you say he is, she'll figure it out soon enough."

When Rainey opened her mouth to answer, a wail rose from deep inside her, turning her inside out, robbing her of her bearings. Children thought it was so easy, so easy to lay out simple reasons, like lines on a highway — not the way it really was, like trying to untangle one of Grace's golden chains. No — worse — as if someone had plucked all those webs from their velvet boards, thrown them inside a wheel, and turned that wheel for ten years, twenty, until they had become a single mass, knotted and crushed. Where could she begin any telling? With the baseball field? With the house in Siler — opening the bedroom door, the Vaseline jar on the pillow, the skewed pictures, and those . . . *monsters?* Or would it be better to leap forward to a hospital where a doctor told her there was no other choice but to tie her child to the bed, to fill her thready veins with drugs enough to bring down a giant? What if she started in between — with the drowning, the lies, the nightmares that told the truth? Or maybe she would begin just a few years ago, when Lynn's fits suddenly vanished and she sealed up like a marble wall. Rainey sank to the floor, her back against the bed. She hugged herself against the pain, rocking. "You don't know. You don't know. You just don't *know*."

Grace picked up a new piece of gold wire and started twisting it, but it broke in her hands. "That's just it. We don't know." She tossed the wire onto the desk. "At least Lynn had a name to start with."

Shock stopped Rainey's tears. "What are you talking about?"

Grace wouldn't look at her.

"Grace? What do you mean — a name? You know his name. Grace?"

Her daughter picked up the wire again and began turning a new shape with the pliers. "I know," Grace said bitterly. "I know he's not my father. Lynn told me. Years ago." She gripped the tool so tightly her knuckles were white. "Maybe you'd like to tell me about that."

Rainey put a hand to her throat to steady her trembling voice. "No, Grace. Oh no.

No." She pulled herself up and grabbed her daughter's arm — too hard — trying to make her turn. "You *mustn't*." She let go and said more quietly, "You mustn't, *do you hear me?* You mustn't ever try to find your father."

"How can I?" Grace's voice was as concentrated as her skilled hands. "You won't even tell me who he is." She turned and stared at Rainey. "Are you going to tell me now that you're keeping me safe? I guess he must be the biggest bastard that ever lived."

Rainey's open hand, out of her control, slashed across Grace's face.

She stared, uncomprehending, at her stinging hand, and the angry mark on her daughter's soft cheek.

"I'm sorry! Oh, sweetheart," Rainey cried, wrapping Grace tightly in her arms, kissing her hair. Grace sat stiff, unyielding. "I'm so sorry, Grace. *Please.* I'm sorry, baby."

When Rainey released her, Grace returned to her tiny, elaborate turnings of the wire.

"Oh, Grace. My Grace. Your father," Rainey said. "He was — lovely . . ." But even as the words still hung in the air, the sentence waiting to be finished, she knew there was no untangling Marshall, either. How could she explain that even before she had felt the first flutter of Grace in her womb, she had decided for all of them, decided to keep silent — decided to let everyone around them believe a lie — so that Marshall could stay on his path? And even if somehow she could explain, even if Grace in time could recognize the sacrifices Rainey had made — how? How could Grace not believe that she herself had been forced to pay the greatest part of the price?

"He never knew about you," Rainey said. "It was for the best. You have to believe me. Please, baby." She rubbed Grace's shoulders, but the girl wouldn't have it. "He was good and kind, your father. And very smart. Isn't that enough?"

"No, Mother," said Grace. "It's not enough."

SEVENTEEN:
THE NEW MAN

Summer's End 1981
Newman, Indiana

GRACE

He had a good seat, the new man, even better than Hiram, though she'd never say so
out loud — not if she wanted to keep her
job anyway. She did. Grace thought she'd
heard Hiram call the man Ken when he first
came to the stable a couple of weeks ago.
They seemed to know each other — the way
Hiram slapped his hand into the other
man's, pulling him in for a half hug; the
way they laughed really loud and then put
their heads close together, like men did
when they shared a secret or a dirty joke —
and though Grace had been listening as
closely as she could without seeming to, she
hadn't heard Hi call his friend, except that
once, anything besides Crab.

That first day, Hi had put him on Ashes,

the big gelding, which made everyone at the stable gather around the ring, asking in whispers if maybe Hi had something against the guy, whether he was pulling some practical joke. Unsaddled, Ashes could be led by a child, but saddled, nobody except Hiram could hold the horse's head — he fought the bit, even with Hi's brother Merle, who had so many show trophies he'd taken to using the tall ones as stakes for his tomatoes and pole beans. But Hiram put his old friend on Ashes, and from the moment he entered the ring, the man held the horse high and tight. In every way they looked a team, and in the sun, the gleam of the horse's coat, freshly curried, matched the shining pewter color of the man's thick hair.

This was the fourth time Crab had been to the stable, so he was old news to the men and women who spent their days there — he was a gifted rider, they'd give him that, but there wasn't any need to act like he'd dropped from heaven to take a gallop on a unicorn. Still, Grace couldn't resist watching him, and when he turned up, she would suddenly find work to do in one of the stalls that looked out on the ring. This morning, hoping the man would come, she'd left Delia's stall for last. Hi had raised his eyebrows at her when he saw her skipping it to go on to the one next to it, but Grace said she figured since Delia had been taken off in a trailer at dawn to meet her stud, she had first better clean the stalls of horses who would be coming back by midmorning.

From Delia's stall, the outside window gave a clear view of the ring. As soon as she saw Ashes and his rider pass, Grace let the pitchfork drop in the straw and pushed open the wooden shutter to watch them. After two walks around the ring, they moved into a trot, then a canter, back to a walk, another canter, and then the man shouted to Hi, and they came out of the ring at a gallop and breezed past the barn.

Never had Grace seen a back so straight, and she envied the way he and Ashes seemed a single nerve, the way they seemed to share a mind.

— No, not a mind. Nothing so rational. It was instinct. It didn't take any special sight to notice that when he rode, this man wasn't an ordinary man, but Grace liked to think she was the only one who could see that when mounted on Ashes, he wasn't a man at all. He was — he just . . . *was.* Not like anything else.

She heard Ashes's hooves pounding the dirt on the far side of the barn, slowing up as they rounded the back corner. By the time they passed the open window again, the man had Ashes in a cooling walk. When he looked straight in at her, Grace turned and grabbed the pitchfork to finish mucking out the stall.

The sweet odor of straw and manure wound around her and she breathed deeply. Mother complained that Grace carried the smell in with her, all through the house, but Grandma said she couldn't smell it and that Rainey needed to leave the girl alone, so long as she left her boots outside. Neither of them had liked the idea of her working at the barn, but after Grace had brought them over to meet Hiram and Grandma realized he was a nephew of Bill Crother, Grandpa's old boss, she accepted Hiram's promise to look after Grace.

"I expect she's safer there, Rainey, than she is closing up that store in the mall," Grandma said.

Mother, though, still thought Grace was crazy, doing all the grunt work at a dirty old stable just for the sake of riding lessons with Hiram. "What do you want to ride for?" Mother would say. "You don't have a horse, and I don't see you being able to buy one."

"That's just the point," Grace said. "If I work at the stable it's almost like having my own horse — lots of horses."

What she didn't tell Mother, because it would have led to a real fight, was that Hiram had worked it out with the farrier to let Grace learn to shoe. She didn't mind the shoeing, but what she really wanted from J.J. was to learn blacksmithing, and this was her way in. J.J. wasn't keen on having a nineteen-year-old girl hanging around red-hot lengths of iron because, like most men, he had the foolish notion that girls burned more easily than guys did, but even he had to admit Grace had a way with the horses, that they lifted their feet more willingly for her than they did for him. Little by little she was breaking J.J. down, proving to him she was strong enough to do the heavy work and that she wasn't afraid of sweat, calluses, or filth.

Like Grandpa Hans, Grace loved physical work, the tightening and tugging of her muscles, the feeling of her developing, sinuous strength. How she missed him. Since his death last year, their house had been all women. Only he could understand Grace's longings — how she waited eagerly for the heat that started with her rushing blood and then rose to her skin in cooling beads; how she gloried in digging the ground, inhaling the smell of the soil, the sweet mineral taste of it when it was freshly turned. Someday she wanted to know the fragrance of every separate plant — not just blossoms, but the acidy, velvet scent of a tomato plant; the light cool smell, like romaine lettuce, of a maple leaf, and how it was different from a crushed redbud leaf, which reminded her of watermelon rind after the juicy flesh had been eaten.

Since the time she'd sat close, at eight or nine, while her grandfather repaired the shed that came down in the hailstorm, and Grandpa, when he was sure Grandma wasn't watching out the kitchen window, had guided her hand for two strokes with the saw, Grace had craved the sensations that came with making things — like the zing that shot up her arm and landed in her chest with every pull of the saw through the plank, the tingling in her fingers that held the sandpaper, and the fragrant almost-itch of sawdust caught in the sweat on her face.

At fifteen, she had fallen in love with how fire, coupled with strong precise blows of a hammer, could turn a length of iron into a cooking pot or a fireplace poker or a gate latch. That autumn, at the Pioneer Days festival, she had stood for hours watching a blacksmith place the fiery iron across the anvil and pound it into the shape in his mind. He noticed her, Grace thought,

371

mainly because she was the only person who stayed for more than a minute, but when he did, he began to explain what he was doing, which caused a few others to linger and ask a question before moving on. Grace listened, all the while fingering a beautiful gate latch he'd laid on a table among other pieces he had for sale.

"It's for your smarter-than-average horse or mule," the smith said, nodding at the latch. He laid his tools aside, took the latch from her, pressed it against the side of the display table and asked Grace to hold it there. "See here," he said, going to the other side of the table. "Imagine this is a gate and your horse is over here. You have a smart horse, he can learn to lift a regular latch with his teeth. And a really smart horse can figure out the kind that slide sideways. But this one . . ." He leaned over to reach the latch, his fingers mimicking the bite of a horse. "The horse might be able to get hold of the top ring in his teeth and lift it, but then he couldn't push down the lever that opens the bolt. Can't get at the bolt without lifting the ring. Takes two hands."

Grace longed to buy the latch, to keep it oiled and free of rust until the day she had her own place out in the country and her own gate to secure against her clever horse.

She had watched the smith work long enough to recognize the latch was worth every penny he was asking for it — more — but it didn't matter because she didn't have enough money.

Three times, thinking she was managing to be discreet, she'd counted the dollars she'd shoved into her back pocket, but of course he had seen her.

"I'll make you a deal on it," the smith said.

"I don't even have half." She shook her head and turned to go.

"I can do part barter." He handed her the latch again and pulled off his work gloves. "That necklace you're wearing. It's nice work. Got a daughter living out in Colorado — she's a potter. I think she'd like it. What do you reckon it's worth? You remember what you gave for it?"

Grace blushed. "My choker? I never thought about it being worth anything," she said. "Except to me. I made it."

The smith stooped to see the necklace better, so Grace unhooked it and handed it to him. He sat down, laid the choker across his lap, and traced the interlocking golden spirals with his finger. "You made this?" Lifting the necklace to hold in the light, he said, "Girl, you could be selling these — right here."

Grace didn't know what to say. It had never occurred to her that anyone besides herself might like her pieces. Her wirework had become a family joke — just like the beading she'd done when she was younger. Lynn usually led the way, asking at dinner what new masterpiece Grace had been rendering instead of finishing her homework, and Mother would roll her eyes when, once again, for Christmas or her birthday, Grace asked for money — money she would immediately hand to Grandma, who would write a check to send mail order for pliers, cutters, crimps, and wire.

"If you're willing," the smith said, "I'll trade you even — the necklace for the latch. Then we both come out okay."

Back home that evening, Grace had laid out all the pieces she had ever made — chokers, chains, pendants, bracelets, earrings. At first, she looked at them lovingly — they *were* pretty — then gratefully. Then critically. Suddenly she could see how to make them better. She pulled her sketches from her desk drawer and, seeing new possibilities — how she could twine or braid the wire before she turned a spiral — she laid strong, confident pencil marks across her original faint designs. From time to time she would take up the gate latch and study it. One day, she promised herself, she would learn ironwork and make an even better one.

"Grace," Hiram called from outside the barn. "Got one coming up."

She finished scattering the fresh straw in Delia's stall and stepped into the breezeway. The new man, Hiram's friend, had dismounted and was leading Ashes to the washing pen. Both rider and horse were powdered with fine clay. Grace held her hand out to take the reins. The man stopped, keeping Ashes just out of her reach, and he looked at her so directly, so frankly, her cheeks flashed hot. She looked to the ground, stepped forward, and put her hand on the horse's lead, high above the man's hand. "I'll take him," she said. "It's my job."

Crab didn't let go. He moved his hand higher, nearly touching hers, his open stare fixed on her all the while, his hot breath stirring the loose wisps of hair around her face.

Still holding the reins, Grace stepped past him to stroke Ashes's neck, clucking softly. The horse dipped his head toward her and nickered back.

"Okay." The man let go of the reins and began slapping the dust out of his jeans.

While she tied Ashes in the pen, turned

on the water, and gathered her bucket and brushes, Grace could sense the man was still there, just outside the pen, watching her. She wiped down the horse with tepid water, his muscles rippling in gratitude with every stroke. With a quick glance as she moved to wash Ashes's other side, she saw the man squatting against the wall, just beyond the flow of water, still watching her.

"You weren't brought up to this, were you?"

Grace turned as far as she could to hide her cheeks — red again — and in her head she ran quickly through the checklist Hiram had made her memorize. Yes, she was doing everything just as he had shown her. She'd been foolish ever to look at this man twice — one of those who was just bent on rattling other people for no good reason. She didn't want to know him now.

"No offense," the man said, standing up, his back against the wall. "It's just you're gentler than somebody who grew up around horses. They're not glass, you know."

Grace ignored him and brushed the water from Ashes's coat in smoother, wider arcs.

"I hope Hiram coughs up for all that extra TLC."

Grace picked up Ashes's left forefoot, checked the shoe and examined the hoof.

"We trade." Picking up the right forefoot, she said, "The shoe's coming loose."

"When's the farrier come?"

"I can fix it." She set the horse's foot back down and walked past the man without looking at him. She came back with her tools, and when the shoe was secure again, she faced him. His stare didn't trouble her now. She stared back.

His gray hair made it hard to read his age, but only partly. At some angles, his face looked young — at most thirty, thirty-five — but there was a deep crease between his eyes, and the eyes themselves looked worn-out, defeated, no light. With his feet on the ground, his back wasn't nearly so straight as when he was on horseback. He was slim and solid, all muscle and bone.

"Come on out with me," he said.

"Outside? Why? I'm not finished here."

"I mean come out with me," he said. "A date. You're not married, are you?"

Grace stood at Ashes's head, scratching his long, taut neck. "Who are you anyway? Do you just go around trying to pick up women in stables?"

"Not always in stables." He'd tried to say this with dash but had failed, and now Grace could see that for all his efforts to appear smooth, a ladies' man, he was really clumsy.

"I'm not married," she said. "But that doesn't mean I'm available."

"Boyfriend?"

"What do you want with me?"

"Jesus, why do girls always have to know that crap? *What do you want? Where is this going?* How the hell should I know? Do you want to go to lunch with me or not? I've got a clean shirt in the car, if that's what you're worried about."

Grace suppressed a laugh and then, surprised at how sorry she felt for him, said, "I can't. When I'm finished here, I have to go home and get ready for work. My paying job."

"Where's that?" He must have caught her look of annoyance, because he said, "Sorry, too many questions. How about dinner, then, or a drink? Are you old enough to drink? Legal, I mean."

"No," Grace said, enjoying his obvious uncertainty about what she was saying no to. "Maybe."

"Maybe you'll come out with me?"

"Maybe," she said. "Sometime. Maybe after you decide to tell me your name and ask mine. Maybe."

He dropped his head in what might have

been shame, but he came up laughing. *"Christ,"* he said and told her his name was Ken, that he was taking some classes at Newman Community College — English and history, mostly — trying to figure out what he wanted to do. He didn't say anything about a job, nor did he mention how it was he had money enough to play around in school at his age. There was a lot he wasn't telling her — even the usual things people share when they're getting acquainted — and something about his manner that forced her not to ask. But she liked him. She was almost sure she liked him.

"Why does Hi call you Crab?" That question seemed safe enough.

"His twist on an old nickname," Ken said. "Hermit. I like to keep to myself."

"And if somebody bothers you, do you come out snapping?

"Sometimes." He winked at her. "But not you. I'd be nice to you. Invite you into my cave." Had it not been for the sweet self-mockery of his tone, she would have thrown the currycomb at his head and told him to go down to the Holiday Inn to prowl the lounge.

Yes, she liked him.

"I'll think about it," Grace said, untying Ashes and turning him to lead him back to his stall. She looked over her shoulder at Ken. "See you around."

It took more than three weeks of Ken's coming to the barn, of his pretending not to notice that she watched him on Ashes, of his hanging around while she washed the horse down, before she finally said she'd go out with him. Hiram didn't like it, but he didn't say anything — not to her anyway. Whenever Grace leaned in the doorway to talk to Ken, whenever she gave him a teasing shove, she could see Hiram somewhere nearby, keeping his eye on her, saying something she couldn't hear to whoever was standing closest. A couple of times she saw him stop Ken at the entrance to the ring, Hi gesturing up toward the barn and shaking his head, Ken tightening his lips and jutting out his chin. They seemed less friendly to each other these days.

Three weeks until she finally said yes to Ken — until she finally said she'd meet him for Sunday brunch at Frisch's. And now he was standing her up.

Grace waited on the sidewalk for an hour, pacing, checking her watch, checking her hair in the window, stepping off the curb to let couples and families pass by her and into the restaurant. Brunch was over by the time she went inside and ordered a Swiss Miss — to go. She had to drive straight to work, and on her way to the mall, she took angry bites of the sandwich at every stoplight.

Then, just before 5:30, when she moved from customer to customer in the jewelry store to say they would be closing in five minutes, she saw Ken sitting outside on the bench, almost lost against the small artificial jungle behind him. She might not have seen him at all if not for his hair.

Grace made a point of not looking at him. She tried to persuade a boy and girl not any older than she was that they could look at the engagement rings as long as they liked — she'd be happy to stay late for them — but they all three knew that Grace had no authority to keep the store open and that even if she did, the boy didn't have any money to spend. Her offer only embarrassed the couple, who quickly left the store.

She asked the manager if there was anything she could help him with, but he said no and waited impatiently for her to pass through the partially opened security gate so he could lock up, tally the day's sales, and go home.

Ken had stationed himself so that she would be facing him when she came out of the store, so Grace glared at him, then made a sharp right, walking quickly. He fell in step behind her, followed her all the way to her car, and knocked on the window before she turned the key.

"Please, Grace," he said, his voice muffled by the glass. "I'm sorry. Really."

She rolled down the window an inch and stared straight ahead.

"Let me take you to dinner," he said. "Right now."

"My family's expecting me."

"Tomorrow, then. Lunch."

"You have class," she said. "You told me you have class on Mondays."

"I'll skip. Say you'll have lunch with me."

"Why? So you can leave me standing around again? No thanks." She started the car and pulled away, leaving Ken in the empty space, looking after her.

Ken didn't come to the barn the next day, or the next. On the third day, he showed up but didn't ride, just spent nearly an hour closed inside the tack room with Hi, their voices raised but the words indistinct. When at last they came out, Ken went straight back to his car without even a glance at the barn, Hi watching him, arms crossed, as if to make sure that's just what Ken did.

Grace flung the saddle up over the white

pony, Whisper, and cinched the girth straps while a little girl wearing a rosy pink cowboy hat and new blue jeans chattered to her. Grace checked the tightness of the saddle and explained to the girl how to grab a handful of the pony's mane, then raise her left foot into the stirrup. "I'll give you a boost up," she said, "and then when you're standing in the stirrup, fling your other leg over. I'll hold on to you until you're steady." When the girl was mounted, her chatter silenced and face rigid with fear, Grace handed the reins to Hiram's son Terry, who taught all the beginners.

Grace headed back to check Whisper's water. She filled the bucket and was pouring it into the trough when Hiram stepped into the stall. "Watch yourself around that fellow, Grace. He's got no business messing with you."

What was she supposed to say? Should she admit she'd wanted to go out with Ken, that she'd agreed and he'd stood her up? She turned to Hiram, the empty bucket swinging from her hand. "Why does everybody make such a big deal about age?" She hadn't mentioned Ken to either Grandma or Mother, because that's what they would have fixed on.

"That's got nothing to do with what I'm

talking about."

No, Grace thought, it wouldn't. What a hypocrite Hiram would be if he warned her off Ken on those grounds. Hi's wife, Mary, was at least twenty years younger than he was.

"Crab's . . . odd," Hiram said. "Not quite right, you know?" He squatted down in the stall and braided a couple of pieces of straw while he talked. "He don't fit this world. Not since the war. Used to come here when he was still a kid, got drafted right out of high school — marines took him — about the time Mary and me got married. He drove the team for the carriage that picked us up at the church." Hi dropped the braided straw and picked up two more pieces. "I knew a lot of fellows that got sent to Vietnam. I ain't never seen a one of them change like Crab did. All them years in that gook prison, I expect."

Grace opened her hand and the bucket clanked softly as it dropped into the straw.

Ken. A prisoner of war.

Where and how had he been taken? How long had he been held? What had happened to him there? Why were his friends — why was Hi — turning away from him? Trying to get other people to stay away from him?

Grace clutched her left wrist and thought

of Capt. Mark P. Stevens. Had there been anyone to meet him when he came off the plane? She remembered scenes of wives and children running toward the men, scenes played over and over on the news, but if someone had been there to greet her captain — her newly promoted major — the cameraman hadn't filmed it. What if he had been alone? What if he was so changed that no one wanted to know him, no one wanted to be patient? Who would listen to him, let him talk about those years in prison? Who — when the world acted like the war had never happened?

Ken was gone and Hi would never tell her how to find him. But even if she did, what would she say? That she understood? Of course she didn't. That she wanted to try? That she cared? That she'd like to know him? She did. But she wouldn't. And it was her fault.

Grace knew the car was squarish and tan, but that's all she could remember. Furious at herself for being so unobservant, she turned to make another pass through the community college parking lot. How could there be so many tan cars? It had another color, didn't it? Maybe blue or a darker brown on part of the doors? She couldn't remember. It was old — she knew that — but so were most of the cars in the student lot. Maybe she wasn't finding it because it wasn't here at all.

Ken was probably long gone, out of Newman altogether.

Hiram had told her Ken had a piece of property way out in the country, an hour or two northeast of Indianapolis. He'd bought it with the payout from a life-insurance policy taken out by his father, who had died while Ken was still a prisoner in North Vietnam. No one seemed to know what had become of his mother. According to Hiram, Ken, ever since he'd gotten back from Vietnam, turned up in Newman every few years, talking big about how he was going to go to school, get a job, settle down. He would stay for a couple of months, maybe as long as five or six, but then he'd vanish again, going back, Hi presumed, to his patch of lonely land.

Grace parked and headed toward the nearest building. Huge bronze letters on the side announced it as the Miller Science Pavilion. There was a girl out front, sitting on a stone bench, so Grace asked her if she knew Ken Vincent. She said she didn't and pointed to a flat building on top of a low hill when Grace asked where students registered. "Drop and add's over," the girl said, and Grace thanked her and hurried up the stone steps to the building. She asked three different people in the registrar's office, each one handing her off to someone, she supposed, with higher authority, but all of them told her student information was private and that they couldn't even confirm that Ken was registered.

She asked about a restroom and followed their directions down the hall, to the left, and down another hall. She took a long drink from the water fountain, stopping only when she sensed that someone had appeared beside her to wait for a turn. "Sorry," she said, wiping her lips with her fingertips.

"Me, too." It was Ken, standing right in front of her.

For days she'd thought of what she would say, but now her mind was blank.

"How's Ashes?"

"Fine," Grace said. "A little edgy, maybe. He needs a good gallop."

Ken shoved his hands in his back pockets and looked away. "I guess Hi will see to that okay." He looked back at her and gave a slight nod. "See you, Grace." He took a step away, and she grabbed his arm. Both of them stood for a moment, looking at her hand on his arm. She let go suddenly, as if her palm had caught fire.

"I was looking for you," she said. "I wanted to bring you something."

He fixed her with that frank stare of his, neither hot nor cold, just unreadable, unnerving.

"Is there someplace else . . ." She couldn't do this standing outside a restroom.

Ken gestured for her to follow, and in a moment they were in a room with café tables and chairs. Awkwardly high wooden booths lined the walls. There were only a few students at the tables, some talking quietly, others with books and papers spread before them. All the booths she could see into were empty. Ken chose one in the corner and Grace slid in across from him, setting her purse on the table between them.

"So what is it?" Ken said. He'd joined his hands together, almost like a giant fist, and he tapped the fist on the table.

"I . . ." Grace watched his hands, lean and strong, dark from the sun.

"I know Hi didn't send you. So what are you doing here?"

She put her hand over his, as if to stop his nervous tapping, but when his hands fell quiet beneath her small cool palm, she didn't take her hand away. She didn't want to.

Ever so slowly, Ken released one thumb and, curling it over her hand, stroked her fingers. And then, without her knowing how it had happened, her hand slipped between his. They were just as she'd imagined, his hands — warm and sandpapery.

"I'm sorry I left you at the mall," she said. "I was pretty mad."

He turned one hand so it cupped hers, and with his other he caressed her open palm. "I get in a funk sometimes," he said. "I never know when it's coming. And when it does, even if I could talk myself into going out, it's no good for me to be around anybody. That's what I wanted to tell you when I came to the store."

She felt a rush of desire for him and longed to fling herself across the table into his arms. She wanted to curl in his lap and pull his head to her chest and hold him and rock with him and stroke his hair.

She loved him. Suddenly. Absolutely.

"I brought you something," she said. With her free hand, she opened her purse and drew out a metal cuff the color of dull pewter. She held it so he could read what was engraved there: *Capt. Mark P. Stevens, USAF, 9-9-66.*

Ken released her hand, took up the bracelet, then stood up to slide onto the bench beside her. He put his arm around her, and laid a line of caressing kisses on her temple, behind her ear, on her cheek, her neck, along her jaw, and finally her lips. She clung to him and he held her ever more tightly and they kissed and kissed.

"Grace," he said, retracing the line of his first small kisses. "Sweet little Grace." He held the bracelet up to read it. "How long did you wear this?"

"Until I saw him get off the plane," she said. "Until I knew he was home again."

Ken held the bracelet before him, sliding his thumb over Captain Stevens's name. "You brought this for me?" He turned to her again, and, cupping her chin in his hand, he looked into her eyes, the same direct gaze, but tender now. "You're sure?" He tugged at the edges of the bracelet to widen it, then pressed it onto his wrist and squeezed it closed. He took her hand and lifted it, kissed the tender underside of her wrist.

There was a tear on his cheek. "I want you to wear mine," he said. "Will you? Somebody sent one back. I never knew who." He pulled her into his arms. "Say you'll wear it, Grace. Will you?"

Grace pressed into him. She wanted to feel her heart pounding against his. She pressed harder, and harder still — and there it was: the beating of his heart, a rhythm matched with hers. "I will," she said. "I will. I will."

EIGHTEEN:
A MIGHTY FORTRESS

August 1987
Indianapolis, Indiana

MABEL

The vestibule was dark and cold, with high ceilings that seemed to be made of stone arching overhead, like a grand tomb. Mabel groped for something to lean on, but her hand found only a slender wooden stand, awkwardly placed at the entrance to the sanctuary. In her reaching for the tilted surface, she knocked off an open book, which fell with an echoing slap to the marble floor.

"Mama, take my arm." Daisy was beside her now, holding her steady, and, as her eyes adjusted to the dim light, Mabel saw her son-in-law, Barry, fetching over a small metal chair. Where had it come from?

"Are you feeling faint?" Barry asked, guiding her into the chair and then kneeling down to take her pulse. "Mabel?"

"I'm all right," she said. "The light was so bright outside. I just couldn't see when I came in." She waved her hand in the air around the seat. "Where's my camera? Did I drop it?"

"It's here, Mama," Daisy said, giving a tiny tug on the strap around Mabel's neck. "Right where it always is. You just sit still a minute and then we'll take you in. The rest of the guests won't be here for another half hour." She could feel Daisy's firm, slender hand stroking her arm. "Are you sure you're okay?"

"I told you," Mabel said. "It was just the light. And the sudden cold — coming in out of the heat like that." She could sense Daisy doubting her — Daisy, who knew every turn of her mood — but Barry and the other people gathered in the vestibule — the priest, a couple of ushers, the hired photographer — seemed to accept her story, as they were chatting about other incidents when a sudden change in light or temperature had made someone ill.

Mabel hadn't been in a church for more than sixty years, not since she was sixteen. She hadn't even stood directly outside one since the Juniper fire, when she and Daisy had paused on the walk before the ruins of the Emmanuel Baptist Church. It didn't matter that this cathedral bore no resemblance to the little stone church she remembered. Even a casual mention of Sunday services tripped a collage of images in her mind — of her father's funeral and then her mother's, of Jim Butcher standing next to her in the pew, loudly singing "Hark! the Herald Angels Sing" two mornings after he'd first raped her, of the churchwomen who had finally driven her away by staring and whispering behind their hands as she passed, of Bertie in her pink graduation dress searching the sanctuary for her and Wallace. She'd hoped to reach the end of her life without entering another church or another cemetery, never imagining that her granddaughter, Jenny, without a single day's instruction in religion, would fall for a boy who had seriously considered becoming an Episcopal priest.

"We'd better call the hotels about open dates," Daisy had said last Christmas, moments after Jenny had startled them all by announcing in the middle of dinner that she was dropping out of college for the spring term so she could plan her wedding to Stephen, whom she had known only three months. "Or there's that new restaurant — you know the one I mean. It's a converted

Victorian mansion. I'm sure we could rent that if they catered the reception."

"No," Jenny said. "We want a big wedding. Stephen has lots of family. And the sanctuary at his church is so beautiful."

"But all that rigmarole," Daisy said. "All that ritual and hocus-pocus. A wedding doesn't have to be in a church to be beautiful."

"I don't think it's hocus-pocus."

Mabel, Daisy, and Barry all stared at Jenny, while their friends Nick and Ted excused themselves from the table, saying they hadn't yet had a good look at the Christmas tree.

"I like it," Jenny stammered. "I can't tell you why exactly. And it's not like I believe everything the priest says. I don't understand a lot of it, but even if I did —" She picked up her fork and scratched at the tablecloth. "I like the way it makes me feel," she said. "Like there's something beyond this world we have to answer to." She nodded toward the ceramic tree that sat in the center of the table. "Why do you even celebrate if you don't believe anything?"

Mabel scooped up the bread basket and said she needed to get more rolls from the oven. Jenny followed her into the kitchen.

"What's wrong, Gran? Don't you like Stephen?"

"I do. We just don't really know him, that's all." Mabel pulled an oven mitt onto her hand, which Jenny pulled off again, saying, "I'll do it."

While her granddaughter opened the oven, Mabel said, "You're too young, Jenny. Finish school first. Get to know some other boys."

One by one, Jenny plucked the steaming rolls from the tray and dropped them in the basket. "Oh, Gran," she said. "When it's right, it's right. What do you want me to do? Wait until I'm thirty-five, like Mom was? Or be like you and never get married at all? It's not like we're planning to have kids right away. Lots of girls my age get married. Lots." She pulled off the oven mitt and covered the bread basket with a cloth. "You're not upset about the church thing, too, are you?"

Mabel shook her head. She turned toward the sink to hide her reddening eyes. "Of course not," she said.

"You are." Jenny stood beside her. "I'm sorry," she said, her voice quiet, "but I want to come out after my wedding feeling like I've been through something — not like

Mom and Dad. They treated it like a big joke."

Mabel's head snapped up. "You don't know what you're talking about." She looked at her granddaughter. "Take that back." Jenny had seen the photographs of her parents' wedding — onstage at the theater following Daisy's closing night performance in *A Doll's House* — and she'd been told the story: how Barry, a theater-loving insurance salesman, talked his way backstage to meet Daisy by claiming to be a florist with a special delivery. From that, Jenny had imagined her parents' courtship as a blithe romance out of a musical comedy — all bells and stardust. But she didn't know what had really happened — like how Daisy, who hadn't been touched by a man offstage in twenty years, fell into hysterical sobs the first time Barry tried to kiss her. He'd lifted his hands to cup her face, and she'd fought him as if he were strangling her. It was hard not to love a man who stayed after that, who sat in a corner until she calmed down, who asked in a gentle way for her to explain what happened, when she could.

Perhaps they had all protected Jenny too much. She was so naïve, understanding the world in the simplistic way of the young —

the very young, who had never faced death or feared any monster that wasn't imaginary. Jenny saw the theater as only make-believe. She couldn't understand — as Barry had come to — that there was no place on earth more sacred to Daisy.

"I didn't mean it," Jenny said. "But why won't any of you tell me why you hate church?"

"Your parents weren't raised on it." Mabel knew Jenny would roll her eyes at that easy answer, so she quickly added, "And me . . . I just didn't want to go back after my mother died." To say any more would have been like throwing her granddaughter into the center of a great maze — and for what? It wasn't Jenny's fault that at twenty-one she remained such an innocent — Mabel and Daisy and then Barry had made those choices. Jenny knew Mabel had adopted Daisy during the war, but she knew none of the circumstances — and certainly nothing of the common past her mother and grandmother shared.

"Those aren't good reasons," Jenny said. "I'm not asking you to join. I just want to have my wedding there."

"Well, what about Nick and Ted?" Mabel knew the question wasn't fair, but she was desperate to divert Jenny to another track.

"Do you want to make them feel they're not welcome at your wedding?"

Jenny sighed and slumped into a chair at the kitchen table. "So I'm supposed to give up even asking questions because some people who go to church think gay men are devils? You know there are plenty of people who don't go to church who wouldn't accept Nick and Ted, either. Why do I have to pay for all that?"

Mabel stroked Jenny's hair. "Oh, honey." All her granddaughter was asking was for them to gather as a family for a few hours inside a church — and for that she did not deserve Pandora's box as her wedding gift. A church was just a place, Mabel told herself, nothing more. She kissed Jenny's cheek. "You have your wedding wherever you like."

The girl brightened instantly. "And you'll take pictures?"

"No, Jenny, I'm too old for that. Can't I just be a guest?"

"Not all of them. Just at the reception — whatever strikes you. We'll pay somebody to do the ceremony and all the formal stuff." Jenny clasped her hands, as if in prayer. "Please? I've told all my friends about my famous grandmother."

"I'm not famous."

"Well, nobody else I know has ever had a grandmother on *60 Minutes.*" She winked at Mabel. "Not a grandmother who wasn't a criminal, I mean." Jenny picked up the bread basket and headed back to the dining room, tossing another grin over her shoulder as she passed through the door.

Jenny's soft-focus view of the world and her generation's obsession with celebrity made the girl recall that interview as cause for rejoicing — entirely forgetting the reason for it. Mabel hadn't wanted to do it at all, but her editor had urged her on. "It's not just anybody," he said. "It's Ed Bradley. He was wounded covering the war in Cambodia."

Mabel's book, *The Never-Ending War,* had grown from the series of photographs she had taken of young men bound for Vietnam. How she wished she could have captured just one moment for all the tens of thousands of Indiana boys who had gone, but working as hard and as long as she could work, she'd managed only a slivered fraction — a few over twelve hundred in seven years. Of those, about half had kept their word and returned to her for one more session. Sixty-three, she knew, would never come back — either killed or reported missing in action. But twenty-nine of the men who returned had joined with Mabel in a new project, letting her photograph them once a year so that others could one day look at the progressive images and understand something of the cost the veterans themselves could not otherwise express. These photos had become the book. If it hadn't been released the same month the Wall was dedicated in Washington, *The Never-Ending War* would have sold very modestly, with little notice, but somehow word had gotten to nearly every news station in the country, and, eventually, to a producer at *60 Minutes.*

Mabel had always liked Ed Bradley, who spoke with the warm rhythm of a man who loved music. He'd come to Indianapolis to interview her, and when he leaned across her own kitchen table and fixed her with those sad, earnest eyes of his — eyes that had known suffering and cherished joy — the cameras she had dreaded melted away. "What did you learn from these men, the veterans?" he asked.

"That for them, that war won't ever be over," she said. "I don't think any real war ever is — large, small, between countries, between people. Even the wars inside ourselves. Something always remains."

"Feeling better now, Mama?" Daisy knelt

before her on the marble floor and whispered, "If you don't think you can do it, you don't have to."

"It's okay," Mabel said. "I'm okay."

"Barry's gone off somewhere with the priest," Daisy said, "and I have to go check on Jenny, but Nick's here. He'll take you in."

She looked up to see Nick in an elegant dove gray suit, offering her his hand with a flourish. "May-belle," he said, "may I have the pleasure of escorting you to your seat?"

Mabel placed her hand in his. "If you had a top hat, you'd look just like Louis Jourdan."

Nick smiled, bowed to her slightly, and wound her arm in his. A half-dozen bearded old men in robes, the sun lighting their faces with the ferocity of heaven, glared at Mabel and her friend as they made their progress up the aisle. She could identify only Moses, who carried the stone tablets. "I suppose they're all prophets," she said.

Nick nodded toward the windows that encircled the altar. "Looks like they put all the angels up front with the priest — too good for the ordinary sinner."

The figures in the altar windows were clearly angels, with their heads ringed by halos and the hint of white wings rising up behind them. Strange how they were all portrayed as young men — beautiful young men, pretty as girls. Like the surly old prophets, the angels were draped in robes, but of lighter colors — saffron and rose instead of mud brown and purple — all except one, who wore bright blue armor. He looked like Nick, nearly forty years ago, when he played George Gibbs to Daisy's Emily Webb in *Our Town*.

At times like these, when someone else would have prodded Mabel to explain her trembling, Nick held her hand, as her Paul would have done. They shared the gift, these two, of understanding without the need to ask questions. Mabel looked again at the blue-armored angel. Was it a blessing or merely luck that she'd had two such rare friends?

Mabel slid sideways into the pew, the second from the front, and sat down. "Where's Teddy?" she asked, pulling Nick down beside her.

"He'll be along later — said something about decorating the getaway car."

"Oh, no!" Mabel clapped a hand over her mouth to keep her laugh from echoing through the sanctuary.

"Don't worry, Belle. Nothing too wild. He promised to stick to the conservative hetero theme — cans and old shoes. Boring!"

Mabel glanced over her shoulder toward the entrance. "Think this crowd will be able to handle seeing you two together?"

"Nary a worry. The priest told me it's been a whole ten years since the Episcopalians voted us children of God. Isn't that good news?" He picked up a hymnal and thumbed through it. "But just in case, Jenny's been feeding the troublesome in-laws a story about Ted and me as bachelor roomies."

"Like in *The Odd Couple*?" Mabel let her laugh go this time. "All ex-wives and stewardesses? Who will ever believe that?"

Nick leaned his head against hers. "Just the ones that have to if they're going to get through the day without a coronary. People believe what they want to believe."

Mabel started to get up. "I'm going to have a talk with Jenny. Right now."

"Geez, Belle, your timing needs work." With a tug on her hand, he drew her back down to her seat. "It's okay, really. Let's not have our Stonewall today. We're here to celebrate. Jenny's still at that age where she's afraid of what people will think of her. And anyway, these are just the special-occasion relatives — all the everyday ones know." Nick squeezed her hand playfully and grinned. "Besides, Ted's determined to get them at Thanksgiving — the familiest of holidays." He fanned the pages of the hymnal. "So many songs about a guy nobody can see."

Mabel took the hymnal from him. "I don't think I know any of these," she said, stopping suddenly on an open page. "There's this one: 'A Mighty Fortress Is Our God.' "

"Well, that's no surprise," Nick said. "Look at all the battle images around here. An angel in armor." He pointed to the marble font. "Shields all over that thing."

"Did I ever tell you? One of my veterans — Charlie Brock — told me his platoon used to sing 'Onward, Christian Soldiers' whenever they got an order to strike a village. Part of the black humor that kept them going: 'Like a mighty army moves the Church of God; / Brothers, we are treading where the saints have trod.' " Mabel pressed a tear from her eye. "Charlie said he never cared about whether it was true — the story going around that a peace symbol was a broken cross. That's why he wore one, he told me. Said there wasn't any way to move forward without breaking the cross."

A rapping sound at the back of the sanctuary caused them both to turn. Barry was waving for Nick.

"My cue," Nick said, kissing Mabel on the cheek. "One of the ushers didn't show, so I've been elected as understudy."

Alone in the pew, she stared down at the open page of the hymnal, trying to remember the tune, but it eluded her, one phrase seeming right while the next slipped away into some odd key. Behind her, she could feel the ancient prophets judging her with their burning eyes. Moses was considering crashing one of the stone tablets over her head.

If she went to the priest to confess — did Episcopal priests hear confessions? — if she told him that in saving Bertie she had lost her, if she told him that even now there were times she could barely lift her head from the weight of guilt she bore over Wallace's death, would he quote the words of this hymn to her?

Did we in our strength confide,
Our striving would be losing —
Were not the right Man on our side,
The Man of God's own choosing.

Bertie and Wallace were gone. In her striving, she had lost them, to herself and to each other. And for all Mabel knew, no mat-

ter how much she might hope otherwise —
that somehow Bertie had survived to have a
family of her own — she herself might be
the last there would ever be of the Fischer
girls, singly responsible for ending the line.

Yes, if she faced the priest, she would have
to admit how much her actions had cost
those she loved best — and the priest again
would nod and chastise her for having relied
on her own mind, her own strength.

But what of Daisy? she would ask. What of
Paul and Daisy and Barry and Jenny and
Nick and Ted — the family that had risen
from the ashes? Could she then, would she,
look into the priest's black eyes and quote
from the same hymn?

And though this world, with devils filled,
Should threaten to undo us;
We will not fear, for God hath willed
His truth to triumph through us.

One day, probably not so very long off,
she would know the answer to Jenny's question — whether there indeed was someone
or something beyond this world that would
hold her to account. And whether what she
had done would be judged as right or ruin.

She turned to look at Moses, raising her
eyes to meet his glare — an ancient assured

that every human choice was reducible to ten imperatives. Didn't he know that time eroded even stone? Behind her she could feel the gaze, less angry, of the angel in blue armor. Like Moses, he felt equally assured of truth, but he wasn't talking.

From overhead, bright warmth fell on her head, pouring over her hair and down her shoulders like fiery water, drawing out the cold. She lifted her face to it. Above her, in the dome, was a skylight, blazing now like the bright wheel of the sun, surrounded by stars. She hadn't noticed it before.

NINETEEN:
WORDS

April 1992
Newman, Indiana

BERTIE
Tuesday, 11:17 a.m.

The vacuum hose was clogged again. Bertie gave it an angry shake, even though she knew that would accomplish nothing. She'd have to get down on the floor to get the hose off and then use a bent hanger to push the clog through. Rainey would fuss when she got home, saying like she always did, "Mother, I've told you to leave those things to me," but if she left it to Rainey, it wouldn't get done for who knows how long and all that time the floor would still need sweeping.

In the kitchen, Bertie rooted through the junk drawer to find the screwdriver, the Phillips. As soon as her hand closed around it, she felt a sharp cold pain, then a tingle, shoot down her arm and into her fingers. She could see the screwdriver in her hand but couldn't feel it, and though it looked like she had a good grip on it, the tool tumbled back into the drawer. Then the room started shifting this way and that, and everything around her — the stove, the refrigerator, all the cabinets — seemed suddenly larger, then smaller, then changing places, with the stove now behind her and the refrigerator on her left, the cabinets sailing near the ceiling.

Another pain sliced through her head and she staggered to where she thought the table was. A faint sense of hard metal touched her palms. With what felt like all her strength, she pulled that metal down and toward her until, very distantly, she heard what might be the scrape of chair legs across the linoleum.

Sitting in a chair now, or at least believing she was, Bertie patted all around the table with her nearly senseless hands to find the thing she needed, the thing she suddenly couldn't name. When she found it, somehow she knew that part of the thing had to come near her face, and that, whether she could feel it or not, she had to press the glowing button that was first in line. From out of a deep hole came words, but she didn't know what they meant. "Accounting. Rainey Brandt."

"Rai-ee," Bertie said. "Rrr ai."

"Hello? Hello?"

Bertie tried again, but though she could feel her mouth working, no words came, only some thin, strained growl, like a dying animal. "Rrrry."

"Mother?"

Was that her name? Her name? Someone calling her name?

"Mother, what is it? Mother, can you hear me?"

"Rry . . . ey."

"I'm calling an ambulance," the voice said. "Mother, I'm on my way."

Tuesday, 5:45 p.m.

She could hear fine, so why was everyone around her yelling and banging pots together?

No, not pots. Not the echoing ring of pots that Lynn and Grace made on New Year's Eve when they ran out to the porch to pretend they were in the ballroom where Guy Lombardo's orchestra was playing "Auld Lang Syne."

No, not pots. But loud banging — so loud it made her nervous.

Until she opened her eyes, Bertie hadn't

realized they'd been closed. She looked around as best she could, but it was too dim to see what things were, and she couldn't quite work out how to turn her head. It was like one side of it was gone. Like one whole side of her body was gone. Maybe it was. Maybe she'd been in some crazy accident that would make the news, some accident that had cut her right in two. But that didn't make sense. She'd be dead.

Some of the noise was voices. Bertie closed her eyes to concentrate on them, to pick out what they were saying. The harder she tried to listen to the voices, the weaker they got and the stronger smells seemed. Nasty smells, like cloth soaked in old pee. Like flowery and fruity alcohol poured all around to cover the pee. There were other smells, too, but fainter, like rusty blood and rubber dusted with baby powder.

She knew those smells. Those and the odor of feet and damp armpits and green beans boiled in tin — the same smells that used to smack into her every day when Hans was dying, those months when Rainey would drop her off in the morning at the main door of the hospital.

To one side of her, the side that was still there, Bertie felt a warm grip on her arm and a soft, pleasant kiss on her forehead.

"Mother, can you hear me?"

Bertie opened her eyes again and looked for the voice. Rainey's face came into focus — tired, smudged with mascara, just a fleck of lipstick in one corner.

"Mother, you're in the hospital. In the emergency room. We're taking you up to your room as soon as it's ready."

Rainey — Rainey was her daughter. Rainey looked away, somewhere past where Bertie's feet should be. "You've had a stroke, Mother."

A stroke, Bertie said. *Did you come after me? Did you fix the sweeper?* Bertie said all this, but the only sound she heard come out of her twisted, half-dead mouth was "Toh."

Rainey's hand tightened on Bertie's arm. It hurt. "Mother, can you hear me?" Rainey said again. "Can you at least look at me?"

I am looking at you, Bertie said with irritation. *Stop squeezing my arm so hard.*

From the missing side of her, Bertie heard another voice — a woman's, loud, confident, flat. "It's too early still to tell if her speech will come back. Or any of the lost feeling. We'll know more tomorrow."

"Can she hear me?" Rainey asked the voice. "Her eyes are open."

"Probably not," the other voice said. "Maybe. It's impossible to say. But keep talking to her. You never know."

"Grandma?"

Bertie woke to a light pressure on her cheek that might have been a kiss. How strange it was, this feeling that was both faint and heavy, the way she imagined it must be for those lions she'd seen on television, after they'd been shot with tranquilizer darts — minds awake, bodies asleep.

Grace was leaning over the bed, wearing one of those funny necklaces she made back in the woods, where she lived with that good-for-nothing gray-headed man that wouldn't marry her. Bertie had thought the necklaces were pretty once, before she got up close. From across the room, they looked like crocheted gold. When she got closer, she saw they were nothing but tiny metal rings — each one no bigger around than a peppercorn, linked together.

"How you doing, Grandma?"

Such an easy way about her Grace always had, able to talk to her just the way she might if she'd come in for Sunday lunch.

Bertie knew now what had happened, or at least what the doctors were saying. She'd had a stroke. She'd lost feeling on one side

414

— but that was coming back. She'd lost her ability to speak, but so far that wasn't coming back. Nobody seemed to know if it would.

Rainey was about to drive her out of her mind, the way she talked really loud and slow — even though Bertie's hearing was fine. And the way Rainey talked to visitors, answering for her, so that after a minute whoever had come to see Bertie was visiting with Rainey. Rainey talked about her like she wasn't there, her voice high and nervous, the sound of tears way down in her throat, all the time pacing like a cat.

Grace's eyes were a little red around the rims, and when she turned just so, Bertie could see the last bit of a tear on one eyelash, but Grace smiled and talked on like Bertie was still Bertie, still Grandma.

"Now if you had to go and do this," Grace teased, "I sure appreciate your waiting until after that big storm that came through. The roads up my way were so icy, I would have had to come in on skates." Grace had pulled a chair all the way up and was resting her elbows on the bed. Nobody else would even have thought about bringing the chair so close. "And it's too early to get my garden in, so there's no worry there — well, the cabbage, the beets, and the carrots are already planted, but Ken can look after those all right. I'll bring you half a dozen jars of pickled beets when I get them put up. You like sauerkraut, don't you, Grandma? I've never tried making it, but I will if you like it."

Blech! Bertie said in her head.

Grace rocked back in her chair and laughed. "Well, I guess you told me!"

Barely, just barely, Bertie could feel her face sliding out of an expression of disgust and into a smile.

"It's Mom that likes sauerkraut, isn't it?" Grace leaned in again and stroked Bertie's cheek with one finger. "I don't suppose I could make it anyway. I can't stand the taste of it, so how would I ever know if it had turned out?"

"Yohg," Bertie said, feeling her face scrunch up again. How a person could eat that old sour stuff was beyond her. No way to tell when it went bad.

Grace gave Bertie's shoulder a playful shove. "You and yogurt."

"Is she talking to you?" Rainey appeared at the foot of the bed, a twisted Kleenex tight in one fist.

"We're doing okay," Grace said.

"So no talking yet."

"Has Lynn been in to see you, Grandma?"

While Grace watched Bertie for sign of an answer, Rainey snapped, "She has not."

"She's got an awful lot to do," Grace said. "Maybe she had to be in court today."

Her granddaughter's voice was calm, but tired. This was an old story — the trouble between Lynn and Rainey — going on since Lynn was in college. No, before that — since the trial, at least. More times than she could count, Bertie had said to Grace, "I wish there was some way to make your mother see she's the one who has to give up the fighting. She has to stop letting what's done and gone upset her so." Rainey would tell her, "I want loyalty. Just a little loyalty from my daughter. Is that too much to ask?" But Bertie knew it was. *Loyalty,* to Rainey, meant that Lynn would have to go back and unwalk roads she'd already walked.

Thursday, 6:20 a.m.
Bertie flailed her arms when the cold rush of the river splashed over her chest, up to her throat. Standing behind her, Mabel wound her arms tightly around her waist and clasped Bertie's hands in her own. *I'm here,* Mabel whispered in her ear. *I've got you. I've got you, Bertie. Just hold on to me.* Their friend Wallace waved from the riverbank. In church last Sunday, when Bertie

417

turned pale over the announcement that her baptism was scheduled for the next service, Wallace waited until all the people congratulating her had moved away and said, *Don't you worry, little gal.* He cupped her cheek in his hand and her heart popped with joy. *I'll be right there to dive in after you if you need me.* The preacher had come up just then, and Wallace's ears turned pink around the edges. *Reverend Small hasn't lost one yet,* he said, slipping away with a final grin at Bertie.

Wallace will save us, Bertie said to Mabel, who laughed and said, *Don't let the preacher hear you say that. He'll toss us out as blasphemers.*

Reverend Small talked on and on, his arm raised, blessing her, but Bertie paid no attention, concentrating on Mabel's beautiful hands that held hers, feeling Wallace keeping watch from the bank.

Here we go, Mabel whispered, and they were down under the water, the sun above them oozing like a burst yolk.

Come up now, Mabel said. "Come on now, Bertie. Come back to us. Come on. Attagirl."

Bertie shook the water from her hair and opened her eyes to a shadowed wall striped with sunlight. "You had us worried there," said a slim girl wearing a hospital-green top that was too big for her. Her shining dark hair was cut short — a bob, they called it. The girl absently stroked Bertie's arm while she looked at the machine beside the bed. "Better. Better. Looking better. Almost." Then the girl smiled across the bed at Grace, who was standing, arms tightly crossed, as if she were freezing, eyes terrified. "Crisis over," the girl said. "We just need to keep tabs on her." She patted Bertie's hand. "You're soaked through, honey. I'll get someone in here to bring you a clean gown and some dry sheets."

Grace disappeared for a moment and returned with a washcloth and a small basin of water. She soaked the cloth, wrung it out, and dabbed at Bertie's face. "Don't scare me like that, Grandma."

"You," Bertie said.

"I stayed the night." Grace rinsed the cloth and wrung it out again. "That was the only way to get Mom to go home."

"K." Bertie strained to listen to her own voice. She made an adjustment. "K?" she said, hearing the rise at the end she'd intended. "You? K?"

Grace wiped Bertie's throat with the cloth, careful not to get the bedclothes any wetter than they already were. "Don't worry about me," she said. "I'm fine."

Bertie looked her granddaughter straight in the eyes. With all her might, she managed the word, "Tell."

"Good job, Grandma. That's two real words. You'll be jabbering up a storm by tomorrow."

Bertie lifted one hand and folded it as well as she could to point a finger at Grace. "Tell. Me."

Grace put the cloth in the basin and pulled her chair beside the bed as she had yesterday. She always had to warm up to speaking, Grace did. Bertie knew the pattern — the eyes down, up, to the side, and down again; a hand at the back of her neck, then fingers lifting her hair and letting it drop; then the same hand sliding under her chin.

"I'm thinking about leaving Ken," she said.

Bertie had never made any secret of how she felt about Ken — a brooding son of a gun, not nearly good enough for Grace, took advantage of her sweetness — so she didn't try to say anything.

"He won't let me near him," Grace said. "You know. I mean inside."

Bertie raised her eyebrows as high as she could.

"Not that he ever really did." Grace gathered the edge of the blanket in her fingers and worked it in tiny circles. Fidgeting was another of her habits. "When we were first together — I mean when we first moved out to the country — he kept busy fixing up the house, plowing up the garden. But now he just holes up in the spare room or the shed, or he goes off alone into the woods. He's gone for days sometimes. Weeks." She laid her head for a moment on the bed beside Bertie and kissed the exposed skin on Bertie's arm. "When he drinks, it's not like when Grandpa would have too much."

"Leg," Bertie said, and Grace nodded. Hans's bad leg. Had she ever told him she understood about that? About how he had to drink because of the pain, which got worse as he got older. Bertie couldn't remember.

"Grandpa just got a little silly — you know, the way he'd sing that song he liked from *Hee Haw,* with all the groans? Ken gets . . ." Grace looked off toward the noises coming from the hall. "It's Vietnam," she said at last.

Grace stood up and went to the window, spreading the slats of the blind open with her fingers. "It's going to be a pretty day," she said. "Should I open these?" She opened them without looking at Bertie and then she came back to her chair, now lit with the sun.

"I'm just worn out with feeling useless, Grandma. Ken says I'm not. He says all the time that he needs me."

Bertie held out her hand. Grace took it and said, "I used to ask him to talk about the war, to help get it out of his head. He says he can't, says anybody who wasn't there can't understand. And of course he's right." Grace sat up straighter in her chair and massaged her throat — the way she always did to keep from crying. "It's not enough anymore," she said. "For me. It's like he was shot through, like he's a sieve. Nothing can ever fill him up again. I'm tired."

"So, what are you two talking about?" Alma came in and stopped at the foot of the bed. She was wearing a crisp lemon-colored suit, so bright it hurt Bertie's eyes. With her matching handbag, sprayed hair, prim makeup, and fragrance of roses, she could be on her way to meet the queen.

Grace stood up to accept Alma's touch-less hug and air kiss. "Did you stay at the house with Mom last night?" Grace asked.

"I left Ohio at three this morning," she

said. "I'd have come Tuesday, but your mother seemed to have everything under control, and Gordon had so many patients he needed to see."

"So Uncle Gordon's here."

"No, no," Alma said, coming to the side of the bed to pull Bertie's blankets up to her neck. Bertie tried to wiggle them down again with her shoulders, but Grace saw her struggle and folded them back to her waist. Alma turned away to find a place to lay her purse. "I couldn't say how long I'd have to be away, so Gordon thought he'd best stay home. He'll come, of course, if there's a real emergency."

That made Grace mad, Bertie could see, and with a small grunt, Bertie managed to stop her granddaughter from speaking her mind. Gordon wouldn't drive down from McAllister unless she died, which everybody in the family well knew. He hadn't come for years, not since his own mother had died, and that was just fine with Bertie.

"And Milton?"

That Grace: She had a way of still sounding polite while she sneered underneath.

"Oh, he's far too busy setting up his practice," said Alma, chatting away as if she were trying to best some other mother at a garden party. "And there's the house. He and Penny haven't really settled in yet." She came to the bed with a fine-tooth comb in her hand and started flicking at Bertie's hair. "He'll be glad to know you're doing so well, Mother."

Grace caught Alma's wrist. "The aides will be here in a minute to give Grandma a bath and change the bed. They'll wash her hair and see to the tangles," she said. "They're gentle."

Two nurses' aides appeared in the room, one carrying a bundle of linens and the other a plastic basin and a big sponge. "What do you say we make you more comfortable, Mrs. Jorgensen? Get you out of that sweaty gown and into some clean sheets?" Alma picked up her purse and said she would go downstairs for coffee.

Bertie squeezed Grace's hand as hard as she could, which wasn't hard at all, and when Grace began to pull her hand free, Bertie clutched at her fingers. "G . . . gace," she said. Grace stopped, leaned down, and kissed Bertie on the forehead. "I'm not leaving you. I'll be right outside the door."

Saturday, 5:15 p.m.
Bertie checked to make sure the cook wasn't watching, and she mounded up a double helping of mashed potatoes for

Wallace. She dipped up a ladle of gravy and poured it over the potatoes and the roast beef and put the bread on another plate, since he liked to keep his bread clean of gravy until he was ready to sop his plate with it. When Bertie pushed through the kitchen door into the dining area, she stopped.

Where were the wooden booths? Where was the counter with the cash register, and where was Doris, who never looked at people when she took their money? There was just one empty table beside the big window, which ought to have looked out on Main Street in Newman but instead gave a view of the Juniper train station, the Emmanuel Baptist Church, the high school — none of those places really close enough together to see all at once — and the barn with the doors open so she could just see Jim Butcher's dangling, black-shoed feet. Covering the whole wall between the window and the door was a photograph of Mabel dressed in white lace, sitting on a swing, her long dark hair draped around her shoulders.

Now the table was occupied, two nice-looking young men facing each other, playing cards. The thick-shouldered one with the dark blond hair, who had his back to her, twisted to see her and grinned. It was Wallace. When he turned again to the game, he moved just enough for Bertie to see it was Hans across from him. Hans looked at her too, like he did when they stepped out together to go to the pictures, eyes full of friendly hope.

Bertie stood beside the table between them, trying to follow the game. There were rules and plays she couldn't understand. When the men both folded their cards and stood to shake hands, she still didn't know who had won. Wallace turned to leave, and Bertie took his arm. He stopped, kissed her cheek with lips like cool water, and very gently unhooked her arm from his and placed it tenderly around Hans's waiting arm. Wallace vanished out the door, somewhere into Juniper, and though Bertie looked and looked through the window, she couldn't see him anywhere. Sorrow welled inside her, until she thought she would be drowned by it.

Then Hans took her in his arms and rocked her. Rocked her until all she could think of was how solid he was, how like a small warm house smelling of freshly sawn wood.

I love you, she said. But she didn't say it. It was only in her mind. She tried again and again because she wanted him to know, but her voice wouldn't obey her. Still Hans rocked her, but she could feel him vanishing, as Wallace had vanished before him. She struggled to speak. She had to say the words so he could hear them before he disappeared.

Bertie clenched her fists, concentrated and clenched every muscle in her body to help push the words out. "Ove you."

"She's waking up," a woman's voice said.

"She's just talking in her sleep," said another woman's voice, tight and sour.

"I love you, too, Gran," said the first voice. "I think you're right. She must be dreaming."

"Well," said the bitter second voice. "At least you give me credit for a little sense."

Hans was gone now, along with the window, the table, and Mabel. Bertie tried to pull herself from the darkness, toward the voices.

"Why did you come? Just tell me that."

"Because I wanted to see Grandma."

"Oh, yes. You think she might die, you come for a day." The bitter voice was Rainey's.

"I would have come sooner, Mother, but you told me yesterday morning she was getting better."

"That's my point. Your grandmother gets a little better, starts talking again, and you decide to stay put. That asshole has a bellyache, you move him in with you."

"It was cancer," Lynn said. "Daddy's been dead for almost two years."

"Well, all I know is, you'd never come for me. No more than two hours away, but it's years. Years, and you haven't been back here to see me — just to see me — even once. There's always some other excuse, to see your grandmother or to go to a reunion — never just to visit your mother. You're only here now because of her. You'd never think about how maybe I need you here to help me."

Bertie could hear Lynn's voice knotting up. "I have to work, Mother. Grace and Aunt Alma are here. What more do you want? I can't just walk out on my clients. Really, you don't have any concept of how busy I am."

Bertie couldn't quite see clearly, but she could see the back-and-forth, back-and-forth movement by the window. Rainey was pacing. "Oh, well, how *could* I? What do I know about the life of a lawyer? You've always thought I was an idiot."

"I never said that."

"I'd just like a little respect for once."

Lynn was angry now. "And you don't think I would? Do you ever put yourself in my shoes, think about what it was like for me trying to explain to my friends that my own mother wouldn't come to my law school graduation?"

"That was your doing, not mine." Rainey was crying. "I wanted to be there. But I was not going to sit in the same room with that —"

"It's been thirty years, for God's sake. More than that! Whatever you think he did to you, can't you just drop it?"

For a moment there was silence, broken only by the sound of pacing and angry, exhausted breaths.

"Besides," Lynn said, "why the hell shouldn't Daddy have been there?"

Rainey's voice was oily black. "One has to pay the piper, I suppose."

"So what are you saying? You'd rather I be like Grace — no education, stuck in a shack in the woods with some nut, scraping a living from making goat cheese and chain mail?"

"Well, Grace didn't have a father to pay all the bills for her."

"And whose fault is that, Mother?"

"Nnno!" Bertie couldn't let this go on. *Stop,* she wanted to say. *Forgive. Forgive.*

But all she could manage was "Gv."

Lynn was at her side now and Rainey at the foot of the bed. "Grandma, what is it? What do you need?"

"Gv," Bertie said again, suddenly in fury at her own body for paralyzing her this way.

"She doesn't know what she's saying," Rainey said. "This has happened before. You haven't been here to see it."

"Liuh."

Bertie felt Lynn's touch on her shoulder. "Yes, we love you, too," Lynn said.

"Liuh. Riah." Bertie shook her head in frustration.

"I think she wants to ring for the nurse," Rainey said, coming now to the other side of the bed and pressing the call button.

Bertie groped in the air, trying to catch at Lynn's hand. Oh, where was Grace? Grace would make them understand. "Gace," she said.

At last, Lynn's hand closed over hers. But when Bertie tried to pull Lynn's hand toward Rainey's, Lynn released her grip and Bertie groped the air again.

"Her face is getting all red," Lynn said. "Where's that nurse?" She reached across the bed and pressed the call button.

Bertie waved both her hands now, trying hard to make them move toward each other, as a signal to Lynn and Rainey, but the hands moved by some wild design of their own that had nothing to do with her will.

"Mother, try to calm down," Rainey said. She was staring anxiously at the machine beside the bed. "Please, try to calm down."

"Yyou," Bertie said. The ceiling pressed down on her chest and she was being pushed deeper into the bed, through the mattress, down and down and down.

"Yy . . . gv." She was crying now, dry tears deep inside. Lynn and Rainey still stood beside her, but she was vanishing like Wallace, like Hans, like Mabel.

Somewhere far above her, a small red light pulsed, and there was a wailing sound, like a high, long scream, holding and holding and holding on the air, but all the time fainter until it was so faint it was only the memory of sound.

TWENTY:
ACCOUNTING

Late Winter 1994
Cincinnati, Ohio

ALMA

February

Once again, a figure appeared in the waiting room door, and Alma put down her magazine to look up in hope, but it wasn't Milton. This time it was another young man, twenty-five at most, wearing a faded yellow hospital smock that had been pulled on hastily over his bloodred T-shirt. His face shining with sweat, he stood speechless until a middle-aged couple noticed him and leapt up, crying in unison, "Boy or girl?" Tangled in an embrace, they all three managed to wedge back through the door to scurry off down the hall, laughing and crying.

For the first time since her 4:00 A.M. arrival, Alma was alone in the waiting room. Milton had called them in McAllister a little before one o'clock to say Penny had gone into labor, three weeks early, and that they were on their way to the hospital. "Meet me there," her son had said, and she'd started flinging clothes into her suitcase while Gordon was still trying to wake up enough to grasp the news.

"It's probably a false alarm," Gordon said. "I'm not driving two and a half hours to Cincinnati in the middle of the night for a false alarm. They'll have sent her back home before you get there." He rolled toward the wall, pulling the blankets over his shoulder. "What do they need you for anyway?"

"You go back to sleep," Alma said. She was too happy to try to reason him into happiness. A baby! Her grandchild. "I'll call you when I get there."

"It's over." Milton now stood in the waiting room door. His voice was dry. "A girl."

"Milton!" Alma went to him, lifting her arms to wrap around his neck, but then she thought better of it. Her son had never liked being hugged. With a quick, light touch on his arm, she said, "A girl — how wonderful!"

Nervously, Alma waited for Milton to smile and give her more details, but he did neither. How tired he looked.

"Son?" she said at last. "The baby — she's

all right? Isn't she?"

"Oh, fine," Milton said, and Alma breathed again.

"What are you calling her, dear?"

Milton picked up Alma's coat and purse and handed them to her. "Sarah, I think. That's the one Penny picked."

Alma flushed, embarrassed by her forgetfulness. "Oh, Milton, I'm sorry. How is Penny? Let's go to her."

"She's asleep," he said. He reached into his pocket and pulled out his keys. "I'll get my coat and we can go. You can follow me to the house."

"But, Milton . . ." So many words rose up, demanding to be said, that Alma couldn't get hold of any of them. He wanted to leave now? He wasn't going to stay the night with Penny? What about the baby?

Milton returned his keys to his pocket and sighed. "I guess you want to see her. Well, come on, then."

He led Alma down the hall, through several turnings, and down other halls, but finally she saw the windowed wall of the nursery and pushed ahead of her son. "Where is she? Oh, where is she?" Alma scanned the rows of little cribs, each with its tiny swaddled bundle, and then at last —
Baby Girl Crisp — a little redder than the

others, being the newest, with just a few wisps of silky hair. Alma pressed her hands to the glass and leaned in, steaming the window with her whispered declarations of love.

"Are you a grandmother?"

Startled, Alma looked up to see one of the maternity nurses leaning out the door.

"Is this your mother, Dr. Crisp?" asked the nurse. "Well, we can bend the rules for her." She motioned for Alma to follow.

A moment later, Alma was covered in a smock and being led by the nurse through another door into the nursery.

"She's a little small," the nurse said, bending into the crib, "but not bad for a preemie. She'll be able to go home when her mother does."

And then the baby was in Alma's arms. "Sarah," she said, more tenderly than she had ever said anything. "Sweet, sweet baby." She caressed her granddaughter's velvety little head with her cheek, wet from tears she couldn't stop — tears she never wanted to stop. From somewhere inside her, a tune rose, and even as she began to hum it, thinking, *Sarah, Sarah,* she tried to recall what it was. A lullaby? No — an old song from the radio. "Blue Moon." Something Daddy used to sing. As she hummed it through, the story of the song nudged up to her through the melody — and suddenly she knew that, until this moment, she had been that person, longing beneath that lonely moon, waiting for the love of her heart.

Alma sang softly on. She no longer noticed the lights, the low talk of the nurses, or the cries of another baby just waking. There was nothing in the world except this child in her arms. She gazed into the tiny face, dancing her darling in dips and sways, the two of them, together, under the blue-black sky, bathed in the brilliance of the newly golden moon.

Safely wound in her blankets, Sarah stirred like a leaf in a breeze, and Alma kissed her once, twice, three times.

So this is what a soul feels like, Alma thought — weightless but solid, a mystery that could warm beyond its warmth. Here was love that expanded. Love that multiplied, past measure.

March

It had surprised Alma — surprised her, but also made her proud — that Milton wanted to go right back into the office the day after Sarah's birth. "I have patients scheduled," he said. "If I cancel them, I'll have to double-book for the rest of the week."

"Of course, dear." Alma poured him another cup of coffee. "I understand. Your father never liked to let his patients down, either. I'll go to the hospital to help Penny."

"I want you to come to the office with me," Milton said. "Judy can't check everyone in and do all the triage, too. You can go pick them up at the hospital after work, if it pleases you."

Much as Alma had longed to return to the nursery — to hold little Sarah, to rock her and tell her of all the things they would one day do together — she was touched by her son's need of her. Not that *need* was a word he had ever been able to say to anyone. Naturally, it was too short notice for him to hire a temporary replacement that first day, but he made no mention of it for the next day or even the next week. It was his way of showing Alma he trusted her. Like Gordon, Milton had always been strong, in control, incapable of showing vulnerability. It would have been unfeeling of her to press for explanations at that moment, when everything about his life was changing.

Though still it tore at her when she had to leave baby Sarah behind each morning, now, nearly five weeks after she'd arrived in Cincinnati, Alma had to admit she enjoyed replacing Penny as Milton's office manager.

In all his years of practice, Gordon had never asked her to tend his office for him, not even for the short while between one girl quitting and another hiring on — sometimes as many as four or five in one year.

That first day, as Milton showed her around the front office, she'd found herself growing excited about her new responsibilities.

"The patients' medical files are organized by last name in the green filing cabinets, and," Milton said, tapping a few keys on the computer, "in the files here, on the hard drive." He pointed to a set of low black cabinets with double-width drawers beneath the window. "The insurance records are in there, filed in numerical order by the patients' Social Security numbers. You won't need to bother with those. Penny will catch up on all that when she's back full-time."

He plucked three black pens from a cup on the desk and fixed them in his jacket pocket. "All you have to do is check the sign-in list when someone comes in, pull the patient files, and leave them on this ledge for Judy. She'll do the rest. If I've asked the patient to schedule another appointment, Judy will tell you that. There's no reason for you even to open the folders."

"What about billing?" Alma asked.

Milton shook his head. "When Judy hands the folders back to you, put them here." He lifted a portable file case from the top of the nearest green filing cabinet. "I'll take them home to Penny. She'll transcribe my notes, put everything on disk, and on Saturday, you can stay home with Sarah while Penny and I come in to transfer the files and do the billing."

Alma had never been happier, but Gordon was furious with the arrangement, especially after Milton told his father over the phone that it wasn't worth hiring someone else, since Penny might decide anytime she was ready to go back to work. "He wants to talk to you," Milton said, handing Alma the phone. When Gordon had blown out the worst of his fury, she did her best to explain to him how to do the laundry and prepare simple meals for himself. Ten days later, he showed up at Milton's, grumbling that he had run through all his clean clothes and swearing he would never eat another frozen lasagna. Once he settled in, though, it wasn't any more difficult to tend to Gordon than it would have been at home, and Alma simply set about establishing a pattern for their blended household.

In the mornings, she got up first, lightly

bouncing Sarah in her arms while the bottle of formula warmed on the stove. Then Alma would make the coffee, wake the others, and start breakfast. When she'd finished loading the dishwasher, she would go and get dressed for the office, check Sarah's diaper, and sit with her for a few moments in the rocker before handing her off to Penny, who seemed to appreciate the orderliness of the schedule, taking the baby into her arms with mechanical efficiency.

When Sarah woke in the night, Alma — remembering how exhausted she had felt as a new mother — would slip carefully out of bed so as not to disturb Gordon, stop outside Milton and Penny's closed bedroom door, and say quietly, "I'll see to her. You two need your rest."

After work, she'd do the grocery shopping, then come home to cook dinner, cleaning up the kitchen afterwards while the others relaxed in front of the television. More often than not, Sarah lay in her carrier, cooing and blowing bubbles, perched safely in the center of the table while Alma put away the dishes.

How strong she felt — *invigorated.* Back in McAllister, she had always been exhausted by seven or eight o'clock and struggled to stay awake until ten so she'd sleep through the night. Now sometimes she didn't lie down until past midnight, and even if she'd been up with Sarah two or three times, she would wake again at five thirty, perfectly refreshed.

"You look younger every time I see you, sweetie."

Alma looked up to see Mr. Radford, who came in once a week to have his hemoglobin and his blood pressure checked. He was eighty-seven and was dropped off by the downtown shuttle from the Senior Center, where he spent the days while his grandson was at work.

"I'll tell Judy you're here, Mr. Radford," Alma said, starting up from her chair.

"No, no," he said, laying a bundle of papers on the counter, frayed from having been folded small enough to fit his back pocket. Alma now remembered it wasn't Mr. Radford's usual day.

"I need you to look over these papers for me," Mr. Radford said. "Gladys says she thinks they're not right." Gladys, Alma knew, was Gladys Bishop, a friend of Mr. Radford's from the center and another of Milton's weekly patients. Mrs. Bishop had to watch her blood sugar.

Mr. Radford unfolded the papers and smoothed out the creases with his fist. "It's the insurance has made the mistake, but they won't talk to me about it — just treat me like some old fool that doesn't know what's what." When he grinned, Alma caught a flash of the gold crown he'd shown her once to prove that his teeth might not be what they'd been when he was twenty, but they were all still his own.

Mr. Radford reached through the window to hand the papers to Alma. "You tell them you're calling from the doctor's office, and they'll listen to you," he said.

Alma adjusted her glasses and tried to make sense of the claims report. Separated into columns were codes that corresponded on the back to various procedures. In the next column was listed the doctor's charge, followed by how much of the charge the insurance would pay, followed by the difference owed by the patient. The amount owing after insurance for each procedure seemed awfully high — anywhere from $30 to $150 — and Alma started to speak. Seeming to read her thoughts, Mr. Radford said, "It's not that last bit I'm worried about, where it says I owe the doctor. Dr. Crisp has been awful good to me — to Gladys, too. Well, to all of us down at the center. He's always said he'll take only what the insurance pays, never has asked a one of us for a penny. Can't ask for better than that."

"Yes," Alma said. "Milton's a good and kind boy."

"It's all those numbers at the start," Mr. Radford said. "They make it kind of hard to understand, the way they just use the numbers and put all the words in that doctor's language on the back page in that ink you can't hardly see." Alma turned over the page and saw the details corresponding to the codes written in type so small, in such ghostly gray ink, that even she had trouble reading it.

Mr. Radford went on: "Then Gladys had the idea that I bring in one of my other statements — seems like I get three or four a month — and I read off the numbers while she checked them against what it says on the back the charge is for."

"It's always handy to have a second pair of eyes," said Alma. "What's the trouble, do you think?"

"It's the charges," Mr. Radford said. "I don't know what those insurance people are up to. Probably just not paying attention." He shifted from one foot to the other and then back again. "You know I come in here every week so Judy can stick me to make sure my blood's still red enough."

"Yes." Alma nodded. "The hemoglobin count."

"And then she blows me up with that cuff of hers."

Alma flipped the paper over again and quickly identified the codes for those two procedures. Each code was listed twice, followed by different dates corresponding to two consecutive weeks in January, before she had come to help. She opened the appointment book and noted that Mr. Radford had been scheduled those days, and had come in. With a pencil, Alma made a light check mark for each code she could identify, but two other codes, also each listed twice, with different dates, remained. She checked these dates in the appointment book and couldn't find Mr. Radford's name.

"You always come on Wednesday, Mr. Radford. Isn't that right?"

"I do. So what I want to know is why they've charged me for a couple of Fridays."

Alma checked the codes again. According to the claims statement, Milton had been paid for two cholesterol screenings and two regular office examinations. "Doesn't Judy always do your blood tests?" Alma asked.

"She does."

"Do you remember if you saw Dr. Crisp for anything else last month? I don't have you in the book, but maybe he worked you in?"

Mr. Radford shook his head. "Last time I was in for anything but the blood was about a week after Thanksgiving," he said. "My grandson had all the family down — did I tell you I have five great-grandchildren so far? There was a lot of commotion — you can understand — and I ate some things I shouldn't and didn't sleep so well, so it wasn't any wonder I picked up a nasty chest cold from one of the kids. I saw the doctor for that, but nothing else since. My hemoglobin's been so good, I haven't had to go for a transfusion since last summer."

Just to be sure, Alma studied all the codes and dates once more. "I expect they've confused your records with someone else's, or maybe Penny accidentally billed you for another patient's procedures," she said. "Having a baby can make a woman's mind awfully fuzzy."

Mr. Radford laughed at that and told her a story about how his wife, after their first baby was born, kept putting stamps on letters without ever addressing them.

Alma looked at the statements again, wishing she knew more about how the insurance was filed so she could figure out what had happened. She hated to burden Milton and

Penny with it. Last Saturday, when Penny woke up with a headache and told Milton she thought the billing could wait another week, he'd taken her back to the bedroom, where they had argued in loud whispers for nearly an hour. It would help ease so much anxiety for them if Alma could solve this problem.

"I thought about showing these to my grandson," Mr. Radford said, "but I don't like him thinking I can't handle my own business. Peter has his own trucking company. He's used to dealing with papers and red tape and such."

"Oh, I don't think we need to bother him just yet," she said. "You leave this with me." Alma refolded the pages and tucked them into her purse. "I'll get to the bottom of it."

Later that afternoon, after Judy had left and Milton was pulling on his overcoat, Alma said, "I have a few things to finish up, dear — four or five reminder calls to people scheduled for tomorrow. And then I have some errands to run."

Milton stared at her.

"Don't worry," Alma teased. "Dinner's all ready. There's beef stew in the Crock-Pot, so all you have to do is heat up some rolls if you want them. They're in the freezer. Penny can manage those."

"It's getting dark out," Milton said. "I'll wait for you."

Alma blushed at his concern. She squeezed his hand. "Really, dear, it's all right. I'm a big girl." When her son hesitated, she added, "Yes, I know how to reset the alarm when I leave." She bumped his shoulder playfully. "You go on. I know you're tired."

Milton stood in his place for another moment, his fingers clutching a button of his coat, but at last, without another word, he left, pulling the outside door hard behind him.

Alma took Mr. Radford's statements from her purse and opened the appointment book to the first date when he was mistakenly charged for the cholesterol screening. It took a few minutes to pull the patient files for the people listed that day, but now they all lay before her. One by one, she opened the folders, looking for some evidence that someone else on the same day had come in to have a cholesterol check. This was more difficult than she had expected, because, in spite of Milton's notes having been transcribed to typed pages, the procedures were shortened to four-digit billing codes — in most cases, three, four, or five codes for each patient. Several of the records showed the code for cholesterol tests, but there was no surprise in that. Old people had to watch their cholesterol.

Alma took Mr. Radford's folder from the bottom of the pile and opened it. The only way to do this, she decided, was to be methodical and look at least briefly at every sheet of paper. The first several sheets, which she laid aside one by one, were Penny's typed notes. Then came a photocopy of Mr. Radford's insurance card — he was one of the lucky ones from the Senior Center who didn't have to rely on Medicare. He'd worked for the railroad for nearly fifty years, and they still paid for his coverage. Behind that was his original patient record, filled out during his first visit. Alma noticed the date, just a few weeks after Milton had opened the practice.

Next, gathered with a binder clip, were the forms Judy and Milton used for their notes during the patient's visit. At the top of each, Mr. Radford's name was scribbled in Judy's handwriting. Most of the notes were Judy's, but Alma did find Milton's notes from the early-December visit Mr. Radford had mentioned. They were hard to read, but when Alma got the hang of it, nothing seemed amiss. She wasn't going to find the answer this way, she decided, so she carefully tapped the pages back in place and fastened the clip.

Alma gathered the loose sheets she'd set aside and was just about to place them back in the folder when she caught a glimpse of writing in the lower left corner of a notes page. She pulled the stack out again to look — a pair of four-digit numbers written in fine black ink, followed by a plus sign and another single digit. She lifted the first page to see the second, and there was one number marked in the same space. On the next there were three, and on the one after that, two again, then one. Every page of notes had codes listed in the lower corners.

Surely they were the codes for the procedures listed in the notes. Of course they were — to make things quicker for Penny in transcribing and billing. To prove it to herself, Alma reached for Mr. Radford's claims statement. By now, she knew the dates by heart, so she found the pages of notes for Mr. Radford's January visits. Just one for each of the weeks, as she expected. On the claims statement, she had checked off the code for hemoglobin testing — 7418, and the one for the pressure check — 6100. The numbers in the lower left were 8146 +2 and 2002 +2. She didn't understand the +2, but the four-digit numbers were the codes for a cholesterol check and a regular office exam. Alma looked again at Penny's transcriptions. For the January dates, all four codes appeared in the narratives as services performed.

Sweat beaded along Alma's nose and at the nape of her neck. She closed Mr. Radford's folder and chose another randomly from the pile she had made. The papers were in the same order, multiple codes listed in every transcription. And in the lower left corner of every page of working notes, more black ink codes, followed by a $+2$ or $+4$, sometimes even a $+7$, were jotted in a small but legible hand. Judy's numbers were large, sloppy, with twos that looked like sevens and fours that might be nines. Always in bright blue ink.

Alma pulled another file, then another.

It couldn't be.

There had to be some terrible mistake, some reason other than the one that was in her mind.

Patient after patient, page after page, codes for every test that could be performed in the office, ordinary procedures that were common for elderly people — flu shots, pneumonia vaccines, allergy treatments, stress tests, EKGs, X-rays, heart monitors, and every possible blood test — tortured

Alma from those lower left corners.

The plus signs added days — days between the patient's actual appointment and the invented ones. She saw that now. Code upon code upon code for procedures never performed, visits never made.

Every one of them written in fine black ink by her son's hand.

Alma slapped the folder shut and pushed it away from her. Her face burned, as if she'd been struck. A great pain pounded in her chest and poured out as she wept.

"Sarah . . . oh, *Sarah,*" she cried.

At the sound of her granddaughter's name, Alma quieted. She saw exactly what she must do.

First, she dried her eyes. Then, she took Mr. Radford's insurance statements and folded them again inside her purse. Tomorrow, she would give them back to him, saying how sorry she was that she couldn't help him. *Penny will have to see to them,* she would tell him. *But in the meantime, perhaps you would feel better letting your grandson have a look?*

Next, Alma restored the pages in the files to perfect order and returned the folders to the cabinet, making sure each settled in again as if it had never been removed.

She would drive back to Milton's house,

and, after dinner, after putting Sarah to bed, Alma would find a moment to speak with Penny. She would remark, casually, that Penny seemed bored at home — and no doubt Penny would confirm this, so Alma would quickly suggest that, in a few days perhaps, she and Penny could begin to split hours at the office, and by the middle of next week, Penny could take over again and Alma could stay home with the baby. If Penny balked at all, Alma would mention Mr. Radford, describing his concerns in a clumsy but pleasant way.

Then, if she had to, she would go further and show Penny the statements, remarking on how she had tried her best to help Mr. Radford but had quickly discovered the problem was well beyond her. "I'm afraid it's up to the young people now," she would say, mentioning Mr. Radford's grandson. If necessary.

It might take ten days, perhaps two weeks, before she could muse aloud about taking Sarah back with her to McAllister — just for a little while. Just until Milton and Penny were settled again in their routine — that's what she would say. Gordon would be so glad to go home he wouldn't argue about taking the baby.

Milton and Penny wouldn't protest at all

— they wouldn't even pretend. Though it froze Alma's blood to think of it, this was the one thing she was surest of.

Only two weeks of careful stepping — three at the most. What was that after a lifetime of practice?

Let come whatever end must come for the wrongs Milton and Penny had done. Nothing mattered but Sarah. Nothing. Not Milton or his practice. Not Gordon. Not anyone here or in McAllister. No one but Sarah — her Sarah, whom Alma would keep safe, bound forever in her arms.

TWENTY-ONE:
ARMORER

April 1995
Pilgrim's End, Indiana

GRACE

"Where do you buy all these tiny links?"

It was the question Grace got most often at art fairs, and, when answered, was usually followed with an incredulous "You *make* them?"

The woman asking the question now was a type Grace recognized, an expensively dressed weekend crafter up from Greenwood who trolled all the booths at fairs, looking for ideas she could knock off and sell in some little shop her husband had set up for her in the children's abandoned playhouse.

Grace pointed to the mandrels in plain sight in front of her, explaining these were two of the half dozen she'd made herself with blocks of wood, clamps and old hand drills, or variously sized iron rods heated and bent to form cranking handles. On one, she'd left a fine gold wire partly coiled. Guiding the wire with one hand, Grace turned the crank slowly so the woman could see four new links take shape. *Not so difficult,* she imagined the woman thinking, which was why Grace was glad she'd set up the second mandrel with a finished coil of heavy-gauge bronze. She tapped cutting nicks with her chisel and then showed the woman another bronze coil she'd already nicked and released from the mandrel. Grace stretched the coil slightly open, then snipped off a dozen rings. She offered the snips to the woman, who grasped the tool confidently, but even with the strength of both hands, she had trouble cutting a single link.

Grace took the snips back and quickly cut the rest of the coil. Then she set one ring in the mouth of her pliers and, with a second pair of pliers, showed how to butt the ends together to close the ring. "When I'm doing mail armor," she said, "I solder them."

She worked until she had a tiny pile of closed rings, which she then began joining to open rings in a complex variation on a King's Chain. She could have demonstrated with an easy four-in-one, but she didn't like

these dabblers who called themselves arti-
sans. In a few minutes, she had a slender
bronze cocoon, which she laid across her
fingertip and held out to the woman. "It's
an awful lot of work for what you get," the
woman said before stepping off to the next
booth to try to figure out, Grace supposed,
whether there might be a shortcut to making raku pottery.

She wished now she'd brought the hauberk with her. The men especially liked to try
on the shirt of mail, but no one ever offered
to buy it, and it took up too much display
space. It was the jewelry that sold, the
jewelry and the mesh evening bags that
would make it possible for her and Ken to
fix the roof, put tires on the truck, and keep
Pilot in grain and hay if the summer turned
out to be dry.

Grace opened the box of bronze links
she'd cut last night and spread the strip of
mail cloth on the table in front of her. She
was making the coif with Ken in mind, just
as she had made the hauberk and the
chausses, hoping he'd finally let her gird
him with her armor, but he would refuse
even to try the coif on, just as he had the
other pieces, and Grace would have to snip
apart the finished head covering and make
it larger so more average-size men at craft

fairs could pretend to be knights for five minutes.

Mail was what she and Ken argued about most. He didn't mind her making the jewelry, like glistening lace. But the armor — he wouldn't hear her reasons for that, not that she'd ever managed to express them very well. When she offered him the mail shirt, he burned a hole in her the same as if she'd tried to force an M16 into his arms.

She stumbled to explain. "It's beautiful," she said. "Mail tells us who we are. How vulnerable life is. How precious." But he pushed away from her, not even trying to understand what she meant.

Grace thought of mail like she thought of her POW bracelet, like she thought of wedding rings — her own wedding ring. They weren't guarantees against the treachery of life; nor were they talismans with the power to prevent any breach. The bracelet, the ring, the mail were only commitments to hope, to what might be — full of longing, with best intentions.

Grace had tried again to tell Ken this morning while he packed his rucksack with water, cheese, and the flatbread she'd made last night. She tried while he saddled up Pilot, tried to tell him all she wanted was to wrap everyone she loved in mail made just for them — Ken, Pilot, the cats, the goats, and Charlemagne, now stretched dozing at her feet, one magnificent ear pricked up to catch any sign of danger. Grace would wrap up Mother, who wouldn't understand any better than Ken did. And if Grandma were here, Grace would make special mail for her, too — the strongest, with tiny riveted rings, so tightly woven no arrow could pierce.

Millions of years of human life, and still there was no more arduous battle than crossing the border into someone else's heart. Or to stand aside and wave him across your own. Maybe it wasn't possible to know another person, not entirely. Maybe it wasn't possible to do more than show the desire to know, offering some sort of symbol, creating a touchstone.

Or perhaps the struggle was only in her own family. They had all been raised up on secrets — things never expressed but linked through time to all the other members. Though Grace was sure she didn't know her sister at all — knew her less than anyone else, in spite of the shared events of their childhood — she sometimes wanted to gird Lynn, too, against the tangled secrets and what they had wrought. Grace yearned to believe Lynn was more than she appeared — a woman obsessed with money and public attention — but she suspected that a lot of her sister's causes were driven by the thrill of being on the local news or the subject of a front-page article. Still, there must be something else, something deeper that had made Lynn give her first dollar to Amnesty International, something besides a photo op that made her raise her first picket sign.

Mother was nearly as much of a stranger, making allusions to dreams she'd once had without ever saying what they were. What was it, Grace longed to know, that made her mother so perpetually unhappy, always looking at the rest of them as if they'd done something to betray her? Ken had that look sometimes, too, oftener every year since she had moved with him to Pilgrim's End. She didn't know him, either, after all their years together, but at least she understood, or thought she understood, why she never would.

He'd told her in fragments about Vietnam — the constant feeling of slime and filth from the heat; the way you learned, the very first day, to tense at the snap of a twig or the rustle of grass; the way you had to get close to the men in your unit and then had to forget that closeness in a second if the guy stepped on a mine in front of you. The way, after the explosion, you were ready to burn everything in sight, blow up anybody who got between you and your pain. He'd learned all this, he said, and much more, in less than three weeks in the bush.

Then, on his twentieth day, he was captured by the Vietcong and he began to learn how to be a prisoner of war. The only thing he'd ever told her about those fifty-seven months — 1,739 days — was the time when four jailers held one of the other prisoners down on a rough-cut table while another guy with a knife sliced into the prisoner's belly to extract his appendix. The screaming was something he'd never forget, Ken said, and Grace wondered what worse must have happened to him if this was the thing he could manage to tell.

Of all the people Grace had ever loved, it was Grandma Bertie she'd known best, but that knowing had come so late, in the one lucid day she had before the second stroke. They had all been so hopeful. Grandma had awakened the Friday morning after the first stroke, talking normally and asking for some breakfast. Mother called Lynn, and though she was angry when her elder daughter said she would delay her visit for another day,

Mother had felt easy enough to go on to work when Grace said she would stay.

For a long time that day, she and Grandma had talked about nothing, the way people do — the fact that the eggs weren't hot and needed salt; the way the nurse with the red hair bossed all the others; whether or not the weatherman would be right in his prediction that it would snow overnight. And then Grandma had asked about Ken, and Grace had said, as she had the day before, that she was thinking of leaving him.

"It's because he won't marry you," Grandma said.

"No, that's not it at all. It's the other way around. Whenever I say anything about leaving, he tries to talk me into getting married." Grace could see this upset her grandmother, so she clarified. "I'm not against marriage," she said. "But he only asks me when he thinks I'm about to walk out. I love him. I do."

And she did. Grace knew she did. Hard as it was to really recognize what was love and what wasn't, she knew she loved Ken because any time she tried even to think maybe she didn't, every hair on her body stood up in protest. She reached out for Bertie's hand. The grip was strong. "I just feel sad when I'm with him — just a little sad, like you do when it's rained all day. And then when he goes off into the woods — he stays sometimes for a week, ten days — I feel better. Happier. Even though I miss him."

She did not tell her grandmother then what remained true even now: that she and Ken still — after twelve, thirteen years together — made love with more intensity than in their first weeks, as if somehow their bodies believed that the only answer to anything lay in the other's flesh. They clung to each other all night, but in the morning, they untangled their limbs without looking the other in the eye, and if they hadn't been arguing the day before, they went about their chores, talking quietly, but only when necessary. When they were angry, there was little difference: In the glow of the oil lamp, they still kissed and clawed hungrily, still wound themselves together in the darkness, still separated in the morning, talking a little less than usual, a little more coolly.

There was a brief commotion in the hallway outside Grandma's room, with men and women rushing past with carts and IV bags, calling out codes. "Somebody's in trouble," Grandma said, squeezing Grace's hand and looking into the hall, where the people had been. She said, "It tore your

Grandpa up awful bad when they wouldn't take him for the war — on account of his leg. I told him he didn't have any business trying to sign up at his age — I guess he was about forty then, maybe a little older — but he said every man had to do his part. I said to him, 'What about these children? You mean to tell me you're going off and leaving me with these children?' and he said, 'There's lots of other men with children going over. For their children.' When he got back home, after they'd turned him away, I was glad. But I wish now I hadn't acted so much like I was. It put something up between us that never did pass."

"But it's different with Ken, Grandma. He was drafted."

"Let me finish." Her grandmother gestured toward the plastic water pitcher on the table beside the bed. Grace poured her a cup. She drank it all and held the cup out for a refill. "There was a boy that lived a few doors down the street," she said. "He went off to the war like he was going to a party. He came back and wasn't never the same. Wouldn't talk to anybody, hardly ever poked his nose outside the house, couldn't work."

"But you hear that kind of thing all the time," Grace said impatiently. Grandma was missing the point about Ken. "It's how we've been taught to think about Vietnam vets — all those reports about the drug abuse, Agent Orange, all those analysts looking for a way to explain why some guy shoots his family, thinking they're the enemy. Nobody ever talks about the ones who came home just fine, got on with things. There must be thousands of them. Everybody just points backward at an old cliché that doesn't really mean anything. Of course war changes people — everything does. You can't blame everything on the war."

"That's not what I'm saying, girl." Grandma drank the rest of her water and settled back against the pillows. "Not what I'm saying." She closed her eyes, as if trying to see the words ready before her. "Your grandpa, that boy down the road, that gray-headed man of yours, and Jim Butcher, I'm pretty sure —"

"Who? Who'd you say?"

"My stepdaddy."

Grace struggled to remember if her grandmother had ever mentioned this man.

"My daddy was about to get sent over to France, but then he died of that bad flu that was everywhere. I was too little to remember, but Mama kept the telegram. Seems like she told us just before she married him that he'd been over there, too — Jim Butcher, I mean. In the war." Bertie shook her head as if to clear it. "I think sometimes about how maybe that was what made him so mean — or maybe just meaner. I don't know. What I'm saying . . . it's not just wars — and maybe not the things that go on, the fighting and such, which I guess is mighty hard to go through. I mean it's when something happens — like a war, but not only a war, not just that. Something that makes you see that what you thought would happen won't ever be. Not ever. Something can happen to change your life so sudden, you can't get over it fast enough. And so you do things you wouldn't ever have thought of doing. Maybe hurt other people. And that changes things for them, too, all in a line."

Grace had never heard her grandmother talk like this. She worried that the effort of trying to gather what seemed like meandering thoughts would be too much for her overburdened heart, and Grace eyed the monitors nervously.

"Like me," Grandma said. "I never got over my sister leaving like she did."

"Mabel?"

Her grandmother lifted her head from the pillow and looked at Grace, startled. "What

465

do you know about Mabel?"

"Her picture, remember? It fell out of a book we were looking at together. I was just a little girl. It fell out, and when I went to pick it up, you said her name really quick and then made me leave the room. That was the only time."

Grandma nodded and let her head fall back on the pillow. "I remember now."

Then, in fits and starts, as if she were pulling out stitches that had grown deeply into the skin, she told Grace a strange story about how she'd been in love with a boy named Wallace, how she and her sister, Mabel, used to plan that one day they'd get away from their stepfather, and how on the day she was happiest — her graduation day — she came home to find the sheriff at the house, cutting her stepfather down from a rope in the barn and telling her that her sister and Wallace had run off together.

"I never saw him hanging there — not with my eyes — but I still see it in my head," Grandma said. "And I used to get letters. From Mabel. Never from Wallace. They'd come to me from the post office in Juniper — for years, they came. I wouldn't read them. Burned them all in the stove. Your grandpa, he never knew anything about it. Didn't even know I had a sister."

"Oh, Grandma."

Bertie rubbed her eyes hard with her fingertips. "I'd give a lot to have just one of those letters. Maybe so I'd know what really happened. If they were sorry." Grace pulled some tissues from the box on the table and pressed them into her grandmother's hand. "I thought I saw her once." Grandma dabbed her eyes and nose with the tissue. "What's that program comes on Sunday nights? With the ticking clock?"

"60 Minutes?"

"That's the one. I thought I saw Mabel on there one time. Years ago, now. I was in the kitchen doing the dishes and I could swear I heard her voice, so I came out to the living room, but there was just this old woman on the television. Of course, Mabel would have been old by then. They called her something else, Miss Something Else — but I guess that could have been a married name. Only I think they said Miss. Or it could have been that funny one the women make you say now — Ms." Whenever Grandma said it, the *S* buzzed like a bee.

"So do you think it was her? What was she on for?"

"I don't remember too much, talking about some men she knew — seems like they might have been soldiers. It was that nice-looking colored man with the woolly beard doing the interview. But I remember they said she made her living taking people's pictures, so it couldn't have been her. Mabel hated pictures."

After that, Grandma had fallen asleep, and she'd slept the whole afternoon. She stirred awake for a few minutes when Mother got there. Grace kissed her good-bye, told her she'd see her in the morning, and Grandma clutched her hand, motioned for her to lean down so Rainey, who was busy fumbling in her purse for her cigarettes, couldn't hear. "You go home and get that picture for me," Grandma said. "It's up in the high cupboard, over the hall closet. All the way in the back in a long box. There's a glove in there, too. And a hair ribbon. You bring it to me."

Grace had gone straight to the house and found the slim gray box, nearly invisible against the back wall of the cupboard. She remembered the picture exactly, as if it had sat in a frame on her dresser all these years. Mabel in her lace dress, pretty, with long, shining hair. Just like Grandma said, she had the look of a girl who didn't like to have her picture taken. Were the glove and the ribbon Mabel's as well? Or Grandma's? They were yellowed a little, but looked like they'd both been put away nearly new. And there was one other thing Grandma hadn't mentioned — a lovely antique silver button, carved like a rose bloom.

By morning, Grandma had lost her speech again, and then late in the afternoon, when Grace had gone downstairs to the cafeteria with Aunt Alma while Mother and Lynn stayed in the room, Grandma died.

Grace called Ken and asked him to come, to bring her some fine silver wire and the small mandrel, and that night, in the dim glow of the table lamp in her grandmother's bedroom, while Ken slept, Grace turned and cut hundreds of rings, weaving them into shining blossoms, joined to meet in the center at Grandma's rose. She'd worn it to the funeral. She'd worn it on into the next morning, when she woke Ken and said, "Marry me. Today. Tomorrow. As soon as possible." And she'd gone on wearing it every day since, the oils of her skin dulling the silver to a rich, soft gray.

"Does he bite?"

Grace looked up from her work to see a man trying to hold a toddler back from Charlemagne, who was sitting up in his splendid height, panting and whipping the grass with his tail. "He's a pussycat," she said. "Really."

The man looked uncertain. Even for a German shepherd, Charlemagne was large — enormous, in fact — but when Grace lightly pressed his shoulder, he dropped to his side, rolled onto his back, and lolled his head to gaze up at the little boy and beg for a belly rub.

"Registered?" The man was now squatted down beside the dog, scratching his neck.

"Stray," Grace said. "Starved rib-thin. All our animals were — except the goats. We even found our horse wandering loose in the woods — no bridle, not even a rope, hooves split — just turned off, I guess."

"So you live around here? I figured all you people came up only for the fair."

Did he think they were Gypsies? Had the man not at that moment given Charlemagne a final pat, said "Let's go, pal," to his son, and swung the boy up onto his shoulders, Grace might have demanded he tell her why it was so remarkable that anything people might actually think was worth spending their money on could come out of a place called Pilgrim's End.

It was a good thing Ken wasn't here. He'd have put the guy straight. Ken loved this place, their place — they both did — though it had been Ken's far longer than it had been hers. The day he got his orders for

Vietnam, he'd walked out the door of his father's house and taken off in the car, just driving, he said, driving as far as the gas tank would take him, not looking for anything except maybe some limestone cliff he could drive off of. Deep in the country, far from Newman, the car sputtered to a stop and Ken got out and walked. Hours he dirt roads he wasn't sure were roads. But he wasn't sorry, he said, because it was a bright blue day and around him there was the kind of quiet that's not quiet at all — the wind through the autumn leaves, the tiny whoosh of birds settling among the branches. He swore to himself then that he would find out the name of the place, and if he made it through the war, he would buy land and live in the quiet that wasn't quiet, quiet soft enough to sleep through but loud enough to pull his thoughts away from all the talk in his head.

That's what he went out to the woods for, Grace thought, what he went looking for. He was always searching for that quiet of his dreams, but though Nature fulfilled her part, Ken couldn't muffle the voices inside his head, not for long anyway. He never said so, but Grace imagined those voices staying with him all the way into the woods, wait-

ing in the branches while he set up camp,
chattering when he lay down to sleep. For a
few days after he came back, things would
be worse between them than they'd been
when he'd left, but then he'd get better and
for a little while, a few months sometimes,
he'd be able to abandon himself to the
present and stop in the middle of wee...
the corn to turn his face up to th...

Though the Ken she had fallen in love
with was the one who had come back from
Vietnam, Grace wished she had something,
anything — a photograph, a crumpled third-
grade report of his summer vacation, a high
school love letter, or some tale from his
childhood — that could shape for her an
image of the boy he'd been before, the boy
who had stood on the precipice of that all-
changing moment when he opened the
envelope from the selective service. But long
before she knew him, Ken had left all traces
of that original boy behind, shedding that
self like a winding-sheet to seek transfigura-
tion in Pilgrim's End.

Grace wanted to go home. Right now.

There were still a few hours left for the
fair, but the crowd was thinning and they
weren't buying — not from anyone today
— so she nudged Charlemagne's foot with
her own and said, "What do you say, Maj-

esty? Pack it in?" They could be back on the road in an hour; she could be cooking supper in two.

Maybe Ken would change his mind, satisfied by a long ride in the woods, and come home tonight. If he did, she would fling herself into his arms and tell him that she loved him, that she was glad she'd married him, that she blessed him for having brought her to this place with the sweet, funny name no one seemed to know the origins of.

Her packing was slowed by three or four people who suddenly appeared, wanting to buy things they'd noticed earlier in the day, but Grace managed to get rid of them without too much talk.

In the truck, Charlemagne rode like a passenger, sitting up, looking around at the scenery and peering at the people in passing cars. The sun was just going down when they got home, and she let the dog out of the truck for his evening run and went to feed the goats. Pilot wasn't in the barn, so Ken hadn't come home, but he might yet. She'd keep the soup simmering on the stove just in case.

The soup was nearly cooked down to stew by the time Grace turned off the burner and went to bed. In the morning, she tended to her chores, patting the animals, talking to them, shooing the cats out of the lettuce patch. By afternoon, Ken still wasn't home, so she worked on the coif, first measuring it on her own head and then putting on one of Ken's hats to estimate his size. In the last of the light, when she was in the yard, tossing a stick out over the field for Charlemagne, she saw the low beams of a car winding down their road. She couldn't make out the color, but from the shape, it looked like a trooper's car.

It was.

When he got out of the car, the trooper touched the brim of his cap to her, looked into the field where Charlemagne stood alert, and said, "Fine dog there." He asked her was her name Grace Vincent and she nodded. "Kind of hard to find you out here." He waited while she called Charlemagne to her. Grace knelt on the ground, her arm tightly around the dog's chest. And then the trooper said a name she didn't recognize, explaining the man was from Chicago, just down to do a little hunting.

"When he heard the shots, two shots, he got worried, since he'd brought his son along — nice boy about fifteen, his first hunting trip. Father said the boy'd gotten away from him, so when he heard the gun, he was afraid his son might be in some trouble."

The trooper took a small black notebook from his pocket, didn't open it, and told her the rest.

Ken had shot Pilot first. Clean through the head, quick.

Maybe then, or maybe before that, he'd set out his gear far from where he was going to lay his own body down, far enough so there wouldn't be any blood spatter. He'd made sure the piece of paper with his name and address was the first thing anybody would see when they unzipped his rucksack.

Grace still knelt on the ground, her arm tightening around Charlemagne as the trooper held out a piece of paper, a neatly folded square. "I believe this was meant for you, ma'am."

When at last she reached for it, the bracelet on her wrist flashed Ken's name at her: *Pfc. Kenneth Raymond Vincent, USMC, 7-12-68.*

She released Charlemagne, but he continued standing guard beside her while she unfolded the note, smoothing it open against her thigh.

Ken had written — in letters so prettily made, he must have taken his time — *My Grace. My sweet little Grace. Sorry. Sorry.*

Twenty-Two:
Archaeology

November 1997
Newman, Indiana

RAINEY

"Well, you're going, aren't you?" Even across two thousand miles of telephone wire, Sally's tone came through as clearly as if she'd been standing right in front of Rainey — one hand on her hip, the other on her forehead, her eyes agape with astonishment, her mouth a twist of impatience.

"I hadn't even thought of it," Rainey said.

"Of course you have. That's why you called me."

Sally was right. Of course she had. Ever since she'd opened the newspaper this morning.

Reading the weekly college page in the *Newman Herald* was a habit started years ago — not long after Rainey had heard the buildings of the old Anderson County

Junior College had been bought, renovated, and renamed Newman Community College. She'd only just walked in the door from work one evening when Mother handed her a clipping and said, "Didn't you go to school with that girl?" It was just a tiny notice, but Mother read the *Herald* word for word — even the court docket. Ann Naylor, a girl Rainey had known slightly in school — they'd shared a cutting table in home economics once — had, according to the newspaper, been named to the dean's list.

"Imagine that," Mother said. "In college at her age. Whatever for?"

Before, Rainey had only scanned the paper, never more than glancing at the college page, but the notice about Ann had made her curious. In the years since, she had occasionally seen the name of someone else she had once known, and she would linger over the words, wondering what had driven them back to school — whether they had lost their jobs or were just bored and had nothing else to do.

This morning, it was the photo that had struck her first. And then, for the rest of the day, after she'd read the accompanying article, she had merely watched her body going through its motions — doing the billing, lunching in the company cafeteria, driving home, watching the evening news and then a few silly programs, waiting for the long-distance rates to drop at 11:00 P.M. so she could call Sally and figure out what to do.

Marshall — identified in the newspaper as Dr. Marshall Turner, Professor of Archaeology at Arizona State University — was coming to speak at Newman Community College.

"It's really just for the students," Rainey said to Sally. "It's during the day."

"Stop avoiding the issue. You just told me the article says 'free and open to the public.' That's you. Surely you've got a sick day you haven't used yet. Go."

"But why? To do what?"

"Curiosity. To say hello. To reignite the flame. How should I know? You're the one who called me." Sally sighed, "You can always tell anyone who asks that you just want to learn something about archaeology."

"Oh, Sally."

"I know you've been thinking about it all day. Tell me."

"Really," said Rainey. "I doubt he'd remember me."

"Why would he forget? He might not

recognize you, but you could always remind him."

Rainey had recognized Marshall instantly — the eager eyes and the same slight build that somehow gave the impression of great height. Though the photograph was in black and white, she could see the Arizona sun had baked his skin to taut leather. It was perhaps this more than anything else that had made her know him even before she read the caption. He looked like Grace, who worked her body lean in the sun.

"Why Newman, anyway?" Sally asked. "It's such a small school. I bet they don't even teach archaeology."

In spite of its brevity, the article had been very thorough. "Some other guy who teaches there apparently knew him in college. He found out somehow that Marshall was going to speak at IU, so he invited him to come here, too."

"There goes the reunion-show fantasy," Sally said.

Rainey shivered at the thought. "I hate those things." Seemed like a person couldn't turn on a talk show these days without seeing somebody crying about how they felt incomplete for never having known one or both parents. Then, after the host had wrung out every detail of the sad story, he would say, *Karen* or *Leon* — followed by a big pause — *we have a surprise for you!* The camera would catch the tearful face, looking around desperately, and then the lost person would step out from backstage, arms open. Rainey wondered if anybody else ever noticed that the lost one, recently found by a detective hired by the talk show, nearly always looked resistant and anxious, not at all joyful as the audience demanded. It was an epidemic, these programs. She feared the day would come when she would turn on the television and see Grace in the interview chair, weeping over the father she'd never known.

"So what else does the article say about him?" Sally prodded. "Anything personal?"

"Just that he lives with his wife — a social worker. And his sons — one a sophomore at Arizona State, the other a graduate student in thermodynamics. Whatever that is." She wondered if Marshall's parents had ever been able to build their house near Flagstaff, or if, after all these years, he still spent his summers digging up the property.

"So — no daughter?"

"Stop it, Sally."

"I'm just saying . . . I mean, you never know."

"I wouldn't do that to him," Rainey said.

"It wouldn't be fair. He's got a family. What would he think? And why should he even believe me?"

"Come on, Rainey. Don't tell me you haven't thought about it. He's a big boy — all grown up. Maybe hooking them up would help things between you and Grace."

"I think it's probably too late for that," Rainey said. So much had come between them, so much more than her steely silence about Grace's father. For one, Rainey hadn't been able to hide her disappointment that all her life Grace had let Lynn show her up in school. Grace was every bit as smart as Lynn — smarter in a lot of ways — but she'd thrown it all away on that strange man. Rainey had never liked Ken. After he killed himself, there might have been a chance to repair the rift with Grace, to get her back to Newman where she belonged, to get her straightened out, but Rainey had made the mistake of saying too much too soon: "Now that you're free of your burdens," she had said, stroking Grace's arm after the funeral, "there's nothing to stop you. You're still young. You can be anything you like." She hadn't meant it quite the way it came out — hadn't meant to suggest she didn't realize her daughter was grieving — but she couldn't take it back and expect to be believed. Even now, now that it was impossible to change what had happened, Rainey wished she had insisted on staying with Grace after the funeral — at least for a few days — whether Grace wanted her or not, but the moment she had spoken the words, she felt her daughter stiffen against her, and she lost her courage, afraid anything else she might say would open the ground between them even wider, so wide, perhaps, that it would swallow them both.

Grace hadn't asked about her father in years — Rainey couldn't even remember the last time — but it was Grace's way to go quiet when she was angry or troubled. Now that Rainey had some real information, something more than just a name and a few memories, would Grace want to know? Would it help her find her path? Perhaps she could just mail Grace the clipping with a little note saying, "See — this is what you come from." Would that knock some sense into her, make her realize there was something more for her than the half a life she was living in that place with the absurd name — a place nobody had ever heard of? Nothing but fields and trees and cattle as far as you could see.

"Who can say when it's too late for anything?" Sally said. "I think you should just go. I know you want to. You don't have to make up your mind absolutely before you get there. Maybe you'll introduce yourself and maybe you won't. Just go and see what feels right."

It was well past midnight when Rainey hung up the phone. She had thought it would help when she admitted that Sally was right — yes, she did want to go, she did want to see Marshall — but it hadn't helped, because no matter how much they talked, Rainey couldn't say exactly why she wanted to see him. Again, Sally had urged her to go to the presentation, and, once there, to follow her instincts. But that was just the problem: She didn't know what her instincts were. How was she supposed to separate her instincts from fantasy and nostalgia, from selfishness and fear? At times, she even felt jealous — but of whom? Of his wife? Or of Marshall? And for what? She did feel an intense longing to see Marshall again, but she also felt just as intensely that going would be wrong in every way.

Rainey turned out the lights and pressed the pillow into a perfect cradle for her head, but she couldn't sleep. She imagined walking into the auditorium, taking a seat near the front, but off to one side. She would sit at attention in her chair, and then, when Marshall came in, laid his papers on the podium, and began to talk, he would glance her way and she would smile, nod reassuringly. She could see him sorting through his memory as he continued his lecture, finally looking at her again with warm recognition. The ice broken, she would wait patiently until the crowd of students wanting to ask questions had dispersed, and Marshall would come toward her, clasp both her hands, hold her at arm's length to say how little she had changed, and then embrace her, whispering an invitation to dinner, where he would ask about Lynn, and nod in shared pride as Rainey said, "She's a judge now. Married to another lawyer. Last year they adopted a child — a little girl. Taylor." When he asked Rainey about herself, she would smile and shake her head — *no, I never remarried* — and he would assume there were no more children, so how could she tell him of Grace? If she did manage to find the words — saying how she hadn't realized she was pregnant until months after he'd left, explaining how she'd decided not to contact him, not wanting even to risk that he would give up graduate school to provide for them — would it shame him, a university professor, to know his daughter had squandered her chance to go to college to run off with a crazy ex-soldier who didn't deserve her? Or would it be better not to speak of Grace at all? Perhaps there would be no need — this was only catching up between friends, after all. But if she didn't tell, what would she do if he wanted to keep in touch, if he asked to see her again?

Rainey twisted furiously in the bed. *Dinner. Another meeting.* The scenario was ridiculous. If he recognized her, his reaction might be far from warm. There wouldn't be any reason for him to be hostile. But indifferent? That was very likely. And why shouldn't he be? Thirty-five years ago, they'd known each other for three months. How many men since had she dated — some of them for nearly a year — men she'd slept with that she would be neither happy nor unhappy to see if she unexpectedly ran into them? If she stayed behind then, to reintroduce herself, Marshall's indifference might quickly turn to alarm. How would she explain why she had come? Just because his picture was in the paper? Why him, after all these years? What would he think? That she was stalking him? And then if he became upset and tried to get away from her, would she lose control, get upset too, demand he listen, and shout after him as he tried to push out the door with his host, *And what about our daughter?*

Perhaps she could sit in the back of the auditorium, pretend to take notes, drape her hand over part of her face whenever she looked up, and when he was finished, she could get lost in the crowd and slip out, make it all the way to her car before he was even able to get to the door.

Insanity. Rainey sat up in bed and flung her pillow across the room. If she wasn't going to speak to him, why go at all? What was she hoping to gain, anyway? Her memories of Marshall were lovely. In his company, she had felt beautiful and desirable, capable and smart. Seeing him now might damage those memories somehow, replace them with new and less satisfying images.

But that had happened already. Now that she'd seen the photograph, now that she knew he'd married and had sons and an important career — none of it having anything to do with her — she wasn't sure she would she be able to remember the darling, nervous young man who had made her feel for a time that almost anything was possible. Once, when they'd been together for about a month, they'd sat in the court-yard of her apartment building on a warm afternoon, watching Lynn practice her somersaults. She kept rolling to the left, getting more and more frustrated, until Marshall got up to help her, laying one hand on her left knee, guiding her over until she began to feel the balance in her own little body. In a few moments, the somersaults were perfect, and Lynn couldn't stop, in her success forgetting all about the adults and the attention she usually demanded from them.

"You'll be a wonderful father," Rainey had said. "So patient."

Marshall shrugged but looked out at Lynn. "Did you always just want to get married?" he asked after a long while. "Have a family?"

She looked at him, astonished. "No," she said, as though he ought to know better, but then she realized he knew almost nothing about her. She told him then about Carl, about that first job she'd loved, her classes at the junior college, and her hopes of someday being an independent woman with the freedom to marry — or not. "I never wanted to feel like I had to get married just to have a man to take care of me," she said. "My sister did that." She looked at Lynn, her dress and panties stained with grass, her face red with the joy of effort. "I

487

messed things up pretty bad. A child. No husband. No education. Barely getting by."

Marshall's silence terrified her. She ought not to have been so frank. Did he think she was trying to trap him? What could she say to make him understand that she knew he wasn't going to marry her, that she didn't expect it, or even want it? That she just wanted to enjoy what time with him she could?

At last he took her hand, lightly squeezing her fingers. "You can still have your independence, Rainey." He laughed when Lynn leapt up in triumph from a particularly fine somersault. "You have it now." He looked at her. "You really don't know how strong you are, do you?"

Rainey hadn't thought of that in years. Hadn't thought of it, she was sure now, since the moment Marshall had said it. She had raised her girls — perhaps imperfectly, but she had raised them. She had taken care of everything Mother either couldn't understand or had been too upset to deal with when Daddy was dying. And then for years after that, she had taken care of Mother, seeing to it that all the bills got paid, supplementing the Social Security check with her own small income, always finding some other way to cut the budget when she was sure they were at bare bones.

That long-ago afternoon, while Lynn, newly confident in her somersaults, entertained herself by chaining them in combinations with hopscotch and jumping jacks, Rainey had asked Marshall, "Why archaeology?"

"Two things," he said. Reaching into his pocket, he brought out a small drawstring pouch, and from that, a flat stone the color of a desert sunset. He laid it in her palm. "This is the first fossil I ever found — I must have been seven or eight." He placed a fingertip on the stone and said, "See here? It's a beetle. For weeks after I found it, I couldn't think about anything else except that beetle. How it must have died. How it must have gotten trapped, maybe suffered. But then how, if it hadn't died this way, locked in the mud, it wouldn't be here in my hand, making me think about my life. About all life."

Rainey looked harder at the stone, as if she could look deep enough to see beyond the beetle to find Marshall as a scrawny boy of eight. "You said two things."

"I found the fossil while I was collecting potsherds. I didn't really know what they were then — no idea how old they were, or even that they were bits of old pottery," he said. "I had noticed one on the ground one day, saw that it had a design on it, and decided to find all I could — a shoe box full — you know how kids do? Collect things without any reason to collect them?"

Rainey nodded. One summer of her girlhood, she hunted the ground for bottle caps which she dropped into a mason jar. At night, she rattled their music in her ear before she slept.

"After I found the fossil, I wanted more. I put the shoe box in a garage and forgot about it." Marshall took the sunset stone from Rainey and slid it back into its pouch before speaking again. "A long time later — two, maybe three years — I came home from school, and there was my mother, sitting at her worktable, that old shoe box open beside her. Did I tell you she's an artist?"

Rainey shook her head. "What then?"

Marshall laughed. "Stupid kid I was, I said, 'Hey! Those are mine!' My mother just kept on working, setting the sherds one by one into plaster. 'They're not yours,' she said. 'They belong to the people who made the pots, painted them and used them. And to the people who respect them.' I just sat and watched her for the longest time, not saying a word — I'd never done that before

— and after a while I started to see what she was doing. She was making something beautiful, something new and whole, out of what had been lost and broken."

A few weeks later, when Marshall, off to graduate school, said goodbye to her, he gave her a small box, asking her not to open it until he was gone. Inside, wrapped in a soft cloth, was one of the potsherds he had shown her the night they met — a jagged triangle, not quite two inches long from its apex, half that wide at the base. Most of the other sherds in Marshall's collection were in shades of brown and red, the colors of mud and clay, but this was a lovely aged white, like old ivory. Dropping diagonally across its broken shape was a pattern of faded black lines, each like two sides of incomplete triangles, or like two paths diverging from the same point, keeping each other in sight — three repetitions of the pattern and part of a fourth, traveling across the sherd like time.

Somewhere, deep in a drawer or maybe a forgotten box in the attic, the sherd waited for her to find it again.

Rainey made up her mind. She would go to hear Marshall's talk. And afterwards, perhaps, she would speak to him only long enough to thank him. She wouldn't be able to tell him she had always been confident of her own strength, but at least she could thank him for telling her he had seen that strength in her. No one else, not even Daddy, ever had.

The campus was much larger than Rainey had imagined, sprawling across an area she remembered as a collection of small farms. So much had changed that, on the way in, she'd missed the main entrance and had to drive a little further on to a subdivision where she could turn around and come back. The parking area was a confusion of signs, most of them saying either RESERVED or PERMIT ONLY. Finally, on her second go-round, she saw a sign that said VISITOR PARKING, and she was able to get a spot someone else was just pulling out of.

She was no less confused when she got out of the car. Five or six buildings arced around the parking areas. Still others stood beyond those. There were people every-where — not all of them young — with arms full of books or bags slung over their shoul-ders, walking from one building to another, sitting hunched in their winter coats on benches, huddling in entryways to smoke. She tucked the newspaper under her arm and headed for the nearest building, where she stopped a woman about Grace's age, showed her the article about Marshall's talk, and asked for directions. The woman pointed her to the center building, a flat-roofed structure that seemed to be made of nothing but windows.

Once inside, Rainey took a moment to catch her breath. She looked around and unbuttoned her coat. There was a handmade poster advertising Marshall's visit, with a sign-up sheet at the bottom. A stout woman with frowzy blond hair was writing on it. Rainey put a hand up to her own hair before stepping up beside the woman. "Is this for the archaeology lecture?" She noticed there was a line not just for name but for address, phone number, and e-mail, as well. "I didn't realize it was reservation only."

The woman shook down the ink in her pen and finished writing her address. "It's not," she said. "This is for anyone who wants to go on a dig." She turned to Rainey, offering her the pen. "Interested?"

"A dig?"

"In Arizona, in March. Spring break, I guess."

"And you're going?" The woman was over sixty, with splotchy pink skin that would blister in the desert.

"Something I've always wanted to do,"

the woman said. "My husband's not too keen on the idea, but I just said to him, 'Nobody's asking you to come.'" She smiled at Rainey conspiratorially. "Kids are all grown. What's to stop us, eh?"

"I never really liked the sun," Rainey said. "My daughter does — but her work keeps her too busy to do anything like that." The woman was looking at her so intently, Rainey felt she had to explain her presence. "I just saw the article in the paper and it sounded like it might be interesting — the talk. Maybe some pretty slides. I had the day off work, so . . ."

The woman looked at her watch and then bent down to pick up a large tote. "We'd better get going, then." The tote was open at the top and Rainey could see a couple of thick books and a fat green binder.

"Do you take classes here?" Rainey asked.

"Oh, sure," the woman said. "Three or four a year. I always think I've taken about all there are, but then I get the schedule and I see something else that looks interesting. How about you?"

"Me? No," Rainey said. "I started here years ago, just after high school, when it was still the junior college. But I had to quit." She felt a surge of tears behind her eyes and struggled to think of something else to say without revealing too much.

The blond woman nodded at her words. "I know what you mean. Life happens."

The room wasn't an auditorium, as Rainey had expected, but more of a meeting room, with long tables pushed together to form an open rectangle. A wooden lectern sat on the end of one table. A white screen had been pulled down behind it. There was no crowd to get lost in. Only one other person was seated — a boy of perhaps twenty who looked like he hiked for a living. Rainey looked for the least conspicuous seat. If she sat at the furthest end of the room, she would still be no more than twelve feet from Marshall.

"How about these two?" The blond woman was already scooting sideways behind the chairs to the seats with a center view of the podium.

Rainey followed. The woman set her tote on the table, pulled out a chair and started wrestling out of her coat.

"You know," Rainey said. "I think I'd better find a restroom before this starts."

"Oh, yes." The woman winked at her and whispered, "I miss those good old days of bladder control, too." She lifted her tote into the chair next to hers and nodded toward the door. "Go left. It's five or six doors down. I'll save your seat."

In the restroom, several very young women — Rainey supposed they were only eighteen or nineteen — giggled and talked as they leaned in toward the mirror, checking their hair and makeup. Rainey pushed into a stall and locked the door. She dug in her purse for her cigarettes and lighter and then dropped them with irritation back into her bag. She'd seen at least four NO SMOKING signs since she'd come into the building. It would be humiliating to be caught sneaking a smoke in the bathroom like a teenager. She tried to remember a calming exercise she'd seen once on television. She had never tried it, but now she hooked her purse on the stall door, stood as straight as she could, relaxed her shoulders, and tried to breathe very slowly from below her belly button, counting to twenty. She took one breath, then another. On the third, she realized it was working: she'd stopped trembling and her mind was no longer spinning around like a carnival ride.

She waited until she heard the girls leave, then came out of the stall and set her purse on the counter over the sink. She washed her hands, reached into her purse for her comb, dampened it with water, and flicked it lightly through her hair. Putting the comb back, she worked her fingers along the bottom of the purse to find the potsherd, still wrapped in its soft cloth. After hours of looking, she'd found it in a box of old photographs taken during the two years she'd lived happily in Indianapolis — first with Sally and Lynn, and then, briefly, on her own, with Lynn and baby Grace. She slipped the sherd in her pocket, in easy reach if Marshall needed a reminder. With another deep breath, she picked up her purse and stepped back out into the hallway.

Two men wearing jackets and ties passed her. They were talking, focused on their conversation about how a design on a pottery fragment could identify its place of origin, even if it had somehow been carried hundreds of miles away. Marshall's hair was streaked with gray, but his body still danced with boyish energy. He and his companion turned into the room where Rainey's pink-cheeked friend with the flyaway hair waited in happy anticipation.

Every doubt, fear, question, and silly dream Rainey had had about coming instantly dropped away and burned like a launch engine from a rocket. Just like that.

Rainey had to clap her hand over her mouth to keep from laughing. She was glad she'd seen Marshall one last time. Seeing him without being seen — it was enough. Nothing of what she had expected, but all she needed.

Leaning against the wall, she took the sherd from her pocket and held it in her palm. Someday, perhaps, she would press it into Grace's hand and tell her, "This is from your father." And Grace, her lovely Grace, would see what it was, see that it was something beautiful but broken, waiting to be born anew.

Rainey buttoned her coat and started back down the hallway, her step light, almost buoyant. How would she ever explain all this to Sally? "I followed my instincts," she would say, and leave it at that.

Outside, she pulled her purse strap high on her arm and put out her hand to stop a young woman who was just going into the building, possibly to hear Marshall's lecture. "Could you tell me where the admissions office is?" Rainey asked.

"Right next door," the young woman said. "First floor. You can't miss it."

"Thank you," Rainey said, not quite realizing she was speaking to the air, having already stepped away from the young woman toward her destination. "Thank you so much."

TWENTY-THREE: FAMILY COURT

October 2005
Indianapolis, Indiana

LYNN

The piece on *Good Morning America* wasn't kind to her, but Lynn supposed it could have been worse. She had expected worse. The producers made no attempt, so far as she could see, to conceal their prejudice in favor of the adoptive parents, to whom they had devoted two full segments, with the leggy blond reporter leaning in towards the trembling mother and saying in her rich, warm, Dixie-tinged voice, "Tell us, Lila, if you can, what it's like knowing that in less than twenty-four hours, Judge Brandt may order you to return little Julianne to her natural father."

It was a question designed to make the woman collapse, sobbing, against her husband's chest, choking out, "She's our

499

daughter . . . our daughter," so the reporter waited for what seemed a compassionate five or ten seconds, the camera catching her look of shared sorrow, before she addressed the man: "Keith, how have you prepared your daughter for this? How do you explain to a four-year-old that she may have to go and live with someone she's never met?"

Keith Howard repeated much of what he'd said in court yesterday afternoon in his final appeal, though now allowing himself greater emotion for television. He claimed he bore no ill will toward the birth father, Julio Ortiz, that he respected Mr. Ortiz for fighting in Afghanistan, that he believed Mr. Ortiz loved Julianne and would have been a good father to her had he known about her from the beginning. And he said he was sorry Mr. Ortiz had been lied to by the birth mother, Casey Lockwood, but that her lie to a former lover did not reflect on the Howards' right to Julianne, who had lived with them since she was five weeks old.

At home, in private, Lynn railed to Sam about the court of public opinion whipped to frenzy by television news, but when she passed the crews, she knew to keep a pleasant, professional poker face for the camera, acknowledging them with a nod as she entered and left the courthouse. An intern from *Good Morning America* had called her for comment, which of course she couldn't offer, as even an intern ought to know, but Lynn knew how the people on these programs liked to foment controversy while implying their own fairness by being able to say, truthfully, "Judge Brandt declined our request for comment."

Sam appeared beside her, holding out a cup of coffee. "Are they making you out to be the Merry Monster of Meridian again?" A few days ago, when the media began implying that Lynn was showing considerable sympathy toward the birth father's case, some cheeky reporter from a TV tabloid claimed that picketers in support of the Howards had labeled Lynn "the Merry Monster." An image of Meridian's street sign, with the courthouse in plain view, flashed on the screen beside a video of Lynn striding into the building. Since then, the nickname had been flying all over the Internet. Though Lynn hadn't looked at it — and wouldn't — her daughter, Taylor, had told her there was already a spoof on YouTube, showing Lynn's transformation from a smiling middle-aged family court judge to a leering, snaggletoothed monster in battle fatigues who, along with a man in a cheap black Halloween wig, broke down the door of a suburban home, trained their assault weapons on the Ozzie and Harriet parents, and dragged a screaming little girl into the darkness.

"No, no," Lynn said, sipping her coffee and winking at her husband. "This is *quality* journalism."

Sam rubbed her shoulders and leaned down to kiss her on the head. He picked at the roots of her hair with his fingers. "Not a sign of gray, Judge."

"They did make a point to say I've ruled in favor of the adoptive parents in other cases," Lynn said, "but then they as much as took it back by saying those were mostly surrogacy disputes. They said I have a history of social activism — showed some photo of me in college, waving a sign for immigration-law reform — and then they implied I may be politically motivated to rule in favor of the Hispanic father."

"Motivated? Why? He's not an immigrant. What — do they think you can't win your seat again without the Hispanic vote? In Indy? All four percent of it?"

Lynn set her coffee on the table, pulled Sam down to the couch, and swung her feet into his lap for a massage. "They're just making something out of nothing, as usual," she said. "Have to keep those viewers from turning over to CNN." She leaned back, eyes closed, and stretched her legs while her husband worked the tight muscles in her calves. "Oh, yes, they did make sure to mention that Taylor's adopted. And they found out somehow about Daddy, too — about my finding him after being kept away from him for years — and so they're twisting that into evidence of bias."

But if they were looking for bias, Lynn thought, they were reading her far too simply. Though Julio Ortiz was the child's biological father, if she ruled in his favor, she'd have to watch Julianne Howard being torn from the arms of the parents she loved, the parents who loved her. Just imagining that moment had rekindled Lynn's childhood nightmare, squalling and reaching out with all her might to her receding father.

What would those reporters think — always so busy trying to guess a person's motivations to get the jump on the competition — what would they think if they knew how much she had struggled, especially in the early years, to be fair to the more vindictive parent in custody disputes? It was usually the mother, determined to cut the children off entirely from the father. Two or three times, Lynn had ruled fully in the woman's favor, but only when the evidence of danger to the children from the father was insurmountable. More often, she had played it safe, granting at least visiting rights to the other parent, and frequently joint custody, but at times she had paid with nagging doubts about whether she'd done the right thing. Maybe the bitter parent was bitter for a reason.

The phone rang, and Lynn said, "That'll be Mother."

Sam stretched toward the end table to read the caller ID. "Yep," he said. "I can tell her you're not here."

Lynn held out her hand for the receiver. "I might as well get it over with."

Rainey waited only for Lynn's hello before starting to talk. "Don't tell me you're going to take that child away from her parents and give her back to that Mexican."

"He's not Mexican, Mother. He's American. Third or fourth generation. And he's her parent, too."

"I've been watching the news, listening to him talk," Rainey said, "and I don't believe he really wants that little girl. He just wants the attention and he's trying to make everybody feel sorry for him because he's been in the war."

"Well, if that's all he wants, then why —" Lynn caught herself, annoyed that she had once again nearly let her mother embroil her in an emotional debate. "Look, I can't talk about the case. Why do I have to explain that every time?"

"Well, you just tell me one thing." Mother's voice pricked Lynn like cold spurs. "What would you have done if some other judge had tried to take Taylor away from you?"

"The cases are altogether different," Lynn said, feeling her skin hardening to steel. "The mother, as you know very well, OD'd on crack. The father won't be out of prison until Taylor's in grad school."

"Then tell me this," Rainey went on. "How do you think a man like that Ortiz fellow can take care of a little child? The army's liable to send him to Iraq."

"I really can't talk about it, Mother." With the press of Lynn's thumb on a button, Rainey evaporated. For now, anyway. Eventually, Lynn knew, she would have to apologize for her brusqueness — her truce with her mother was ever fragile and needed tending. But it could wait. Later, when she called to check her messages, Lynn would tell her secretary to send flowers — white poppies, if one could get them. For peace.

Still, her mother, as a fairly typical representation of the American television viewer, had raised the specter of what questions the media, ravenous for scandal, might ask. Since they had already introduced the subject of Taylor's adoption, might they next begin to speculate on whether Lynn had taken advantage of inside information to adopt a child who could never be reclaimed? Or would they study the local news archives and soften in her favor when they found the features applauding her good citizenship for adopting an older, at-risk child?

As with all things public and political, the pendulum of mood might swing either way, but right now, it seemed that pendulum was swinging for her head. No — that image was as absurdly overdramatic as the You-Tube video. And yet, given the media's current feelings about her, it wasn't unreasonable to imagine that one of those reporters could spin the facts to suggest that Lynn and Sam's reasons for adopting Taylor had been less than pure.

Hadn't her own sister once hinted at the same thing? They hadn't talked much, she and Grace, not since they were girls, and when they did, their conversations were brief and strained, but in spite of this, Lynn had let herself believe Grace would celebrate the news of the adoption, so she'd made the call.

The seconds of dead air on Grace's end had set the tone for what followed. "You're adopting?" Grace said at last. "Wow. Congratulations."

Now it was Lynn's turn to be silent, so Grace could think about what she'd done.

"What I mean is," Grace stammered, "I'm just surprised. I didn't know you wanted children."

"Sam and I have been trying since we were married," Lynn said, too angry to admit she'd probably never told Grace that. "It's not going to happen, and it seems wrong — to both of us — to go through the long process for in vitro or surrogacy when there are so many children who need homes."

"That makes sense," Grace said, not sounding truly convinced. "But why this child? I mean" — Grace's voice lifted toward the lighthearted — "I know there's a long waiting list for an infant, but wouldn't they pop a judge to the head of the line?"

"I would not take advantage of my position like that," Lynn snapped.

Though Grace stumbled through an apology, her remark had unnerved Lynn. If her sister had thought to mention it — whether in earnest or in jest — others might do the same. The truth was, when she began considering adoption, Lynn had weighed her options carefully. Healthy white infants were hard to come by, and their adoptions were far more vulnerable to being challenged. The chance of any adoption being contested was slim, but Lynn had learned in law school to consider all the odds. As for her influence — and Sam's — was her husband supposed to pretend that he wasn't the most sought-after human rights attorney in Indiana? Was she supposed to apologize for being a newly elected judge and therefore of interest to reporters? But even the appearance of her and Sam's taking advantage of their public status might make the adoption less secure, so, together, they had decided an older child would be safer — perhaps three or four years old — and they were open to taking a mixed-race child, too, which would increase the chances of completing the adoption sooner. And, yes, they had talked about the impact their adopting Taylor would have on the low adoption rate for nonwhite children. If their choice to adopt in this way could bring attention to other needy children, so much the better. What was wrong with that?

She could have said all that to Grace, but she didn't. She had long suspected that Grace resented her success, and this confirmed it. Poor Grace — living in that sad little house in the middle of nowhere, left to her by that crazy Vietnam veteran who shot his horse, and himself, in the head. After he was dead, Grace might have done something with her life, gone back to school at least — even Mother had done that. Over the years, Lynn had told her sister two or three times, "Sam and I will help you with the cost. You could study graphic design. Or architecture." But no, time after time, Grace thanked her without even considering the offer, saying she was content to spend her time growing vegetables, shoeing horses, and making armor. *Armor,* for God's sake.

When Lynn had made that call to tell Grace about Taylor, she had wanted more than anything to share the whole story: how she had gone to the orphanage simply to make a few inquiries, never expecting Taylor would peer out from around a corner and penetrate her with her eyes — eyes so deeply brown they were nearly black. Lynn was utterly helpless after that, helpless against the absolute love that overtook her. When she went home, she told Sam she'd found her child — at the time she didn't even know the girl's name or age, nothing about her except that she was meant to belong to Lynn.

Never had Lynn felt so calmly on fire, and it was this strange sensation that allowed her to say to Sam that if he objected, she would divorce him. "She can be ours, or she can be mine," Lynn said, entirely without rancor. It was just a fact she was expressing. "But she will be mine."

Because he loved her, Sam had accepted Lynn's decision, and when he met Taylor — she was TannaRayla then, so named by her Filipino mother and black father — he fell in love with her, too, so everything was all right.

Lynn turned up the volume on the television again. The *Good Morning America* hosts were all lined up on their couch, talking about her case.

"Hey, babe," Sam said, playfully squeezing her foot, "You're the topic Around the Water Cooler this morning."

"Hooray for me."

The particular point they were discussing was how Julio Ortiz, if he was granted custody, would deal with Julianne's memories of the Howards. That was another question Grace had raised about Taylor.

"You said the little girl is what? Five?"

"Yes."

"So how will you handle it?" Grace's voice was tentative. "I mean, have you thought

510

about what you'll do when she remembers?"

"What are you talking about? Remembers what?"

"Her old life," Grace said. "Her real parents."

"Sam and I will be her real parents."

"Lynn, you know what I mean. She's bound to remember some things. Whether they're good or bad, you'll have to be ready to talk to her about them. Think about how you felt. You remembered."

"I was older. That was different."

"Lynn . . ."

She didn't speak to Grace for nearly a year after that, not until she had to be polite over Christmas dinner at Mother's. Thankfully, there hadn't been much need of that. After they'd opened the gifts, Grace had made up her mind she was going to teach Taylor how to play Twister, and by the time they'd finished their second round, it was late enough that Lynn could say, "It's time for us to say good night and head back to Indianapolis."

It was a relief now to be able to point to Taylor, at fifteen, as a model of adjustment, and an even greater relief for Lynn to be able to say truly to herself that she had been right: At five, Taylor had been too young to remember her former life in any detail. And

Julianne, only four years old, would soon forget her time with the Howards if Lynn ordered the child be returned to Mr. Ortiz.

But here was another factor to be considered — one that the *Good Morning America* reporter had brought up when she asked the Howards, "If you lose custody, will you appeal?"

Before handing down any decision, Lynn weighed the likelihood that her judgment would be overturned by a higher court, but this time, in the case of Julianne Howard, the question seemed especially heavy. If she granted custody to Mr. Ortiz, it would be several years before the Howards could hope to win the child back again — years during which Julianne would have adapted to a new life, a life that she might then be torn from — and what damage might two such tearings do — one at four and another at seven or eight, very nearly the same age Lynn had been when Mother tore her, a second time, from Daddy.

Lynn's sharpest memories of her father, and the dearest — even after all these years — were of those few months when she was a child, after she'd overcome her initial fear of him, after she'd realized in the instinctive way of little children that he truly wanted her. How she had loved being so small that she had to look up to him as he bent to hand her a huge ice-cream cone, so small that he lifted her on his shoulders to watch a parade, so small that he could carry her effortlessly back to the car when she was tired from the day's adventure — as if he were her personal storybook giant, noble and gentle, sent to serve and protect her.

Back in college, on that first trip to Siler, her boyfriend, Derek, had asked her, "What do you really want from him, Lynn? If we find him?" If she had told him about her fantasy, he would have scoffed — maybe even broken up with her right there in the car. Derek — like her — was a person of reason who trusted logic drawn from verifiable evidence. It was why they were together.

"I've heard my mother's side of things," Lynn said. "Now I want to hear his."

But emotion had overtaken her reason on her father's front porch when first she saw him, and again on the next three or four visits, months apart, through her senior year. And then suddenly she was in law school, with even less time to spare — she saw him just five times in those three years. After that, she took an internship in Indianapolis, which led her to a job at the law firm, where she worked seventy or eighty hours a week in order to prove herself worthy of a partnership. So it was a long time before she began to consider the facts and to think reasonably about her relationship with Daddy.

In the beginning, they were linked by their shared bitterness toward Rainey for having kept them apart, but after a while, when Lynn realized her mother could no longer wield that power, the anger fell away, taking the bridge between her and Daddy with it. Whenever they met, after the first few excited hours, there was nothing to talk about. Daddy had no interest in politics — he didn't watch the news or even take a daily paper — and Lynn thought she'd go mad if she had to sit through another car race or listen again while Daddy held forth on the idiocy of people who overfed and overpetted their guard dogs. She could see he was bored when she talked about her classes, and even her announcement that she was to graduate with highest honors didn't impress him much. At this same news, Mother had alternately wept and giggled for two days, and that whole summer after, whenever Mother ran into someone she hadn't spoken to for some time — despite her feelings about Lynn's visits to her father — she told the tale of her brilliant daughter, first in her university graduating class.

Daddy wasn't any more impressed when Lynn was accepted into law school — he said lawyers made him think of termites, feeding off trees felled by storms. "Well," she told him, "the acceptance doesn't matter much. There's no money to pay for it." She had applied for the few fellowships the law school offered, but she'd done her research, and she knew these never went to girls from working-class families. She'd been able to pay for college by patching together awards from speech competitions and small scholarships from the university, her high school, local civic clubs, and the electric company. Grandpa made up the rest by cashing in the last of his war bonds, and, for spending money, Mother gave her what little she'd saved in hopes of one day buying a house.

"I'll take care of it for you," her father told Lynn, but he said it as if he were buying her a longed-for toy, not because he admired her ambition or intelligence. A year or two later, upset from a fight she'd had with her mother, she learned from Grandma Bertie that Rainey had spent months trying to borrow the money Lynn needed for law school, going to every bank in southern

Indiana, only to be turned away time and again as a bad risk.

But at least, Lynn had told herself back then, clinging to the eight-year-old inside her, *he's mine. Daddy's mine.* She didn't have to share him with Grace, as she'd had to share Mother, Grandma, and Grandpa — knowing always, *always,* they preferred her younger sister. Though it shamed her now to think of it, especially when she thought of her love for Sam and Taylor, as a young woman she'd been happy to find her father alone in the world. Their need for each other, she had believed then, would weld them together. She and Daddy were family — and over time she trusted they would prove this by coming to know each other's secret selves.

Lynn waited — visit after visit, she waited — for her father to tell her who he was, what he really cared about. She'd even prodded him once, gently, by describing the photograph she remembered. In it, she was standing in front of a Ferris wheel with Daddy and another man, who held up two fingers behind her head, for devil's horns.

"He was a big man, I remember — like a bear," Lynn said. "I think I was a little afraid of him." *And jealous,* she thought, but she didn't say it.

"That must have been Vernon," Daddy said. "Good fella." He shifted in his chair and looked straight into Lynn's eyes for a moment. "It's on account of him you're sitting here — alive, I mean. He knew how to do that mouth-to-mouth stuff — got you breathing again after we fished you out of the lake." He took a swallow of his beer and looked at his watch. "The race'll be on in a minute." He started to stand up, but Lynn caught his hand.

"What happened to him? Vernon? Do you still see him? Were you . . . *friends?*"

"Lost track of him years ago," Daddy said. "Just disappeared from town one day."

He said nothing more about it — not then. Not ever. And not once in all their time together — even in Daddy's last year, when he was dying and she moved him into her house in Indianapolis to take care of him — did her father ever tell her what his real relationship with Vernon — or with Mother or anyone else — had been. Daddy died without Lynn's ever knowing for sure if he was a man who preferred men, as the long-ago gas station attendant had told Derek, or if the talk that had cost him his job, his friends, and the custody of his daughter was only that — talk.

Those years of trying to join herself with

her father had driven such a great wedge between her and Mother that, at times, the old bruises still ached. Once, Lynn had divided a sheet of paper with a heavy black line and labeled one column *Mother* and the other column *Daddy*. She wanted to see clearly, in writing, what aspects of herself — her nature, her desires, and her accomplishments — she owed to each of her parents, but she tore up the paper, angry at the balance sheet, when she could think of nothing to write under *Daddy* but *law school.* That in itself was enormous — she wouldn't be who she was now without it — but still, she couldn't help but wonder: If she had been brought up in her father's house, if he had been the one in charge of guiding and encouraging her, would she have cared for school, would she have been able to imagine any future for herself beyond rural mud?

Lynn now tried to imagine little Julianne Howard as a young woman of eighteen or twenty, struggling to soothe the scars that love — so much possessive love — was now searing onto her, trying to appease whichever parent or parents the court had finally declared to be her true owner, while perhaps also trying to link herself again somehow to the family that was lost.

Sam flicked Lynn's big toe to get her attention. "Get you anything else, Judge?"

Lynn swung her feet back to the floor, kissed Sam's cheek to thank him for trying. "Better go write my ruling," she said.

She closed the door to her study, tapped the keyboard to wake up her computer, then picked up a legal pad and settled in the window seat. The red leaves of the oak tree, where they'd had a tree house built for Taylor, darkened against the gray clouds that were coming in. If it rained, most of the leaves would be on the ground by tomorrow morning. Funny. She couldn't remember ever seeing Taylor in that tree house — they'd planted roses along the fence so the scent could waft up to her — but she'd heard Taylor talk about it nostalgically with her friends, and Lynn wondered if she still sometimes took her homework up there on warm afternoons. She was probably too old for that now.

At the top of the legal pad, Lynn wrote *Ortiz v. Howard.* She pressed the tip of her pen on the page, but she couldn't think what the first sentence would be, let alone the second or third or beyond.

The Howards were good parents. There was no evidence otherwise. But the Howards' lawyer had tried to argue that Julio Ortiz wasn't fit — first, because he hadn't filed an immediate challenge to the erroneous birth certificate, and, second, because he was unmarried and in the military. The lawyer had argued this because there wasn't anything else to argue. Ortiz's lawyer had proven that his client had not known about Casey Lockwood's pregnancy until she wrote him a taunting e-mail, months after his deployment to Afghanistan, telling him she'd just signed away his two-day-old daughter. Lynn had studied the text of the e-mail, the validity of which Lockwood had confirmed in her testimony, sneering over how she had felt especially good about naming the kid after Julio while putting another guy's name on the birth certificate as the father. Lockwood admitted she had never even dated the other man; he was just somebody who'd shared space once in a high school classroom.

After receiving Lockwood's e-mail, Ortiz had done everything he could from Afghanistan, which wasn't much, but he had managed to get a lawyer to order a DNA test and, in the last three years, had submitted to half a dozen of them himself, both overseas and in the States, every one of them showing with statistical certainty that he was Julianne's father. Ortiz was smart and methodical. He had kept every scrap of correspondence — paper and digital — and was able to prove that he had begun fighting for custody of Julianne from the moment he learned of her existence, even before he knew Casey Lockwood had lied on the birth certificate. Ortiz was even able to show e-mails indicating he had told Lockwood many times that he wanted to have a large family. Ortiz's lawyer argued that Lockwood, bitter that Ortiz had broken up with her just before being deployed, had taken her revenge by not telling him about the baby until she thought it was too late.

In spite of having this evidence before them, the Howards refused Ortiz's every request to see Julianne when he returned to Indiana in 2003. They justified their refusal by saying they didn't want to take any chances that Julianne would become attached to him, since it was likely he would be redeployed within a year or two. In response to this, Ortiz, who, according to his parents' testimony, had never wanted anything more than to be a marine, had decided he would not reenlist when his term of service ended early next year.

Not that Ortiz was the irreproachable, wronged hero his lawyer tried to portray. There had been a lot of girls before Casey Lockwood, at least two others at the same time as Casey. He'd strung them along, giving them the impression that he was going to propose marriage. And his military career was undistinguished. He had the reputation of being a troublemaker, a malcontent, frequently on the edge of insolence toward his superior officers, doing what he could to fob off more dangerous assignments on other men. Though none of the fellow marines called as witnesses would say so directly, Lynn could see very well that had there not been a war on, Ortiz would not have been encouraged to reenlist, so his departure from the service was not really so self-sacrificing as he made out.

From what she knew of them personally, she liked the Howards much better than Julio Ortiz, and though their decision to bar him from seeing Julianne was ill considered, Lynn understood it. She would have broken every law ever conceived to protect Taylor from harm. Perhaps Mother had felt that, too, for her.

But this case was not a question of personality or feeling. And as a judge, Lynn could not consider desperate acts of love as justification for poor choices. The only truly relevant issue in this matter — since there was no evidence to suggest that Julio Ortiz would be a neglectful or abusive father —

was that he had been denied his rights through Casey Lockwood's actions. Lynn's duty now was to right that wrong.

She heard paper being slid under the door and caught a glimpse of Taylor's glittering purple fingernails. "Honey," she called. "Tay, that you?"

The door opened just enough for Taylor to peek in. "I don't want to bother you. I just thought you'd like to see this e-mail from Aunt Grace."

Lynn tossed the legal pad and pen onto the window seat and turned her face away long enough to compose it. She was annoyed, but she didn't want Taylor to think she was the reason.

"What's it say?" Lynn stood up and motioned for her daughter to come all the way in.

Taylor did, stepping carefully on her slender feet, as if afraid to make a sound. The girl picked up the paper and held it out to Lynn. "She just says to tell you she's thinking about you and that she can send you a sword to balance your scales if you want her to."

Lynn pressed her lips together and stared at the page in her hand without reading it.

"I think she meant to be funny," Taylor said. "Aunt Grace always says stuff like that when things get serious. She also says she knows you're a good judge and will make the right decision."

"I didn't know you were in touch with her," Lynn said. "Does she e-mail you a lot?"

"A couple of times a week, I guess." Taylor was looking at her cautiously now, measuring how much to say. She could cultivate that to become a good lawyer, if she could get her emotions under control.

"You remember last Christmas she told us about her Web site? I found it one day and e-mailed her to tell her I liked it. You ought to see it," Taylor said, forgetting to parse her words, her voice becoming lighter and quicker. "She's got this thing on there that lets you pick a body you think looks like yours — of course you can pick any body you want — and then you can put a picture of your own head on top and drag over pieces of armor to see how you look as a knight."

"Does she?"

"It's fun." Taylor was growing nervous again. "I like Aunt Grace. She really helped me with that paper I had to write last spring about *Sir Gawain and the Green Knight* — you know, the part where Gawain gets ready to leave on his quest and there are all these lines about his armor — his horse's, too."

Lynn nodded as if she did know, but she didn't. Who was Sir Gawain? "I would have helped you with your paper."

Taylor looked down and buried her hand in her short black hair. She'd done that since she was a little girl, hung on to her hair when she felt embarrassed, dipping her head to hide the way her milky caramel skin flushed a shade darker. "I hated to ask you. It's just, you're always so busy. You have too much to do as it is." Taylor started to hum softly, another nervous habit.

Lynn picked up a folder from her desk and paged through it. "So what was your paper about?"

"You mean the one about Sir Gawain? Aunt Grace explained what all the pieces of the armor were, why they were important, how the design shows the way he thinks about himself — and then she showed me how the Green Knight never wears a harness — the armor isn't a suit, she says; it's a harness. Anyway, I got the paper from that. Mr. Quentin really liked it. He said everybody else just wrote about what he'd already explained in class."

"Well," said Lynn, pulling open the silver box on the desk to see if she'd left her reading glasses there. She hadn't. "I'm glad

525

Grace's occupation has some value."

"Oh, you ought to see the prices of the stuff she makes. Just one helmet. She says she's got so many orders, she's had to give up her farrier's work — that's putting shoes on horses — for all except her oldest customers." Taylor still clutched her hair, but she tried a small smile. "You really ought to take her up on that offer of a sword, Mom. Sounds pretty valuable."

Lynn folded her sister's e-mail, pressing a crisp crease with her fingertips. "Thank you for bringing this in, sweetheart. I really do have to write my ruling now."

Taylor looked down to the floor and hummed again. What was that tune? When Lynn caught the next phrase, she knew. It was the tune Taylor had invented herself, a tune she'd invented to turn her name, TannaRayla, into a musical pacifier. Even before they brought her home, Lynn and Sam had been teaching their daughter to think of herself as Taylor. It was for her own good, they told each other. To let her be TannaRayla would only make her an outsider once she started school. It was important she fit in. Lynn remembered bragging to a colleague that Taylor loved her new name: She answered to it immediately, Lynn said, and wore proudly the gold locket engraved with it. Months after that, on the nanny's night off, when Lynn passed Taylor's room, she heard a muffled tune. She thought Taylor had turned her CD player down low, so she opened the door to check. The music was coming from Taylor herself. She was lying with her face to the wall, curled up, the covers pulled up to her eyes, and she was rocking in rhythm to her tune, singing to herself, *TannaRayla . . . TannaRayla . . . TannaRayla.* Lynn stepped out into the hallway again and closed the door. She had never told Sam about it. She'd never told anyone about it.

But here was the tune again, just under Taylor's breath.

"I better get to school," Taylor said. She turned to go, then stopped and looked back over her shoulder. "Are you giving her back, Mom?"

Lynn held her arms open, catching Taylor by the shoulders as she approached. Looking into her daughter's dark, dark eyes, she said, "I wish I could tell you, baby, but I really can't. You'll just have to wait to hear it on the news, like everybody else." When Taylor reached up for her hair, Lynn caught her hand and held it gently in her own. "Now, just think about it," she said. "Do you believe it's right that you should know before the Howards and Mr. Ortiz do?"

Tears sparkled in the corners of Taylor's eyes. She looked to the floor again and shook her head.

"All right, then," Lynn said. "You go on to school and I'll see you at dinner."

When the door closed, Lynn sat down at her desk. Her computer had gone to sleep again. She tapped a key. She'd just write it on the computer this time, and if she got stuck, she'd go back to the legal pad.

Maybe she ought to anticipate her detractors and resign her seat, citing family reasons — no one questioned those. She'd talk to Sam about it next week, after the media had forgotten about this case and were busy mucking around in somebody else's business. She would talk to Sam, yes, and Sam would tell her, just as he did every time she doubted herself, that her resigning would be a betrayal of the public trust. And of course he would be right. She couldn't do that — wouldn't do that — to the people who'd put her into office.

Twenty-Four: Gathering

June 2007
Pilgrim's End, Indiana

Bertie's Girls

Rainey stopped the car at the crossroads. Was she supposed to turn right, past the brown-and-white cows standing behind their fence, or was it left, between the two broad fields of ankle-high corn?

"Where did you put those directions?" Lynn said, sliding her hand along the space between the seats. "We could wander around out here forever. No road signs. Grace should have come out to the highway to meet us." She punched the buttons on her cell phone. "No reception. Big surprise."

"I'm pretty sure it's this way," Rainey said, turning past the cows, though she wasn't sure at all. She hadn't been out here since the day of Ken's funeral — twelve, thirteen years now. Before that, she had been to

529

Pilgrim's End only twice, but the advantage of the house being so far out in the country — no doubt the only advantage — was that the landscape had changed very little in the twenty-five years Grace had been here — a place so completely nowhere that developers ignored it. Rainey caught herself nodding at the cows as she passed, wondering if it was the corn they were staring at, plotting somehow to open the gate and cross the road to feast on the succulent young shoots.

"I'm sure I've worn the wrong shoes," Lynn said, looking down at her strappy high heels.

Taylor leaned up from the backseat. "Mom, I told you to wear flats or running shoes."

"I don't own any flats. Or running shoes."

Lynn was still angry with her daughter, but more angry with her sister for having cooked up the plan for this gathering. A few weeks ago, without any warning and in the middle of their Saturday-morning breakfast, Taylor had said, "Aunt Grace wants to have the family in to celebrate my graduation. And my scholarship."

There were so many explosive possibilities in those few words, Lynn hadn't known which to defuse first. *Family,* as it turned out, was meant to include Aunt Alma and

Sarah, the granddaughter become daughter. In Lynn's mind, they hardly counted as family, as she hadn't seen either of them since the first Christmas after her cousin Milton and his wife had gone to prison. While Lynn was in the spare bedroom wrapping the gifts she'd hidden in her suitcase, Alma came in, closed the door, and said, "I need you to tell me what I have to do to get permanent legal custody of Sarah. Every step."

Lynn flushed with panic. Only days before, she had filed as a candidate in the judge's race — no one even knew about it yet besides Sam. But if she helped Alma, it wouldn't be long before her political enemies found out about Milton, and then all it would take to ruin her career would be a few artfully edited ads and speeches linking her name with Milton's misdeeds. Lynn turned from Alma and began gathering the scraps of paper and ribbon, speaking mechanically about state laws and licensing and how she couldn't adequately advise on a case in another state. She ended by saying, "I'll have my secretary call you with a list of phone numbers for lawyers near you who specialize in family law."

Alma would not give up. "I could do as well looking in the Yellow Pages," she said, and when Lynn tried to leave the bedroom, the packages in her arms, Alma blocked the door. "You owe me a favor, Lynn. You wouldn't have found your father without me."

So Lynn had done what she could. After the holidays, she shut herself in her office and spent half a day phoning through her contact list until she found an advocate for Alma's suit. After that, she worked on her own time as a shadow consultant, studying all the documents the Ohio attorney faxed her, offering advice over the phone, being careful to destroy her paper trail. Even though everything had worked out — her campaign had moved forward without so much as a whisper of impropriety, and she had won handily with 62 percent of the vote — she had not forgiven Alma for holding her to an ancient obligation. Other than the printed card of acknowledgment for the flowers Lynn had sent when Uncle Gordon died, she and Alma had had no contact since that Christmas. Sarah, just a baby then, must be thirteen by now. A complete stranger. What could they possibly find to say to one another?

Lynn felt similarly disconnected from Grace, who made it to Mother's house in Newman for maybe one out of every three

Christmases, always using the excuse that she couldn't find anyone to tend her animals long enough for an overnight trip. "If you ever decide to have Christmas at your house," Grace had said to her a few years ago, "I can make it a day trip. It's only a little over an hour for me to Indianapolis. Of course you're all welcome here anytime you want to come. If it snows, it's gorgeous, and not too tricky to drive unless it's right after the snow. One thing we aren't short of out here is plows."

Presumptuous, that's what Grace was. Practically inviting herself to Indianapolis, then implying everyone else ought to defer to the complexities of her life. What on earth could Grace know about complexities? And now this party. How dare Grace take it upon herself to make plans for Taylor? The two barely knew each other, except for sending messages over Facebook and talking on the phone now and then. Well, this proved what Lynn had long suspected: Grace had been stirring up and encouraging Taylor's starry-eyed ambition to become a composer. Lynn and Sam had always believed Taylor would grow out of her fantasies, as little girls grow up to recognize they aren't really princesses, and so they had worked hard and put enough by to pay Taylor's tuition to any school she wanted. Taylor herself had given them reason to believe everything would turn out all right, for, in spite of her repeated claim that she cared for nothing but music, she had kept her grades up in every subject and had scored high enough on the SAT to guarantee admission anywhere in the country.

Taylor had run into the house, screaming and waving the acceptance letter from the state university over her head. Though Lynn had forced herself to smile and give her daughter a congratulatory kiss, Taylor must have caught her look of dismay. "It's tops in composition, Mom. They hardly let anybody in as a freshman, but they picked me."

Later, when Lynn and Sam were alone, he said, "It could be worse, Judge. It could be one of those arts schools without any general-education requirements." He hugged her to him and laughed. "Don't forget — I thought I wanted to be a gym teacher." Lynn had smiled at that, the image of Sam in too-tight short shorts advocating for push-ups instead of for fair hiring practices. "Let's just give her a chance," he said, "She'll take those other classes and find out there's a lot more she could be interested in."

Sam was right: Just being in college — all

that opportunity to recognize her potential — would get Taylor back on the right path, and then in a year Taylor could transfer to a college more worthy of her gifts. But that didn't mean Lynn was going to forgive Grace's meddling. She'd tried to defuse Taylor's enthusiasm for going to Grace's by saying, "We'll have a graduation party here. As grand as you like." Ignoring her daughter's downcast look — a ploy — Lynn said brightly, "Invite anyone you want. You can invite Grace. Think of all the trouble you'll save her by asking her here."

Taylor wiped tears from her eyes and spoke without looking up. "I don't want a fancy party, Mom. Just my friends over for pizza or something." She wiped her tears again and took three deep breaths. "It's just . . ." As if suddenly gaining courage, she raised her eyes to meet Lynn's. "It's just that Aunt Grace is the only one who is happy for me about the scholarship."

Lynn had left Taylor with a promise to talk over the matter with Sam, fully believing her husband, who could discuss Grace without having to cut through a tangle of emotions, would offer a way to avoid the invitation by suggesting a plan so reasonable that even Taylor would have to accept it. To Lynn's astonishment, Sam had said,

"Maybe it's not such a bad idea after all. Maybe seeing how her 'artist' aunt really lives is just the wake-up smack Taylor needs." Sam said he could excuse himself from going to Grace's, citing an engagement to speak at a Lions Club meeting, but what he would really do with the day was shop for a new car for Taylor. Their daughter would find it upon her return, parked in the driveway and adorned with a giant bow.

Rainey slowed the car, watching for mailboxes. "Somebody please tell me again how Grace managed to persuade Alma to come."

"I'm not exactly sure how they first hooked up," Taylor said. "Probably Aunt Grace's Web site or Facebook — like we did. Anyway, somehow Sarah found out that a Girl Scout troop was visiting the farm for different projects, so she asked if she could come for a week or two. She can do enough there to earn about a million badges — arts and crafts, organic gardening, small business operation, wildlife, botany — she sent me the list."

"Fine," Rainey said. "If that little girl wants to run around in the woods and get eaten up by bugs, that's her business. But why does Grace have to torture the rest of us?"

Taylor slumped back against the seat.

"She's doing this for me. For my party."

"There are a lot of other places to have a party besides the wilderness."

Lynn could have backed up her mother, whose obvious annoyance with Grace pleased her, but she didn't want to add fuel to her disagreement with Taylor. Silence was the best choice. Even after fifteen years, the bond she had with her mother remained tenuous. Being together in the hospital room when Grandma died, weeping as one when they realized what had happened, had changed things. From that day forward, whenever they spoke, they silently agreed not to talk about Carl, each of them taking care not to detonate the mine that lay between them. And then came Taylor, their love for her becoming a natural barrier against hidden trip wires.

"Oh my God," Lynn said, pointing up the road. "That's got to be it."

A great painted shield, bright gold — at least nine feet high — stood several yards ahead of a gravel road. A strange design, painted in red, filled the upper part of the shield. At the center, a large scrolling letter *F* split its stem into an *M* on the left and a *B* on the right. From the joined initials hung the words *Grace Vincent, Artisan & Armorer*.

Rainey was trying to work out the meaning of the three letters — *F, M, B* — when Lynn touched her mother's arm and nodded at what stood on the other side of the gravel road. "It gets worse." There was no missing that what served as a mailbox was an immense knight's helmet, gleaming green and at least three times the size any ordinary man might wear. It bore the same images as on the shield, only smaller and painted in red edged with gold, with the practical addition of a delivery address.

"Ha!" cried Taylor. "The Green Knight!"

The women in the front seat ignored her. "Think of the poor guy stuck with this route," Rainey said. "Having to lift up that visor and shove his hand in just to deliver the mail."

The gravel drive was so long Rainey was on the point of turning back when she saw the house — tiny, made of weather-grayed stone, like hermits' houses in fairy tales. The two barns, one behind and one to the left of the house, were far larger. The barn on the side was the newer one — Ken and Grace had built it themselves and painted it a ferny green instead of traditional red, so it blended with the woods that encircled the property and stretched beyond sight. The older barn, as old as the house, was tar black, and, though taller and wider than the stone dwelling, the barn would have been nearly invisible behind it, easily mistaken for a hollow in the woods, were it not for the slender windows that wrapped the building just below the roofline.

Rainey recalled now that this was Grace's workshop. She hadn't really looked at it on the day of the funeral, but she remembered Grace's excitement over the phone, just after it was finished: "You have to see it. We took out the loft so the whole center fills with light all day. We're building worktables and benches with the wood from the loft floor. It was all Ken's idea."

"It must get awfully hot with so many windows," Rainey said.

"Oh, no," Grace insisted. "You'll see that when you come. The afternoon sun filters through the trees. It's perfect."

Rainey could sense Grace waiting for her to say something else, but she couldn't think of a thing. Not one thing. Far from planning a visit to that godforsaken place, back then she was still waiting for Grace to come to her senses, leave Ken, and get on with her life.

"He's good to me, Mom," Grace said to the silence. "Ken loves me."

Yes, Rainey now thought. Loved her so much that not a year later he went and killed himself. She still despised him for hurting her daughter that way, leaving Grace to deal with the shock and embarrassment of his suicide. Disloyal, that's what it was. Selfish.

How she had longed to wrap Grace in her arms then like an infant and carry her back home to Newman to take care of her. But Grace had not wanted her comforting. Four or five times since then, Rainey had been on the point of giving Grace her father's potsherd — the jagged little triangle with its faded black lines, diverging paths — but the moment had never seemed right. Why, she couldn't say. Rainey loved her younger daughter more than anyone else in this world, but Grace remained a mystery to her, a puzzle she would live out her life without ever solving.

Two immense white dogs, their coats stuck all over with bits of twigs, leaves, and mud, leapt around the car and barked, their noses high in the air. Lynn sighed in irritation, Taylor tapped at the window, calling, "Hey, doggies!" while Rainey sat rigid, her fingers white-knuckled around the steering wheel. What was Grace thinking, letting those beasts run loose like that?

Grace came jogging down the path from the house, calling, "I've got them!" She whistled and the dogs bounded toward her. Somehow she made them sit, lie down, then rise and follow her in relaxed walks toward a fenced area where thick straw lay around a pair of doghouses. Once past the gate, Grace pointed at the openings to each of the doghouses, and the dogs went in, turned around, and poked their heads out to wait for Grace to hug each of them around the neck and plant kisses on their giant brows.

Only after Grace had twice tugged at the gate to prove the latch was secure did Rainey open her car door. She was barely on her feet when she was nearly knocked off them again by Grace's running hug. "Hi, Mom!" While Rainey brushed dog hair and God knows what else off her blouse, Grace turned to her sister. "Lynn, I'm so glad you're here!" Rainey watched as her elder daughter awkwardly patted Grace's back.

"Now," said Grace, holding her arms open to Taylor. "Here's our family star!"

They clapped each other in a tight hug, rocked together, then pulled back to smile into each other's faces, and, as if signaling in secret code, they began to giggle and jump, arms still locked.

"Let me in!" cried a young voice, and a slim girl with what appeared to be shining blue hair sprinted towards them.

Grace and Taylor opened their arms to the girl and the three linked hands and pulled one another around in a circle.

"Whoo!" cried Grace. "I have to stop." And she did stop — abruptly — pulling her laughing companions onto the ground with her.

Rainey and Lynn stood over the group, staring at the girl with the blue hair. She flashed a smile at them and held out her hand for someone to pull her up. "It's a coif. I made it — almost all of it," she said. "Grace helped me get the shape right." When she twisted her head back and forth, the light caught the electric blue links, turning her into a sparkling waterfall.

"Isn't it heavy?" Lynn asked, for something to say.

"Lift the end," said the waterfall, leaning her head toward Lynn. "It's titanium. Very light — but strong."

"I'm Lynn."

"I figured." The girl bowed. "I'm Sarah. And you're Aunt Rainey. I mean Great-Aunt Rainey."

Seeing Rainey's look of alarm, Grace put her hands on Sarah's shoulders and said, "We've been working on a family tree. For Girl Scouts, so Sarah's trying to get all the labels right."

They all turned toward the sound of an approaching car. "Grandma!" Sarah darted toward it and started chattering at the window before Alma had completely stopped.

As Lynn had only a moment before, Alma expressed her worry about the weight of the coif, whether it would damage Sarah's fine blond hair or scratch her scalp.

"Do take it off, sweetheart," Alma said. "We'll get a wig stand so you can put it up in your room. It's really just meant to be looked at."

"I want to wear it all the time," said Sarah. "It's pretty."

"No, Sarah." Alma was already lifting the head covering, catching the clinging hairs in her fingers to keep them from pulling out. She'd barely slept for the last eleven days, worrying what Grace might lead Sarah into. Today at last she could collect her child and begin restoring a little order. Not that she didn't think Grace meant well — Alma was sure she did — but her niece had never been a mother and couldn't be expected to know when she was getting carried away.

There was nothing to do about it, of course, but facing this particular truth was a disappointment to Alma. She should have trusted her first impulse, the impulse that cried *No!* when Sarah had brought up the idea of spending time with Grace. As part of her strategy to get her way, Sarah had pulled up Grace's Web site on the computer and then made Alma sit beside her at the desk. "Look," Sarah had said, pointing to the screen, "she let all these Girl Scouts blog about the things they did there. In a week, I could earn enough badges to go up two ranks — easy!" Looking at Sarah in that moment, a child on the verge of adulthood, Alma had taken herself in hand, recalling that it was she who had urged Sarah to become a Scout, with the hope that her granddaughter might grow into a responsible young woman. She would simply have to stand aside and let Sarah do this.

So Alma had made the long drive from Ohio to drop Sarah off. She'd even stayed overnight in Grace's little house, doing her best to behave as if it were a charming country inn rather than the primitive hut it more closely resembled. During the visit, she had chatted with her niece and smiled, admiring what she had the strength to admire — like a blossoming pear tree in the front yard — keeping her fears to herself. But she had concealed her hopes, as well.

On her next birthday, Alma would be seventy-eight, and while she remained in good health, she had to face facts. Gordon had died suddenly eight years ago. What if something like that happened to her? What would become of Sarah? Ever since they'd been released from prison — Penny after eighteen months and Milton after three years — her son and daughter-in-law had suffered the twice-yearly visits to Sarah as if these were extensions of their sentences. And while Alma had taught Sarah to behave warmly toward her parents, she knew the child felt nothing for them because they made it so clear they felt nothing for her.

Who was she to look to? After Milton was arrested, the news spread all over the state, and on the day Alma and Gordon returned to McAllister to make final arrangements for selling the house, people stared at them from a distance, whispering to each other and nodding toward them. Then, when the trials were over and her son and daughter-in-law had gone to serve their sentences, Alma and Gordon had taken Sarah and moved to a simple house in a town they'd picked randomly from an Ohio state map. It had been impossible to make friends. Those first several months, whenever she would fill out papers in a doctor's office or write a check at the grocery or print her name on a raffle ticket, she felt sure the person behind the desk or the cash register or in the booth at the fair was looking hard at her name, was longing to know but trying not to ask if it was really her — the mother of Milton Crisp, convicted and sentenced for insurance fraud."

By the time Alma realized the case was not so widely known as she had imagined, she had been marked by her new neighbors as prim and standoffish. It was a small town, and labels were hard to overcome. Once or twice, she had suggested to Gordon that they invite a few people in for coffee or dinner, but he'd just glared at her, fixed another drink, and started again on his lecture about all the ways she had gone wrong with Milton and all the ways she was sure to go wrong with Sarah.

People at Sarah's school and the parents of other children were nice enough to her granddaughter, but there was no question the child had suffered from Alma's lack of social connections — around others, Sarah was clumsy with pleasantries, fidgety, liable to blush without reason. The Girl Scouts had helped with that, but then as Alma had watched Sarah begin to find her way, she had begun to worry about the future. No matter how kind a teacher or Scout leader or friend's mother might be, they couldn't be relied on to look after Sarah. If Sarah was not to be lost to foster care, Alma had to think of family — but what family? She'd never seen eye-to-eye with Rainey, and though she admired Lynn's drive, her elder niece had provided only the most grudging help years ago when Alma needed her. There was no one except Grace.

With Sarah beside her now, dragging her toward the others, breathlessly reciting all the things she'd done on the farm, Alma felt glad her girl was happy, but also dismayed to recognize that Grace — her one hope — several years past forty, was just an overgrown girl, clearly not at all a suitable guardian for Sarah. Not permanently.

Grace's hug caught Alma by surprise, and when she managed to release herself from the embrace, she nodded her hellos to Lynn and Rainey. Grace's gesture was only more evidence of how childlike she was — unable or unwilling to recognize that hugs were too intimate to be proper greetings among family become strangers.

But — seeing them now, together. When Sarah looked at Grace, she beamed. And Grace beamed back.

"Aunt Alma," Lynn said, drawing forward a beautiful, caramel-skinned girl. "This is Taylor. My daughter."

As Grace led them toward the house, the women asked each other about their general health, the length of the drive, the price of gas, and whether it might rain tomorrow or the next day.

"Sarah," Grace said, draping her arm around the girl's shoulders, "how about if you show everybody around? I want to borrow Taylor for a few minutes." She smiled at the others. "Sarah knows the place almost as well as I do now."

Sarah, clearly delighted with her task, announced she would begin her tour at the duck pond and motioned for the others to follow her.

"Lynn, wait," Grace called. She jogged a few yards to a covered porch and brought back a pair of rubber clogs, the once-brilliant yellow stained with dirt. "My garden clogs," she said, offering them to her sister. "I don't want you to ruin your shoes."

Lynn hooked her finger into one of the clogs and held it, dangling, at arm's length.

"They're clean," Grace said. "I hosed them down this morning." She laid the other clog at her sister's feet, then turned to Taylor and took her hand. "Come with me to the workshop."

When Grace pulled open the wide door to the old barn, Taylor blinked in the light and then stood openmouthed, her eyes traveling the walls, covered nearly to the high windows with pieces of armor.

"It's mostly commission work," Grace said. "Pays the upkeep on this place."

Taylor traced the intricately etched design on a silver breastplate. "It was your husband's, wasn't it? The house, I mean. Mom told me."

Grace nodded and said, "That's a French pattern. See the fleur-de-lis?"

"And you made all this?"

"And more. But then, I've been doing it for years." She gestured toward a dull shape that hung beside the door, so different from everything else in the shop, Taylor had to ask what it was. "That's my first piece."

The first piece — born so unexpectedly the night of Ken's funeral.

Beginning with the night the trooper had come to tell her about Ken, and each time in the days following when she called to update her mother about the arrangements, Grace tried to ask Rainey if she would stay over, just for a few days, but whenever she started the question by saying, "After the service . . ." her mother would say, "You should just come home with me."

"I can't do that, Mother," Grace said. "I have a farm to take care of." She didn't have the energy to argue back when her mother asked, "Isn't it time you left all that behind?"

When the funeral was over and she and her mother walked away from the church toward the car, Grace was again on the point of asking her not to leave, but then Mother said, "Now that you're free of your burdens, there's nothing to stop you. You're still young. You can be anything you like."

For a long time after her mother left, Grace had stood in the driveway, wearing her hastily bought dress and high heels, holding the startlingly small urn that held Ken's ashes. What was she to do with them? She and Ken had never talked about such things.

She couldn't face the house, not then, so she whistled for Charlemagne, went into the barn she and Ken had built together, and, seeing his coveralls hanging there, stripped off her dress, pulled on the coveralls, and shoved her feet into her husband's work boots. She had already started filling the bucket before she remembered Pilot wasn't there to drink the water she would pour into his trough. With the dog trotting at her heels, she fed the goats, put out food for the cats. She picked up Charlemagne's bowl and put it down again on the shady side of the barn, where he liked best to eat in the spring and summer; then she sat down on the stump she and Ken had long ago decided to preserve as a stool. The maple tree they had planted beside it now shaded her seat. After nosing his food for a moment, Charlemagne came to sit beside her, laying his head in her lap. They stayed like that for a long time.

She remembered that feeling of blankness, of feeling that somehow her body had vanished even as, like a collection of phantom limbs, it was too heavy to move. Always she had wondered what it meant in books when people described a suspension of thought, and now she knew. She was aware of her own mind, aware that it was there, but just as much aware that it turned itself to nothing other than the sense of her invisible, burdensome body.

She might have sat there through the night, frozen on the stump, if the setting sun had not caught the sheet of tin Ken had left lying in the grass. Just the week before, when he'd pulled down the decaying shed, he'd said something about keeping the tin, making use of it somehow, but she couldn't remember what.

Now, she could not remember thinking about going to pick up the tin before she did it. But she could see herself then, in the twilight, dragging the rusted sheet into the workshop, starting a fire in the stone hearth. She set out her tongs and hammers, and when the heat was right, she laid an edge of the tin first across the fire and, when it was hot, across her anvil. She could see herself beating out the ridges in the tin, beating as hard as she could, all the while remembering a line from a book or a poem that she had never since been able to locate: "on an age-old anvil wince and sing — then lull, then leave off."

She did not leave off until the tin was flattened, not until she had curved it around her anvil into the crude, arching shape and seen in that shape a shirt of armor. In the morning light, with the promise of armor, she suddenly knew what to do with Ken's ashes, so she took up the urn and shook some out under the oak where they had picnicked the day Ken had first brought her to see his land. She went into the barn and set the urn on the ground while she opened with two hands the latch that had made her want to become a blacksmith, opened the door the latch had secured against their clever horse, and scattered some of the ashes in Pilot's empty stall; and then in the grape arbor Ken had built with hopes of jelly and wine; to the garden he had made;

then to the creek and into the woods — but not to the clearing where the stranger from Chicago had found him.

She emptied the last of the ashes outside the door of the workshop Ken had created for her out of the black barn that had once been left to tumble. And then, she crossed the threshold to the newly smoothed tin. Through the rest of that day and into the night, working and resting, working and resting, she cut the tin at the curve and shaped for herself a crude breastplate, then a backplate, which she fastened together with strips from a snapped bridle Pilot had once worn and that Ken had set aside to repair.

"You make jewelry, too?" Taylor was standing at the center work-table, holding in the sunlight a necklace, an asymmetrical web of gold.

"I started with jewelry," Grace said. "You can ask your mother. Little bits spread all across my desk — instead of homework. Used to drive her and your grandmother crazy."

Taylor laid the necklace down again and traced an imaginary line on the table to balance the design. "It will be so beautiful when it's finished. Will you send me a picture?"

Grace came to the table and lifted the golden web, draping it across her hand. "It's for you," she said, holding it out to her niece. "And as finished as I can make it now."

Taylor blushed with embarrassment. "I'm sorry. . . . I didn't mean to . . ."

"Never mind," Grace said. "Let me show you."

It was a glimmering garden, a carpet of blossoms — daisies, roses, pansies, tulips, birds-of-paradise, the fluted trumpets of lilies. But only when Grace began to follow the pattern with her finger did Taylor see the letters — each formed of fine braided wire, each stretching out to other letters, running like vines through the garden. Grace laid her finger on a scrolling *F* placed at the center of the chain. The stem of the *F* curved and split, forming the edges of a letter *M* on the left and a *B* on the right.

"That's on the shield out front," Taylor said.

"The *F* is for Fischer." Grace stroked its swooping lines. "That was my grandmother's — your great-grandmother's — maiden name. She was Bertie. And see here?" She touched with her fingertip a ring that connected Bertie's initial to an *H*, for Hans, and traced the connection down to the lovely letters representing Alma and Rainey. From Rainey's *R*, Grace let her finger follow through another generation. "You're here."

Taylor touched her *T.* Not only had Grace linked her mother's *L* to her father's *S* for Sam, she had drawn the ends of the initials down and around the *T*, like an embrace.

Taylor sat quietly, gazing at the necklace and following with her eyes the intricate web of her family. "This is your husband," she said, fingering the link that joined Grace with Ken. "He killed himself, didn't he?"

"Yes."

"Why?" Taylor looked down, as if in shame. With one hand, she clutched her hair. "I mean . . . What I mean is, was it too much for him? Living? Was he . . . Was it . . ."

Grace looked into Taylor's eyes and there saw fragments of a feeling that had pierced her child's heart, a feeling her young woman's mind now struggled to name. Grace took her niece's hands in her own. "Was it despair?"

Taylor nodded.

"No. Partly — but not just." Grace brushed a lock of hair away from Taylor's eyes. "I think it was sacrifice."

"I don't understand."

"Neither do I," said Grace. "I think that's how it is with sacrifice. It matters. But we don't always know how."

A tear spilled over Taylor's cheek. She looked again at the necklace. "What's this question mark linked to Grandma Rainey?" She looked closer. "There's a heart inside it."

"That's my father," Grace said. "I don't know his name." She traced her finger back along the vine to Bertie. "Look here. What do you see?" The letter was clearly a *B*, but only by looking intently could one see that Grace had shaped the lower loop ever so slightly as a heart, and that floating within it was a tiny *W* turned from wire finer than a hair. "Before she died," Grace said, "just before — Grandma told me she had loved a boy named Wallace. Whatever we carry inside us shapes everyone we touch."

Taylor lifted the necklace from the table and let the golden garden drape across the back of her hand as Grace had done earlier. "And this *M?* Who is it?"

"My grandmother's sister."

Grace told Taylor then all that Bertie had told her — of Mabel, of Wallace, of her graduation day and Jim Butcher. "Someday," she said, taking the necklace from Taylor, "if you want, I can add in the family you make." She stood up to close the chain around her niece's neck. "But the pattern will always be out of balance. I can't tell Mabel's story."

Taylor let another tear spill over. "Thank you for this."

Grace leaned down to press the girl's cheek with her own. "Now," she said, "how about you go join the party?"

Taylor turned to look at her with a sly grin. "You mean my party."

"Yes, darling." Grace laughed. "Your party. You go on. I'll be along in a minute."

Grace leaned in the doorway, watching her niece walk, skip, and then dance in twirls toward the house. The others came out on the far side of the barn — Sarah must have been showing them the goats romping in their lot, clattering up the gangplank and butting each other off the platform Ken had built for the first pair, years ago. She saw Taylor wave, and a moment later, their family of women gathered around her bright light, leaning in — she must be telling them about the necklace. It pleased Grace to think of Taylor telling the story, learning it by telling it. She would let the tale belong to her niece for a little while, and only when she was sure Taylor had told all she remembered would Grace join them.

The others probably wouldn't believe anything Taylor said about Mabel and Wallace, and they would tell Taylor she must have misheard. Grace turned back to her worktable and slid open the shallow drawer that ran nearly the full length of the table. "For the jewelry parts," Ken had said. He'd made it to open from either side of the table, so she could always work on the side with the best light and still keep her wire and rings and small tools at her fingertips without cluttering her work surface. Long ago, further back in the drawer, she had placed the slim gray box Grandma had sent her from the hospital to find. In it still lay the glove, the pale green ribbon, and the photograph of Mabel. She would take the box to her family, and, wearing the necklace she had worn every day since Grandma died, the chain of flowers with the silver rose button at its center, she would open the box, show them the photograph, and tell them all she knew.

She sat down at the table and took Mabel's photograph from the box, tilting it to keep it out of the strongest sunlight. She wished she could know what had become of that pretty dark-haired girl on the swing and wished even more to know what had caused the fear that seeped through those eyes.

Grace smiled at the beautiful young face. Whatever the reason for it, Mabel's departure had changed the direction of Bertie's life, and from that change had grown their family. The necklace Grace had made for Taylor, an orderly tangle of links, vines, and blossoms, was in many ways a map of sadness and loss. Only by standing back a little could one see how beautiful it was — like a forest floor renewed by fire. Grace's life — this life and place she loved — had risen out of the ashes of so many.

She closed the box and clutched it to her chest, stooping at the door to stroke her fingers across the ground that had long since drawn in the last of Ken's ashes. Words of gratitude and love swirled in her mind like motes of dust sparkling in the sun, settling on Mabel, on Wallace, on Bertie and Hans, on Ken, and then — as she took her first step out of the barn and toward her gathered family — on all of them.

TWENTY-FIVE:
DEPARTURE II

June 2007
Indianapolis, Indiana

MABEL

"Mama? Are you asleep? Mama-bel? Jenny's here with Bonnie."

Mabel heaved her eyes open to look for Daisy. It was Daisy's voice she heard, but there was only a blur before her, and inside the blur was an old, old woman.

"Where's my Daisy?"

"I'm here, Mama," said the blur. "Right here."

"You're old."

Daisy smiled and stroked Mabel's cheek. "Sure am," she said. "But not as old as you."

When the blur came closer, Mabel could see her lovely Daisy. The old woman was gone and in her place was the girl with the copper hair, pinned up in a clumsy twist. "Your hair's pretty that way," Mabel said. "I can help you fix it so the ends don't come down."

Daisy lifted her hand to her hair and became an old woman again. "Jenny's here," she said. "Jenny and Bonnie. They've come to see you."

"Bertie?" Mabel tried to pull herself up, tried to see the door her sister would come through.

"No, Mama. Bonnie. My granddaughter. Your great-granddaugter."

A young woman appeared by the bed. "Hey, Gran." The young woman's hands rested lightly on the shoulders of a little girl, about ten or twelve, who stood in front of her. The little girl wore a soft pink dress.

"Sweetheart." Mabel reached out to the child. Her hair was cold, stringing wet and cold. "I'll hold on to you, Bertie. I won't let you drown."

"It's Bonnie, Gran. This is Bonnie. We've just been swimming. The pool opened today." The young woman turned her head toward Daisy and said, "How long has she been like this?"

"She just woke up," Daisy said, her voice breaking. "She might know you later on."

"You'd better tell me, Mom."

Mabel reached out again for little Bertie, trying to tell her not to be afraid of the water, but her sister kept pulling away, as if she were frightened somehow of Mabel. The others talked on.

"The hospice nurse is here. She says the kidneys are going. It's why I called you. Could be anytime. She won't really know what she's saying, but the nurse said it won't last long."

"I'll take Bonnie home and come back," said the young woman. She bent down to the child. "Bonnie, say good-bye to Great-Grandma."

The little girl in the pink dress drifted across the room. Bertie was going.

Mabel struggled to rise. She would go after her sister.

Far away, a door was opening and Bertie was going through it.

Tugging free of the weight that held her, Mabel followed. She opened the door and there was Bertie, standing before the dresser in her pink chiffon dress, settling a small comb into her upswept hair.

"Oh, Bertie!" Mabel motioned for her sister to twirl around and they both laughed with pleasure at how the dress floated and settled, floated and settled, like a spring breeze.

"Does my hair look all right?" Bertie asked.

"Hold still," Mabel said, taking the small finishing brush from the dresser. A single lock threatened to tumble, so she took out a couple of pins, smoothed the lock, and fastened it into place. "You're beautiful," she said, wrapping one arm across her sister's chest, pressing her own cheek against Bertie's. "Mama would be so proud," she said to their smiling reflections.

"You'll be there by a quarter to three?" Bertie smoothed the front of her dress and fastened the buttons on her sleeve bands, little silver roses. "Any later and you might not get a seat."

Mabel hoped her smile was convincing. "Of course I'll be there."

How she longed for that to be true. If only she could make this day as happy as Bertie had imagined it would be — but in half an hour, Wallace would sneak into the barn and settle himself in the loft to wait for her. After that, there would be no turning back. For now, though, for this moment, she would pretend that today would be nothing more or less than Bertie's eighth-grade graduation day.

"Wallace is coming," Bertie said. "He promised he'd dance with me at the party."

"You can't dance in a Baptist church." Mabel laughed.

"I know," Bertie smiled, her cheeks pink. "But Wallace keeps his promises." Suddenly serious again, she touched Mabel's arm. "You think that's all right, don't you? After all, *he* won't be there."

"Of course it's all right." Mabel hugged Bertie tightly. "You don't need to worry about him spoiling anything." She took her sister's hands, stepped back, and held her at arm's length to have one last look at her. "You'd better get on, now. The principal likes to have everybody in place before the families get there."

When Bertie left, Mabel closed the door and sat down on the bed to watch the clock. She and Wallace had timed everything as carefully as they could. Early this morning, Wallace would have walked two streets over to Henry Layman's house to catch him while he was doing his chores and give him the sealed envelope to pass to Bertie at the graduation party. Inside was a train ticket, along with the instructions Mabel had written: *Go straight to the station. Don't go home. Take the late train to Louisville. We'll leave another ticket for you there at the window in Mama's maiden name. Don't be afraid. Trust us. We'll be waiting for you. Love M&W.*

If anything had gone wrong — if Wallace hadn't been able to find Henry or if Henry had refused the task or asked too many questions, Wallace would have found a way to let her know. Everything was already in place in the loft. Now, she needed to wait a full ten minutes just to be sure Bertie didn't turn back for something she might have forgotten. Then, Mabel would write one more note, very brief, and slip it into her dress pocket. She needed this time to breathe deeply and prepare to go to the back porch to wake Jim Butcher from his Saturday nap.

How easily in these last few days had he taken to believing she welcomed his hands. Instinct alone had allowed her to swallow her revulsion and act when she saw the way Butcher was looking at Bertie standing before the mirror in her pretty new dress. Even from the back, as Mabel stepped into the hallway to tell him his breakfast was ready, she could see it in how he was leaning into the room, the way his head tilted, the way his hand pulsed on the knob.

She had moved without thought or hesitation: a light touch on his arm. A smile. A question about supper. Enough to break the spell, but for how long?

The moment Bertie stepped out the door on her way to school, Mabel let her stepfather take her in his arms and kiss her as if she were his bride.

All that day at Kendall's Dry Goods, she couldn't stay still, unfolding and refolding neat stacks of shirts, taking tins off shelves only to put them right back again. Ten minutes before the senior high school was to let out for the day, she faked a stomach pain and begged Mr. Kendall to let her go home to lie down. She waited outside the school, waved down Wallace and persuaded him to send Henry Layman to tell Bertie he wouldn't be meeting her for their walk home for the rest of the week.

She told Wallace the whole story — not every detail, but enough to make the blood drain from his face and then rush up again until she thought he might explode. He was the one who put it into words what they had to do, and that was when she knew that there was one other person in the world who loved Bertie as much as she did.

The core of their plan came to them quickly, and it was with astonishing ease that they agreed on each point. Over the next few days, they let people in town see them together — but they gave the impression they were trying not to be seen by sitting in a corner of the balcony at the movies, their heads together; by holding hands as they slipped round the back of the church after Wednesday-evening service; by tucking almost out of sight to embrace behind a display of washtubs at the hardware store. Between them, they had almost enough for three train fares, and to get the rest, Wallace sold his pocket watch and his bicycle, while Mabel begged for an advance on her pay, saying it was for Bertie's graduation gift.

Mabel raked her fingers through her hair. Time to go. She simply had to trust that Wallace was in place in the loft. It was too risky to check.

Just last week, Butcher had met his bootlegger for his summer supply of whiskey. He took a lot of trouble not to let anyone see him heading out for the meeting, but once the whiskey was in the house, he didn't care who knew about it. In the kitchen, Mabel took a new bottle from the cabinet and set it on a tray with two clean glasses. She chipped a bowl full of ice off the block because she knew in summer he liked his whiskey cold.

On the back porch, he was stretched out across the swing, swaying in rhythm with his breath. She set down the tray, filled the glasses with ice, opened the bottle and poured. She picked up one glass and took a drink, bathing her lips in whiskey, then set the glass back on the tray and approached the swing. Now she must do it, just as she had done so many times this week in her mind.

She bent over him. "Daddy," she whispered, waiting until he stirred before stroking his cheek with her fingertips. "Daddy." When he opened his eyes, she leaned down to kiss him. The kiss, she knew, would tell her whether he believed her. She closed her eyes and tried to imagine they were both other people, as if Mabel Fischer and Jim Butcher had never known each other, or even existed. His response was immediate. Without breaking the kiss, he rose up in the swing and pulled her onto his lap.

"Bertie's gone now." Mabel slid the tip of her tongue over his lips. "She won't be home for hours."

At this, Butcher laid rough kisses along her throat and clutched at her breasts. He began unbuttoning her dress.

She put a hand up to stop him and then remembered, *No, gently,* so she wrapped her fingers around his and lifted his hand to her lips. "No rush, Daddy," she said. "We have hours." She got up from his lap but continued to hold his hand. "Look, I've brought you a cold drink."

She handed him one glass and set the other and the bottle on the ledge closest to the swing. He drained the first glass, so she gave him the second and poured a refill. After three whiskeys, he pulled her onto her feet and started to steer her back inside the house.

"I've a better idea," Mabel said, smiling. "It's so much cooler in the barn. And" — she wrapped her arms around Butcher's neck, pressed her head to his chest, and cooed — "if Bertie should could home early, she won't find us."

Butcher answered by lifting Mabel into his arms. She reached out to pick up the whiskey bottle as he carried her down the steps and across the yard into the barn. When they reached the loft, he took a few more swallows of whiskey while Mabel lay down on the floor. She didn't dare look toward the far corner, where Wallace would be hiding, so she looked at the heavy beams above her. When Butcher put aside his whiskey and came to her, she closed her eyes and opened her arms to him.

While he unbuttoned her dress and laid her bare, she kept up a steady moaning, like a chant, and concentrated. Her body was a fortress and could bear anything. He could pummel away at her, try to break her down, but he would never breach her.

He would never take Bertie.

So she let him thrust and pound. She let him believe that the sounds she made were the sounds of the conquered. And then, just as they had planned, just as the bastard cried out, believing in his victory, Wallace sprang from behind the bales, hooked Jim Butcher's ecstatic throat with a length of short rope and twisted the breath from him with all the wrath of God.

Wallace held the limp body upright with the rope so Mabel could pull out from under, and while she dressed, he fastened up Butcher's pants. They didn't speak. Mabel knocked over the whiskey bottle so it would drain onto the floor and then opened the sack of seed corn to dig out the two empty bottles she'd hidden there. She dropped them randomly near the other. Wallace shook apart two bushel baskets to remove the long rope he'd coiled between them. Already he had tied a crude noose at one end, and now he flung the untied end over the lowest beam, pulled, and flung it over twice more to loop it.

They stood together beside the corpse and stared silently at the noose dangling just beyond the edge of the loft. Mabel took Wallace's hand, but she couldn't look at him. After a moment, he stepped closer to the edge and leaned out to pull the rope in.

When he had the noose end, he passed it to her and she moved aside while he pushed and pulled the body toward the drop-off. A few feet from the edge, Wallace held Butcher upright and Mabel slipped the noose over his head, tugging the rope back a little to tighten the slipknot. Then, at Wallace's count, they shoved the body over. Mabel heard the tiniest of snaps as the weight dropped. Good, a broken windpipe.

Wallace picked up the short rope, wound it to a small coil, and shoved it deep inside his pocket. Later, when it was dark, he would find an empty space on the train, open a window, and let it slip off into the wind.

They took a few moments to look around for anything they might have missed. Mabel found a button that had pulled off her dress, but nothing more. They climbed down from the loft and Wallace waited by the door while Mabel went to stand just below the place where Butcher's body swung gently. She looked up, estimating the spot, and drew from her pocket the note she'd written earlier — less than an hour ago — unfolded it, as though it had been read, crumpled it in her fist, and let it drop to the floor. Finding it, the people of Juniper would believe that she and Wallace had run off together and that Jim Butcher had hanged himself out of foolish jealousy. They would think, too, that, having no one left, Bertie had fled.

This, Mabel prayed, would be what they would think. It must be.

Seeming to know her thoughts, Wallace came to her, embraced her, and led her toward the door.

If only there were some other way.

But there wasn't.

Bertie had to pay this little price — these few hours of believing herself abandoned, betrayed; then a night and day of confusion and fear, traveling far from all she had known, not sure where she was headed, not sure she could trust Wallace and Mabel to be there at the end of her journey.

But Mabel would be there to meet the train in Chicago, to rock away Bertie's terror and wipe her tears. And later, when Wallace came back to lead them to their new home, after they had all eaten and slept, then she would take Bertie's hands in hers and tell her sister everything. Bertie would understand. Bertie would forgive her and comfort her in return. They would be closer than ever. And for the rest of their lives, no matter what else happened to them, they would never be parted.

ACKNOWLEDGMENTS

For their steady encouragement and wise guidance, I am deeply grateful to the three exceptional women who formed the chain that brought *The Sisters* to its present place. First, I thank my dear friend Sena Naslund, who urged me on from the earliest stirrings of Mabel's and Bertie's story, who spurred me forward with eager questions as new characters emerged, who spotted where I stumbled and restored me to my path by offering her advice on many successive drafts, and who introduced me to my agent, Lisa Gallagher. Second, I thank Lisa Gallagher for saying yes to the book with the kind of enthusiasm rarely known outside one's sweetest fantasies. I thank her for her penetrating analysis of the story and her clarifying criticism, both of which helped me to revise the book in unexpected and joyous ways, and I thank her for leading me to my editor, Hope Dellon. I thank Hope

Dellon — the splendid, strong third link in this chain — for shining the bright light of her intelligence and experience into the murky corners of the novel, and then standing back, so I might, in my own way and time, find what was missing.

I am grateful to the Kentucky Foundation for Women and the Kentucky Arts Council for their generous grants, which, in addition to providing practical financial assistance, gave me much-needed boosts of confidence in the early and middle stages of writing *The Sisters.*

Finally, I say thank you to those in my family and among my friends who, on hearing the good news, cheered loud and long — and even danced a bit: Phyllis and Bob Herzfeld, Harry Siler, Stan Price, Donna Heffner, Annie Patterson, Rayford and June Watts, Mandy Pursley, Miranda Howard, Jolina Petersheim, Jamey Temple, and Mia Culling.